# mandrake

*Also by Paul Eddy*

Flint

# mandrake

PAUL EDDY

headline

First published in 2002
by HEADLINE BOOK PUBLISHING

10 9 8 7 6 5 4 3 2 1

ISBN 0 7472 7116 X (hardback)
ISBN 0 7472 7117 8 (softback)

Typeset by Avon Dataset Ltd, Bidford-on-Avon, Warks

Typeset in Sabon

Printed and bound in Great Britain by
Mackays of Chatham plc, Chatham, Kent

HEADLINE BOOK PUBLISHING
A division of Hodder Headline
338 Euston Road
London NW1 3BH

www.headline.co.uk
www.hodderheadline.com

For Sara, always

# New York City

# one

Grace Flint is marooned in a secure US Customs covert observation post, helplessly watching a CCTV monitor, watched herself by too many men who are fast losing faith in Operation Pentecost. And, rightly so.

*Got all your bases covered?* Cutter had asked, calling from his car on the way to La Guardia. *Everything as it should be?*

*Well, yes and no, Mr Cutter,* for what shouldn't be, what is causing the back of her shirt to stick to her skin as though it is glued, is mounting evidence of her own failure to expect the unexpected.

The chance of April showers and skittish gusts of wind had been the meat of the weather forecast. No mention – not a hint – of the vicious squall that has come racing across Upper Bay, signalling its arrival with a rolling grey fog that now obscures Staten Island.

Across the East River yacht basin flecks of spume are flying horizontally and the plaza of the SeaWorld Leisure Center is deserted. No sign on the CCTV monitor of the milling lunch-time crowds that should be providing cover for the back-up team. No sign of the back-up team either.

'Crawdaddy, talk to me,' Flint says into the microphone of the headset she wears. 'Where are you?'

'Inside,' says Crawdaddy, whose real name is Crawford, his booming voice broadcast to the operations room by high-fidelity speakers. 'Can't go back out there. They'd make us in a second.'

'Can you see them?'

'That's a negative, not any more. They're on the boat.' Crawford pauses and then he adds, 'We think.'

Behind Flint a voice says 'Jesus', spoken softly like a sigh.

'You *think*?' Flint demands into her microphone.

Jarrett Crawford does not apologise for his uncertainty. 'We lost visual contact when the storm hit and everybody scattered. But, Grace, where else would they be?'

'Call it off,' says the voice behind her, the voice of Joint Assistant Director (Operations) Nathan Stark, formerly of the FBI and Flint's equal in the hierarchy of the Financial Strike Force.

But Flint will not be panicked. She knows all too well that most undercover operations flirt with calamity; that the nagging, whining voice inside her head is ever-present at times like this, par for the course. As Aldus Cutter never tires of saying, there is no such thing as a perfect plan. Undercover, you are always close to the edge, waiting for the target to develop a sixth sense, or for one of your colleagues to screw up or the technology to fail. 'Pilgrims,' Cutter will remind his people, 'you gotta have a Plan B.'

Flint concentrates on a second monitor that is directly in front of her and says, 'Lily, can you hear me?' and on the covered bridge that links SeaWorld to The World's Greatest Emporium (no false modesty here), the woman who make-believes her name is Lily Apana raises her right hand to touch her hair – the pre-arranged signal that tells Flint the FeatherLite receiver Apana is wearing, disguised as an earring, is working as it should.

Her real name is Ruth – Ruth Apple – but Flint has erased this from the collective memory of the Financial Strike Force. In the active present tense, she is always and only Lily.

'Lily, you're going to be out there alone,' Flint says. 'You'll have no back-up within two hundred yards. I need to be sure that you're going to be okay with that.'

Lily Apana cannot reply, for Flint would not permit her to wear a concealed microphone or a transmitter. A well-disguised passive receiver is one thing – an acceptable risk, in Flint's view. But Flint knows there is no transmitter signal that cannot be detected, and no microphone too small to be found, and under her left breast she bears a scar to prove it. Even now, five years after the event, she still relives in Technicolor nightmares the moments when an animal named Clayton Buller found a microphone hidden within her bra and stomped it deep into her abdominal wall with the heel of one of his hand-made Italian boots. Before starting on her face.

'Because if not,' Flint continues, 'look in your bag as though you've forgotten something and turn around, come back to base. Have you got that?'

Once more Apana touches her hair to acknowledge receipt of Flint's message but she does not break her brisk stride. In her flat shoes and her tailored silk suit that is coloured a striking Hooker's Green, she looks what she is pretending to be: a rising bank executive running fractionally late for a meeting.

Still on edge, Flint says, 'This is not a one-shot deal, Lily—' though she fears it is exactly that. Easily, without the need for the slightest hesitation, she continues to dissimulate: 'We can work out some excuse that won't sound phoney. I mean, who in their right mind would turn out on a day like this? Right?'

Barely perceptibly, Apana shakes her head. She is nearing the end of the bridge, approaching the Rubicon, her point of no return.

'Heads up,' says Crawford over the speakers. 'Movement on the boat. Someone coming up on deck.'

To Rocco Morales, on secondment from the US Customs service, who sits alongside her at the console Flint says, 'Give me a picture,' but Morales shakes his head. *No can do.*

'All the cameras on that side of the building are FP,' he explains, meaning fixed position. Flint grimaces and he feels obliged to offer her something. 'Look, give me a few minutes. I'll see if I can get a hand-held on the roof.'

'Lily, slow down,' Flint commands. 'There's been a hitch.'

Apana does not immediately alter her pace but after passing through the revolving doors that lead from the bridge to the mezzanine gallery of the World Emporium she stops and searches her shoulder bag until she finds a mirror. Glancing at her watch, she apparently decides there is still time to check on her appearance.

'Smart,' Flint whispers to herself. To Crawford she says, 'Who's the perp?'

'Looks like Hustler,' Crawford replies, using the codename that the Strike Force has assigned to Karl Gröber, its most significant target of the moment. 'Difficult to be sure because he's wearing foul-weather gear, but I'd take a bet it's him.'

'What's he doing?'

'Looking around. Looking for Lily, I guess.'

On the edge of her vision Flint sees Nathan Stark raise his eyebrows as he takes a chair beside her and inwardly she groans. 'Crawdaddy, you know better than that,' she tells Crawford. 'Don't guess. Just tell me what you see.'

'You'll have a picture in five minutes,' says Rocco Morales, putting down the phone.

Too long, Flint knows, for in less than one minute Lily Apana will be late for her meeting with Karl Gröber, alias Hustler, and she cannot credibly continue to bother about how she looks when there is so much at stake, and when – in all likelihood – she is under the intense scrutiny of hostile, wary eyes.

Flint swivels her chair and finds Felix Hartmann where she expects him to be, his arms folded, leaning against the wall.

'Felix, you've got the cellphone number?'

He nods. 'You want me to call?'

'In a couple of minutes, when she gets down to the atrium. Make it from the booth.'

Hartmann nods again and pushes off from the wall, loping with his long stride towards the soundproofed glass cubicle that occupies one corner of the room.

'Grace, you have to pull the plug,' says Nathan Stark, as Flint knew he would.

She does not respond and switches on her microphone. 'Lily, we need to buy some time. When you get downstairs you'll get a phone call from Felix. As of now, he's your boyfriend. I want you to tell him that you can't talk, that you're late for an appointment, and I want you to say it nice and loud so that everybody around you can hear. Okay so far?'

Apana gives her hair another affirmative pat and puts away the mirror in her bag.

'But Felix is going to persist,' continues Flint, glancing at him to make sure he is listening. 'Your mother's had a fall, a car crash, some kind of accident. She's in hospital. She's asking for you, needs you there ASAP. Now, I want you to get upset. You're torn. Your mother needs you but you've got this appointment you can't break. You don't know what to do. Felix is going to argue with you: no appointment is that important when your mother needs you, and so forth. Start moving.'

On the monitor Flint sees Apana begin her descent of the stairs.

'So you plead with him: "Felix, go to the hospital, hold her hand until I get there. I'll be there in an hour. Felix, honey, will you do that for me?" You know the sort of thing, just keep it going. Make it clear to anyone who's listening that he's giving you a hard time, but you're determined to keep the appointment. I'll tell him when to quit.'

Apana is moving out of frame, and out of Flint's view, until Rocco Morales switches the feed to another camera, this one fixed on a teeming atrium that is called the Winter Garden. Sixteen Robusta palm trees stand in incongruous rows like the columns of a temple.

'Hustler's making a phone call,' Crawford reports and Flint gives Rocco Morales a look that says, *I really need that picture.* He replies with a helpless shrug: *I'm doing the best I can.*

Stark moves his chair closer to Flint's and leans towards her until she can feel his breath on her neck. He suffers from chronic halitosis which he camouflages with a mouthwash that reminds her of the smell of quince.

'Grace, listen to me. They'll use the weather as an excuse to get her on the boat. We can't hear her and, when that happens, we won't be able to see her either. They can do what the hell they like and we won't know a thing about it. You have to call it off.'

'Nathan, get out of my face.'

She turns, reaches out with her hand and pushes him away with a strength that surprises him.

'Lily,' she says into the microphone, 'when you get out there, you make Hustler come to you. You don't go anywhere near the boat no matter what he says or does. Have you got that? Felix is going to call you now and the first thing I want to hear you say is, "Yes, I understand", or I'm going to abort this operation. Is that clear? Lily, whatever happens, you do *not* get on that boat.'

Flint nods at Felix Hartmann, now inside the booth waiting by the phone, and says to Morales, 'Put it on the speaker.'

While Hartmann dials the number, Flint pushes the switch that allows her next transmission to be heard by all twelve Strike Force agents who comprise the back-up team, though not by Lily Apana.

'Gentlemen, listen up. Let's be clear about this. I'm about to put a federal agent in harm's way. One of ours – one of *yours*. She needs your very best attention.'

'Grace,' says Stark standing up, 'Lily's too inexperienced to pull this off. You could do this, she can't.'

'Hello,' says Apana, her voice coming over the speaker.

'Lily, this is Felix.'

Hartmann and Flint watch each other through the glass, waiting through the pause.

'Yes, I understand,' Lily replies.

Stark seems about to continue the argument until Flint says, 'Nathan, this is not your call.'

'Felix, I can't talk now. I'm late for a meeting.'

'Lily, listen, your mother's been in an accident.'

'What?'

'I was at the apartment when they called. She got hit by—'

'My mother's *hurt*?' says Apana, her voice rising.

'Listen, calm down. I'm at the hospital now. I just spoke to the doctor and she's not dying but—'

'*Oh my God! My mother's dying?*'

'Lily, I said she's *not* dying. But she needs you. You have to get over here.'

As Hartmann presses on, embellishing Flint's improvised script with inventions of his own, and as Apana repeats the gist of what he says for the benefit of those around her, Stark shakes his head. 'I'm calling Cutter,' he announces in an undertaker's tone.

'Go ahead,' says Flint as though she doesn't care, turning away from him, turning to Morales to renew her appeal.

'The camera's in position,' he says. 'I'm getting you the feed.'

On the first monitor the picture is as fuzzy as Staten Island. *A day late, a dollar short*, as Cutter would surely say.

'I need it now, Rocco,' she says urgently. Sooner would be better, she thinks.

Part of her is aware of Stark – standing away from her, talking quietly on the phone – but she puts that aside and concentrates on the conversation between Hartmann and Apana; not just the content but the tone. She must assume that some of Hustler's hoods are mingling among the exceptionally large crowd on the atrium, looking for Apana, looking even more keenly for any sign of a trap. If they know their business, as Flint assumes they do, the watchers will have found Lily and will be reporting back to Hustler that she is talking on a mobile phone. Furthermore – and this is important – Flint knows that mobile phone calls are easy to intercept, and she must also assume that Hustler has the necessary equipment on the boat; that, by now, he will have found the frequency. Thus, she takes it as a given that Hustler – or one of his apostles, as Cutter calls them – is listening to every word.

'Lily, I don't believe this,' Hartmann is saying, having reached that point in Flint's fiction where Apana is refusing to meet his demands. 'We are talking about your *mother*.'

Hartmann is German, on secondment from the *Bundesnachrichtendienst*, and although his English is excellent his grasp of the vernacular is shaky. To Flint's uneasy ears his indignation sounds too forced, too brittle.

'Felix, please,' says Apana. 'I have to take this meeting. What difference is an hour going to make?'

'And what do I tell your mother?'

'I don't know ... Tell her my phone's turned off. Tell her I'm stuck in traffic. Tell her anything you want, Felix. Just hold her hand until I get there. *Please*.'

Running out of arguments, Hartmann pauses and gesticulates to Flint through the glass: *What now?*

Inside the booth he cannot hear anything she says so she mouths to him his cue: *Which hospital? Ask her!*

Hartmann grasps the point immediately. 'Get where, Lily? You don't even know where the hell I am.'

'Okay, Felix,' Apana says tightly, as though she is struggling to keep her patience. 'Where are you? Which hospital?'

'That is not the point,' says Hartmann, buying a few more precious seconds. 'Why didn't you ask me that before?'

'Shit, Felix, I don't have time for this. You want a fight? Fine, we'll have it later. Now, just tell me where—'

'Lily,' Hartmann interrupts. 'Your attitude, it's fucking unbelievable!'

On the monitor Apana is pacing a tight circle on the atrium, the phone clasped to one ear, waving her free hand in obvious frustration.

Into her other ear, through the FeatherLite receiver, Flint whispers, 'Good stuff,' and to Hartmann in the booth she gives the thumbs-up sign and then rolls her hand to tell him: *Keep it going*.

But for how much longer, when there is still only fuzz on the monitor, and nothing that Rocco Morales does with his switches and dials makes any difference? And Nathan Stark is coming towards her, his bony face expressionless, holding out the phone.

'Cutter wants to talk to you,' he says, his voice neutral, still giving nothing away.

Flint's stomach churns as she takes the handset from him but her voice does not betray her when she speaks into the mouthpiece. 'Yes, sir?'

'So, Nathan tells me it's all screwed up,' Cutter says with his customary approach, cutting to the quick. 'You've got no back-up in place and no Plan B.'

'I don't think so, Mr Cutter.'

'Terrific,' says Cutter. 'Glad to hear it. So, what is Plan B? You wanna share it with me, Flint?'

At times like these, Cutter's voice takes on a distinct Texas drawl.

Stark is watching her and she turns her back on him. Closing her eyes, she succeeds in blanking out the escalating row coming over the speakers.

'The back-up is not as close as I would like, but it *is* in place. They can reach Apana in about thirty seconds if they have to. I've already told her she's not to go anywhere near the boat and I'm about to tell her that if Hustler starts anything she's to go down on the ground and start yelling her lungs out.'

'Got a sniper in place?'

'No,' she says, telling him what he already knows. 'That wasn't in the contingency because there are supposed to be a couple of thousand civilians out there and you didn't want them getting shot – remember? Anyway, it's too late now.'

Cutter grunts and says 'Right' and then he pauses and in the background Flint can hear airport terminal noises. Stark must have reached him as he stepped off the plane. 'So, Hustler's got all the time in the world to do what he likes to Lily?'

'That and think about his future, Mr Cutter. If he starts something, he's going to have twelve armed men coming at him, telling him to freeze. That should get his attention.'

'She's got a weapon?'

'Of course not,' Flint snaps, and instantly regrets the sharpness of her tone. She takes a breath and adds, more evenly she hopes, 'She's supposed to be a bank executive, Mr Cutter.'

'And Lily's what – not much more than five foot in her heels and a hundred and ten pounds soaking wet? What's to stop him picking her up and hauling her off to the boat?'

'I don't think he'll do that, sir, not unless he's got suicide in mind.'

'Humour me, Flint. He's got his apostles on the boat?'

'Yes.'

'Armed?'

'Presumably.'

'So, he's got Lily as a shield if he wants, and he's got covering fire if he needs it. Go on assuming the worst. Say he gets her on the frigging boat and they take off? What's Plan B?'

Flint is ready for that.

'They won't get half a mile,' she says firmly. 'I've got two fast NYPD marine units, one either side of the basin, and if they don't stop him I've got a Coast Guard launch waiting downstream. It's armed with a cannon, Mr Cutter. If Hustler wants to pick a fight with—'

She gets no further because Cutter interrupts. 'You think Lily's immune to cannon fire?'

Flint hears herself sigh. 'Mr Cutter, sir, there are always risks. I've given her the option to abort and she doesn't want to take it. She knows the score.'

'Does she? You sure about that?' Cutter lets the question hang and then he says, 'Don't want to bury another pilgrim, do we, Flint?'

This is a low blow, for Cutter is referring now to Kevin Hechter, late of the US Treasury department. Hechter, riding on a Learjet that Flint should also have been aboard, blown out of the sky with a Semtex bomb – a catastrophe for which Flint irrationally blames herself. She was the one who formally identified Hechter from the wedding ring on his severed hand.

'No,' Flint says quietly. The hand was all they found of Hechter, all there was to bury.

'Nathan thinks you should call it off, set it up a second time.'

'There won't be a second time, Mr Cutter. Hustler's too cagey. If we pass on this chance, we won't get near him again.'

There is another pause while Cutter considers his decision. Flint opens her eyes to glance at the booth and sees Hartmann signalling to her once more. He's running out of gas.

'Grace,' says Cutter softly, 'you think Lily can pull this off?'

'Yes, sir, I do. Or she wouldn't be out there.'

'Then, so do I,' says Cutter. 'You've still got the call.'

There is no picture on the monitor, and no more time. Flint swallows hard and gives Hartmann the sign he's been waiting for.

'All right, Lily,' she hears him say over the speakers, resignation in his voice. 'Go to your precious meeting . . .'

# two

In the bitter aftermath of Operation Pentecost, after Ruth Apple has been laid to rest in a forlorn cemetery in Boca Raton, two lawyers from the Department of Justice – two taciturn men named Murtagh and Mosley – will travel from Washington to New York City to challenge Aldus Cutter's contention that risk is inherent in war, and sometimes you lose because that is the nature of risk.

In his office that hides behind the tired red-brick façade of the Marscheider building overlooking UN Plaza, they will confront Cutter with what they have perceived as his moment of failure. It is the word 'then', taken from the transcript and supported by the tape, that they will dwell on: as in Cutter's phrase, '*Then*, so do I.'

With their sly questions the lawyers will imply – in many different ways, until Cutter is tired of it – that this qualification of his statement proves that when he allowed Operation Pentecost to proceed helter-skelter to its disastrous conclusion, he relied on Flint's judgement, rather than his own. Despite the repeated, prescient objections of Assistant Director Nathan Stark.

'Get this,' Cutter will say when he's had his fill of their insinuations. 'Pentecost was Flint's operation, her command, her call. She'd thought through the risk, and she thought it was worth taking, and I agreed with her. Still do, as a matter of fact. None of us knew about the damned Bradley. None of us could have known, including Stark.'

'But it was on the roof,' Murtagh will protest, while Mosley fast-forwards the CCTV tape to locate the shot that proves it.

'Where the lifeboat should have been and covered with a tarp,' will be Cutter's firm response. 'You won't see that on the tape' – and he will wave a hand at Mosley, telling him not to bother – 'because the feed wasn't working until too late. But I've got twelve pairs of eyes that saw it, thirteen if you count Flint's. The assholes sucker-punched us.' Cutter will smile. 'They sometimes do.'

While Murtagh and Mosley absorb this truth, and note it on their legal pads, Cutter will continue, 'My professional responsibility ...' causing the lawyers to start, for they come from a department that is called the Office of Professional Responsibility. Within Justice, the OPR is the pious guardian of standards and ethics and, when things go wrong, the fixer of blame. With Ruth Apple's family about to file suit against the federal government, claiming three million dollars in compensatory and punitive damages for the 'gross negligence' they say caused their daughter's murder, the OPR has never been more ready to fix blame.

'My professional responsibility,' Cutter will repeat, 'is not to second-guess my directors in the field. I make sure they're competent; I vet their operations; I make damn sure they get the resources they need – and then I let them get on with it. Pentecost was a textbook operation and it was flawless, right up until the end.'

'Ah,' Mosley will say, tapping his lips with the barrel of his fountain pen, 'but you had *two* directors in the field. Two directors who disagreed. All right, you say that Flint was nominally in command, but why did you discount Agent Stark's warnings?'

'There's nothing nominal about command,' Cutter will say briskly. 'Not on my team.'

Mosley will not acknowledge this rebuke so Cutter will continue: 'You want a better reason? Okay, I'll give you one. On something like this, I'll take Flint's call over Stark's any time. Nathan's got qualities I can use, but when it comes to running an undercover op he's not in her league. Know why?'

Mosley will leave it to Murtagh to say, 'Go ahead.'

'Because she's been undercover more times than I can count. Nathan, the closest he ever came to walking the line was in his Bureau days, breaking into some violator's house to hang a wire.'

Seeing them stiffen, and their sudden frowns, Cutter will ask straight-faced, 'What's the matter? You think he didn't have a warrant? Trust me,' he will continue, giving them just a glimmer of a smile, 'Nathan doesn't take a piss without a warrant.'

Then, serious once more, Cutter will say, 'Stark doesn't have Flint's sixth sense. Because he's never been there, he doesn't have her feel for how far to push the envelope. Every grey op we run –

and that's most of them – is built on a lie that can come back and bite you. You know what we do? We build houses of cards on shifting sands, and knowing when they're about to fall down is something they don't teach at Quantico.'

'But Flint's not infallible,' Murtagh will say.

'Close enough.'

'And, on the basis of her record,' Murtagh will continue, ignoring Cutter's caveat, 'you might describe her as headstrong? Reckless, even?'

Cutter's faded-blue eyes will not show the disdain he feels for Murtagh. 'You might. You've read the files and you think Flint's got some kind of death wish. Well, you're not the first to come to that conclusion – and you're dead wrong. She's got guts all right, *and* she's got smarts. She knows exactly how far to push it, and when to pull back, which is why she's as good as she is.'

'Ah,' Mosley will begin again, a verbal tic that irritates Cutter, 'but being an undercover operative is not the same as directing another operative, surely? An operation that might not be reckless for Flint to undertake could be extremely reckless for someone less skilled. Or, less experienced. Isn't that precisely what we're talking about?'

Mosley will pause while Murtagh searches the tape transcript for the proof. Finding it, Murtagh will clear his throat and say, 'This is Stark to Flint verbatim. Quote: Lily is too inexperienced to pull this off. You could do this, she can't. End quote.'

'Wasn't he right?' Mosley will add.

Cutter, now hunched forward across his desk, getting closer to the agents, will say, 'Let me tell you something about Ruth Apple. When Flint found her, Ruth was working undercover for DEA, and you don't get to do that unless you're pretty damn good, because you don't stay alive if you're not. She was down in Miami, working the inside of the Raúl Gonzalez cartel for the best part of a year, and she lived to tell the tale in court. Even so, when she came to the strike force, Flint re-trained her, polished her, tuned her like a violin. She made her into Lily Apana and into one of the best undercovers we had and the legend Ruth got for Pentecost, that was pure Flint and platinum-plated. What Nathan said was horseshit. Ruth was plenty experienced, and well-prepared.'

'But, in light of what happened, not sufficiently,' Mosley will say gravely. 'Unfortunately.'

Within law enforcement circles, Aldus Cutter has a famous intolerance for what he sees as Monday morning quarterbacking, and a temper to go with it, but for once he will not explode. Leaning back in his chair, clasping his hands behind his head, he will regard Murtagh and Mosley with what they might mistake as benevolence and ask, 'You fellers want to know something? Experience don't count for a hell of a lot when the target shoves a loaded Magnum in your mouth.'

# three

It is the morning after the murder of Ruth Apple and Grace Flint is slumped on the skimpy cushions of a government-issue couch, watching herself on a flat screen that hangs like a painting on one wall of Aldus Cutter's office.

On the screen her face is animated, her eyes brilliant, her mouth working furiously as she says things we cannot hear. In real life her eyes are dull with fatigue, her face white and as frigid as a mask. Daubs of dried blood – Ruth's blood – mark her clothes.

Cutter is seated at a small conference table with Jarrett Crawford to his left, Rocco Morales to his right. There is a chair at the table for Felix Hartmann but he prefers to stand by the window, staring down at UN Plaza on the other side of First Avenue where manikins the size of dolls hurry through the lashing rain.

A telephone warbles and Cutter snatches at it.

'I said no calls.'

Nevertheless, he listens to what he is told and then he relents. 'Okay, put him through.' Covering the mouthpiece with one hand he says to Rocco Morales, 'Pause it, will you? They've found the chopper.'

The video freezes on a frame that catches Flint glancing up at the camera, and Morales, having nothing else to do, idly enlarges it until her face fills the screen. Her eyes are now on fire, her nostrils flared, her lips parted. It seems she is about to scream.

Cutter says into the phone, 'Nathan, go ahead,' and he begins taking notes, his left hand scurrying across the page of an unlined pad. Flint, who feels oddly detached from the events taking place in this room, notes that Cutter is still wearing his wedding ring. This raises a question in her mind, for within the Strike Force it is common knowledge that Mrs Cutter is in the process of obtaining an acrimonious divorce.

Flint gets up stiffly from the couch and sees once more the ruined state of her skirt. She runs her hands down her thighs as if she might somehow iron out the creases, triggering a spasm in her left leg. The pain makes her gasp and Crawford gets up quickly from the table and comes to her side.

'You okay?' he asks.

She smiles and lies. 'I'm fine,' she says.

'Well, let me tell you, you look like shit. You want to get that looked at, Grace.'

He is referring to her left femur, the patella and the tibia, and the attending ligaments and tendons. In the emergency room of Saint Vincent's hospital – where Ruth Apple was pronounced dead from the cumulative trauma of massive internal injuries – they had, as an afterthought, offered to X-ray Flint's leg. She had declined but she did allow a young intern with an earnest face to probe her neck and clavicle where a vivid bruise was already spreading like a stain, a cocktail of purple, red and blue. He had reluctantly conceded there was nothing broken, so far as he could tell.

Flint touches Crawford's arm to reassure him but he's not buying.

'Why are you punishing yourself?' he asks, keeping his voice low. 'You think that's going to help?'

She shakes her head as if to say, *No, it doesn't help.*

'It wasn't your fault, Grace,' Crawford insists. 'If there's blame going around, it's mine.' She gives him a look that says *That's ridiculous* but he presses on. 'I was the point man, wasn't I, the closest one to her? I should have drilled that asshole when I had the chance, and I did have the chance, didn't I? You know that.'

Again, Flint shakes her head. She wants to tell him to stop it but she can't find the words.

And, anyway, Crawford is growing angry – with himself as much as her, his Celtic temper getting the better of him. 'It's not been twenty-four hours and I've already relived what happened a hundred times. I had a clear head shot, and I wouldn't have missed, and I didn't take it. It was me who screwed up, not you, so stop this bullshit.'

'Crawdaddy,' she says, 'it wasn't your call.'

'The fuck it wasn't!' he explodes. 'You think I was waiting for your permission?'

Cutter breaks off from the phone call to say, 'Hey, pilgrims, keep it down.'

Crawford flaps a hand in apology. 'You know what, Grace?' he continues in a near-whisper, taking her arm and turning them both away from Cutter. 'There's a side to you I just don't get. You're about the smartest person I've worked with even if you are a Brit, so tell me something. Any time shit happens, how come it's always got to be your fault? Does self-pity turn you on or is this your ego talking? I mean, tell me, Grace, what is it that makes you so goddamned important?'

Gently, Flint retrieves her arm. She thinks but does not say, *Ruth was my friend.*

'Hustler's gone,' Cutter announces with weary certainty as he puts down the phone. 'Long gone.'

On Cutter's command Rocco Morales has resumed the running of the tape, and Flint has taken a place at the table. Felix Hartmann still gazes out of the window, as though he wants no part of the events being depicted on the screen.

So he misses seeing his walk-on role in the replay of the drama, the moment when he comes into shot, leaning over Flint's shoulder, one hand resting on the console. We can see his mouth moving and Cutter asks Morales, 'Can you give me sound?'

'It's not synced. I haven't had time.'

'Even so,' says Cutter, and Morales freezes the picture once more. He lugs a bulky sound recorder on to the table and puts on a pair of earphones and says, 'Give me a minute to set it up.' The recorder is a reel-to-reel with a cushioned drive mechanism that makes a soft sigh each time he reverses the direction of the tape, searching for the cue.

In a flat tone Flint volunteers, 'Felix asked me if I was sure. Sure about going on with it.'

Cutter nods, as if he had expected this. 'And you said?'

'No, not really, but that it was too late to abort.'

'What changed your mind?'

Flint hesitates because she doesn't know the answer. Then she speculates, 'We still didn't have a picture of the boat and it was making me uneasy.' Cutter waits for more and she says. 'A gut feeling, I suppose. That they were going to pull something.'

'You got that right,' says Cutter, and he might as well have slapped her.

'Didn't I just?' is all that she responds.

There is a brooding silence that Morales breaks. 'All set,' he declares, taking off the earphones, turning on the speaker. 'More or less.'

The picture on the wall comes alive and Flint sees herself turn her face towards Hartmann's, and hears herself say – the words not quite in sync with the movements of her mouth – 'Oh, Christ! It's a set-up!'

What she's thinking now is: *How did they know?*

Still no picture on the monitor. Crawford's voice urgent, booming over the speakers: 'He's pulled a weapon!' Flint coming out of the chair like it's on fire, Felix Hartmann reeling back to get out of her way.

'Nathan, take the desk,' she yells and she's barely said it when Stark comes into frame.

'He's put a fucking gun in her mouth,' Crawford reports.

'Take him down,' says Stark.

'He's dragging her to the boat.'

'Go!' commands Stark. 'All of you. Take him down!' He turns his head and says, apparently to Morales, 'Give me that picture, *now*!'

Off-camera there are sounds of frantic activity in the operations room, sounds we cannot fully comprehend until we hear what is unmistakably the slamming of a door.

Over the speakers Crawford is shouting, 'Federal agent! Clear the way!' He sounds breathless, as though he is running, and on the screen on Cutter's wall the picture makes a jagged cut, from the operations room to the scene on the atrium. The crowd scatters like a flock of startled pigeons as a dozen men, brandishing weapons, converge on the exits leading to the plaza. Crawford, coming down from his vantage point on the mezzanine, has the furthest distance to travel and we see him barging his way down an escalator, cannoning through bodies. Morales pulls a close-up of his livid face and we can easily lip-read the new mantra he is now mouthing: '*Get out of the fucking way!*' We can hear it, too, coming over the speakers with a momentary delay, like a rifle shot heard from a distance.

Then the picture makes another jagged cut and we are on the bridge that runs between the two centres, and we see Flint emerging from the lobby of SeaWorld, brushing her way past startled security

guards. She pauses to take off her shoes and then she is running
along the bridge, running like the wind, Hartmann coming on
behind trying to catch up.

There is no sound to accompany the pictures from the bridge.
What we hear instead are the noises relayed by Crawford's
microphone: a volley of gunfire, the crash of breaking glass, a
faded wail of screams.

'They're firing from the boat,' Crawford tells us, and Stark's
disembodied voice says, 'Goddamn you, Morales!' and a moment
later Morales replies, 'Got it. Coming now.'

The screen on Cutter's wall goes white before we catch our first,
brief look at the plaza and then it flickers into black vertical lines
that obscure our view and there is a loud thud on the soundtrack
as though somebody – Stark, we assume – has slammed a fist on to
a hard surface close to the microphone. Above the howl of
approaching sirens there is a second volley of shots and then a
third, this one louder and longer, until Crawford shouts, 'Hold
your fire!'

'Hustler's using her as a shield,' he hurriedly explains, 'and now
they're too damn close to the boat. I could have taken him out but
I didn't.'

'River One, this is Pentecost,' says Stark's voice. 'Hear this. Code
Red. They have a hostage, one of ours. Acknowledge.'

The vertical lines on the screen are slowly dissolving, thinner
now like the bars of a cage. Between them, we have glimpses of the
sodden plaza on which nothing moves.

There is a crackle of radio static and then, 'Roger, Pentecost, this
is River One. We're monitoring your traffic. Come back.'

'Stand by,' says Stark.

'River units, standing by.'

Now Morales splits the screen into segments to provide us with
a kaleidoscope of views of this bankrupt operation. There, on the
left, is a close-up of Stark, staring at the monitor, talking into the
phone. Alongside, in the next segment, we can see the end of the
bridge and the entrance to the World Emporium, Flint hitting the
revolving doors without slowing. An instant later, or so it seems,
she bursts into the third segment that shows the mezzanine, and
then she's in the next, taking the stairs down to the atrium at
reckless speed. Hartmann follows her from segment to segment,
still lagging behind.

'He's got Lily on the boat,' Crawford tells us, and there is another flurry of shots. 'He's taking her up to the top deck.'

Flint has moved on. She is crossing the atrium like a hurdler, vaulting over live bodies that lie prone on the floor, heading for the exit and the last segment of the screen that now shows a clear view of the plaza and, in the distance – too far to make out much detail – our first indication of the corporate charter boats moored in the yacht basin.

There is a loud crack on the soundtrack and the whine of a ricochet and Crawford grunts and mutters, 'Jesus.' Then, puzzlement in his voice, 'What the fuck's he doing?'

'Tell me,' says Stark. 'I'm still blind.' And so are we.

'There's something on the roof,' Crawford tells us. 'I can't make it out. Looks like—'

He breaks off as though he can't believe his eyes; as if he is waiting for the camera operator to pull the focus, allowing us to see for ourselves and confirm his startling conclusion.

And, obligingly, the picture on the screen flickers and grows and we seem to be sucked into a vortex, racing across the plaza towards the basin at madcap speed. The superstructure of a boat looms into view and then dissolves into a meaningless purple mush that resembles the aura of the sun. The operator of the camera has evidently overdone the magnification but he quickly recovers. With a violent shake, we are lurched back until our viewpoint steadies and sharpens and, right on cue, Crawford continues, '. . . some kind of toy chopper.'

Indeed it does. Perched on the roof of the flying bridge of a substantial motor cruiser is what looks like an expensive item from the Hammacher Schlemmer catalogue: a faithful, pint-sized reproduction of a helicopter, one that a pampered child of indulgent parents might be given to fly over Central Park via radio control.

But Stark knows better.

'It's a Bradley 5LD,' he says crisply. 'And it's not a frigging toy. River One, do you copy?'

The picture on Cutter's screen shimmers with a milky opacity and it is difficult to make out much of the two huddled figures that seem to melt into the Bradley's Perspex canopy.

'Pentecost, copy that. Do you want—?'

We do not catch the rest of the radio transmission from the

police boat for it is obscured by a grunted exclamation, the rattle of sustained gunfire and, almost simultaneously, a deafening bellowed command from Crawford: '*Get down!*'

Flint has arrived on the scene, evidently, for Crawford next says, 'Christ, Grace! Are you trying to get yourself killed?' And then, alarmed, 'What are you doing?'

Panting for one thing, sucking for air, her mouth very close to the microphone that is clipped to Crawford's shirt. We imagine her lying on the ground beside him, seizing him by the tie, pulling him towards her.

'Nathan,' she manages to say between the gasps, 'Hustler has wings.'

'He knows,' Crawford tells her.

'Air support on its way,' says Stark, and Crawford repeats it.

'Too late,' says Flint – and we can see what she means.

On top of the Bradley the rotor is turning, building speed until it becomes a black blur. The tail lifts and the little machine leans forward into the wind. Hesitantly it rises into the air and there is a puff of smoke from the stern of the cruiser and we hear the muffled roar of powerful engines. Then two loud cracks, and from the deck of the boat come two smouldering projectiles that look like flares arcing towards us.

They fall on to the plaza well short of our position.

'Smoke,' we hear Flint shout. 'They're trying to blind us!'

And quickly they succeed. From the projectiles, belching plumes of dirty white clouds rise up like a curtain as thick as cotton wool. The last we see before our view is obscured, the cruiser is pulling away from the dock, the Bradley hovering above it.

'They're getting away,' says Crawford uselessly.

The camera pulls back to lengthen our perspective, until we can see the whole of the plaza. Beneath us figures huddle by a wall, one of them breaking away, running towards the cloud.

'River units, intercept,' calls Stark.

'Roger, that's a go. River One and Two underway.'

Again the camera pulls back, and pans left, and we see the flashing blue light of an NYPD launch pulling away from the near bank of the East River.

Then we are yanked back to the plaza where the smoke is thinning, scattered by the wind, and the Bradley is rising above our viewpoint. We are staring at its black underbelly when something –

someone – comes spilling out of the cockpit. Lily Apana is falling, falling like a brick.

Crawford howls like a wounded animal and there is another lurch of the camera and we see Flint sprinting across the plaza, making thirty yards, only to misjudge the point of impact. She overruns the spot and has to turn back, and she is straining, her head up, reaching out her arms as though she is a defensive back trying to intercept the pass.

We assume that she is trying to break Apana's fall, or cushion it at least, but this is a vain hope born of absolute despair. The velocity that small body has achieved sends Flint sprawling and, an instant later, Lily Apana smashes on to the unforgiving paving stones of the plaza of the World Emporium.

The distant report of the impact captured by Crawford's microphone is not in sync with the picture. There is a good second's delay before we are made to hear that dreadful sound.

# four

Felix Hartmann is on his way to the small airstrip in Suffolk County where the Bradley sits abandoned, guarded behind police tape. Jarrett Crawford is at Number One Police Plaza, observing the futile interrogation of three of Hustler's hoods who, on the advice of their expensive lawyers, decline to say a single word. Rocco Morales is at his bench in the basement of the Marscheider building, enhancing the soundtrack in anticipation of the inevitable inquiry.

Flint has been given nothing to do.

She lies on the couch in Cutter's office watching him at his desk through half-closed eyes. She wishes to believe that if she concentrates hard enough on what he says into the telephone she can banish the sound of Ruth's death that her memory keeps replaying.

This is not true. She can alter the mental picture she sees, transforming the event, but she cannot change the resonance.

What she hears over and over, above and beyond Cutter's meaningless words, is the sickening thud of a frightened sparrow hitting a windowpane of her childhood bedroom; the snapping of bone, the squash of flesh, the sudden expulsion of breath. She had lured it inside the room for company and closed the window and, consequently, caused its panic. Her fault.

The bird had made no cry as it fluttered and died and nor had Ruth.

Cutter puts down the phone and looks at her and says, 'Grace, go home.'

It takes a moment for his words to register. 'Yes,' she says tentatively. She looks at the bloodstains on her shirt as though she is seeing them for the first time. 'Yes,' she says again, 'I need to change.'

Cutter shakes his bull's head. He doesn't mean her apartment. 'Go home to your husband, Grace.'

She looks at him bewildered, as though he's speaking a language she doesn't understand.

'I want you out of here, out of the city.'

'Sorry?' She tries shaking her head to get rid of the fog.

'For a few days,' Cutter continues. 'Until things calm down. There's going to be a lot of shit flying around and I don't want you covered in it any more than I can help.' He pauses. 'Come back for Ruth's funeral, if that seems appropriate.'

Flint's sad eyes are hazel but now they're darkening, the colour coming from much further down the spectrum. The torpor she has worn like a cloak all morning has abruptly vanished. She swings her feet on to the floor and sits upright.

'Excuse me?' she says, her tone no longer vague.

Cutter gives her a sharp look. 'Don't go there, Grace. This isn't the time.'

Abruptly standing up, advancing towards Cutter's desk, she ignores his warning and the pain in her leg.

'Are you suspending me, Mr Cutter?'

'No,' says Cutter but then she comes very close to him, jutting out her chin. Given Cutter's volcanic temperament, Flint knows this is an imprudent thing to do but the rage she has suppressed for the last twenty-four hours is now spilling out of her like blood from a severed artery and rage can make her reckless.

'Back off,' Cutter says, wasting his breath.

'Is that it?' she demands. 'Have I been canned?'

'Sure you have,' he replies. Coming slowly out of his chair, standing toe to toe with her, matching her glare, Cutter continues, 'Sure, you're suspended. If that's what you want.'

'You think it was my fault?' she demands.

'I think you lost it, Flint, like you're losing it now.'

'Meaning?'

'Meaning you abandoned the desk. Meaning you had twelve agents out there you were supposed to be directing and you went running off like some dumb broad—'

'Nathan had the desk,' she interrupts.

'It wasn't his command.'

'We couldn't see. There was no picture.'

'You had Crawford's eyes.'

'Not good enough, Mr Cutter. *I* had to see.'

'Morales was getting you the picture.'

'Not soon enough.'

'He *got* you the goddamned picture.'

'*Not soon enough!*'

She shouts this last retort and a spray of her spittle splatters Cutter's face, causing him to flinch. He raises his hand and for a half-moment she thinks he's going to strike her. Instead, he wipes his cheek.

'I'm sorry,' she stutters and then, 'You weren't sodding there, Mr Cutter. You were in sodding Washington . . .' Her voice trails off as she loses the thread. Cutter waits.

Suddenly deflated, as though all of her spirit has left her body, she asks, 'How did they know? How did they know that Ruth was a plant?' She cannot remember ever feeling so tired.

Cutter puts a hand on her arm, offering a truce. 'That's down to Nathan,' he says. She instantly stiffens and starts to protest but he shushes her with a squeeze of his hand and presses on. 'He's good at that, better than you. He'll put together a pack of terriers and take Pentecost apart line by line until he finds the leak, if that's what it was.' He softens his face. 'You don't have his patience, Grace. It's not your style.'

'Hustler's mine,' Flint says defiantly.

'Not any more he's not.'

Again she bridles and Cutter cocks his head. 'Think about it. This is now a homicide investigation and you can bet the bank the Bureau will claim jurisdiction, since Ruth was still technically a fed. Matter of fact,' he nods at the telephone on his desk, 'I was just talking to Bob Palmer at Justice and that's exactly the way he's reading it: Karl Gröber murdered a federal agent.'

Flint's own words come swimming back to her. *Gentlemen, listen up. Let's be clear about this. I'm about to put a federal agent in harm's way* . . . Well, she'd certainly done that. She suddenly feels faint and closes her eyes. On the left side of her frontal lobe there is a pinprick of intense pain.

'You okay?' she hears Cutter say. 'Got one of your migraines coming on?' Not for the first time she thinks, *You know me too well*.

She opens her eyes and shakes her head. 'I'm just tired,' she says.

Cutter moves his hand to her undamaged shoulder. 'Then go home, Grace. Go home to Ben.'

*Ben's not there*, she thinks, but there seems no point in telling Cutter that.

# Miller's Reach
# Connecticut

# five

By Cutter's rules, the intelligence files of the Financial Strike Force are never photocopied and they never leave the confines of the Marscheider building. Other than when they are logged out to an agent for specific and specified use, they remain locked in the Archive, watched over by cameras and accounted for by a formidable woman whose name is Kitty Lopez.

But even Cutter's rules bear exception, and Flint and Kitty Lopez have reached an understanding.

Inside a two-hundred-year-old red barn, Flint keeps the beam of her small torch pointed at the floor while she waits for the bats to re-settle. Ben has persuaded her it is a myth – 'a slander,' he calls it – that bats are blind. Disturbed from hibernation, they will panic and feign attack, heading in a whirling cloud directly for the light. The bats that have colonised Ben and Grace's barn are Little Browns no bigger than field mice but there are uncounted thousands of them roosting in the abandoned walls. The smell of their guano that carpets the floor is overwhelming.

As taught by Ben, Flint talks into the darkness in reassuring tones. And when at last their fluttering has ceased, she dares to step on to the ladder that leads to a platform beneath the rafters where she has hidden a near-complete copy of the Pentecost file. The fourth rung is missing and the seventh has been weakened, half-sawn through, so that it will break under human weight; two traps – deterrents – that Flint has laid and that she must now negotiate. Needing both hands, she reluctantly douses the torch and stows it in the back pocket of her jeans.

In the four months since she brought home the Pentecost file she has climbed this ladder in the pitch dark a dozen times but it gets no easier and the pulsing ache in her left leg is sharpening her senses. Whatever Ben might say in defence of bats – and for all of her father's cheerful, teasing corroboration – she remains terrified of their mythical power. If she allows herself, she can feel them in her hair.

Reaching the platform, she squats on her haunches and gratefully turns on the torch. Shielding the beam with one cupped hand, she uses the glow to guide her other hand to the loose panel that conceals her niche. She pushes it aside and reaches in and her fingers find the oilskin in which the precious file is wrapped. It consists of some eight hundred pages, and is consequently heavy, and she locks her wrist in anticipation of the strain. There are sleeping bodies hanging within inches of her face that she really does not wish to disturb.

*Come on! Do it!* she tells herself, and slowly, very slowly, she retrieves the package and slips it into a nylon backpack that is hanging from the shoulder that is not hurting. Extinguishing the torch, returned to total darkness, she edges backwards on her knees until her toes find the top rung of the ladder.

Going down is the most dangerous part, for it is easy to miscount the steps, and the prospect of imminent release from the barn can tempt you into careless haste.

Flint forces herself to go slowly, take it one rung at a time, concentrate on the count, keep her weight on the right leg as much as possible. That's fine as far as it goes but the nerve endings in her damaged shoulder have now come alight with pain and she has to bite her lip to stop herself from squealing.

*Like some dumb broad*, as Cutter had said, and the sudden recall of his gratuitous insult brings with it a flush of anger made even more righteous by the unfairness of his verdict. *Hustler's not yours – not any more. Hustler belongs to Nathan. Nathan will find the leak. He's good at that. Better than you.*

Reaching out with her gammy leg, testing the next rung to confirm it isn't the weakened seventh, Flint says louder than she means, 'Well, screw you, Aldus Cutter,' and, somewhere too close to her, creatures stir.

Flint pushes open the barn door and squeezes into the sunlight feeling a surge of relief that makes her heady. She waits until her eyes have adjusted to the light, and until the giddiness has passed, and then she starts towards the house, skirting a pond that on this shining April morning presents a surface like polished glass.

It is not always so placid. Two weeks ago, the last time she was here, after lunch and with Ben asleep by the fire, she chanced to look out of the window and saw one corner of the pond molten, boiling with unexplained activity. Hurrying to investigate the cause, she found a deer swimming for its life, and three snapping coyotes dancing at the water's edge. At the sight of the intruder they broke off the chase but they soon regained their courage, and then it was Flint they were stalking, attempting to circle her, and it was she who was backing away. Only when she'd gained some distance from them did she turn and flee for the house.

Bursting into the living room, searching for her gun, she woke Ben and gave him a hurried explanation. Still groggy from sleep, he yawned and muttered some banality about allowing nature to take its course.

'Bugger that,' she said, the vet's daughter that she was.

But it was not necessary to shoot the coyotes. When she got back to the pond, the largest Irish wolfhound she'd ever seen stood like a sentinel with its back to the water, watching the coyotes slink away into the woods. The deer was free and clear and well on its way to the safety of the far bank.

'So, does your hound have a name?' Ben asked, smiling at her, amused by her breathless account of the deer's salvation.

She said she had no idea – and she still has no idea, but the dog is there, the height of a small pony, standing on her deck, watching her come limping from the barn.

She goes inside the house and unwraps the Pentecost file and places it on a glass-topped table beneath the picture window that occupies one entire wall of her den. From here she can see most of the five acres that she and Ben own, a wedding present bought outright with her father's money.

Actually, her mother's – his wife's – money, inherited by Dr John Flint after Marie-Madeleine Flint disappeared when Grace was not yet six years old, but that is a subject father and daughter still find too haunting to talk about. The only acknowledgement of the fact is the picture of Grace's mother, set in a silver frame, that sits on the table facing the window, sharing her fine view of Miller's Reach.

Still too restless to settle to her task, Flint goes to the kitchen to make tea and, while the kettle boils, she goes upstairs to collect the towels from the bathroom and the sheets from the bed and puts them on to wash. Ben was supposed to do this before he left but he's not had time, or, more likely, he's forgotten, which is just like him. He's also neglected to leave her one of his funny farewell notes, adorned with his drawing of some exotic bird, which is not like him at all. She searched for a note in all of the usual places when she got home from New York last night, and not finding one has left her feeling unsettled.

When the tea is made she returns to the den, bringing with her two sweet digestive biscuits for the dog. Given his condition, he is clearly not a stray. She expects he belongs to one of the neighbours she has never met and she also expects to find a name and perhaps a telephone number on the tag she has seen embedded in his collar. She opens the French doors and calls for him to come and, sensing no fear in her, the hound obeys. He sits at her feet and allows her to scratch the hard, rough coat under a jaw that looks strong enough to crush stone, and then he gently takes the biscuits from her hand. The tag bears only a name: Sirius, after the Dog Star, the brightest in the sky.

'Haven't you got a home to go to, you brute?' she says affectionately, but Sirius shows no intention of leaving. He settles on the deck while she settles at her table and, pulling the Pentecost file towards her, aware that she is about to raise unwelcome ghosts, she admits to herself that she is not at all displeased to have his silent company.

# six

On the cover page, beneath the logo of the Financial Strike Force, there is a stark warning, emblazoned in red, that this fat file is CLASSIFIED and, beneath that, the single word PENTECOST, printed in slender capitals.

'Okay, I'll ask,' Flint had said wearily as Cutter grinned, waiting for the question. 'Why Pentecost?'

'The day of Pentecost had come,' intoned Cutter in a deep mock preacher's voice, taking hold of the lapels of his bathrobe like a bishop's pallium. 'And the *Holy Spirit*,' he went on, rolling his eyes as though he was possessed, 'descended from the sky as a *driving wind*, a *great noise* which filled the *whole* house where the Apostles were gathered. And there appeared unto them *flames*, flames like tongues of fire distributed among them . . .' He had broken off and chuckled at the expression of astonishment on her face. 'You're the flames. What do you think?'

'Excuse me?'

'Way I see it,' said Cutter, perching one plump buttock on the corner of the kitchen counter, 'around about next Pentecost, if you do your job right, you'll be coming down on Gröber and his apostles like the wrath of God. Get it?'

Flint had groaned.

'There's a supplementary,' said Cutter, even more pleased with himself. 'Now, you may not know this, but in the Jewish faith Pentecost is called Shabuoth and one of the observances during Shabuoth is readings from – guess what?'

'I've no idea.'

'The Book of Ruth! How do you like that?' He'd slapped the counter with his hand. 'I thought about calling it Operation Shabuoth,' he went on, 'but Nathan wouldn't know how to spell it. Matter of fact—'

'Aldus,' Flint had interrupted, 'were you awake all night dreaming up this stuff?'

In the Marscheider building, or almost anywhere else, she would never have called him Aldus, but they were in the kitchen of his apartment on East 63rd Street, Cutter reluctantly on sick leave, convalescing from emergency surgery for a strangulated hernia. There was no sign of Mrs Cutter and Flint hadn't liked to ask.

Suddenly all business, Cutter had enquired, 'Got a legend for her yet?'

'Yes,' she'd said, and told him of the complex web of deceit she and Ruth Apple had been busily spinning.

'That's good,' he'd agreed. 'Ruth got a name?'

'Lily,' she'd replied. 'Lily Apana' – and Cutter had nodded his approval.

Which is how Ruth Apple, special agent of the Financial Strike Force, became Lily Apana, an ambitious bank executive open to corruption, and for the last eight months of her life nobody had ever called her Ruth. On her very rare visits to the Marscheider building, slipping in through the basement door; at the more-frequent progress briefings with Flint, held covertly in her new apartment; at the Delta Bank of New York where she worked assiduously to enable Karl Gröber's organisation to launder some two billion dollars; on every record and document that falsely testified to Lily Apana's existence; to everyone outside the Strike Force, and everyone within it, she was never Ruth, always Lily. It was Flint's aim, and eventually her achievement, that even Ruth came to think of herself as Lily, the only name to which she would instinctively respond.

To her parents in Boca Raton – and former colleagues at the Drug Enforcement Administration in Miami, her few friends, her one-time lover – she remained Ruth Apple, of course, but in absentia. The legend said Ruth was on a one-year assignment in Pakistan, from where reassuring postcards in her hand would occasionally be sent. And, indeed, Ruth Apple *was* the officially accredited FSF liaison officer in Islamabad, though any attempt to reach her there was invariably met with a recorded apology on her answering machine: Special Agent Apple regretted that she was away from the office for a few days; in the field, by implication, doubtless advising the Pakistani police on some complex and time-consuming financial inquiry related to the illegal narcotics trade.

And had any of those who knew her as Ruth Apple – even her lover, even her *mother* – come to New York and bumped into her on the street (one of the nightmares of every undercover agent), they would have been hard-pressed to recognise her. Under Flint's guidance, Lily Apana was fifteen pounds lighter than Ruth Apple. Her hair was jet black and brushed the back of her neck, not short-cropped and fair. Thanks to contact lenses, her eyes were deep brown, not blue, and cosmetics made her complexion paler. Above her top lip – a nice touch, this – ran a thin scar, the apparent legacy of a childhood accident that had not befallen Ruth. Hours of practice, and tight shoes, gave Lily a gait that was shorter than Ruth's, and added to the hint of the Orient about her. Lily Apana was born in Hawaii – if you believed the official records; a fifth-generation descendant of Asian immigrants who had come to work on the sugar plantations, and yet more hours of practice, this time with a voice coach brought in from Hollywood by Flint, had given Lily a dialect that weighted the lie.

Yet for all that, for all of the platinum plate applied to the legend of Lily Apana, it had cracked like cheap glass. At some point in the last eight months, Karl Gröber had not only discovered that Lily was an elaborate invention, he'd also learned her true name.

The proof of that was in the envelope found stuffed inside Lily's bra when they'd stripped her body prior to autopsy: an envelope neatly addressed to 'Flint' that contained one page, torn from a copy of the Revised English Bible.

Page 226. The first page of the Book of Ruth.

In her den, watched over by Sirius and the spirit of her vanished mother, Flint turns the cover page and reads the first two lines of the opening report, lines she wrote herself.

SUSPICIOUS BANKING ACTIVITIES.
Possible Money Laundering by Delaware Corporations
Formed for German Nationals.

Next comes the explanation that this is a 'Narrative Summary of Interview with Confidential Informant #00217,' and then the date, and then the identity of the authors: 'JAD/O Flint & SA Apple.'

She was still Ruth then, for Operation Pentecost – and Lily Apana – had not yet been spawned.

'This individual, who has provided reliable information to FSF on several previous occasions (see in particular CR00-BONY at pages 27–31 and CR00-CITYB at Appendix II),' the report begins in the familiar dreary prose of all of its kind, 'contacted Joint Assistant Director (Operations) Flint by telephone call on 04/26/00 and requested an urgent meeting. Subject declined to come to the office and insisted on a rendezvous at 0100 hours the following morning in the parking lot adjacent to The River Café, Water Street, Brooklyn. In accordance with procedures, JAD/O Flint was accompanied to the meeting by Special Agent Apple, a circumstance which caused the Subject some initial agitation.'

Initial agitation? In hindsight, Flint now feels that was something of an understatement.

*What are you doing? Who the hell is she?*

Little Vincent Regal screaming at Flint, waving his arms, scuttling across the frozen parking lot towards her like some deranged crow, his black, oversized overcoat flapping at his ankles.

*I told you to come alone!*

*Vincent, calm down.*

*You'll get me fucking killed.*

*Vincent, CALM DOWN!*

'Why does he do it?' Ruth had asked as they'd driven across the Brooklyn Bridge, Flint keeping one wary eye on the rear-view mirror.

'Why do any of them do it?' she'd replied. 'Settling a score? A power trip? Taking out insurance for a rainy day?' She'd thought about it for a moment and then said, 'I think that's probably it. Because, with our Vincent, you know there *is* going to be a rainy day.'

Vincent Regal in the front passenger seat of Flint's car, twisting his head on his thick, short neck to glare at Ruth with his rheumy eyes.

*How much does she know?*

*She knows nothing, Vincent.*

*Then why is she here?*

*Because those are the rules, Vincent. I can't meet you alone, you know that.*

*You people, you're fucking unbelievable.*

She had heard this before and she'd had enough of him by then. Leaning across his lap, she'd opened the passenger door.

*Out, Vincent!*

*What the fuck are you talking about?*

*Either stop behaving like a jerk or get out of the car. You don't want to talk to me – fine. I've got better things to do than listen to your foul mouth.*

'Subject was eventually placated,' the file says without elaboration, 'and volunteered information about a large number of shell corporations that have been formed in Delaware on behalf of German individuals and entities by WeTry Business Solutions, Incorporated (WETBS), of which the Subject has direct knowledge. The Subject further stated his belief that these Delaware corporations are part of an organised scheme to launder funds through US banks.'

*They're wash, fold and dry,* Vincent had said, teasing them with one of his euphemisms.

*Meaning?*

*Dixie cups. Disposables. You set them up, open an account, do a couple of transfers. Then the big one – the money comes in, the money goes out, all nicely laundered – and then you fold them.*

He'd turned his head again, this time to smirk at Ruth.

*The dry part? Well, that's you guys. You go looking for a paper trail and there isn't any – or nothing that's going to take you anywhere. You come up dry. You get my meaning?*

There was a cowlick of black hair staining his forehead, held there by the perspiration that was oozing out of him. Despite the chill outside, Flint had cracked open her window to give herself some air.

*How many corporations are we talking about, Vincent?*

*Sixteen hundred, give or take.*

*And why Delaware?*

As Flint had posed the question, a dark blue Buick that had seen better days pulled into the lot, passing their position, parking by the riverfront alongside Vincent's shiny Mercedes. Two men inside and neither of them got out. In the mirror, Flint had seen Ruth feel inside her bag where she kept her gun. Flint's own weapon was under the driver's seat, within easy reach.

The Buick had made Vincent nervous and once again cantankerous.

*Jesus, don't you people know anything?*

*Just tell me what you know, Vincent.*

He'd affected a weary tone, trying to pretend he wasn't scared.

*Because in Delaware they don't want to know a damn thing. Who are the principals? They don't give a shit. What's their nationality? Who cares? Where are they based? Fuck knows. All the client needs is a registered address in Delaware that I can rent for fifty bucks a month. What's the corporation for? Now, that's a good one. Know what we put on the registration form?*

He was about to recite what he knew by heart when he heard Ruth talking softly into her mobile phone, reading out the digits on the Buick's licence tag.

*Hey! What are you doing? You think they're interested in us?*

He'd grasped the door handle, ready to bolt, and Flint had grabbed his arm.

*That's what we're finding out. Just sit tight.*

*Jesus!*

Ruth had stopped talking but she still held the phone to her ear, waiting while they ran the plates.

*What do you put on the forms, Vincent? Tell me exactly what you put.*

He'd chanted it in a monotone.

*The purpose of the corporation is to engage in any lawful act or activity for which corporations may be organised under the General Corporation Law of Delaware.*

Flint, glancing in the mirror, saw Ruth mouth, 'REPORTED STOLEN.'

*You know that fucking Saddam Hussein?*

Flinted had waited, knowing she was about to receive one of Vincent's little homilies.

*Or that bin Laden guy? The Arabs, they could have a thousand Delaware corporations buying themselves nuclear materials, bombs, whatever they want, and Delaware wouldn't know, wouldn't give a shit.*

Keeping her eyes on the Buick, Flint had asked, *What's the going rate, Vincent?*

*Three-fifty a pop. You get a five per cent discount if you buy ten at a time.*

*That's it?*

*You want a bank account, that's another four-fifty.*

*What about due diligence?*

*Are you kidding me?*

And then Vincent had suddenly laughed, a prolonged giggle in a high falsetto that she can still hear – and hearing it now she can smell his sweat, see the thick black hair on the back of the hand that he had belatedly put to his mouth.

*You are kidding me, right?*

*Just tell me what you know, Vincent.*

What he knew, the file says, was that some American banks do not abide strictly by the US Treasury's 'know your customer' rule that is supposed to be one of the main planks of the defence against money laundering.

'Subject stated that accounts are routinely opened at banks in both New York and California on the basis of a stipulation by the president of WETBS that he has conducted due diligence investigations of the principals, but this was never true,' the report says.

*And do you check them out, Vincent?*

*Sure, we do. First thing that happens, they send us a cheque for our four hundred and fifty bucks – and we wait until it clears.*

*That's it?*

Another of Vincent's giggles, though this time quickly stifled.

*That's it. That's all we need to know.*

Flint turns the page.

'Subject stated that certain of the banks that WETBS deals with insist the customers should appear at the bank with appropriate identification – such as a passport and credit card – within thirty days of opening the account. But during that thirty-day period, the accounts are fully functional, allowing wire transfer capabilities.'

*If they don't show – and most don't – the account gets closed, usually. Big fucking deal! You know how much money you can move in thirty days?*

*You tell me, Vincent.*

He had given her a sly look.

*Well, put it this way. A fuck sight more than you're going to need for your honeymoon.*

She must have shown some reaction – and, God knows, why wouldn't she? – for he had twisted in his seat to watch her, now with a how-about-that grin on his face. He'd even had the gall to wink, and reach out with his hand to touch her arm.

*Congratulations! It's Ben Gates, right? Good-looking guy.*

*Let's stick with your business, Vincent, shall we?*

There was acid in her voice and he'd raised his hands in a gesture of surrender.

*Hey, no offence. I just like to know the people I'm dealing with.*

Vincent Regal was a creep by her definition, pond scum only marginally redeemed by the fact that he served as her occasional informant, and the revelation that he knew anything about her private life – indeed, had been *able* to learn anything of her private life – had almost made her gag. She'd suddenly felt cold and somehow soiled, as though she'd come into her bedroom and found him picking through her underwear.

Even now, the memory of it makes her uneasy and she gets up from the table. Outside, on the deck, Sirius also rises to look at her with curiosity.

'I'll get you some water,' she says distractedly, heading towards the kitchen, her mind still bothered by questions she cannot answer: How had he known? *Who* had he known? – for she had told few people of her impending marriage to Ben Gates and none of them, surely, would have shared her business with the likes of Vincent Regal.

For a moment she had been tempted – sorely tempted – to get it out of him then and there; take him out of the car and put him up against the wall if needs be, and only her training had stopped her. Never, *never* let an informant see that they've got you rattled, the instructors at Hendon used to say. Nothing they can tell you comes as a surprise because you're omnipotent, all-knowing – or that's the way it's supposed to be.

And then the moment had passed because Ruth had coughed and, checking the mirror again, Flint had seen the headlights of an NYPD blue-and-white come bouncing on to the parking lot, two unmarked cars from the Detective Bureau coming on hard behind.

The convoy had passed Flint's car as though it wasn't there and corralled the Buick, the detectives' cars close up, one on either side, the blue-and-white behind, its emergency lights now flashing, pressing the rear bumper. The brake lights were still on when six men spilled out of the cars, pointing handguns at the Buick, yelling instructions that demanded a life or death response.

Flint had seen the occupants of the Buick hurry to put their hands on their heads. A uniformed sergeant toting a pump-action shotgun had glanced in her direction and given her the briefest of nods.

*What the fuck are you doing?*
*We're going to take a little drive, Vincent. Continue our chat.*
*What about my car?*
*What about your car? You think the police are going to steal it?*

Standing in the kitchen she has to remind herself why she is there. She finds a fruit bowl and fills it with water from the tap, watched over by a kestrel – one of Ben's collection of carved wooden birds that perch throughout the house. Thinking of him, trying to imagine what he is doing, she glances at her watch and calculates the time difference between Connecticut and East Africa. He's seven hours ahead and she guesses it will already be dark in the bush.

She has overfilled the bowl and she carries it carefully to the den, holding it with both hands to avoid spilling water. The dog is not waiting for her by the French doors. She steps on to the deck and calls his name while she scans her territory, but Sirius has vanished as abruptly as he came.

# seven

Now the sun has also disappeared, taking with it the promise of the day. Flint can hear a raven's mournful call and there is a mist gathering over the pond, dulling its surface to match her mood. It's getting on for five o'clock in the afternoon and, though she has worked diligently, she's no more than one-tenth of her way through the Pentecost file, her progress stalled by her gut certainty that, somewhere within the first eighty pages, there is something she has missed; something that might have led her to the truth.

It registered on her iconic memory, she is sure, but she did not recognise its significance in time, like a missed turning on a country road. And no amount of flipping through the pages, retracing her steps, has brought her back to that point. She knows that the process is becoming self-defeating.

Pushing away the file, she returns to the kitchen half-intending to find something to eat but there is nothing in the freezer that appeals to her. She would go to the store in Essex to stock up on provisions if that didn't require a ten-mile drive there and back. She'll have to go before Ben returns, but since he's not due home for another four days she decides she will delay the expedition, spare her aching shoulder and her stiff leg.

From the larder, she takes a small can of Heinz cream of tomato soup that her father ships to her in bulk from England, a sugar-laced brew to which she is dangerously addicted, or so Ben says. She heats the soup in a saucepan and pours it into a mug that she takes upstairs to the bathroom to drink while she fills the tub with hot water. It is a large Jacuzzi that she and Ben have installed so they can bathe together – though, more often than not, bathing turns out to be just the prelude.

She smiles at the thought and then pushes away the pang of longing that it brings. Returning once more to the kitchen, she collects a glass and a half-bottle of white wine from the fridge. Ben would disapprove of her drinking in the afternoon but then Ben's not there to disapprove, she tells him tartly.

Back in the bathroom she pours a glass of wine, and a generous dollop of bath oil into the tub. Then she goes into the bedroom and strips off her clothes. Standing before the mirror, she carefully examines the contusion that runs from her neck across the width of her left shoulder and is gratified to see the first traces of a yellow tinge that tell her the injury is on the mend. On the surface at least, her thigh is unblemished and there is no sign of swelling.

She puts on music and, as an afterthought, goes downstairs to collect the Pentecost file. She will not read any more of it – not now – but she will keep it in the bathroom with her while she soaks in the tub, thus fulfilling at least the spirit of a promise she has made to Kitty Lopez: when the file is not hidden, to never let it out of her sight.

At night, filtered through the trees, Flint can see the faint glow of light coming from the house of her nearest neighbour but not the house itself. For all practical purposes, Miller's Reach is hidden from the human world, which was part of its attraction to her. In some respects it reminds her of the Georgian farmhouse in middle-England where – after her mother vanished – she grew up in self-imposed solitude, coming home from school to shut herself away in her room at the top of the house, waiting for the comfort of the dark. To the consternation of her father, she was a joyless, solitary little girl who had no friends and no apparent need of any. Much of that remains true. Darkness still soothes her and – Ben apart – she rarely feels the need for human company.

Dressed in Ben's flannel bathrobe that faintly bears his scent, she sits on the floor in the living room, her back propped against a chair, nursing the last of the wine. There is a log fire burning in the hearth, but otherwise the house is dark and silent. At least for now, she has banished Ruth's ghost and the memory of her death and focused her psyche on the certainty that is evading her.

Cutter calls it her sniper's eye, this ability Flint has to fix the cross hairs of her mind unwaveringly on a target thought.

For a long while she sits motionless, staring into the fire, willing herself to recall the fleeting snapshot of what it was she saw in the

Pentecost file before the memory was erased or masked by new information.

The fire is dying when she finally gets to her feet and walks slowly to the den, taking with her the file, feeling now a sense of dread.

On her table is a halogen lamp that floods the glass top with a brilliant light, and when her eyes have adjusted she instantly sees what she only faintly registered in the meagre light of day. On the first page of the narrative summary of her interview with Vincent Regal, there in the top right-hand corner, is a faint blue smudge no larger than an infant's fingernail.

She fetches a magnifying glass and sees that the smudge is shaped like the petal of a rose. She also sees that there is a near-identical petal in the corner of the next page of her summary, and the next, and the next. Quickly she riffles through the whole file to confirm what she fears: every page she glimpses bears the same telling hallmark.

She feels a swell of panic and forces herself to take deep breaths. It is more difficult to suppress the tumult of cries and accusations running through her mind; to concentrate on what must now be done.

It is almost two o'clock in the morning when she picks up the phone and calls the night-watch supervisor at the Marscheider building to ask for the unlisted home telephone number of Kitty Lopez.

No, the supervisor rightly tells her. It is another of Cutter's rules that the FSF does not disclose information about its employees to any caller, not even one who *says* she is the Joint Assistant Director (Operations).

'Then call her and get her to call me,' says Flint, minding her temper.

'Now? At this time of night?'

'Tell her I've found rose petals. Do it, please. Now.'

The darkness is no longer soothing. While she waits for Lopez to call Flint busies herself, passing through the house, turning on every light. She puts strong coffee on to brew and rebuilds the fire. She is getting dressed, putting on a business suit, when the phone rings.

Kitty Lopez does not waste time on recriminations. 'These petals of yours, what colour are they?'

'Blue,' Flint tells her.

There is a moment's hesitation while Lopez considers how much to risk on a line that both of them know is not secure. Then, 'I'd say it's more a *cobalt* blue, wouldn't you?'

Cobalt chloride, a translucent dye that reacts to strong light; one that turns blue if the pages with which it has been invisibly marked are run through, say, a photocopier.

'Yes,' Flint acknowledges.

'Then it's what I think you think it is.'

'The bottom line, Kitty?'

'The bottom line,' Lopez replies before cutting the call, 'is we've been screwed.'

Flint knows Aldus Cutter's home telephone number by heart. She dials it on the speaker phone in her bedroom and listens to the ringing tone while she finishes dressing. There is no reply – and no reply to his mobile, either.

It takes another call to the Marscheider building, and another tussle with the night-watch supervisor, and a twenty-minute wait before she finally has a disgruntled Cutter on the line.

'I need to see you,' she tells him.

'Do you know what time it is?'

'I've found the leak.'

She waits through his silence, imagining him rubbing the sleep out of his eyes.

'I'm in Florida.'

'Oh?'

'I came down to see Ruth's folks.'

'Okay, I'll get the first flight I can to Lauderdale.'

'No,' says Cutter. 'Miami.'

'Excuse me?'

'I'm not in Boca any more. It didn't go well with her folks.'

When he does not expand on his explanation Flint says, 'Right, Miami. I'll call your cellphone when I get in.'

'Do that,' says Cutter and then he adds, 'Trust me, Grace, this had better be good.'

*No*, she thinks after he's gone, as she stuffs the Pentecost file and a few personal necessities into her overnight bag. *Trust me, Mr Cutter, this is anything but good.*

It is a little after 4 a.m. when Flint secures the house and begins her journey. She does not leave a note for Ben.

# Gatwick Airport London

# eight

When they instructed Mandrake in the art of maintaining his false identity they cautioned him that no matter how long it survived, or how comfortable it became, there would be moments when doubt would come sneaking up to bite him; self-doubt, a gnawing feeling in the viscera that his cover was about to be blown. Typically, they said, and based on their long experience, these moments of disbelief might very likely come as he waited to submit his passport – his inherently bogus passport – to the scrutiny of some customs or immigration official. And that's the worst time, Mandrake, they said – though Tully was supposed to be his name – because the people who guard the frontiers, or the best of them, at least, will pick up the signals you're putting out and home in on you like precision-guided ordnance locks on to a target.

*They've got profiles, Mandrake. Based on their long experience they know how the guilty stand, how they fidget, how they walk, how they smell. They can see things in your eyes you don't even know are there and they've got cameras to help them look. Think about it,* they said: *You're still fifth in the immigration queue and there are people in a back room looking at your face on a monitor, seeing your edginess, seeing your doubt.*

*Do you know what happens when you're nervous, Mandrake? Your blink rate goes up. You're trying to keep your face a mask but your eyelids are fluttering like a butterfly's wings, and that's only one of the telltales. Your sweat glands are excreting – and it doesn't matter what the temperature is. You might be in Siberia and it's cold enough to freeze your breath but the right hemisphere of your brain is transmitting worry signals and the receptors in your dermis are going berserk, and then your sweat glands get into the act and before you know it you've got a telltale sheen on your face like grease.*

*They'll see it, Mandrake, sooner or later, one of these days;
they'll see it in your face, the people in the back room, and then,
unless you're good – unless you remember exactly what we're
telling you*, they said – *you're fucked.*

Rayland Tully stands in the immigration line at Gatwick's South
Terminal awaiting his turn, his eyes fixed on the broad, ebony-
coloured neck of the woman in front of him. She is exceptionally
tall, almost as tall as he is, and the pyramid of braided hair that is
piled on top of her head probably obscures his face from most of
the watching cameras.

Even so, just in case they're watching, Tully slowly chews gum to
mask any involuntary twitch of the muscles of his mouth – another
of the giveaways he was warned about – and concentrates on the
music he is playing inside his head. To soothe the unease within his
auditory cortex he has selected the slow movement from Bach's
Sonata in G minor, the master's exquisite marriage of the flute, the
cello and the harpsichord.

The queue shuffles forward and now he's second in line.

At most airports that Tully has passed through you get to choose
the line in which you stand and therefore the official who examines
your documents and, if their instincts are aroused, asks the
awkward questions – and Tully knows better than to pick the
young ones, the ones you might be conceited enough to think you
can beguile with your good looks and your easy charm. In Tully's
experience the young ones are the worst because they still believe
they can make a difference, and young women are the worst of all
because they've still got something to prove. Given the choice,
Tully always chooses an older guy; calls him 'sir', shows him a little
respect.

But at Gatwick there is no choice – just a single, snaking line that
takes you to the head of the queue and then spits you out towards
the next available podium.

'Next,' says a mechanical voice, and the woman with the ebony
skin and the piled-high hair approaches her fate. Then, before he
has time to reassess the situation, it's 'Next' again and it's Tully's
turn, and now he knows this is not his lucky day.

Twenty-something, female, with sallow skin and a tight, disapproving mouth that slants down towards the corners like an
inverted V.

She does not respond when Tully approaches the podium saying 'Hi' in a neutral tone and hands her his documents; his passport, his landing card, his return ticket. Opening the passport, she glances from his photograph to his face and then begins flicking through the pages, pausing to study each of the entry and exit stamps she finds, as though they might tell her something important about this man who claims to be Rayland Tully.

'And where are we coming from?' she asks, unnecessarily since the answer is written on his landing card. Her voice is more pleasant than he has expected, a soft contralto pitched a half-octave below middle C.

'Boston,' he replies evenly. 'By way of New York.'

'And what is the purpose of your visit?'

'A little business,' he says, 'but mainly pleasure.' He resists the urge to smile. 'Mainly, I'm on vacation.'

*Don't get clever, Mandrake. Don't elaborate and don't volunteer information they haven't asked for – because that's what guilty people do. Just answer the questions.*

She's still not looking at him, still flicking relentlessly through the pages of the passport.

'And what business is that?'

'Advertising,' he lies, though in his wallet there are business cards that declare Rayland Tully to be a Partner with Baikoff, Ducas & Tully, Advertising Practitioners of Lexington Avenue, New York. If examined, the records of the firm will show that Tully is indeed a partner though he has never crossed the threshold, never met or even spoken to Messrs Baikoff and Ducas.

'And when were you last in the United Kingdom?'

This is a trick question for she already knows the dates of his arrival and departure, evidenced by the stamps in his passport.

*Memorise them, Mandrake. Make really sure you remember when and where you're supposed to have been.*

'Last September,' says Tully. If she wants the precise dates – and his entire itinerary for that entirely fictitious trip – he has them ready but he volunteers nothing more.

It is all too obvious that something is bothering her. She examines his ticket, now the landing card, now the passport once more. Tully stands completely still, keeping his hands out of his pockets, studying her face. To distract himself he takes a broader view of her attributes. She is not wholly unattractive, he decides. Good hair, nice eyes, a pert nose that turns up at the tip. And from what he can see of her body, it's supple and trim, a body you could bend. Anywhere else, in any other circumstances, he concludes, he would make a play for her just to see how far he could get.

Behind him, at one of the other podiums, a commotion is building, not one he can credibly ignore. Tully turns around and sees the woman with the ebony skin pulling papers from a voluminous bag. Her protesting voice is growing louder, escalating towards a wail. He turns back to the podium and risks a shrug and a sympathetic smile. *These people!* he wishes to convey.

'Wait over there,' she says, nodding away from the podium, vaguely to her left.

*They're just doing their job, Mandrake – that's the way you see it. You understand; you're grateful, even. You want them to be thorough – to keep out all those terrorists, and drug traffickers and paedophiles. Now, it wouldn't be natural if you didn't show just a little bit of impatience –* Tully glances at his watch before nodding and stepping to one side – *but you're on their side. Look at it this way, if they need to keep you waiting for a few minutes while they run you through the computer, it's not a problem. Right?*

There must have been a hidden button she could press, or perhaps they were watching from the back room.

Stone-faced, thick-necked, burly inside a charcoal grey suit that was not made to measure and brown brogues on his feet, the man coming to the podium has 'copper' written all over him. Special Branch, Tully decides. Not a rocket scientist, not if he works for the Branch, but dangerous nevertheless.

Tully watches as his documents are taken away for further examination, his face registering not a flicker of emotion. The truth is, he's fireproof. They can run his passport through their computers all the way back to its genesis, and it will still stand up – verified by the documents on file with the US Passport Office.

But any substantial enquiries made by the Branch could raise alarms among his 'friends' about his vulnerability and, to those 'friends', Tully is sure, he represents the weakest link. Now that his part is done, he would be a fool not to recognise that he's both redundant and a potential liability.

For the next fifteen minutes – until, with no enthusiasm, he is finally granted permission to enter the United Kingdom – Tully tries not to dwell on the unnerving fact that he has most to fear from his friends.

'Problems, were there?'

Ridout asks his question while lounging in a doorway of the Gatwick Express, watching Mandrake on the platform smoking a quick, forbidden cigarette.

'Only, you were a long time coming through.'

Mandrake answers carefully, 'Nothing serious.'

'But they ran a check, did they?' Ridout smiles sympathetically. 'Put you through the wringer?'

Given his friends' resources, Mandrake knows there is little point in lying. 'I drew a bitch. She was in a bad mood.' He pulls on the cigarette. 'Maybe she had a fight with her boyfriend.'

'They're the worst,' says Ridout.

Up and down the train, doors are slamming shut. One minute to departure.

'So,' continues Ridout, 'perhaps friend Tully has reached the end of his useful life, don't you think?'

'I'll take care of it,' says Mandrake.

Ridout steps down on to the platform. 'Better if you leave that to me,' he says, holding out one hand.

Mandrake tosses away the cigarette butt, reaches into his pocket and surrenders his Rayland Tully passport; the only passport he has.

'We'll fix you up with something else, of course.' Another smile from Ridout, as empty as the first. 'It'll take a day or two. Be in touch.'

As the man who is no longer Rayland Tully – who no longer has any identity – goes to board the train, Ridout grips his arm. 'And young Ben Gates?' he asks. 'He's no longer with us, I assume? Gone to meet his maker, has he?'

'History,' is the reply.

'Sure about that, are we?'

Receiving an affirmative nod, Ridout releases his claw.

# Coconut Grove
# Florida

# nine

Before he was pressed into becoming the founding Director of the Financial Strike Force, moving to New York to spearhead what they said would be the most intensive, the most focused, the most funded attack ever mounted on international money laundering, Aldus Cutter ran a federal task force out of Miami and made his home in a sprawling wooden A-frame on Poinciana Avenue; set on a large lot, shaded by dense tropical vegetation, a swimming pool in the back yard. It was the prospect of quitting this little bit of paradise as much as what he knew to be the overblown nature of their promises that had caused him to hesitate, to play hard to get. Eventually, they had sweetened the pie, adding a rent-free apartment in Manhattan to an already-generous employment package, allowing him to keep the house in Coconut Grove.

'So, you can spend as much time here as you want,' he'd gratefully told Mrs Cutter, who regarded anywhere north of Virginia with a true southerner's distaste.

She had taken him at his word. Having done what she saw as her duty in furnishing the apartment, she had never set foot in New York again. And while at first Cutter had made regular weekend pilgrimages to Florida, the pressure of the Strike Force's business – as well as a hint of coldness he thought he detected in Mrs Cutter – had sapped his will to make the effort. Though he had missed the house, he'd consoled himself with the knowledge that his mandatory retirement was not all that far away and there would then be ample time to fix all those things that needed fixing around the place. And, if necessary, he had assumed, he would fix his marriage.

Not any more.

Squeezing past a moving truck parked in the front drive, coming through his wide-open front door, Flint finds him in the split-level living room, surrounded by packing boxes and swathes of bubble

wrap, most of the furniture gone. He is red-faced, naked except for
a pair of baggy shorts, his body almost hairless and glistening with
sweat, pulling on a can of Miller Genuine Draft. Over his shoulder
Flint can see there are a half-dozen empty cans floating on the
surface of the swimming pool and it's not yet noon.

'Thirsty work?' she asks, keeping her tone light.

'Don't start,' says Cutter sharply as though she is a nagging wife.
'You want one?'

'One what?'

'A beer, for Christ's sake,' says Cutter, waving the can.

She doesn't want a beer but the belligerence of Cutter's tone
warns Flint to humour him. 'Sure,' she says. 'Why not?'

Cutter waves his free hand in the direction of the kitchen. 'In the
fridge. If there still is a friggin' fridge.'

The source of his irritation is to be found on the kitchen counter,
an inventory of the contents of Poinciana Avenue printed on a
sheet of a Miami law firm's notepaper and headed 'Cutter v. Cutter'.
Out of habit – or maybe compulsion – Flint turns the page around
to steal a better look and rapidly establishes that the division of the
marital property is anything but even. Mrs Cutter gets most of it,
apparently, including the fridge.

'Know what gets up my nose?' says Cutter calling to her
from the living room. 'That you're dumb enough to think *I'm*
dumb.'

Having no idea what is going on in his convoluted mind, she
makes no reply. Even so, waiting for the truth to drop, she can feel
her face redden.

'I mean, how much time have you wasted dreaming up whatever
crock of bull it is you're about to give me?' There is a pause before
Cutter continues, 'About the file.' Another pause and then, 'Fridge
still there?'

'Yes, sir,' she manages to answer.

'So stop reading what doesn't concern you and get yourself a
beer. And then get back in here. I need some answers, Flint.'

*So do I*, she thinks, and she draws a deep breath. *Okay, Mr
Cutter, we'll dispense with the bullshit, shall we?*

She takes two cans of Miller from the fridge and slams the door
and marches into the living room with her chin up.

'Good morning to you, too, Mr Cutter, and – thank you for
asking – the flight was fine, and – since you ask – I was going to

lie.' She pulls open the tabs on both cans with satisfactory snaps.
'About the file.'

'About how you got it?'

'Right.'

'Like, Kitty didn't give you a copy of the file, didn't know
anything about it?'

'Right again,' she says and takes a swig from one of the cans,
offering Cutter the other.

'Got yourself a story?' asks Cutter, taking the beer.

'Almost there.'

'Jesus, Flint, I *told* Kitty to give you a copy of the file. I also told
her to mark it so we'd know if anybody made a second generation
copy.'

'I just worked that out, Mr Cutter. Question is, who else did you
tell that I had it?'

Flint is by the swimming pool, sitting in the shade, morosely
watching Cutter taking pot shots at the floating beer cans with a
small .38 revolver that he usually keeps in an ankle holster. Any
minute now she expects to hear the sirens of Miami PD units
coming to investigate reports of gunfire but, given Cutter's dark
mood, perhaps this is not the first time today that gunfire has been
heard on Poinciana Avenue. Inside the house, the two quarrelling
Hispanics who are struggling to manoeuvre the fridge on to a dolly
don't seem in the least alarmed.

By now Cutter has revealed that Kitty Lopez called him in the
night to tell him about the cobalt blue telltales on Flint's copy of
the Pentecost file; had reached him even before Flint called with her
half-evasion: *I've found the leak.*

'You might have said!' she had blurted out, and then looked
away from his mocking stare.

By now he has also convinced her that nobody at the Strike
Force – nobody but he and Kitty Lopez – knew or could have
known that she kept a copy of the file hidden at Miller's Reach,
and this has brought them to the brink of the only other possible
explanation. Uncharacteristically, Cutter has stopped short, not yet
asking the question he must ask, the question Flint has been asking
herself over and over for the last ten hours, always coming up with
the same and only answer.

*Who else knew, or could have known?*

*Ben.*

Still putting off the moment, Cutter asks, 'You want to swim?' and then catching the look she gives him he quickly answers the question himself. 'No,' he says, 'I don't suppose you do.'

For, as Cutter well knows, Flint has an aversion to swimming pools. Not two miles from here, in the course of one of Cutter's undercover operations, she once lay near-naked by a pool at the Buccaneer Hotel, watched over by a Russian goon named Vladimir who had been ordered to kill her if things didn't work out the way they were supposed to. Well, things were never going to work out the way Vladimir wanted and he would have killed her, she has no doubt, if he hadn't made a momentary mistake: making her come to him, reaching for her crotch, biting her breasts, giving the SWAT team the chance they had been waiting for.

But that wasn't the end or the worst of it, at least not for Flint. The last shaming moments of Vladimir's life – shaming for Flint, that is – were captured on surveillance video that, a year or so later, some creep had stolen from the evidence room and uploaded to an Internet porn site called Action Babes. When she'd found out, and gone ballistic, Cutter had moved heaven and earth to get the site closed down but it was by then far too late for the clip had spread across the net like a contagion. It is still out there and any half-decent search engine and a little persistence will find it.

'Dumb question,' says Cutter giving her a rueful smile.

'Got another?'

'Like what?'

'Like . . .' She swallows hard and then continues, 'Did Ben know about the file?'

Cutter takes careful aim at one of the surviving cans, squinting along the barrel. 'No,' he says, 'because if that was the case you'd have already told me.' He squeezes the trigger and grunts his approval as the can leaps into the air. 'Right?'

'How about, *Could* Ben have known?'

'That's not such a dumb question,' says Cutter, turning to look at her. 'That's got legs. Asked him yet?'

'He's away on a field trip – East Africa,' she tells him and Cutter nods.

'Bird watching?'

'*Birding*. They call it birding, Mr Cutter. He's due back on Monday night.'

Again Cutter nods and then turns his attention back to the swimming pool. There is still one can that doesn't have a bullet hole in it.

'So, that's when you'll ask him,' Cutter says – not a question, a statement of fact. 'Monday night.'

Later, when she is alone, when she is in the room at the Buccaneer Hotel that she has taken for the night, too fatigued to face the journey back to Connecticut, Flint poses herself a question: Why did she mount no defence of Ben – no rebuttal to Cutter's manifest suspicion of her husband?

Lying on the bed in the half-dark, the phone unplugged from its socket on the wall, she does so now.

*Ben? You think Ben copied the Pentecost file? Oh, come on, Mr Cutter, that's ridiculous!*

*Could Ben have known I kept something in the barn? Yes, I suppose he could – probably did – but he wouldn't care. Trust me, Mr Cutter, there's nobody alive who takes less interest in what I do for a living than Ben Gates. He lives on a different planet – which is one of the things I like about him; one of the many things, Mr Cutter. I only have to say 'money laundering' and his eyes glaze over. All he cares about – except me, I hope – all he thinks about is grebes: great-crested grebes and grackles and cardinals and towhees and flickers – especially flickers. Oh, don't get him started on the subject of flickers, Mr Cutter, or you'll be there all day.*

*Birds, Mr Cutter, that's Ben's thing. Okay, he's wild about Bach and he's also into caterpillars and seashells and bits of old rock – oh, and Siamese fighting fish and polar bears – but birds are what he lives for. That and sailing and flying – beat-up old airplanes that are tied together with bits of string.*

*Know what 'jizz' is, Mr Cutter? It's derived from old RAF slang for plane spotting and it's a short form for 'General Identification Size and Shape' – or something like that. Anyway, 'jizz' is what birders use to build their 'lifetime list' of birds they've seen, and Ben started his when he was seven – in New York, if you can believe it. He used to run around the Ramble in Central Park with Teddy Roosevelt's great-grandson and his mother's opera glasses and that's where he saw his first gold-crested kinglet, or maybe it was a chickadee – one or the other.*

*Mr Cutter, sir, this is a man who takes it as a personal affront that he'll never see a live dodo! When it came to our honeymoon, Ben wanted to go to Mauritius, only because that's the only home the dodo ever had. 'No way, Jose,' I told him, because I had my sights set on Australia, the Great Barrier Reef and, in particular, this island called Hayman, which is just a hotel, nothing else except for a chapel where you can have your marriage blessed – which is what we did. Amazing place. So, anyway, we go halfway around the world to cement our vows and wallow in a little luxury and you know what we do? We go birding, Mr Cutter. They've got eighty-five species of bird on Hayman and I promise you we saw every damn one of them. And, at four o'clock in the morning – and we're on our honeymoon, remember – Ben is waking me up so we can see the fruit bats – bats the size of pelicans – returning from a night's carousing.*

*Coming back, we flew to England to see my father and then France, because we both have French ancestors, not that he cares. Anyway, I wanted to show Ben La Rochelle, which is where my mother's folks came from. You know what, Mr Cutter? We spent all of half a day in La Rochelle because what Ben wanted to do was visit a biological station in the Camargue – in the middle of nowhere, I might add – which is where we spent five whole days. One night, Ben was out in the hills, trying to spot an eagle owl or some such, and I snuck a look at his diary.*

*I know, I know, but we're still on honeymoon, remember, and I thought he might have written something about me because that afternoon . . . Well, never mind why, I just did.*

*Know what I found?*

*'Woke up to the call of the hoopoe. In the afternoon' – he meant the early afternoon, before I finally got his attention – 'saw flamingos taking off from the battlements of Aigues Mortes. Watched roosting harriers at sunset.'*

*Are you getting the picture, Mr Cutter?*

*Ben Gates is other-worldly. He doesn't care about food or clothes or cars or money – he can't even balance the chequebook. He cares about me, birds, sailing boats, flying planes and Bach, and not necessarily always in that order.*

*Now I ask you, Mr Cutter, does that sound to you like a man who would copy every bloody page of the Pentecost file?*

Satisfied with her summation, the defence rests as Flint feels herself drifting off to sleep. She does not trouble to undress.

# ten

Flint's nightmare is episodic, a fragmentary confusion of actual events and her worst imaginings.

She is lying in a stairwell of a multi-storey car park in Belgravia and Clayton Buller is stamping on her face while he calls her a bitch – but the voice she hears belongs to her first husband, Jamie, who, in a sudden change of scene, is now rising up from a table, hurling down his napkin, giving her a look that says he wishes she was dead.

'Bitch, bitch, bitch' – but now the voice belongs to Ben Gates, her second husband – this is *Ben*, for God's sake, the gentlest man she's ever met – who is shattering her teeth with the heel of his boot.

Now she is lying on her back watching Ruth Apple come tumbling towards her through a leaden sky, not making any sound.

Her father is saying, 'I love you more than life, Gracie,' turning to face her, bloodstains on his surgical gown, a hammer in his hand.

Flint is at her mother's graveside, watching a JCB dump earth into the gaping hole, hearing only the insistent pounding of sodden clay as it lands on the lid of an empty oak coffin.

Snapping awake, she hears the door splinter and she's rolling off the bed, using it for cover, assuming a defensive crouch, feeling under the pillow for the butt of her gun.

Jarrett Crawford peers around the doorframe and says, 'You know, Grace, you'd make life a whole lot easier if you'd just answer the fucking phone.'

Behind him in the hallway she can make out two uniformed cops, dressed all in midnight blue, one of them holding what appears to be a sledgehammer.

'Cutter's pissing himself,' Crawford continues. 'You know how long we've been trying to reach you?'

Still on her knees beside the bed, still trying to decide if this is part of her dream, she watches Crawford coming towards her through the half-light. Picking up the handset of the phone, listening in vain for the dial tone, pulling on the lead until he establishes that it is unplugged from the socket, he grunts. 'Yeah, that's what I thought,' he says.

She is getting stiffly to her feet as Crawford goes to the window and snatches open the curtains, filling the room with sudden, searing light that makes her flinch. She closes her eyes and keeps them closed until Crawford says, 'Some party.'

She dares to look and sees that he is picking through the debris on a room service tray: a half-eaten club sandwich, some congealed French fries; an untouched pot of stone-cold coffee; an empty wine bottle lying on its side. There are also three empty Red Label miniatures from the mini-bar and Flint has a vague recollection of using the last of the whisky to wash down some Extra Strength Tylenol – a pre-emptive strike against the migraine she had anticipated last night. She supposes that might explain why her head is throbbing and why her tongue feels swollen, too large for her mouth.

'What time is it?' she asks thickly.

'What *day* is it?' Crawford retorts. 'You got any idea?'

She has to think about this. 'Friday,' she eventually decides.

'Grace, it's *Saturday*, and coming up to noon. You've been out of it, stone cold, for thirty-six hours!'

*Oh, Christ!*

Crawford has now found the box in which she keeps her Tylenol and Inderal tablets and he's examining the contents. 'Hey, booze *and* pills,' he says, 'that'll do it!' He closes the lid and tosses the box on to the bed. 'That's really smart, Grace, *real* smart.'

Flint wants to say that it is none of his business – 'None of your *goddamned* business, Crawdaddy' – but she's not entirely sure she can manage the words. She turns her head away from him, and now she can see that one of the cops has come edging into the room, that he's standing there with brawny, bare arms folded across his chest just below the silver badge and the name plate that says he's called García, regarding her as though she's dirt. She can imagine how she looks to him in her rumpled clothes, wild-eyed, her hair dishevelled. Angrily she nods her head in his direction.

Picking up her meaning Crawford says, 'Hey, thanks a lot, buddy, I'll take it from here,' but García is not ready to be so easily dismissed.

'What am I supposed to put in the report?' he demands sourly.

'False alarm,' Crawford suggests.

'And that?' García means the door that hangs askew from its hinges.

'We'll take care of it.' García still makes no move to leave so Crawford goes over to him holding out his hands, adding, 'Listen, we owe you.' Now he takes García's shoulder and turns him and gently steers him towards the doorway. 'You've been real helpful and your watch commander's going to hear about it. That's a promise you can take to the bank.'

García appears to be mollified but when he's in the hallway Flint hears him call to her, 'Lady, you've got a *real* problem, you know that?'

Better now, halfway to human, Flint stands under a hot shower feeling the stiffness ebb from her limbs. The chambermaid has collected her suit for pressing and a couple of maintenance men have fixed the door. Coffee and something to eat are on their way. Crawford is on the phone to Cutter – who is back in New York, evidently – filling him in on the state of play.

She is confident that Crawdaddy will be discreet.

*She was exhausted, Mr Cutter, just needed to sleep – hung out the do-not-disturb sign, locked the door from the inside and unplugged the phone.*

Something like that. No need for him to mention the booze and the pills.

When the fug has receded from her brain she steps out of the shower and wraps herself in one of the Buccaneer Hotel's soft cotton robes. She towel-dries her hair and brushes it back from her forehead and then examines her face in the mirror. There is a pinkish tinge to her eyes but all in all, she decides, she looks better than she might; better than she deserves.

Crawford is sitting on the edge of the bed, still on the phone, when she returns to the room.

'Yeah, okay,' she hears him say. 'There's a flight out of here around fifteen hundred with a connection in Houston.' Then he falls silent and scribbles on a hotel notepad that rests awkwardly on his knee. He glances up at Flint as she squeezes past but he does not respond to her enquiring smile.

The coffee arrives together with a basket of warm croissants and Flint rewards the waiter with an extravagant tip.

Crawford says into the phone, 'Not yet. But I will, as soon as we're done.'

She pours a cup of coffee and takes it over to him but Crawford shakes his head. He's scribbling more words on the pad and he catches Flint trying to steal a look. She looks away, acknowledging the futility of the attempt. Even if she wasn't trying to read it upside down, she decides, his writing would still be entirely illegible.

With nothing else to do she wanders out on to the balcony that overlooks South Bayshore Drive and Dinner Key beyond. It must be eighty degrees and the breeze coming off the ocean is barely sufficient to disturb the palm trees, and it occurs to Flint that it was on a day very like this, and very near to here, that she and Ben had their first date: a lunch that had meandered through the afternoon and into the evening until their waiter had put a lighted candle on the table and Ben had said, 'Pushing my luck, will you have dinner with me tonight?'

'Yes,' she'd said, laughing, 'but if you've also got breakfast in mind, forget it.'

It was meant as a joke but he hadn't taken it that way. 'No, no, no,' he'd protested. 'Not here. I know *exactly* where we're going to have our first breakfast.'

'You do?'

'In Maine, about three hours north of my office, I have a small cottage . . . Well, it's really my parents' place, but since Ma got ill . . .' He'd broken off and Flint had watched his face while he found his composure. During the afternoon she had learned that Ben's mother suffered from the scourge of Pick's disease; that she had, to all intents and purposes, vanished into an unfathomable world of her own.

'Dad thinks it's too isolated, in case anything should happen with Ma, and, anyway, she needs a warmer climate so they don't go there any more. So, Lizzie and I share it – except it's a long way for her to come so, mostly, it's mine.'

Lizzie was his sister, four years older than Ben, a paediatrician with three daughters – boisterous daughters, judging by the photograph he'd shown her – and a thriving practice in California's San Mateo county.

'Anyway, it's set on a ridge – what they call an esker, created when the glaciers retreated – overlooking an inlet with the most perfect beach you've ever seen. I've been going there since I was a kid and almost nothing's changed. It's not easy to get to and you feel as though you're the only person for miles around – which you will be.' He'd grinned and added, 'Except, I'll be there, I hope.'

'There are birds, I expect,' Flint had said, for she'd already gathered what it was that Ben Gates lived for.

'Oh, yes,' he'd replied, his walnut brown eyes reflecting the light of the candle. 'Herring gulls and cormorants and terns and herons' – and on and on the list had gone, punctuated by his impressions of bird calls and sweeping animations of their flight. He was moving on to describe other forms of wildlife when she'd interrupted.

'This cottage of yours,' she began doubtfully, 'it has electricity, I suppose?'

'Hell, no!' For a moment he had looked genuinely alarmed. 'I mean, it would cost a fortune to run a power line in there and, anyway, utilities would ruin it. Dad would never allow that.'

Dad, Flint knew, was Joseph Gates, professor of art history at McGill University in Montreal.

'So,' Flint had asked, 'what do you do about, you know, er, heat? Light? Water?'

'Rain water,' Ben had replied cheerfully. 'There's a cistern on the roof to collect it and, believe me, up there we're never short of rain. And there's oil lamps and wood burning stoves, and since we're right in the middle of a pine forest, there's no shortage of fuel either.' For the first time, he'd taken her hand. 'Trust me, it's magical.'

'Well,' Flint had said, 'it's not exactly what I would call irresistible' – but she was wrong about that. In the end that's exactly what it was.

Crawford coming out on to the balcony to join her, chewing on a croissant, flecks of pastry adhering to his walrus moustache.

'How are you feeling?' he asks.

He's got that dour Welsh Baptist's look on his face and suddenly she's tired of his disapproval, tired of his games. She wants to know why he's here. Ignoring his question she asks one of her own: 'Okay, Jerry, what's going on?' He begins to gesture towards the room until she says sharply, 'Cut it out! You didn't need to fly all the way down here just to get some PD goons to kick in my door. You could have just phoned them, you know? So,' she says, her voice now very strong, 'why are you here?'

He's wondering how to tell her when they hear the call of the chambermaid bringing back her suit. It looks as good as new and Flint shells out another generous tip.

'Why don't you get dressed?' Crawford suggests when she returns to the balcony. 'We've got a plane to catch.'

'Because we're not done, Jerry, and we're not going anywhere until I get an answer that makes some sense. One more time: What's going on?'

He stalls a little longer, taking out a handkerchief to wipe his mouth. Then, 'Grace, I need to ask you a question.'

'Fine,' she says, not really meaning it.

'You said Ben's in Africa, right? On some kind of bird watching trip?'

'Tanzania. And it's called *birding*,' she says pedantically. 'So?'

'He flew out there two weeks ago? Out of Boston?'

'Right. Via Amsterdam and Nairobi.'

'And he's due back on Monday?'

'Monday. Right again.' Prickles of anxiety are tingling her skin and she snaps, 'Oh, come on, Jerry! What's your point?'

He gives her a look that says, *I don't want to do this*, and then, 'We ran the airline manifests, Grace – Cutter's call. In the last twenty-one days nobody called Ben Gates, or anything remotely like it, has flown out of Boston to any part of Africa and nobody with that name is booked to come back.'

She's staring at him, hearing his words perfectly well but struggling to make sense of their meaning.

'It's not just Boston, Grace,' Crawford continues. 'We ran all the manifests for every international flight out of every airport in the northeast and Ben doesn't show. Either he used another name and another passport or he didn't fly.'

*Another name!* Her instinct is to say, *That's ridiculous!* Instead she says, 'Or somebody screwed up.'

'No, they didn't,' Crawford says, but she's no longer listening to him. Hurrying back into the room, pulling her robe undone, picking up the suit from the bed, she heads for the bathroom and begins getting dressed, not bothering to close the door.

Crawford watches her from a distance.

'This is such a crock of shit,' she calls to him angrily. 'You know what airline manifests are worth. Every time there's a crash, it takes them days to work out who they've killed.'

'Maybe you should call Ben's office?' Crawford ventures. 'Find out if he changed his plans?'

She comes out of the bathroom still buttoning up her shirt. 'That's exactly what I'm going to do. Where's my bag?'

'There, on the chair,' Crawford says, pointing the way. 'That would be the Maine Audubon Society in Portland, right?'

'Falmouth,' says Flint who is now rummaging through her overnight bag, looking for her address book. 'Same thing.'

She still has her back to Crawford, still looking for the book, when she hears him say, 'Grace, I already called the office. They've never heard of Ben Gates.'

# The Marscheider Building

# eleven

In a conference room on the fifth floor of the Strike Force headquarters where the terriers assembled by Nathan Stark to dig among the bones of Operation Pentecost await his arrival to report their progress, a young analyst named Justin Hamilton grows bored with the delay and wilfully steps out on to dangerous territory.

It is dangerous because Stark has specifically forbidden what he calls useless speculation about Grace Flint's relationship with her husband. It is wilful because Hamilton knows full well he will get a rise.

'Am I the only person alive,' he says laconically breaking the silence, 'who thinks this is weird? She *never* called her husband at the office?'

'Meaning?'

This is Kate Barrymore – team leader of the terriers – who is regarded by Aldus Cutter as the brightest of the bright young minds he has recruited to the FSF from Columbia University. Until Ruth Apple became Lily Apana and moved into her netherworld, Kate and Ruth shared an apartment.

'Meaning,' says Hamilton, 'they'd not been married a year, right? They were hot for each other, right? *In love*,' he adds, the syrup in his voice emphasising the sexual connotation. 'She's here and he's in Maine, and they see each other every third weekend if they're lucky, and she *never* calls him at the office!' There are five other analysts lounging around the table and he holds up his hands to them in a gesture of mock surrender. 'Hey, call me old-fashioned, but I'd say that's pretty weird.'

'Your wife calls you all the time, of course,' says Barrymore evenly. 'Is that what you get up to in your cubicle all day? Phone sex?'

Hamilton gives a theatrical groan. 'No, Kate, since I don't have a wife – and that's just a cheap shot.'

Kate Barrymore nods a small acknowledgement and then continues to probe Hamilton's logic. 'How do you know she didn't call the office?'

'Because she *can't* have done.'

'Go on.'

'We're here to find the weak link, okay? And right here, right now, the prime candidate – no, strike that; the *only* candidate – is the husband of our esteemed deputy director; a husband who, it turns out, does not and never has worked for the Maine Audubon Society – which is what our esteemed deputy director *says* she believed until she was so cruelly disabused this morning by Jerry Crawford. And how did the relentless Crawdaddy establish that fact?' He challenges Barrymore with a righteous stare. 'With *one* phone call, Kate.'

Hamilton cocks the little finger and the thumb of one hand to mimic a telephone handset that he holds to his ear.

*Hello*, he says in a fair imitation of Crawford's resonant voice, *I'd like to speak to Ben Gates.*

*Who?*

*Ben Gates.*

*Never heard of him.*

'One phone call, Kate. That's what it took. So it stands to reason she never called the office or she would have found out. Or maybe she did call.' All of the jokiness has gone from Hamilton's tone. 'I don't think we can dodge the issue.'

'And the issue is?'

'The issue is this, Kate. Is our esteemed deputy director simply dumb, or naïve – or is she complicit?'

One floor below, in Aldus Cutter's office, Nathan Stark lays out the bare facts that the FSF has now established about Grace Flint's husband.

'He's got a Social Security number issued on the basis of a birth certificate and a Connecticut driver's licence.' Stark pauses and then adds, 'I'll come back to the driver's licence in a second.'

Cutter stirs in his chair, watchful as a cat. From Stark's viewpoint he is framed by a window that shows a sky of unremitting grey; the tail end of Monday's storm that still hangs around like a forbidding omen.

'Benjamin Gates,' Stark begins reciting from a facsimile of the birth certificate, 'no middle name. Born May 11, 1967, in Laval, Quebec. Father, Joseph, mother, Françoise Louise, née Lamoureux.'

'Spoken to them?' asks Cutter.

'Not yet. According to what Flint told Crawford, Mrs Gates has got Alzheimer's, or something like it, and Gates senior took early retirement on account of her illness. He was a prof up at McGill University.'

Cutter nods. 'Yeah, I remember him from the wedding. Smart guy. Come to think about it, he mentioned his wife was sick.'

Stark also nods, wearily. He's not been out of the building for forty-eight hours, surviving on catnaps and sandwiches imported from a nearby deli. The same is true of his impatient terriers but they are half his age and it's on his bony face that the strain is showing.

'Anyway,' he says, picking up the thread, 'Flint told Crawford that they moved to southern France about ten months ago, after McGill did the decent thing and made him Emeritus Professor. Supposedly, the climate's better for Mrs Gates's health.'

Cocking an eyebrow Cutter says, 'That make sense to you?'

'No,' Stark admits, 'but it checks out so far. McGill's not being what I would call super-cooperative, but they have confirmed that Gates is in France so far as they know, at some place near Nice, apparently, and if he's registered with the consulate we should have an address or a phone number for him before the day's out.'

When Cutter's mind is racing he sits very still, like now.

'So, Flint hasn't seen her in-laws for the best part of a year?' he asks.

'She told Crawford she's never met the mother. Never spoken to her either. Wrote to her once, after the wedding, and got a "bless you" reply. Nothing further. So far as the father is concerned, she met him first time the day before the wedding and one time after that for dinner in the city. Says she's spoken to him a few times on the phone – and that's it.'

'Some people get all the luck,' says Cutter dryly, but Stark does not seem to hear him.

'She tells Crawford,' he goes on, 'that on a couple of occasions Ben proposed they go to France to see his folks but that never happened because, every time he brought it up, Pentecost was on the boil.'

'Figures,' says Cutter, leaning down to open the bottom drawer of his desk, rummaging through its contents. 'Go ahead,' he continues. 'What about the driver's licence?'

'He needed primary and secondary ID to get it. The primary could have been his Canadian passport but he elected to produce his birth certificate – duly certified, all the bells and whistles you'd expect. For the secondary, he came up with a pilot's licence, which Connecticut accepts as satisfactory ID. So,' Stark concludes, 'there's no record of his passport.'

'What about INS?' Cutter asks, still rummaging in the drawer. 'He'd have needed a visa, wouldn't he?'

'No,' Stark replies gloomily. 'As a Canadian, and assuming he's got professional qualifications – or forged them – he's pretty much guaranteed entry under the NAFTA treaty. No written application, no prior approval. Just turns up at the border with proof of citizenship – the birth certificate again – a letter offering him a job in the States, and fifty bucks for the fee, and he's in. Gets an I–94 form stamped "multiple entry" and he *never* has to show his frigging passport. Supposedly, the I–94's only valid for one year but under the treaty he can renew it indefinitely, more or less.'

The drawer does not contain what Cutter seeks, apparently, for he gets up from his desk and heads towards an ornate highboy that seems out of place in these austere surroundings. 'God bless NAFTA,' he says, meaning the opposite. 'It's a fucking paper tripper's charter, isn't it?' Reaching the highboy he pulls open the top drawer. 'Got the Canadians on board?'

'Yes,' says Stark with a distinct lack of enthusiasm. 'I've got their passport office running a check but they say it'll take five days – minimum.'

Cutter says 'Shit' and opens the second drawer.

'Most of the other records are kept on a province-by-province basis and there's no central register or cross-referencing so, if he is a paper tripper, and he's any good, it could take forever to nail him. The CSIS,' Stark continues, referring now to the Canadian intelligence service, 'has got informal access to most of the provincial databanks and – strictly on the quiet – they're doing a trawl for us. But' – he gives a shrug of resignation – 'I'm not holding my breath.'

'What we need,' says Cutter, turning away from the highboy, a grin growing on his face, 'is a little edge.' He has found what he's been looking for and he holds it in his hands, showing it to Stark. 'What do you think?'

Cutter's edge is a photograph, four-colour, ten inches by eight, four people in a tight shot, smiling for the camera. Flint and Ben Gates are centre stage, she radiant in an antique-white dress that leaves her shoulders bare, he proud in a dress shirt and a morning coat with a grey cravat held in place by a diamond pin.

Getting up from the couch, coming over to take a closer look, Stark points to the beaming, gangling man who stands by Ben's side and asks, 'That him?'

'No,' says Cutter, 'that's Flint's daddy. This' – he is pointing now to a distinguished-looking but much shorter man who stands by Flint's side, her arm resting on his wide shoulders – 'is Joe Gates. Except, Nate, I've got twenty dollars that says he's not.' Cutter hands the photograph to Stark. 'My twenty dollars says that if you wire this picture to the folks at CSIS, and get them to run it by the folks at McGill, they're gonna tell you that, whoever he is, he is *not* their distinguished Emeritus Professor of Art History – or any other frigging history. And,' continues Cutter, flying now, on top of his form, 'I've got another twenty dollars that says that whenever you reach the real Joe Gates in the south of France and ask him about his son, he's gonna tell you that Ben died in childhood.'

'No bet,' says Stark.

'Won't have died in Quebec, of course,' Cutter presses on. 'Some other province, or maybe even here in the States; anywhere there was no chance of some registrar stamping "deceased" on the birth certificate. Or maybe he just forged the certificate. You know there are books out there that tell you how to do all this shit?'

Stark nods as if to say he knows only too well.

'Okay, let's get this on the wire,' says Cutter, handing the photograph to Stark. 'Meantime, I know a cop in Paris – a good friend of Flint's as it happens. I'll give him a call' – Cutter checks his watch and calculates the time difference – 'and see if he can't find Joe Gates for us.'

Stark is halfway to the door when he stops and turns and says, as if it is an afterthought, 'What are you going to do about Flint?'

Cutter, now back at his desk, picking up the phone, replies, 'Let's see what they come up with in Portland. You said they don't get in until midnight so it's going to be tomorrow at the earliest before we know anything.'

'You'll have to suspend her, won't you?' Stark asks. 'That or send her on leave?'

'She *is* on leave. Has been since Tuesday.' Cutter considers the implicit contradiction and corrects himself. 'Well, she would be on leave if it wasn't for the frigging file.' He pauses again before adding, 'Yeah, you're probably right. In any event, I want her kept out of the loop.'

'Of course,' says Stark. 'And out of the building, too. For her sake as much as ours.'

'Out of here and out of New York, until we know.'

'There's going to be a lot of heat,' Stark suggests.

'There already is,' Cutter tells him, 'and they don't even know about the file – yet. Justice called,' he explains, 'and OPR are sending a couple of shit kickers down here on Monday.'

'You going to tell them?'

'Not yet. Not until we have some answers.' Cutter presses one of the speed dial buttons on his telephone. 'Because if I do, they'll go jumping to half-assed conclusions like they always do and we'll find ourselves in the middle of a pissing contest.'

There is an edgy silence which Stark breaks. 'Aldus, you're sure she's not . . .' he begins and then breaks off as though he is unwilling to ask the unthinkable question.

'Dirty?' Cutter says it for him. 'Yeah, I'm sure. There's a lot of stuff I'm not sure about right now but if Gates turns out to be the grade-one creep we think he is you can take my word for it, Flint didn't know.'

'Strange, that,' Stark muses. 'Being married to someone and you don't even know who they are.'

'It happens,' Cutter says. Any further insights he has on the subject go unspoken as, some 3,000 miles away, a telephone is answered and he breaks into a polyglot language of his own eccentric composition.

*Gilles! ¡Hola! It's Aldus, Aldus Cutter. Comment ça va, good buddy, comment ça va?*

# Portland Maine

# twelve

Crawford said they should give the guy a break, shouldn't they? Wait until a decent hour? Because hammering on his door again before God's good light had risen would imply a suspicion that was not strictly merited by the facts. Sure, Crawford had conceded, Tyler's answers to their questions had not been entirely satisfactory but it had been one o'clock in the morning, and they had dragged him out of bed, and Flint had been . . . well, a little rough.

'Crawdaddy, get some sleep,' Flint had said. 'I'll see you in the coffee shop at seven.'

'Seven thirty,' Crawford had countered and Flint had smiled her agreement, lying through her shining teeth.

Returning alone to Thomas Tyler's house Flint leaves her Hertz car at the corner of the street, parked defiantly alongside a fire hydrant, asking for trouble because that's the mood she's in.

It's cold enough that she can see her breath pluming from her mouth like cigarette smoke caught in the porch light above the front door. Huddled in her parka she leans her undamaged shoulder on the bell and listens to its shrilling ring coming from some distant corner of the house.

While she waits for the inevitable to happen she psyches herself up by rehearsing the reasons for the anger she feels towards the comfortable occupants of this white clapboard house on this quiet smug street in this safe smug town that seems a million miles away from the blood-splattered plaza of the World Emporium; a smug town she already hates for its association with feelings that threaten to overwhelm her. For now, she refuses to think about her husband. She prefers to focus on her immediate target.

*You lied to me, Thomas Tyler, because I know that you're part of it, part of Ben's legend.*

'My dear,' he'd said to her not four hours ago in an accent that was part English and part New England and as difficult to pin down as the mid-point of the Atlantic, 'I would be delighted to help you, but I really can't. I know absolutely nothing about Mr Gates.'

*Oh, really? Then explain this to me, Mr Tyler, sir: How come that on the one occasion when I misdialled Ben's direct line – transposed the last two digits – I got the Audubon Society and I was put through to you, and I told you I was Ben Gates's wife, and you said you would have him call me back – and he did call, not five minutes later? How come this man you don't know got the message, Mr Thomas Fucking Tyler, sir?*

The front door is not substantial and she knows from her earlier visit that it is secured by a simple Yale lock. Even with her gammy leg and her painful shoulder, she is confident she can force it open if she has to. And she will, if she has to.

A light has come on, reflected faintly through the glass panes that occupy the top half of the door. The glass is frosted and there is no spy hole so he'll have to open the door to establish who is leaning on his doorbell at a little after five o'clock on a Maine Sunday morning. That, or call the cops.

Now that there is more light coming through the glass and she can see his silhouette approaching, she takes her shoulder off the bell and prepares herself for verbal combat.

'Who is it? Who's there?' – said *sotto voce* but laced with alarm.

'It's Agent Flint, Mr Tyler, I was here earlier. I need to speak with you again.'

He hesitates and then, 'I've told you, I know nothing and I have nothing more to say to you. Go away.'

'Open the door please, sir.'

'*Go away!*'

She reaches out with her right hand to press and release the bell: once, twice, a third time, a hundred times if she has to – and the door is wrenched open and Tyler is standing there in his bathrobe, his bearded face a picture of indignation. It suddenly strikes her that, above the beard, there is some similarity to her father's face: a certain angularity to the cheek bones, the broad forehead, the deep crow's-feet creases running from the corner of his eyes.

'*Are you mad?*'

Not *sotto voce* this time, more like *fortissimo*, and from within the house a child's voice calls out in alarm, '*Dad?*'

Tyler takes a step back and turns away and doesn't notice Flint coming up the final step and into the doorway.

'It's all right, Sally,' he calls up the stairs to the unseen child. 'Go back to bed.'

'*Thomas?*' – this a woman's voice and her implicit enquiry is not so easily dismissed. She calls again: 'Thomas? What on earth is going on?'

'Nothing. Nothing important. *Please*' – there is an edge of panic in his tone – 'just get the children back to bed.'

Now he turns back to face Flint and finds her much closer to him than he has expected and sees that she has wedged one foot against the door, and sees that she is looking at his feet, which are bare, and perhaps he thinks she will stamp on them if he tries to close the door. He takes another step back.

'No, sir, you're wrong. It *is* important,' Flint says quietly.

'Do you know what time it is?' – the inevitable question of just about every miscreant and reluctant witness she has disturbed at such an ungodly hour.

She glances at her left wrist. 'Eleven minutes past five, but' – she frowns – 'this is a cheap watch so I could be a couple of minutes out.'

She is goading him, attempting to keep him off-balance but she can see that this is not your average creep; that, despite her provocations, he is composing himself, fighting against his instincts and getting his temper under control.

'Do you want to step outside, sir?' she says abruptly in her sternest copper's voice. 'So we don't disturb your family any further?'

No go. He is putting his hands in the pockets of his robe; she can see the anxiety leaving his eyes.

'You might want to put on some shoes,' she advises. 'It's cold out here.'

He watches her with an expression that's difficult to interpret because she can't really see his mouth – because of the beard – but Flint believes she can detect the first hint of a smile.

*You don't know how close you are to the edge, Thomas Tyler*, is what she thinks. 'I'm waiting, sir,' is what she tells him.

'Say what you've come here to say.'

'Are you sure you want your family to hear . . .' She breaks off because now the set of his face is growing imperious. 'Very well,' she continues. 'Earlier this evening—'

'This morning,' he corrects her.

'*Earlier*, you told me and Special Agent Crawford that you'd never heard of Ben Gates, that you knew nothing about him.' She pauses and waits for him to repeat the lie but he does not reply. 'Well, I have information – very good information – that what you told us was not the truth.' Another pause, another stubborn silence. 'If you don't talk to me now, sir, the next time you're asked questions about your knowledge of Ben Gates you'll be under oath.'

*Or tasting the barrel of my gun, Mr Tyler, because that's what your friends did to Ruth; put a gun in her mouth before they threw her out of a helicopter.*

'Because on Monday morning,' she presses on, keeping her darker thoughts to herself, 'I'm going to ask the US Attorney in Portland to convene a grand jury and subpoena you to answer questions about a criminal conspiracy to launder money, about wire fraud, tax evasion and – oh, yes,' as though this last thought has only just occurred to her, 'the murder of a federal agent.'

Now she is sure he is smiling, no question about it.

'And while you're pleading the Fifth Amendment like some cheap hoodlum, I'll be at your office seizing every record you've got.' She has to hurry this along because the pain in her leg is growing exponentially and sooner rather than later she's going to have to take her foot away from the door.

'And then I'll come back here with another subpoena for your phone records, your bank records . . . I'll be particularly interested in your bank records, sir,' she continues, 'because my agency has asset-seizure powers and if I find one dollar that you can't account for, I *will* seize your assets, Mr Tyler.'

It's no good. Her left knee feels as though someone has torn gaping rents in the meniscus and she has to take the weight off her foot. As casually as she can, she shifts her position.

'Have you finished?' he asks with the nonchalance of a bored waiter come to clear the table.

'No,' she says, 'I've barely started.'

'Well, I have' – and now there is resolve in his voice. He removes his hands from his pockets like a man who's decided that he is, after all, willing to fight and takes a firm hold of the door. 'What you're accusing me of is fanciful beyond belief and your threats are equally bizarre. If you have anything further to say' – he begins closing the door – 'you can address it to my attorney.'

'One last thing,' she says quickly, causing him to pause. 'Do you have any notion what it's like to be the subject of a federal homicide investigation?'

'Goodnight, Agent Flint – what's left of it.'


Tyler's house is set back from the road on a grassy lot scattered with evergreen bushes that has no fence; no impediment to Flint's cautious approach to the wooden deck that surrounds an expensive rear extension.

This is Tyler's new study that he has stocked with costly toys and it is one more reason why Flint knows in her bones that Tyler is dirty.

'Never underestimate the gall of the greedy,' she tells the trainee agents she occasionally lectures at the FBI Academy at Quantico as part of her duties. Then she regales them with the story of a mid-level banker in San Francisco – whose name, ironically, was Prudence – who took to money laundering late in his career and who, in just fourteen weeks – as though he was making up for lost time – spent more than four million dollars on a Mercedes-Benz sports car, a diamond ring, a Rolex watch, a condo in South Miami Beach and a powerboat to go with it – and nobody noticed. 'Or, rather,' Flint tells her students, '*everybody* noticed, and nobody called the cops. His cover story was that he'd got lucky with dot com investments and people were lining up for his advice on which hot stocks to buy.' At this point in the story she usually smiles. 'And, fortunately for us, Mr Prudence was very *imprudent* – stupid enough to believe his own bullshit. Bad advice is what he gave and one day there was this young woman, a secretary down the hallway, sitting there thinking, "He's got a Merc and a condo and I've got a margin call for $150,000" – and *then* we got the phone call.'

Flint's point is that avarice and recklessness are handmaidens and it is a rare bird indeed who can resist the temptation to spend what he has sold his soul to obtain. 'They reward themselves for their own temerity,' she says. 'If you're looking at a suspect institution and trying to figure out who's dirty and who's not, always begin with financial checks and look for significant changes in spending patterns. Nine times out of ten the perpetrators will identify themselves.'

Like Thomas Tyler, who has a shiny new extension to his home, and a shiny new computer, and a hi-fi system that must have cost him a month's salary and, open on his desk, seductive catalogues for the four-wheel-drive Isuzu he's planning to buy. She'd had to fight the urge to ask him, 'Your auntie died, did she, sir? Left you a nice inheritance?'

Now she's on her belly, crawling across the frozen ground, refusing to acknowledge the pains in her leg and shoulder, keeping out of the rectangle of light that is coming through the sliding glass doors of Tyler's extension. Whenever she looks up she can see him pacing the room, one hand pushing through his hair, talking on a cordless phone. She can't hear what he's saying – not yet – but every gesture he makes betrays his agitation and – to Flint – the extent of his lies.

'Gates?' he'd said when she'd called on him with Crawford four hours ago, still affable then and not unduly put out at being called from his bed at one in the morning. 'Doesn't ring any bells, I'm afraid, but then I do meet rather a lot of people. Perhaps he works for the *national* Audubon Society? Different animal to us, of course. I could check my contacts book.'

'No, sir,' Flint said. 'He was very specific that it was the *Maine* society. And he had business cards that said he worked for you and an office phone number that was almost identical to yours.'

'Really? How extraordinary.'

He was good; Flint would give him that. To this point he hadn't shown a hint of nervousness, calming his wife who hovered halfway down the stairs with a bit of jocular banter. 'They're *federales*, darling, come to see if I can help them find some *bandito*.'

Then to Flint he'd said, 'Do you have a photograph, perhaps?'

*Actually, I do, Mr Tyler, sir. In my wallet I do indeed carry a photograph of my husband; a rather fetching photograph that I took myself in the course of our honeymoon and one that perfectly captures his liquid eyes and his winning smile. But if you think I'm going to admit any of that to you . . .*

'No, sir,' she'd said. 'Not to hand.'

'Pity. Well, come on through to my study' – Tyler ushering her on with a ladies-first gesture – 'and we'll see if I can find your Mr Gates on the computer.'

*My Mr Gates! How do you know that he's my Mr Gates? Is that a figure of speech, Mr Tyler – or a slip of the tongue?*

She had given Crawford a fast look but he'd pretended not to notice.

'Now, let me see,' Tyler had said, flaunting his new computer, 'I know there is some clever way to search the entire database.'

Now Flint has reached the edge of the deck and is crouching alongside the three steps that lead up to it, rubbing dirt on her face to mask the whiteness of her skin. Very slowly she lifts her head until her eyes are just above the line of the deck and sees that Tyler is no more than six feet from her position, standing motionless by the glass door. He still has the phone to his ear, listening to someone or holding the line.

*Talk to me* she wills him but his mouth does not move.

'Talk to me, Mr Tyler,' she'd said when he'd completed his charade of searching the computer for a name that was not there.

'I beg your pardon?'

'Look, sir, he didn't just print up a few business cards. It's very clear to us that Mr Gates has detailed knowledge of the workings of your society, and of you – you personally, that is.'

'Detailed knowledge?' Tyler had repeated vaguely.

'Wouldn't you say so?' Flint said to Crawford.

'Encyclopaedic,' Crawford had replied.

'For example,' she had continued, 'thanks to what Mr Gates has said, I can give you a pretty good description of your office routine; how Mary's always the first one in, and always makes the coffee, but sometimes she forgets that you don't drink decaffeinated in the morning – you like the real stuff – and once you blew up at her, and bawled her out, and she had to remind you that making the coffee wasn't part of her job description and she said that you – all of you – could make your own damn coffee from now on, and after four days of nobody making the coffee you almost had a strike on your hands. Remember that, Mr Tyler? How am I doing, sir?'

'I don't understand,' Tyler had said.

'You like tofu and a sliced tomato for your lunch, don't you, Mr Tyler, and you got rid of John Somebody-or-other because he had an alcohol problem and Fran, your wife, is currently upset with you because your younger child – that would be Sally – wanted to go on a ski trip with the school and you wouldn't let her because her grades weren't up to scratch—'

'*Stop it!*'

Flint had reached out and taken his arm as though to steady him. 'How does Mr Gates know so much about you, sir?' she asked gently. 'How does this man you don't know, this man you've never heard of – how does he *know*?'

Tyler had shaken his head as though he had been punched. Afterwards, as they were heading for the hotel, Crawford had argued that Tyler's reaction to her onslaught could have been innocent – 'Christ, Grace, if you ever hit me with that kind of personal shit watch me fall over' – but she was adamant: 'No, Crawdaddy,' she said. 'That was one scared perp staring into the void.'

Now he is staring through the glass into the near-darkness, his sightline several feet above her head. Now he's opening the door and coming out on to the deck, so close she could reach out and touch him – or he could touch her.

'Come on,' he says, apparently to himself.

# thirteen

When Jarrett Crawford was a rookie police detective in Washington DC, working his first undercover assignment, he went to a rendezvous with his informant at the appointed time and walked headlong into a crack dealer's ambush. He was shot at five times with a .38 and hit twice in the buttocks and afterwards he was made to endure – along with the surgeon's probe – his lieutenant's mocking derision: 'Fuckin' horse's ass, what did I tell you? Always get there *ahead* of time' – and since Crawford took the advice to heart, 'Early Bird' is another of his nicknames.

Out of habit Crawford arrives at Friendly's restaurant in the Howard Johnson hotel twenty minutes before he said he would to find that Flint is already there. At first sight she looks spruce and fresh but the hotel has no emergency pressing service at this time of the morning and when he reaches her table Crawford can see that her clothes are badly stained, and he guesses what she has done.

'Christ, you went back there, didn't you?' he says before he has sat down. When all she does is motion to an empty chair with her eyes Crawford leans on the table and continues, 'Grace, are you set on getting yourself sued for harassment? Because you're sure as hell going the right way about it.'

There is still no response and now Crawford does sit down, taking the chair opposite her, but he is not yet done with his questions. 'You know what you look like?' he demands. 'You look like you've been dragged through the dirt and – let me guess – you've been snooping around Tyler's property without his permission or – more to the point – without a warrant, which is called trespass, in case you didn't know – and we're talking here about a guy with some standing in the community, not some lowlife; not some creep you can push around because you feel like it. And for what, Grace? What do you think you've achieved?'

'Close enough,' says Flint breaking her silence.

'What?'

'I wasn't dragged, Jerry, I crawled, and I've been pissed on, and when you've finished giving me your pious lectures get yourself some coffee – and then I need you to make a phone call.'

He doesn't like 'pious' but though her voice is very calm there is a warning light in her eyes that tells him she is close to boiling point. Wisely, he pours a cup of coffee from the Thermos and waits for her to tell him why.

'Because *he* made a phone call, Jerry.'

She is reaching into her bag, pulling out a notebook.

'Citizen Tyler,' she resumes, 'your upright pillar of the community. At approximately five twenty this morning, after I'd rattled his cage. About two minutes after he closed the door on me I called him on my cellphone and his line was engaged. So, yes, I trespassed on his property to try and overhear his side of the conversation and I did hear at least part of it. You want to know what he said?'

The question is rhetorical for Flint has opened the notebook to the first page, and turned it around, and she's pushing it across the table so that Crawford can read what she had written as soon as she'd got back to the Hertz car: her near-verbatim recollection of Tyler's whispered words.

*You assured me this could never happen. You gave me your word . . . Damn it, she knows . . . How do I know how she knows? What I do know is that she's been here twice and she doesn't believe a word I've said and now she's talking about a grand jury and subpoenas and God knows what else, and I'll tell you this . . . No, you listen to me. I'm telling you now that if she comes back again – and she will come back again unless you stop her – I'm going to tell her the truth and you can . . . I'm not threatening you. I'm simply warning you that you've put me in an intolerable position and unless you do something . . . You gave me your word—*

*You gave me your word!*

He had been standing on the edge of the deck about four feet from her position and all he had to do to see her was glance to his right and look down and before that could happen she had half a mind to come out of her crouch with her gun pointed at his head and take the phone out of his hand and hope to hear the voice on the other end of the line – and she didn't really care if she gave Tyler a heart attack.

But then he'd moved away, heading towards the rear of the extension where the deck overhung a steep bank and, following him to stay within listening range, she'd needed both of her hands to hold on to the supporting beams and stop herself sliding into the gully.

She was directly beneath where he was standing when he'd interrupted whatever palliative he was being offered.

'That's all very well,' he'd said, 'but as she's made perfectly clear to me – *perfectly* clear – she has the power to make my life extremely difficult and, frankly . . . *Will you please let me finish* . . . *!* Because, frankly, if she does even half of what she's threatening to do—'

'Well, say what you like but I'm not prepared to stand for it. I'm not going to be treated like a criminal. I only agreed to help you because you assured me that it was a matter of—'

He had been interrupted again and this time he had lapsed into silence and Flint had felt like screaming at him – and not only because the strain of holding on to the beam was seriously aggravating the injury to her shoulder. Through the gaps between the planks she could see slivers of the soles of his feet and in her mind she'd held them to the flames of an imaginary fire until he'd answered her question: *A matter of what, Mr Tyler?*

'I don't know,' he'd said but speaking into the phone. 'Oh, hold on, maybe I do. She left me her card . . .' He'd found it in one of the pockets of his robe, evidently. 'Here it is. She wrote a number on the back which could be her hotel, I suppose' – and digit by digit he had dictated the number of the Howard Johnson hotel.

'Yes, well, I do hope so,' he'd said after a further pause, less angry now, his indignation deflated by whatever reassurance he had been given. 'Good . . . Then I won't need to trouble you again, I hope . . . And to you . . . Goodbye.'

He had stayed where he was, and so had she, watching the gradual arrival of the dawn light. She had heard him sigh and then what sounded like the trickle of water and then she'd felt the warm splatter of liquid on her skin.

After he'd finished relieving himself and gone inside, she'd let go of the beam and slid down the bank into the gully like a sack of garbage descending a chute.

\* \* \*

When Crawford first moved to Washington DC he lived in his
elder sister's house on northwest M Street, sharing a room – for
reasons of economy – with a friend named Jimmy Bamford. They
had grown up together in the same Pittsburgh neighbourhood,
attended the same high school and then Pitt university, from which
both of them had graduated with only modest grades and no
particular prospects. They were drifting in dead-end jobs when
Alicia took a hand by proposing that Jerry enter law enforcement,
for she was married to DC's K-9 supervisor who had sufficient
clout within the Police Department to ease his young brother-
in-law through the selection process. Thus, under his sister's considerable influence, Crawford had moved to Washington and
Alicia's house bringing Bamford with him, and Jimmy was also
eased through the selection process. They enrolled in the police
academy together, graduated together, patrolled together, became
detectives on the same day and – eventually – partners. They even
dated together and their respective wives are sisters.

'Call the Wizard,' Flint says, referring to Jimmy Bamford who
has since taken a very different career path to Crawford but who
remains his soul mate as well as his closest friend.

Crawford is nursing his coffee cup in both hands as though he's
trying to keep them warm. 'Why would I do that?' he asks
cautiously.

'Because we have to know who Tyler called.' Crawford does not
respond and Flint continues, 'A pen register's not going to do it
because he may not call again and going after Tyler's phone records
will take too long.' Aware that she is breaking an unspoken rule to
never acknowledge the Wizard's existence, let alone his access to
sensitive technology, she smiles to mitigate her offence. 'Call him
for me, Crawdaddy. Please.'

He shakes his head. 'You don't ask, Grace. You know that.'

'I am asking, Crawdaddy. I've got no choice.'

Crawford has a boyish face but now worry lines crease his
forehead, suddenly ageing him in Flint's eyes. 'How come,' he says,
stalling for time, 'that when you want something I'm "Crawdaddy"
and when you're pissed at me I'm "Jerry"?'

'No, when I'm pissed at you, you're Jarrett, *Jarrett*.'

He looks away as though he hasn't heard.

Flint reaches out and touches his hand. 'Crawdaddy, understand
something: *they know where we are.*'

Crawford takes the point and shifts in his chair, uncomfortably aware that he is sitting with his back to the entrance of the restaurant but resisting the impulse to turn around. 'They?' he asks as though it is important.

'They, he, she, it – whoever Tyler called.' She is still speaking calmly, still smiling, but her eyes have grown unnaturally bright. 'You want me to call the NSA, Jarrett? Because I will.'

Crawford bristles at this. 'You're talking crap,' he says, glaring at her, calling her bluff. 'You want to burn him? Go ahead.'

She's doing it deliberately – making her eyes restless, dancing back and forth between his face and the entrance, pressing home her warning.

'Will you quit that?' he insists, but now he swivels his chair so that he, too, can watch the door. 'There are times . . .' he begins.

A waitress interrupts, coming to the table with a plate of eggs-over-easy that Flint attacks as though food is the only thing on her mind. Crawford declines to order. For several minutes – until Flint has finished eating – he remains silent, nursing his resentment.

Then, 'You were kidding, right?' he asks. 'About calling NSA?'

'Yes and no,' she says. 'Jerry, I would never burn a source, but if you won't call him I *will* find him, as quietly as I can, and go to him on my hands and knees if I have to, and . . .' She pushes the plate away. 'Crawdaddy,' she begins again, 'it's never supposed to get personal but I have the distinct feeling that I've been pissed on from a very great height, and it's not Tyler's urine I'm talking about, and it *is* personal, and I really do have problems with that, and . . . Heads up,' she says suddenly, nodding towards the door.

Two men are entering the restaurant and Flint is registering their details with Polaroid efficiency: white, average height, well-nourished, tidy hair, early- to mid-thirties – nothing remarkable about them. They are wearing business suits minus the jackets which suggests they are staying in the hotel and are not carrying weapons they wish to conceal. Or perhaps, Flint thinks, these are false impressions they intend to convey. She never takes her eyes off them until they have chosen a table in a far corner.

But they have barely settled when two more white males enter the restaurant, and then a group of three, and then a lone female – forty-something, about 5 feet 8 without her heels, short black hair showing just flecks of grey, light makeup well applied that disguises a small blemish on her left temple that could be a birthmark, eyes that are coloured somewhere between green and turquoise, small-breasted, good legs if a little thick at the ankles, no jewellery, no wedding band – who takes a table close to theirs, and doesn't even glance in their direction, and seems vaguely familiar to Flint. And then comes a family, and then a gaggle of flight crew in uniforms, and it is becoming impossible to keep track of them all, and Crawford stands up as though he has thought of somewhere to go and says, 'Let's get out of here.'

'What would you do, Jerry?' Flint responds, staying in her chair. 'If you were in my shoes?'

Crawford, impassive, leans over the table to scribble his signature on the bill.

'You'd ask me, wouldn't you – ask me to call?'

The woman is making a show of studying the breakfast menu but Flint is watching her eyes and they're not moving because she is concentrating too hard on listening to what's being said and – unless you're very good – the Wernicke's area of the cortex that handles speech comprehension overwhelms the other sensory perceptions. Not a pro, then, not a trained listener; diligent, nevertheless.

'You coming?' asks Crawford, still ignoring Flint's questions.

She gets up from the table as though she is and then she says, 'Go ahead. I'll catch up with you.'

Crawford turns and heads towards the door and Flint goes to follow him and then suddenly diverts to the lone woman's table and sits down in the chair opposite her and reaches out to yank away the menu, revealing her startled face.

'I know you,' Flint says with certainty.

'*Bitte?*'

'I can't place you right now but I've seen your face before and it will come back to me.'

The woman shakes her head and offers Flint a tentative, apologetic smile.

'*Ich verstehe Sie nicht. Ich spreche kein Englisch.*'

'Not in the flesh,' Flint continues, 'but I've seen your photograph. Maybe on one of the watch lists – you know, people we're looking for?' She pretends to consider a second possibility: 'Or maybe it was an Interpol flyer,' she says while reaching into her pocket for her FSF credentials. 'Yes, I think that's probably it,' she announces, opening the wallet to bare an imposing silver shield of Cutter's design. 'Show me some ID?'

The woman's smile has vanished and she is turning her head from side to side as though she is looking for help.

'*Ich verstehe das nicht*,' she repeats: I don't understand.

'*Ihre Dokumente*,' Flint demands. '*Zeigen Sie mir Ihren Paß.*'

Now the woman is reaching into her bag to find her passport – or perhaps it's not a passport she's reaching for, and Flint shouts '*Nein!*', and lunges across the table to seize the bag, and the woman screams, stunning the restaurant into silence. A waitress comes hurrying towards the table until Flint hisses a warning – 'Stay out of it' – with sufficient ferocity to stop her dead.

'*Hilfe! Bitte helfen Sie mir!*' – the woman is on her feet calling for help but nobody tries to prevent Flint from upending the bag, spilling the contents on to the table, rooting through them looking for the gun or the knife or the can of Mace that isn't there.

No passport either, but Flint does find a German identity card with a picture that bears a reasonable likeness of the woman who is now pulling on her arm and trying to wrest her property from Flint's tenacious grasp. Frau Gisela Lender, aged forty-three and from Berlin, apparently – according to the card – receives a shove that sends her sprawling back into her chair.

There are men on their feet now trying to decide what to do, measuring the depths of their chivalry against the high risks of intervention – but none of them tries to stop Flint leaving the restaurant, the identity card still in her hand. She marches across the lobby to the reception desk and confronts a clerk with her credentials and demands to know if Frau Lender – *this* Frau Lender, the one on the card – is staying at the hotel and, if so, when did she arrive?

Five days ago is the answer she receives – long before there was the slightest possibility that Flint would come to Maine – and she feels herself deflate like a punctured tyre.

She leaves Frau Lender's card at the desk with a half-truth explanation that she 'found it in the restaurant' and takes the lift to the third floor, heading for her room. Beyond caring about the probable repercussions of her mistake she nevertheless speculates on what Crawford is likely to say when he learns about the fracas: 'Oh, so now you've added criminal assault to trespass and harassment. That's smart, Grace; *real* smart.'

*Isn't it just*, she concludes.

# fourteen

Flint in her Howard Johnson room, waiting for her clothes to come back from Housekeeping, dials Crawford's mobile phone for the fourth time and still gets no reply. He's not in his room, or not answering the door, and she holds a flicker of hope that he's changed his mind; gone to find a safe phone to call the Wizard in Crypto City where the routine intercept of Tyler's telephone call by the NSA's vacuuming antennas might not yet have been discarded.

With nothing else to do, she drifts into the bathroom to brush her teeth and apply fresh makeup. Like Frau Lender, she favours the minimalist approach: a little foundation, a touch of gloss on her lips. The image that she sees reflected by the mirror is almost flawless – an enduring tribute to the reconstructive surgeons who repaired the dreadful damage inflicted by the heel of Clayton Buller's boot. It is also a deceiving image, for it reflects not a hint of what she feels.

*Okay,* she tells the nagging voice inside her head that is demanding to be heard. *Say it.*

'You married a lie,' she tells the mirror.

*You don't know that!*

*Everything he told you was a lie.*

*You don't know that!*

*He lied about his job, about where he worked?*

*Yes.*

*So every time you were together, everything he told you about what he'd done, where he'd been – all those field trips, going to Africa – that was all lies.*

*Yes.*

*So, Grace, was anything true? Anything he said? Anything at all?*

There is a teardrop forming in the corner of her right eye that she angrily brushes away with the back of one hand. 'Perhaps,' she tells the mirror.

*When he was touching you, Grace, when he was holding you, when he was fucking you, Grace, how do you know that anything he said was the truth?*

Searching the reflection of the mask of her face she does not find an answer she wants to hear.

All business once more, Flint hits the phone and even though it is not yet nine on a Sunday morning she reaches Rocco Morales at his desk in the basement of the Marscheider building and tells him that she needs an address for an unlisted, and now disconnected, Portland phone number.

This is child's play for Morales, for his sister, Rosetta, is a skip-tracer – or, as she prefers it, an 'information specialist' – who from her base in Minnesota pursues debtors and deadbeat dads and runaway wives and other disparate fugitives (some of them sought by the FSF), combing countless databases on the internet for the trails they do not realise they leave behind. It is Rosetta's money-back guarantee that she can provide any unlisted telephone number in the United States, or the name and current address of the subscriber to any US phone – landline or cellular, listed or not, or disconnected within the last three months. For a price.

'This being Sunday,' says Rosetta's brother, 'it'll cost you.'

'More than you think,' says Flint. 'Rocco, I need it now – not in three days, or however long she normally takes. Today. Preferably this morning. I don't care what it costs.'

Through the silence she imagines Rocco doing the math.

'She'll need to bring in a whole crew on double time,' he eventually says.

'Two crews if she has to.'

'Wow! Is Cutter going to be okay with this?' Morales asks.

*Probably not*, thinks Flint. 'I'll square it with him,' is what she says.

She rings off and tries Crawford's mobile phone number again and then his room and, still getting no reply from either, she calls Housekeeping to chivvy them for her clothes. She has nowhere to go and nothing to do except wait for Rosetta to work her magic and the room is growing claustrophobic. She needs air, she decides, and some kind of diversion – anything that will stop her mind dwelling on questions about Ben that she doesn't want to answer.

Some ten minutes later a maid brings her clothes, and now she has a project to distract her. Housekeeping has done its best but there has been no second resurrection: the skirt of her suit is deeply stained and there is a jagged darn in the jacket where the sleeve was ripped that is anything but invisible. Calling Reception to ask where she can buy clothes on a Maine Sunday morning she learns that twenty-five miles north of Portland there is a town called Freeport that is virtually one huge shopping mall stuffed with outlet stores. Perfect, she decides.

She has finished dressing and is scribbling a note of explanation for Crawford that she will leave at the front desk when the telephone rings. Expecting it to be Crawford, or maybe Morales, she picks up the receiver and says 'Flint' – and hears a lingering moment of silence that is replaced by the dial tone as the line is cut. Instantly, or so it seems, she punches the zero key and waits impatiently for the hotel operator to answer, and then demands to know, 'Did you just put a call through to my room?'

'No, ma'am.'

'So, if somebody just called my room it must have been from within the hotel?'

'Yes, ma'am.'

Her warning to Crawford comes back to haunt her: *They know where we are!*

She does not finish the note to Crawford. Glancing in her bag to confirm that she has her weapon, she slips open the door and cautiously checks the corridor in both directions. Satisfied that it is empty, she sets off at a brisk trot, heading away from the lift, following the signs towards an emergency staircase.

Passing through the exit, pausing only to make sure the stairwell is empty, she takes the steps down to the ground floor two at a time, ignoring the jolting pain in her knee, and pushes through the fire exit into the parking lot, and then she is limping along the side of the hotel towards the main entrance and the lobby where – less than two minutes after the telephone rang – she now stands behind a rack of brochures, feigning a keen interest in the tourist attractions of Maine, watching the lift lights that tell her one of the cars has just completed its ascent to the third floor.

She waits and while she waits she palms the small automatic out of her bag and slips it into the waistband of her spoiled skirt, in the small of her back, where, she hopes, the bulge will not show through her jacket.

Soon – perhaps too soon, Flint thinks, for there has barely been time for anyone to establish that she is not in her room – the lift lights tell her that the car is descending. It pauses at the second floor and then completes its journey, disgorging into the lobby an obese middle-aged woman with unnaturally blonde hair and three sullen brown-haired children who are also overweight – and that's it, Flint believes, until the woman says to the largest of her brood, 'Darren, you forget your manners? You get the door for the lady.'

And while Darren uses his bulk to prevent the doors from closing and reaches into the lift to manhandle a large suitcase with an ease that suggests it is not as heavy as it looks, Flint hears the voice of a woman she cannot yet see – 'Thank you, young man, you are most kind' – and it is the same voice she heard less than two hours ago in Friendly's restaurant – *Ich verstehe das nicht. Ich spreche kein Englisch* – and she's got half a mind to reintroduce herself to Frau Lender.

*Hey*, she might say, *you must be a* really *fast learner.*

Instead Flint takes a step back and drops down into a crouch, apparently taking a particular interest in the brochures at the very bottom of the rack, and watches Frau Lender's legs emerging from the lift.

'Most kind, most kind,' she repeats while Flint's hunch that she has seen Frau Lender before today hardens into certainty. Something about the suitcase has triggered a response in Flint's episodic memory and now she is racing through the indices of her stored recollections, willing herself to recall the connection.

Darren must have offered further help for Frau Lender says brightly, 'No, I can manage, thank you, dear. My car is right outside.' And then she is heading across the lobby towards the exit, towing the suitcase that is set on wheels, and it is that conjunction that provides the key – and in her mind Flint is in London on a pig of a humid day last August, stuck in a stifling office above an electronics shop in the Tottenham Court Road, not wanting to be there, watching a ropey surveillance video shot the previous day in the departure lounge of Terminal Two at Heathrow airport.

Operation Pentecost was in the doldrums and Flint had flown home to England to light a fire under her former colleagues at the Major Crimes Task Force who were supposed to cooperate with the FSF but were doing so lethargically and in their own good time.

'That's her coming through security now,' said a detective inspector named Pat Bakewell, a woman so morose that half a day in her company had sapped all of the energy from Flint. 'The cow on the right.'

Still in a crouch behind the rack Flint closes her eyes and tries to recall the details of a flickering image on a TV screen.

'The name on the passport is Moltke, Friederike Moltke,' Bakewell had continued, 'not that that means anything. Well, bound to be phoney, isn't it? Given her line of work.'

In the parlance of Major Crimes Moltke was a 'mule' for the Karl Gröber organisation, a courier of laundered money – or so Major Crimes strongly suspected.

'This is the eighth trip she's made out of the UK in the last two months,' Bakewell had said. 'Regular as a clockwork bunny, and she always takes the wheelie' – and Flint recollects the image of a woman walking away from the camera's fixed position towing a suitcase that was set on wheels.

'I've had her pulled twice by security but they found nothing, of course,' said Bakewell – and on the screen the woman had turned her head to look over her shoulder and the camera had caught her face, and Bakewell had paused the tape, and Flint can see her now: different hair style and colour but the same wide-set eyes, the same aquiline nose, the same disguised blemish on the left temple.

Frau Lender.

Despite the brilliant, deceiving sunlight the gauge on the dashboard of Flint's rental car tells her that the outside temperature is 38 degrees Fahrenheit and there are still glimpses of frost on the road. She is driving a meandering course through and around downtown Portland, trying to keep at least two other vehicles between her and the bronze Ford Escape ahead, taking it for granted that while Frau Lender could just be lost she is much more likely to be checking for a tail.

Flint has called Morales on her mobile phone and he has run the licence plates and established that the Ford is also a rental, and also from Hertz, and Hertz says that the vehicle is due to be returned to Boston's Logan airport by six o'clock tonight. But Frau Lender has shown no inclination to follow any of the countless signs they've passed in the last half hour that would have taken her to the interstate and south to Massachusetts. So, Flint assumes, getting to Boston is not yet at the top of Frau Lender's agenda.

As best she can Flint follows their random route on a street map that is open on her lap. For the second time this morning they are on Market Street, heading east towards ramshackle wharfs that extend into Portland Harbour like the fingers of a hand. The first time the Ford stopped short of the wharfs, turning left on to Commercial Street and joining US-1A, the arterial road that rings Portland, and it is about to do so again, apparently. Flint hangs back, slipping the automatic gear shift into neutral and allowing the car to coast until Frau Lender clears the junction.

Now Flint waits in line for her chance to make the turn, two cars ahead of her, the first one dawdling until Flint taps the horn. Now she's at the junction making the turn, looking to the right for oncoming traffic and then left – and instantly registering the fact that the Ford is stationary no more than twenty yards along Commercial Street and she's coming up on it fast, Frau Lender watching her approach in the wing mirror.

There is nothing Flint can do, no way to avoid being seen. She accelerates past the Ford staring straight ahead – not a glance at Frau Lender – and continues along Commercial Street towards the arterial road, one eye on the rear-view mirror.

She's five hundred yards away and committed to taking the ramp on to US-1A and there is no way back when the inevitable happens. The Ford noses out into the traffic flow and makes a fast U-turn and Flint can faintly hear the blare of a protesting horn, and then her quarry is gone.

Rage can make her reckless and Flint is looking for a place to stop so that she can make a phone call. She has it in mind to claim the Ford as hers, to dial 911 and report that it's been stolen; that there's a baby on board or some other precious cargo – anything she can think of that will get a potent All Points Bulletin broadcast to Portland's finest. And, frankly, damn the consequences.

She's pulling on to the hard shoulder, still intent on madness, when her mobile phone rings and she scrabbles to answer it, and what Jarrett Crawford has to tell her saves her from herself.

'Where are you?' he demands, not bothering with any pre-
liminaries.

'Running around Portland chasing my tail.'

'I need to talk to you.'

'Go ahead.'

'Not on the phone and not at the hotel.'

There is a bleakness to his tone that makes her feel cold.

'Where?'

'Remember Scratchwood and Peter?'

It takes a moment before she makes the association. 'Yes.'

'Same thing. Go south. I'll be there in about one hour.'

'Okay.'

'And, Grace, turn off your phone. Now.'

'Why?'

'Because it's like a homing beacon.'

'What?'

'Grace, trust me. It's like you said: As long as your phone's
turned on, they know where you are.'

'Okay.'

'No, not okay,' Crawford says.

# fifteen

The charter of the Financial Strike Force, tortuously negotiated by representatives of the seventeen countries that sponsor it, grants draconian powers. On the strength of 'reasonable suspicion' the FSF can request the seizure of assets in any of the member countries; any assets that it believes 'derive from or are part of' a criminal scheme to launder money. On the say-so of Aldus Cutter – or, in his absence, Nathan Stark or Grace Flint (when, that is, she's not in purdah) – the authorities of the United States, Canada and the fifteen member nations of the European Union are likely to freeze your bank accounts and seize your house, your boat – anything of value – and to get them back you will have to prove that the suspicions of the Strike Force are unfounded. Even non-member nations, even the Swiss, have been known to acquiesce to the will of the FSF.

To encourage this uncommon cooperation the charter provides powerful incentives. While one-third of what is seized goes to the budget of the Strike Force – making it not merely self-financing but, as Cutter boasts, 'a goddamned profit centre' – the balance provides bounty: twenty per cent paid into a slush fund that rewards and encourages informants; thirty per cent paid to the law enforcement agencies that actively assist each seizure; the rest, the lion's share, paid into the national coffers of the cooperating states. Given these inducements, it is almost unheard-of for the FSF's calls for confiscation to go unheeded.

But as Cutter is quick to point out, there is a downside to this bargain. For any law enforcement agency with budgetary problems – which is all of them – there is a temptation to keep back information that might, when withheld until the most propitious moment, boost its share of the bounty. Or, as has happened too often for Cutter's liking, agencies sometimes jump the gun, seizing assets worth only a fraction of what is still in the pipeline and not yet identified; in Cutter's words, 'not ripe for the plucking'.

Bloodied by experience the FSF also has a tendency to withhold information, keeping some of its secrets until the last possible moment – and it was in this context that last December Flint returned home to England, supposedly on Christmas leave, supposedly to spend time with her father. For anyone who thought it odd that she would not be spending the holiday with her husband she had a truthful explanation, or one that she thought was true.

'Ben's leading a field trip – again,' she told Kitty Lopez who, like almost everyone in the Marscheider building, was not privy to the real reason for Flint's journey. 'To the frosty shores of Hudson Bay,' she said in a fair imitation of Ben's voice, repeating what he'd told her. 'Polar Bear Capital of the World!'

'This is need-to-know,' Cutter said, 'and there's nobody outside this room who needs to know. Are we clear on that?'

And Jarrett Crawford and Felix Hartmann said they understood, and nodded to Flint, and went their separate ways: Hartmann back to Germany, he said, to visit his parents; Crawford to Washington, he said, where the extended Crawford clan gathers each Christmas at sister Alicia's house.

Rocco Morales was called on to provide the equipment they required to conduct their mission, but even he was excluded from the need-to-know loop.

Two days later Flint took an overnight flight to England – to Manchester rather than London, to minimise the risk of any chance encounter with her former colleagues from the Met – and rented a car and drove the 130 miles south to the small Oxfordshire village of Mid Compton and the Georgian farmhouse where she had grown up.

She found her father attending to his patients in the converted barn that serves as his surgery and he provoked raucous excitement among them by roaring with delight at her arrival.

'Marvellous, bloody marvellous,' he said, wrapping his arms around her, lifting her off her feet. Then he took her up the house to show her the extravagant preparations he had made for her visit: an oversized Christmas tree in the living room festooned with lights; the fridge filled with delicacies sent from London by Fortnum & Mason; her old room freshly painted and with new linens on the bed.

Feeling guilty, she nevertheless allowed him to spoil her for most of that first day before she broke the news.

'I've got a favour to ask,' she said as they set off for a walk across the fields in the pallid afternoon sun.

'Anything, darling.'

'Would you mind if a couple of friends came to stay for a few days? Over Christmas?'

'Friends?' He stopped in his tracks and gave her a quizzical look.

'Well, strictly speaking they're colleagues from the Strike Force but they're also buddies.'

She caught a glimmer of emotion on his face – disappointment, she thought, or maybe alarm – but it was quickly banished with a smile. 'Mind? Of course I don't mind,' he said as though he found the very idea ridiculous. 'The more the merrier, don't you think?'

'Thank you,' she said reaching up to kiss his cheek.

And then she tucked her arm into his and they resumed their descent of the steep grassy rise on which the house stands, and after a while he casually asked, 'So, Gracie, Ben is doing well, you say?'

'Ben's fine, Dad.'

'And, things? Everything all right, is it?' – which was as close as John Flint had ever come to enquiring about the state of his daughter's marriage.

'Perfect.'

Which was more or less true at the time. She thought.

Recalling that afternoon, driving to her rendezvous with Crawford – dawdling in the slow lane of the interstate, now pushing the car to 100 m.p.h., now dawdling again – she feels nothing except numb.

Heading south, keeping a frequent check on the mirror and searching ahead for Crawford's sign, she permits her conscious mind to dwell in the sanctuary of past experiences and emotions.

# sixteen

Crawford and Hartmann had arrived at Mid Compton on Christmas Eve, driving up from London in an oddly matched two-car convoy: Hartmann in a powerful BMW with German plates; Crawford in a lemon-coloured Mazda sports car that seemed almost too small to contain him. At Flint's suggestion they had brought a gift of John Flint's favourite malt whisky and he had greeted them warmly enough. They, on the other hand, had seemed painfully ill-at-ease in the presence of her father; overly polite and far too eager to please. She knew it was only a matter of time before he would lose patience.

'For God's sake, the pair of you,' he'd said when they were all gathered in the kitchen for an improvised supper on that first evening, 'will you stop calling me "sir"? I'm *John* – and I'm also not a complete idiot and I'm sure that in due course Grace will tell me why you're really here and the chances are I'll agree to whatever she wants and even if I don't agree she'll do it anyway ... So, *please*, will you just relax? This is Christmas! And, speaking of which, if anybody knows how to cook this goose,' he'd said, poking with a kitchen knife at the succulent bird on the counter, 'now would be the time to speak.'

Hartmann said he knew something about cooking and he volunteered to take over all of the preparations (which was just as well, Flint thought, for she was no more adept than her father at putting a proper meal on the table; Ben did most of the cooking at Miller's Reach). And – this another revelation for Flint – Crawford turned out to have an empathy with animals and a rudimentary knowledge of veterinary medicine and when, after supper, the master of the local hunt called to say that his best mare was writhing on the stable floor with what appeared to be an acute case of colic, Crawford had volunteered to accompany Dr Flint and give whatever assistance might be needed.

Waiting for them to return, banished from the kitchen by Hartmann, she had killed time making up two beds in the spare room and setting the table for the next day's lunch, and then she'd called home to check for messages on the answering machine and heard Ben's voice coming over a bad connection:

*Hi, loon, it's me. Today you're not a nightingale, I'm afraid. You're a loon because I'm a loon, because a loon's got its legs set so near its ass it can't walk, and when it moults it can't fly – and that just about sums up the way I'm feeling. I have no idea what I'm doing here and why I'm not with you, and I'd give the world just to be holding you. I love you, Mrs Loon. Happy Christmas.*

It was gone ten o'clock before Crawford and her father got back to the house and another hour before she felt she could decently imply that Crawford and Hartmann must be tired and should retire for the night, and another fifteen minutes before they took the hint, both declaring sudden fatigue.

'Sound chaps,' said her father when he and Grace were finally alone together, sitting on the couch before the fire, nursing the glasses of malt she had poured for them. 'Work with them a lot do you, darling?'

'Uh-huh,' she said noncommittally, knowing where this was leading, which was where she wanted it to go.

'I expect you're on some kind of operation at the moment?'

'We never close,' she said, teasing him.

'An undercover operation?'

'They usually are.'

'Here in the UK, I mean?'

'Kind of' – and he'd pulled a face that had made her smile.

'Well, then,' he said grouchily, 'don't tell me.'

'All right.'

'Don't tell me anything and I won't tell you what I *was* going to give you for Christmas – was being the operative word.'

'That's blackmail – or do I mean bribery? Anyway, whatever it is, you can't do that to a copper.'

'Can't I? Well, you just watch me' – and he'd taken a sip of the malt and pressed his lips together as though he had nothing more to say.

'Is it – *was* it,' she said after a suitable pause, 'a great present?'

'Magnificent!'

'Expensive?'

'Ruinous!'

'I mean, a present that any daughter of yours would sell her soul for?'

'Absolutely!'

She had pretended to weigh her conscience. Then, 'Oh, all right.'

'About two weeks ago,' Flint began carefully, speaking in a monotone, 'a woman flying into New York from London – a Brit who runs a small private detective agency in Birmingham – got turned over by immigration at Kennedy airport. There was no particular reason: a hunch, an INS inspector having a bad day – whatever. She was red carded, which means she was turned upside down and inside out. INS searched her luggage and behind the lining of her briefcase they found some documents relating to a Strike Force investigation that I've been running for almost a year: essentially a computer printout of requests for information and surveillance of suspects we had sent to the Met, because a lot of what we're looking into has a London connection. She claimed to know nothing about the documents but after being hauled off to an INS detention centre in shackles she pretty soon changed her mind. We let her sweat for another twenty-four hours and then we brought her in. By then she was practically begging to talk.'

This was not the first time Flint had allowed her father to glimpse inside her alien world but watching his face as closely as he watched hers she could tell that he was no nearer coming to terms with the bleak asperity of her descriptions.

'Not that she told the whole truth, of course, because perps never do – not at first. Anyway, she eventually admitted that this was the fourth trip she'd made to New York carrying documents for a client she knew only as "Peter". She'd never met him, she said. He contacted her through the web site she maintains to promote her business and offered her occasional work as a "personal courier" and she didn't have the sense to turn him down.

'The pattern was always the same: Peter would send her an email telling her to set off along this or that motorway at a certain time – always at night – until she saw a car stopped on the hard shoulder with its emergency lights flashing. Then she would pull into the next service station she came to, which was always within a couple of miles, park the car leaving it unlocked, go inside to use the loo, come back to the car, drive home – and, bingo, she'd find an empty briefcase in the boot, or one that seemed to be empty. Then as soon as she could – but always within three days; Peter was very insistent about that – she'd fly to New York, check into the Hilton on Sixth Avenue, call a voice-mail number Peter had given her and leave a message saying what her room number was.

'Within an hour, two at the most, her phone would ring once and that was the signal for her to slip the latch on the door and disappear into the bathroom. She'd stay in there ten minutes and when she came out the briefcase would be gone. It was all a bit elaborate, perhaps, but basically fail-safe. Nicely sterilised, no face-to-face contact at either end.'

'But why on earth would she do that?' her father said and she'd heard her own involuntary, mirthless laugh.

'Greed,' she said. 'Plain and simple greed. On the bed, in place of the briefcase, there would be an envelope containing ten thousand dollars – cash money, twenty-dollar bills. Even allowing for her expenses, that's not bad for three days' work.'

John Flint had shaken his head as though he didn't understand. 'Couldn't this Peter fellow have just posted the documents?'

'Yeah, he could, or used FedEx, but that isn't Hustler's style.'

'Hustler?'

'The prime target, the creep who runs the money-laundering operation we're out to smash. He's an East German who, in the old days, before reunification, worked for state security and had important connections in Moscow, and now he's washing money for just about every dirty racket that's mushroomed in the East since the Wall came down – and I'm talking about hundreds of millions of dollars. He's good because he's very, very careful and what he fears most, and guards against to the nth degree, is infiltration by people like me – because infiltration is the only way we can destroy him. And the trouble with the post is you can't tell if it's been opened – not the way we do it – and the Customs people do random checks on courier traffic and, however long the odds, there was still a chance that we might stumble on to it – and he wouldn't know. That's the point, you see, Dad. By using a mule – his own courier – Hustler maintained the chain of custody over the documents so he would know if something went wrong – if she got busted, say, or the briefcase was stolen – and that would allow him to begin damage control; alerting Peter at this end, for example, so he could start covering his traces.

'And that's what should have happened. The woman – her name is Nina, by the way – should have kept her mouth shut or stuck to her cover story, which was that she'd found the briefcase on a train and decided to keep it. The worst that would have happened is that she would have been deported, and Hustler would have known, and she would have been fifty thousand dollars better off because that's what he'd promised her if the shit ever hit the fan – and Hustler *always* keeps his promises.

'The only thing Hustler didn't reckon on was Nina's reaction to twenty-four hours in INS detention, sharing a cell with the kind of scum I hope you never get to meet.'

John Flint had grimaced and asked, 'What did these people do to her?'

'Let's just say that when I told her that unless she stopped lying to me I'd send her right back to INS she fell apart and cried like a child.' Flint had held her father's troubled eyes unwaveringly. 'People have died because of Hustler, Dad. Innocent people – or some of them. People like Nina need to understand that if you play the game on his team, and it goes wrong, there are some very tough rules.'

'I'm sure,' said her father and then he'd lapsed into silence, staring at the fire.

'Anyway, she cracked and we fluttered her and—'

'Fluttered her?'

'Sorry, gave her a polygraph, a lie-detector test. And she passed, more or less, and I decided to go ahead with the drop as planned – except it was me, not Nina, hiding in the bathroom at the Hilton – and we got some pretty good surveillance pictures of Hustler's bag man and when the time comes we can probably burn him.'

'Burn him?'

'Turn him into an informant, working for us. Sorry' – she had reached out to touch her father's shoulder – 'I've been hanging around too many cops and creeps. Half the time I must sound as though I'm speaking a foreign language.'

'Does Ben understand only half of what you say?'

'Ben doesn't like me talking about work,' she said, wrinkling her nose.

'I can understand why,' said her father, winning him a smile.

'So, now all we have to do is find Peter and see if we can burn him, and that's why Crawford and Hartmann are here – and I'm sorry for imposing them on you.' She grinned. 'So, what's my present?'

'Oh, no you don't,' said her father shaking his head. 'You've only given me half the story. It's all or nothing, Gracie.'

'I shouldn't have told you a thing! Cutter would have me shot if he knew.'

'And why did you tell me?'

'Because I had to involve you because we needed somewhere secure to stay and I couldn't think of anywhere else, and I wanted you to know just in case—' She had broken off, stalled by second thoughts on how to put it.

'In case of what?'

'Peter – or Peter's source if he's just the bag man – works for Major Crimes. Somebody has to be because access to the computer where this stuff is coming from is highly restricted and protected by password *and* fingerprint verification. You can't just hack into it. Before you can even type in your password you have to put your hand on a reader that scans the ridge patterns, and if the whorls and the loops and the arches and the whatnots don't match what the computer has on file, an alarm goes off.

'That means somebody senior at Major Crimes is dirty, and until we know who it is, that means everybody there who matters is suspect, and that means we can't risk asking them to burn Peter. And Cutter doesn't trust anybody else at the Yard – or rather, he doesn't know who to trust – and I don't blame him, so we're going to do it ourselves.'

'Do what?'

'I'm going to make the next pick-up. Instead of Nina.' She had seen alarm flooding into her father's eyes and quickly continued. 'The sports car that Jerry drove here, that's her car and that's what I'll be driving. And so far as we know, so far as *she* knows, Peter's never seen Nina close up and she and I are about the same age, about the same height. I can fix my hair like she does and put on some extra clothes to bulk up – and I'll pass muster at a reasonable distance, which is as close as I intend to get. Jerry and Felix will get to the rendezvous ahead of me and while I'm in the loo and Peter is putting the briefcase in my car, they'll be putting a tracking device on his car. And then we'll just follow him and find out who he is. Or that's the theory.'

'And you wanted to tell me in case of *what*, Grace?'

*In case this is a set-up, Daddy dear. In case Peter knows. In case Hustler's told him that it won't be Nina who is coming to the rendezvous.*

'Just in case,' she said. 'Things can go wrong and if we end up having to take him down in the car park . . . well, there could be a fuss because we don't exactly have jurisdiction in the UK. I didn't want you reading in the papers about the three of us in the middle of some huge diplomatic row when you thought we'd gone on a day trip to Stratford-on-Avon – or whatever cover story I might have given you. I didn't want to take advantage of you *and* tell you lies.'

'Take him down?'

'Arrest him, subdue him – and then we'll call the cops.'

'Will you be armed?'

'No, that would really start a riot. We left our weapons in New York.'

'Will he be armed?'

'I doubt it. You know that our cops don't normally carry guns.'

'Even your friends in Major Crimes?'

'Only some of them – and they're not my friends – and only sometimes.'

John Flint had slowly got up from the couch and looked down on his daughter.

'Do you know when this is going to happen?'

'In three days' time. Nina has received another email. She hasn't read it, of course, because she's strictly incommunicado. No, Dad,' she hurried on, 'not the INS. She's nicely wrapped up in our protective custody – which, by comparison, is like the Ritz.'

'Grace, can I you ask something?'

'As you would say, anything.'

'This woman, Nina; if she hadn't told you the truth, would you have sent her back to that cell and those terrible people?'

'Probably,' she said.

*In a New York minute*, she knew.

Peter's email had instructed Nina to join the M1 motorway near Rugby and head south and the impostor Flint had driven the Mazda practically all the way to the outskirts of London before she saw a set of blinking orange lights on the hard shoulder ahead of her.

'Okay,' she'd said into the needle-thin wireless microphone that she had sewn into the strap of her bra, 'it's the Scratchwood rest area coming up in about two miles. Come ahead.'

Then she had eased her foot from the accelerator until she was doing no more than 50 m.p.h. when she passed the unremarkable Ford parked on the hard shoulder and she had slowed some more and waited for Hartmann's BMW to overtake her – and it had not.

'I say again, it's Scratchwood, about a mile to go and I've got company,' she'd said watching the mirror, watching the brightening headlights of the Ford as it gained on her. 'Come ahead – repeat, come ahead, now.'

*Nada, nichts, nothing – and thank you, Rocco, and may you rot.* The transmitter for the microphone that Rocco Morales had provided was inside her right boot, strapped to her shin – with two fresh batteries she had installed herself, and the transmit switch taped to the 'on' position so that it couldn't move, as Rocco had instructed – and she had reached down and slapped it hard with her hand, for all the good that did.

She'd had no way of knowing that it was the receiver in Hartmann's car that was on the blink; that all he and Crawford had heard of her transmissions were bursts of meaningless static; that they had continued on their merry way, passing by the Scratchwood exit with no more than a glance, oblivious to the fact that she was coming to the end of the off-ramp with the Ford about one hundred yards behind her and one useless thought on her mind: *Now what?*

They had soon realised something was wrong when they'd found themselves coming towards the end of the M1 and there was no sign of the Mazda. No sign either of the route back to the motorway and Hartmann had negotiated a seemingly endless succession of roundabouts and flyovers, pushing the BMW until the tyres squealed, muscling his way through the traffic, Crawford holding on to the grab handle as though his life depended on it.

Then they were back on the motorway, on the northbound carriageway, with the needle of the speedometer hovering at 250 k.p.h., Scratchwood coming up fast and Crawford bawling at Hartmann to pull over on to the hard shoulder. That was where they had abandoned the BMW and begun their weaving crossing of three lanes of traffic, dodging looming trucks and cars that came at them like missiles, vaulting the crash barrier on the median, plunging into the traffic on the southbound lanes with the same mad recklessness, making it unscathed to the other side, though barely. A steep grass bank up which they scrambled on their hands and knees had brought them to the rest area and from its summit they had looked across the sprawling parking lot and seen the Mazda bathed in a sodium light, set apart from the other cars, alongside a Portakabin.

Hartmann with his loping stride had got there first, and thought at first the car was empty, and then he'd seen Flint huddled in the passenger seat, her chin slumped on her chest, the top of her head only just visible above the dashboard. He had pulled open the door and cursed in German and she had raised her head to look at him uncomprehendingly, a trickle of blood spreading from her nostrils to her top lip like an ink stain, black in the sodium light.

Now Crawford was arriving, taking in the details as though it was a crime scene, opening the driver's door, looking for her phone.

He was about to dial the emergency number when she asked, 'What are you doing?' her voice a little slurred.

'Calling for an ambulance.'

'No,' she'd said, faint but firm. 'Get me out of here. Take me home.'

And against his better instincts that was what he'd done, leaving Hartmann to retrieve the BMW, make his own way to the other side of the motorway any way that he could. On the journey back to Mid Compton Flint had drifted in and out of consciousness, saying nothing of what had happened that Crawford could understand.

In the austere A&E department of Horton General Hospital where John Flint took his daughter – after checking her pulse and noting the dilated pupils of her eyes, brushing aside her protestations – Crawford sat mute and subdued on a hard plastic chair.

He knew that Dr Flint blamed him and Hartmann for what had happened, as they had blamed themselves. Watching the vet wrap his daughter in a blanket and lay her gently on the rear seat of his Land Rover, following him uninvited to the hospital through the twisting back lanes of Oxfordshire, seeing the pallor on John Flint's gaunt face as he'd accompanied the stretcher that hurried Grace to the X-ray department, Crawford had felt the dull weight of their failure to protect her.

That was almost an hour ago and Dr Flint had still not returned.

For something to do, Crawford found a payphone and called the Flint home and got no answer; no Hartmann. For something else to do he went outside for air and saw the Mazda in the parking lot and realised he'd never checked the boot and he did so now, and found it empty; no briefcase.

So now he knew there had been no drop and therefore no chance to burn Peter, and therefore no point to the whole operation – and Crawford could easily predict how scathing Cutter's reaction would be. He was contemplating that prospect, staring into the void of the Mazda's tiny boot, when he'd heard Dr Flint calling his name; shouting it across the parking lot as though it was an obscenity.

'Crawford! Where the hell were you?' Flint demanded, coming up fast on Crawford like a man bursting for trouble.

'Excuse me?' said Crawford backing away.

'Why weren't you bloody there? At Scratchwood, in the car park? Where you were bloody supposed to be?'

The pallor had gone from Flint's face. Now it was livid and veins stood out on his temple.

'Sir, please' – Crawford held out his hands in a gesture suggesting surrender – 'tell me how she is.'

'Alive – no thanks to you and your damn friend.'

'*Please*, Dr Flint.'

'She has concussion, *severe* concussion.'

'And the X-rays?'

'Clear,' Flint conceded. 'But they're keeping her in for observation. You're not out of the woods yet, Crawford.'

'Sir, what has she told you? I need—'

'You know, I don't believe it,' Flint interrupted, aiming a swinging kick at one of the Mazda's rear tyres to vent his rage. 'My daughter falls on to concrete from the top of a shed—'

'She did *what*?'

'She fell! Because you weren't there, doing what you were supposed to do. When you didn't show up she pretended to go to the loo and then doubled back to try and get a look at this Peter fellow. The only way she could do that, she said, was to climb on to the roof of a cabin, some kind of shed near to where she'd parked, and she slipped and fell. And then you turn up in your own good time and—'

'Sir, *please*! Did she see Peter?'

'I don't know. I didn't ask her because I don't care. What I do care about and what I do want to know is this: Why on earth didn't you call for an ambulance or take her to hospital?'

'Because she declined, Dr Flint, and she's my superior and, believe it or not, generally speaking I do what I'm told.'

'For God's sake, man!'

'I know, and you're right. We screwed up.'

'You can say that again.'

'Dr Flint, I need to talk to Grace. I have to know if she saw Peter. It'll just take a couple of minutes.'

'Over my dead body,' said Flint.

# seventeen

On the hard shoulder of a section of Interstate 95 that is also the Maine Turnpike, exactly a mile shy of the turnoff to Ogunquit, Jarrett Crawford sits in the passenger seat of an unmarked and unlikely police vehicle, monitoring Grace Flint's southerly progress. In order to achieve this he has called on the amorphous brotherhood of law enforcement officers but it turns out that he and state trooper Craig Karr – with whom he now shares the cosy cab of a half-ton pickup truck – are more formally related: distant cousins by marriage. This is not the first time that Crawford has turned to the brotherhood for unofficial help only to find himself dealing with 'family' and he no longer doubts sister Alicia's claim that there are Crawford kith and kin keeping the peace in every state in the union, all bar Hawaii.

Over the radio the Highway Patrol reports that Flint's vehicle has just passed Exit 2 and Trooper Karr says, 'That's Kennebunk, so she's got about twelve miles to come' and, checking his watch, Crawford nods his thanks. In the past six hours – since Karr picked him up at the Howard Johnson, and drove him to the York County Sheriff's department to use a secure phone, and waited with him for the return call, discreetly leaving him alone when at last it came – Crawford has grown slowly more taciturn, like a man with a lot on his mind.

No rudeness intended and his cousin has not taken offence and they sit in silence listening to the motor idle and the soft throb of the heater until a mobile phone rings, the sudden clamour of it making Crawford start. Karr is reaching into the breast pocket of his parka when Crawford says, 'You mind turning that thing off?'

'Sure,' says Karr, 'but why?'

'Just in case.' Crawford offers his cousin an apologetic smile and adds, 'I should've asked you before but then I never thought to ask if you had one. My fault.'

'No problem,' says Karr, turning off the phone while his sharp mind races to make sense of this conundrum. As the explanation dawns on him he asks, 'You want me to call for back-up?'

'Shouldn't be necessary.'

'You sure?'

'Yeah, I'm sure. That's not the kind of trouble we're in.'

The hiatus resumes until Crawford checks his watch once more and decides it is time. Asking Trooper Karr to activate the truck's hazard lights, he dons a baseball cap and turns up the collar of his coat and – offering a token 'Excuse me' – steps out of the fug-warmth of the cab into a biting cold.

Flint has seen the pickup truck up ahead and already dismissed it for she is guessing that Crawford will be driving a rental car. Then she notes the man standing at the rear of the truck, leaning with his back against the tailgate watching the approaching traffic – watching her, it seems – and in the instant before she recognises the face beneath the ridiculous cap she feels a stab of alarm.

*That's what guessing gets you* she tells herself as the tingling of her skin subsides. She slows down, though not by much, and glances at Crawford as she passes the truck, and catches the barely perceptible jerk of his head towards the sign that announces the exit to Ogunquit one mile ahead.

Now her mind is sprinting through the questions. *Whose truck and who's the driver?* – for she has seen that Crawford is not alone. *The Wizard?* Not likely, she decides, for senior intelligence analysts employed by the National Security Agency surely don't drive pickup trucks – certainly not ones with over-wide tyres and a tailpipe with the bore of a bazooka and Maine plates. And, anyway, she firmly believes that Crawford would sooner die than let her see the Wizard face-to-face. So, *Who is he? What is he? – and why is he here?* She begins to conjure up a fantastic scenario in which Crawford has somehow found someone who knows Ben, someone who can tell her the truth.

*Stop bloody guessing!*

At the end of the turnpike she pays the toll and dawdles towards the Ogunquit exit, allowing the truck to get there first and lead the way to the rendezvous, which turns out to be the parking lot of

Karen's Pizza Parlor. The truck has barely stopped and here's Crawford coming out of the passenger side, striding towards her, a grave expression on his face, motioning with his hands to tell her to stay in the car. He climbs into the back seat and says – his first words – 'Don't ask.'

'Don't ask what?'

'Anything, Grace, just listen.'

He's leaning forward, resting his arms on the shoulder of the front passenger seat so that his head is very close to Flint's and if she turns towards him they will practically be kissing. Instead she looks straight ahead and watches him in the mirror, feeling his breath on her cheek.

'The number that Tyler called,' he continues quietly, 'doesn't exist. In theory it's a regular 0800 number but no phone company's got a listing for it because it's never been assigned. We can paper every Baby Bell and every regional and long-distance carrier in the country and they'll swear on a stack of bibles a mile high that there's no record of any account because there is no such account and no subscriber, period. And if you call the number what you get is zilch – no ringing tone, no pickup; nothing, silence. You with me so far?' Crawford asks and Flint nods her head.

'But Tyler wasn't talking to himself, was he? And there's no doubt about what number he called, trust me. So, how come Tyler can dial a number that doesn't exist and doesn't answer and get himself connected to the entity he wants on the first ring?'

'You said it didn't ring.'

'That's right.' Crawford waits a beat and then continues, 'Until you punch in the four-digit code.'

Seeing that the knuckles of her hands are turning white, Flint eases her grip of the steering wheel.

'It's what they call a virtual number, a sort of gateway which facilitates a transfer to a valid number without leaving any trace. The only record is at Tyler's end and that would only show he dialled a no-such number. You know what?' Crawford continues. 'The sucker doesn't even get billed for the call. Because there wasn't any call.'

There is something odd about Crawford's explanation, something Flint is trying to tie down. She puts some incredulity into her voice and asks, 'And Hustler can set this up without anybody at the phone company knowing?'

'I don't think so, Grace.' Crawford finds her eyes in the mirror and holds them with his. 'I don't think this has got anything to do with Hustler.'

'Go on,' Flint says, but Crawford shakes his head and sinks back into his seat and now she has to turn around to be able to see his face. 'Jerry?'

Crawford sighs and removes the cap and rubs the reddish mark that the band has imprinted on his forehead.

'*Jerry!*' – anger now in Flint's voice. 'You think or you *know?*'

Another sigh as if she's asking for the earth and then, 'Grace, you can't do it without the phone company knowing and the phone company won't do it without a signed piece of paper.'

'Signed by who?'

'The AG,' says Crawford, meaning the Attorney General. 'Or a senior law enforcement official.'

She hears his words perfectly well. It is processing the information, fathoming the implications, that is causing her some difficulty.

'I don't get it,' she says, buying herself time.

'Tyler's working for the government.'

'The US government?'

'Some branch of it.'

'Which branch?'

'I don't know, Grace, I honestly don't. But it's got to be either law enforcement or intelligence. The Bureau, the Company, Customs, us . . . Take your pick.'

*Oh, Christ!*

She swallows hard and asks, 'Us?'

'It's possible, but I think it's more likely to be another agency running a parallel op.'

There is a multitude of questions demanding to be asked and answered but Flint's brain cannot seem to form them. Feeling stunned, feeling like she did after she fell from the Portakabin at Scratchwood, she can only stare at Crawford as though trying to remember who he is.

'I gotta go,' he says. 'Cutter wants me back in New York an hour ago.'

'What?'

'I said I've gotta go.'

This seems to make some sense to her. 'I'm coming with you.'

'No. Cutter wants you here tidying up the loose ends.' Crawford fishes a square of paper from his jacket pocket. 'Rocco's come up with an address for the phone number you had for Ben. Cutter says for you to check it out.'

He hands Flint the paper and she reads what he has written:

MAS
13A Customs Wharf
Portland, ME 04101

'MAS?' she asks.

'Yeah, that's the name of the subscriber – or it was. It could be an acronym for Maine Audubon Society but I don't think so.'

Replacing the cap Crawford pushes open the rear door and levers himself out of the car. Then he comes to her door and raps on the glass and she opens the window to receive his afterthought.

'By the way, Rocco said to tell you that Rosetta says this one's for free, whatever that means. Take it easy, Grace – and keep that cellphone turned off.'

He's leaving now, hurrying towards the pickup truck – and long after it has left the parking lot, Flint finally finds a thought her wits can cope with: *You never did introduce me to your friend.*

# eighteen

Midway along the boardwalk of Portland's Customs Wharf, beyond the maroon-painted frontage of the Lobster Emporium, is an unmarked door opening on to a passageway that takes you past the holding tanks where doomed crustaceans scavenge for their final meal to a flight of freestanding wooden stairs that leads up to a second door, this one more substantial, on which there is a brass plate engraved only with the letters MAS.

Beyond the door the woman who for now calls herself Frau Lender – though her name is really Krol – stands at the threshold of a two-room office suite admiring her handiwork. If you were to judge by her appearance you might address her as 'Nurse Lender', or even 'Doctor Lender', for everything she wears has a surgical connotation: the sickly green cap that covers her hair and the green mask on her face; the green gown, the green over-trousers, the boots that are also green, the rubber gloves that protect her hands. If she removes the mask we will see that she is smiling, pleased with herself – as she has every right to be.

Four days ago, when she began her assigned task, these two small rooms were a crime scene to stir even the most jaded criminalist, strewn as they were with traces of its sometime occupant and deeply-incriminating clues as to how he had employed his time: among other things, a filing cabinet of purloined documents, many of them stamped CONFIDENTIAL or SECRET or EYES ONLY; a personal computer containing on its hard drive an almost-complete list of the personnel of the Financial Strike Force together with physical descriptions of many of its agents, their potted biographies, the names of their spouses and their children and their home addresses; also on the hard drive, a revealing analysis of the strategic strengths and weaknesses of the FSF that Aldus Cutter – for one – would find alarming reading, and a densely-plotted timeline of Operation Pentecost.

Frau Lender had begun with the documents, feeding a dozen pages at a time into a small shredder that she had purchased for cash at the Portland branch of Office Depot and transported to Customs Wharf in her suitcase. It had taken her most of the first day to destroy the evidence and the debris had filled more than fifty plastic sacks that she put out on the street for kerbside collection. In the morning they were gone and on their way to becoming history, thanks to the efficiency of Maine's waste-recycling programme.

More fodder for the shredder was provided by the considerable collection of literature published by the Maine Audubon Society that described its programmes and activities; for example, detailed itineraries of the many field trips and world tours that it organised – trips of the kind led by Ben Gates, or so his credulous wife had believed. Then, page by page, Frau Lender had destroyed a number of reference books, including the seven octavo volumes of John Audubon's lifework, *The Birds of America* – the rare 1844 edition that combines his 435 hand-coloured plates with the text of his *Ornithological Biography* (and when in due course Thomas Tyler learns of this act of sacrilege he will privately describe it as perhaps the greatest of the many crimes).

When she was satisfied that every scrap of paper had been reduced to ribbon and sent for recycling, Frau Lender had turned her meticulous attention to the hardware. The personal computer and the fax machine, the laser printer, the photocopier, the Enigma voice scrambler attached to the telephone and the telephone itself, the DialMate call-transfer device that enabled Ben Gates to always answer his calls as though he was in the office even when he wasn't; these and other gadgets whose purposes were not entirely clear to Frau Lender were all destined for disposal – but not before they had been thoroughly purged.

From the central processing unit of the computer Frau Lender had removed the hard drive and pried apart the casing and rubbed the surface of each of the platters with a pumice stone until she was satisfied that all of the data stored on them was irretrievably lost. Then she had removed the RAM memory chips and shattered them with a hammer.

From the computer keyboard she had removed each and every one of the plastic keys.

From the photocopier she had removed the glass plate that would inevitably bear minute scratches that a criminalist employing spectral analysis could match with blemishes on any copies made on the machine and, wrapping the glass in several sections of the *Portland Press Herald*, she had employed her hammer once more to reduce it to smithereens.

She had removed the drums from the fax machine and the laser printer. She had taken apart the phone and the scrambler and the DialMate, removing or destroying the circuit boards – as she had removed from all of the other gadgets anything that she remotely suspected might have functioned as a memory.

And then and only then had she begun the process of disposal, placing random selections of the debris into black garbage sacks that she consigned to the bottom of Portland Harbour, dropped one by one from the jetty at the end of Customs Wharf over three successive nights. The final sack contained the shredder.

Now all that remains in Ben Gates's former lair are two desks, a couple of chairs, the empty filing cabinet and bookshelves that are bare – all of them gleaming in the fluorescent light, every surface cleaned by Frau Lender with a robust industrial detergent. She has also wiped clean the light switches and the electrical sockets and the catches on the windows and the door handles and the door-frames and every other place she can imagine where Ben Gates might have left a finger or palm print.

Standing at the threshold Frau Lender removes her protective clothing and packs each item neatly in the suitcase, together with her cleaning materials. She closes the door and locks it with a key that she will also consign to the bottom of Portland Harbour, and then she takes a handkerchief from her pocket and gives a final polish to the brass plate that bears the legend, MAS.

When Grace Flint arrives at Customs Wharf and finds her way past the holding tanks and climbs the stairs and comes to this door – in approximately one hour's time, when the woman who no longer calls herself Frau Lender is boarding a plane not at Boston's Logan airport but at the Portland International Jetport – the shining plate will represent the only tangible evidence that Ben Gates ever existed in this place.

Unreliable evidence for Ben Gates never did actually exist, except in the mind of his wife.

# London

# nineteen

Nigel Ridout lives alone in a terraced house off the Fulham Road that boasts a south-facing garden in which he daringly experiments with varieties of flora generally more suited to a Mediterranean climate. It is not simply the challenge to the presumed order of things that appeals to him but the voluptuousness of the plants' Latin names: *Acanthus mollis* and *Salvia uliginosa* and *Thuja occidentalis* and – most glorious of all, he thinks – *Convolvulus cneorum*. Often – too often for the liking of his subordinate officers in the East European Controllerate of SIS – the codenames of its 'assets' and its 'illegals' derive from what grows in Ridout's garden.

'Mandrake's gone AWOL,' said a flustered Stephanie Cooper-Cole, arriving unannounced on Ridout's doorstep on this unusually fine April Sunday evening, taking him away from his pruning chores.

Mandrake as in *Mandragora officinarum* of the *Solanaceae* family; greenish-yellow flowers and a poisonous root that resembles the human body.

'I like your little joke, Steff,' Ridout said, taking her arm, leading her quickly inside the house. 'Mandrake gone! Very amusing.'

'It's no bloody joke,' she said.

'But of course it is!' Ridout insisted, smiling at her with teeth that seemed too large for his mouth, giving him a predatory look. 'Because we had an arrangement, didn't we, Steff? You and I? Yes? You look after Mandrake, give him your very closest attention, and I'll look after you – that's what we agreed, wasn't it, *Steff*?'

He was still holding her arm just above the elbow and the pressure of his grip was beginning to hurt.

'Now please don't tell me that I misjudged you, Steff. That I overestimated your diligence and your dedication, not to mention your intelligence. Surely not?'

Angrily she pulled her arm free of him and flounced uninvited into the kitchen, obliging Ridout to follow her. He watched in silence as she took a glass from the cupboard above the sink and filled it with water from the tap and satisfied her thirst. There was Italian mineral water in the fridge but he was damned if he would offer it.

'So?' he demanded curtly, all the fake banter gone from his tone.

On her mother's side Cooper-Cole comes from aristocratic Irish stock and she has inherited the good bones and the ripe red hair and the flaming temper to go with it.

'Don't patronise me,' she said turning from the sink to face him. 'It's not my bloody fault. And *Nigel*' – pushing it now, defiant with her afterthought – 'don't call me bloody Steff.'

Give him his due, Ridout did not bridle at her gross insubordination. With Job-like patience he waited, watching her with hooded eyes while she thought better about her outburst and came to her senses.

Eventually, 'It's been a long day,' she admitted.

'So?' he said again, this time withholding the spite.

'Last night,' Cooper-Cole began, 'just after nine, Mandrake asked if he could go to his room. He said he was tired, still suffering from jetlag; said he hadn't slept properly since he'd arrived. Mrs Baxter didn't smell a rat.'

Ridout pursed his lips and she said, 'I know, but it was consistent. He'd been complaining about fatigue since Friday and he looked thoroughly washed out. It's in my log: pallid skin, dull eyes, general lethargy.'

'Your *log*!'

'It's Your Eyes Only. Hand-written, nothing on the system.'

Ridout nodded as if to concede the point and then, 'Been sucking on charcoal, had he, to make himself nice and pasty? Is that in your *log*, Stephanie?'

Ignoring his rebuke she continued, 'Mrs Baxter checked on him at 11.05 and he was still awake, tossing and turning. She offered to bring him a warm drink but he declined. Then, at around 3 a.m., he knocked on her door and asked if she had something to help him sleep. Well, she wasn't keen on that, of course, but she did give him a couple of tablets of melatonin. She thought that wouldn't hurt.'

'And, let me guess,' Ridout intervened. 'He said that if the melatonin worked to let him sleep? Do Not Disturb, that sort of thing?'

'More or less.'

'Less, I think . . . Dear Christ!'

'Easily said in hindsight, Nigel.'

'Oh, don't discount hindsight, Stephanie. Learning from our mistakes – *your* mistakes, Stephanie – is how we may survive. And then?'

'She looked in on him about nine, saw that he was sleeping and decided to let him be.'

'Except he wasn't sleeping was he, Stephanie, because he wasn't bloody there?'

Cooper-Cole nodded her fine head.

'Pillows under the blanket?'

'No,' she said. 'Cuter than that. He'd rolled up the rug.'

'And Mrs Baxter didn't notice her rug was missing? Has she gone blind?'

'The curtains were drawn. It was dark in there.'

'I'm sure it was,' Ridout said with a weary resignation. 'So, when did she *see the light*? When did the estimable Mrs Baxter finally *twig*?'

'She didn't. Fellowes did, just after two o'clock this afternoon.'

'Ah, yes, Master Fellowes. And where was our so-called minder during all of this?'

'Downstairs. In the kitchen.'

'Sleeping on the job, no doubt.'

'He says not. Or not until Mrs Baxter came downstairs just after nine and he went off watch.'

'Hum,' said Ridout, not convinced. He saw Cooper-Cole eyeing the water glass and, relenting, fetched a bottle of mineral water for her from the fridge. 'So, *if* young Fellowes was awake *and* alert *and* vigilant, how did Mandrake get past him?'

'He went out of the bedroom window. Forced the lock with a screwdriver or some kind of sharp instrument and . . . I know, I know,' she said quickly, catching the look of astonishment on Ridout's face. 'They never searched his room – or him for that matter – because they didn't see him as a prisoner. More like a guest, one of the team.'

'And is that how *you* saw him, Stephanie – one of the *team*?'

'Nigel, it's a safe house, not a prison. If you wanted him secured you should have put him in Fort Monkton; that or the rubber room. And, anyway, nobody suspected he was going to make a run for it, did they?'

*I did*, thought Ridout but this was not an admission he would make to Cooper-Cole.

'And, come to that,' she continued, 'why did he run? I don't get it.'

*Because he knew, young Steff; knew that he'd come to the end of his useful life – but that's not a matter that need concern your pretty head.*

'When you find him you can ask him,' Ridout said tartly.

She considered his challenge for a moment and then answered with one of her own: 'Shall I have a quiet word with Five? Or the Branch? See if they can help to track him down? What do you think?'

*Touché*, and Ridout acknowledged her parry with a slight, forlorn smile. 'No, you will not talk with MI5, or Special Branch or anyone else, thank you, Stephanie. I think we would be wise to keep this to ourselves. Don't you?'

'Fine,' she said. 'So what do you want me to do?'

'Think, my dear Stephanie, I want you to *think*. Where can he go?'

It was not an idle question, for Ridout's questions never are. Cooper-Cole wrinkled her brow and set her lively mind to consider Mandrake's options.

'Well,' she began – tentatively at first but gaining confidence by the moment – 'he hasn't got a passport and the rest of his documentation is compromised so there's no easy way out of the UK, except in the back of a lorry or the Irish route or a smuggler's boat. On the other hand, he's got money – bound to have some stashed away given his background – and he knows the right people so he could easily buy some new ID, passport included.

'But, there again, he might think that the right people are the wrong people just at the moment. I mean, if he's running from us for whatever reason then maybe he's also running from them. Otherwise, why come in? Why come to us at all if he had other options?'

'Very good, Stephanie,' said Ridout warmly.

'So it's possible, even likely, that he trusts no one, that he's on his own – or thinks he is. Now, in time he'll make a connection because he knows how to do that but until then he needs somewhere he'll feel safe; a bolt-hole – a room he can rent or a bed and breakfast. The problem is, for all he knows we can have his face plastered all over the media. Missing, wanted, whatever pretext we choose.' She paused to smile at Ridout. 'Because he doesn't know about our local difficulties, does he, Nigel? Doesn't know we have to keep this to ourselves.'

*Touché* again, and Ridout gave the slightest nod of acknowledgement.

'Changing his appearance, that's got to be his first priority I would think. He'll grow a beard, cut his hair, all the usual stuff. Sleep rough for a few days, perhaps. Then get out of London, because that's where we are, and that's where *they* are, but if he's going to make the right connection he's going to need to be in a city. So, Birmingham, Manchester, Liverpool – maybe Scotland? Actually, that's not a bad bet. Glasgow, that's a fine place to get lost in, and a fine place to buy some new ID.'

'Excellent,' said Ridout, 'as far as supposition goes. But think, Stephanie, *think*. What if he has a safe friend, someone he believes he can trust?'

'Not in the file he doesn't.'

'A relative, perhaps?'

It took a moment for the penny to drop and then she got it and she blurted out '*Flint!*' and Ridout beamed.

After Cooper-Cole has gone, hurrying away to make her arrangements, Ridout returns to the garden to clean and put away his pruning tools in the shed where each one has its designated place. He gathers up the clippings and places them on the compost heap and brushes the debris from the path, and only when he is satisfied that everything is in order does he call for a cab to collect him in precisely forty-five minutes, allowing himself ample time to bathe and change.

Except in foul weather it is Ridout's habit to arrive at the office on foot and since this is still a particularly fine evening he gets the cab to drop him on the north embankment of the Thames and strolls across Vauxhall Bridge towards the looming folly that is the headquarters of the Secret Intelligence Service, though in every official publication it is euphemistically listed as 'Government Communications Bureau, 85'. To the more irreverent officers of

SIS number 85 Albert Embankment is known as 'Ceauşescu Towers', on the reasonable grounds, Ridout believes, that only somebody with the hubris of the late and unlamented Romanian dictator could have conceived it.

Entering the lobby through bomb-proof doors, Ridout uses his swipe card and his PIN code to open the first of two Perspex security gates and enters a small chamber resembling an air lock, standing on a pressure plate that ensures he is alone, waiting for the first door to close and the second to open. Finally admitted to the marbled inner lobby, he nods civilly to the security guards in the watch room and heads for the banks of rapid lifts that rise inside two gigantic columns. His destination is the 'Comms' room which – electronically-shielded against eavesdropping, the walls lined with lead up to one foot thick – is, Ridout has been known to joke, the most secure telephone box on earth.

Even so, the transatlantic call that Ridout will make from here will be masked by white noise, a cacophony of all the audible frequencies. And, leaving nothing to chance (for SIS's ethos is defined by its motto: *Semper Occultus* – 'Always Secret') the call will be encrypted by a computer chip that the boffins claim makes conversations indecipherable even to the NSA's awesome computers in Crypto City.

Perhaps, Ridout thinks. But how do we know the NSA can't decipher them? he has pondered. Would they tell us if they could?

He doubts it and there will be no careless talk from Ridout, no claims or admissions that could come back to haunt him. On a pad that he will burn he writes and rewrites the instruction he wishes to deliver until he is satisfied that he will not utter a single unambiguous word.

# Mid Compton
# Oxfordshire

# twenty

Coming from his surgery after the evening rounds, Dr Flint climbs the stone steps leading to his house with no need of a torch for the moon is brilliant tonight, bathing everything in an ethereal silver light. Even inside the house there is a lucent glow sufficient to see by. Not bothering to turn on the lamps, he ambles along the hallway to the kitchen and pours himself a ritual drink and continues out on to the terrace that provides him a broad, sweeping view over Glebe Meadow to Allen's Lane beyond. From this vantage point he can see the white ash tree that Grace planted on her tenth birthday, a quarter of a century ago, to mark the spot from which her mother vanished – from where Madeleine Flint was almost certainly abducted and killed – and it is another of Dr Flint's nightly rituals to stand here alone and offer a silent toast to the memory of his wife.

Tonight he is not alone.

He hears the scrape of a shoe on the paving slabs and sees a long shadow falling over his shoulder and swings around, instinctively raising his glass as a weapon.

'Who the devil—'

'Hi, Dr Flint,' says his son-in-law. 'I didn't mean to alarm you but the door was open and—'

'Ben! Is that you?'

'Yes, sir.'

Flint draws closer to the intruder and now he can see that it is indeed Ben but the relief that knowledge brings is swamped by his confusion.

'Where's Gracie? Is she here?'

'No, sir. Didn't she call?'

'Call? Why would she call?' Now deep alarm is setting in and Flint takes one giant stride and seizes Ben's shoulder in a powerful grip. 'What's wrong?' he demands. 'What's happened?'

'Nothing's happened! Everything's fine! Really!'

Ben is trying to pull away but he can't even though he is Flint's height and a little more than half his age.

'Hey, Dr Flint, I'm sorry. Let me explain.'

'Please do.'

'Grace was supposed to call and tell you I was in London for a conference and since I had a couple of days to spare I thought I'd come and see you. Say hello, that's all.'

'Where is she?'

'New York, running one of her operations. A pretty big one, apparently – which is probably why she forgot to call. Shit!' adds Ben with vehemence. 'I knew I should have called you myself.'

Flint looks unsure, not yet certain he is hearing the truth.

'I *swear* to you that Grace is absolutely fine,' Ben says. He stares into Flint's eyes, oozing an intense sincerity that has often mesmerised Dr Flint's daughter. 'I swear,' he repeats softly.

Flint releases his grip on Ben's shoulder and says, 'You frightened me half to death. I thought—'

'I know and you were right to think that because if anything bad had happened to Grace I would be the one to come here and tell you, and I wouldn't have called first. I know what she means to you, sir.'

'Yes, well . . .' Flint coughs and takes a step back and looks around as though he has come out of a trance and is unsure of his surroundings. 'Next time, if it's purely a social visit, perhaps it would be better—'

Ben grins, lighting up his face, and says, 'Next time I'll call. That's a promise.'

Only now does Flint appear to notice that he is a holding an empty glass in his hand, and assumes the contents must have been spilled in the excitement.

'Yes, well, you had better come inside. I expect you need a drink.'

'Not for me, sir, but you go ahead.'

'Will you please stop calling me "sir"?'

'Sure, Dr Flint.'

'And not "Dr Flint".'

'Okay.' Another winning grin from Ben. 'Should I call you Dad?'

Flint considers the proposition for a moment and then, 'John would be best, I think.'

* * *

Inside the house that is now filled with electric light Dr Flint pours himself a replacement whisky and offers food which Ben declines and dismisses his son-in-law's suggestion that he should find himself a room for the night at the local pub.

'Nonsense, you'll sleep in Gracie's room. This is your home, or it will be one day – yours and Gracie's.'

They sit at the kitchen table while Ben describes, with amusing anecdotal details that provide a high gloss of credibility, the conference sponsored by the World Wildlife Fund that he has just attended in London (a conference that did not take place), and his work for the Maine Audubon Society (that never has employed him), and the field trips (that he has never led or been on), and as he weaves his webs of deceit it occurs to him that, had things been just a little different, Dr Flint's daughter would have married Rayland Tully rather than Ben Gates and he would now be sitting here describing an equally fictional life, this one in the advertising business – and Dr Flint (and his daughter) would not have had the slightest reason to disbelieve him. Come to that, he thinks – and he has ample time to think for his glib lies flow from a part of his brain that functions as though it is on autopilot – he could shed Rayland Tully like a skin and revert to a previous existence; that of Jeffrey Stamp, who was also entirely a figment of clever and mendacious minds.

We would have to go back to the time before Jeffrey Stamp was created to find a real persona – and he would not convince us at all. After they had steeped him in their legend of Ben Gates they had wired him to a Reid polygraph to see how well they'd done and not once did the machine detect a suspicious bodily response as he'd answered their questions with inevitable untruths. Curiously – perversely – it was only when they asked him about his real self that the machine reported he lied.

Ben changes his mind about a drink and under John Flint's gentle questioning he is talking now about his supposed passion for birds. He becomes almost rhapsodic as he describes an encounter on the banks of the Roanoke river with 'an army of grackles making the sky black and a noise like thunder with their wings'. He says they settled in the trees until it seemed they covered every branch. 'You should have heard them calling, John, this amazing chorus building on the breeze'.

There is no reason why Dr Flint should know that a very similar description of such an encounter with grackles appears in a small anthology entitled *The Literature of Birdwatching* – a copy of which was among the books that perished in Frau Lender's shredder.

Now Ben's mood abruptly changes as Dr Flint asks solemnly about his mother in France and Ben speaks of the destructive, demeaning progress of Pick's disease from which she suffers. It is similar to Alzheimer's but in some ways worse, Ben says, and his voice falters as he describes his supposed mother's symptoms: her extraordinary restlessness, her coarse hypersexuality and, at the same time, her childlike behaviour.

'Anything she picks up, she puts in her mouth,' Ben says and that is as far as he can go without breaking down, apparently, and Dr Flint says, 'My dear chap, I'm so sorry. Will you see her while you're in Europe?'

Yes, Ben says, though she now also suffers from bouts of profound apathy and he fears – he says – she is approaching the terminal vegetative state.

'And Gracie,' says her father – because he wishes to spare Ben further pain, and because he is ravenous for news of his daughter – 'how is she really? Tell me to mind my own business if you like, but are you both happy?'

And now Ben soars.

Every shining quality that Dr Flint sees in his daughter, Ben also sees, and they share the same blind spots to her faults – and as Ben eulogises his wife, preaching to the converted, the part of him that is not engaged in these proceedings reflects on the oddity that much of what he proclaims about the woman he has both deceived and betrayed is what he truly feels.

After midnight Flint yawns and says, 'Bed, I think. I have patients to attend to in the morning.'

He shows Ben to Grace's room, and settles him in, and goes to his own room and cannot sleep.

It is sometime after three o'clock in the morning when he comes downstairs to consult the address book that holds all of Grace's telephone numbers – just to call her and hear her voice; just to say, 'I'm so glad that Ben is here.'

There is no dial tone when he lifts the phone in the nook he uses as a study. He is pondering why that may be when he hears a sound behind him and, before he can turn around, he feels the back of his head explode.

It is coming up to 5 a.m., just after sunrise, and in the barn that serves as his surgery Dr Flint lies motionless, gagged and bound, stuffed inside a cage that is meant to comfortably accommodate a large dog – a German shepherd, say – and to make the doctor fit his legs have been bent double and forced hard against his chest.

His son-in-law also lies motionless, on a platform that was once the hayloft, peering through the bottom of a window shaped like a porthole. Below in the quadrangle he can just see part of the roof of a small red car that arrived a few minutes ago, its tyres crunching on the gravel, setting off the caterwauling of Dr Flint's inpatients.

There are at least two of them, he is sure of that, for above the animals' din he has heard voices and caught snatches of their conversation.

*Must be . . .*

*Try the door—* a woman's voice.

*. . . locked.*

*. . . windows. Take a look.*

There is not enough light in the barn to reveal the dog cage's human cargo, and the stout door is indeed locked, from the inside, with Dr Flint's heavy desk wedged up against it. They'll need a battering ram to break it down.

'Let's try the house,' the woman says and now he waits for them to head towards the steps and enter his field of vision.

A man appears and then the woman – and though he can only see her from the back he knows instantly who she is: codename Firefly, an SIS intelligence branch officer and Ridout's feisty assistant.

As he watches her long legs climb the steps up to the house where the evidence of a recent, violent assault still remains, Dr Flint's son-in-law whispers 'Fuck!' to himself, over and over.

# Connecticut

# twenty-one

It is about a four-hour drive from Portland to Miller's Reach and Flint could easily have been home by now, but knowing that she can't trust her own phone – and won't even think about turning on her mobile – she's stopped short by eighteen miles and checked into the Inn at Saybrook Point where she now sits on the pint-sized balcony of her room, listening to the groans of the floating docks in the marina, waiting for Rocco Morales to finish supper and call her back.

She's already eaten her indifferent meal at the Dock & Dine across the way and there is a part of her that is irritated that she is forced to stay away from the home comforts of Miller's Reach until her immediate business is done. There is another part of her – the snivelling part she would disown if she could – that is grateful for the excuse; thankful that she can delay her return to the house until the morning, until it is light.

When Morales finally calls back she apologises a second time for disturbing him at home and he says, 'Hey, we never sleep, right?'

'It's beginning to feel like it.'

'Bad day?'

'Not good,' Flint admits. 'The place in Customs Wharf, it's been cleaned out – and I do mean cleaned. It smells like a chemical factory and all that's left are a couple of bits of furniture. It looks like they sent in a pro to scrub it down.'

'Maybe your German friend, Frau Lender?'

'I thought of that, although the Met have her down as a courier, not a cleaner. But, then again, what do they know?'

'We should have the forensics guys take a look at the place anyway. You never know.'

'Fine by me,' says Flint without much enthusiasm. 'Any news of Lender?'

'Yeah, she turned the car in at the airport this afternoon but that was Portland, not Logan. Cost her a seventy-five-dollar drop-off charge but I don't suppose that's going to break the bank. And then, who knows? She wasn't manifested on any flight out of Portland.'

'Well, she won't be Frau Lender any more, will she?'

'Nope.'

'You know, Rocco, I'm sure the bitch suckered me. This morning somebody called my room at the hotel to see if I was there and I thought I was being set up, and I went charging down to the lobby to try and get a look at them and who do I see walking out of the elevator, coming down from my floor, but Frau Lender. So, of course, I followed her and she led me around in circles, and then she burned me – and I let her do it.'

Morales does not respond.

'Christ, what a mess!'

She can hear the whine of self-pity in her voice – that snivelling part of her again – and she tells herself to get a grip.

'Okay' – her voice much stronger now – 'we need to trace the landlord and see if they left a paper trail – references, previous address, forwarding address, and how the rent was paid. Same thing with the utilities and the phone company.'

'Check,' says Morales.

'The premises are above a lobster market and there's a common passageway, so the people who run the market may be the landlords. In any event, they must have seen the perps – Ben and whoever else – going back and forth and we need to get them interviewed. Either get the locals to do it or send up a couple of ours.'

'Better if we do it ourselves, I think,' says Morales. 'I'll talk to Nathan.'

There is a loaded silence until Flint asks, 'Why would you do that, Rocco?'

'Because he's JAD/O-in-charge of Pentecost, Grace. You know that.'

She remembers Cutter's stinging words – *Hustler belongs to Nathan. Nathan will find the leak. He's good at that. Better than you* – and her anger comes flooding back and she says, 'Yes, well, Nathan didn't find the sodding leak, did he, Rocco? I did.'

'Excuse me?'

'Never mind. Okay, fine, talk to Stark if you want to but he's got to understand that one of the priorities is to establish how much time Ben spent in Portland, and where he stayed when he was there.'

'Where did you think he stayed?'

*Oh, you'll like this, Rocco,* she thinks and she gives a hollow laugh. 'Most of the time, when he wasn't on his field trips, he stayed with Tyler, or so he said. And, speaking of Tyler—'

'He's off limits, Grace,' Morales says quickly.

'What?'

'Cutter's orders. Until we know who he's working for, we leave Tyler strictly alone.'

*Oh, really? Not while I breathe.*

'Yes, well,' she says, preventing her thoughts from becoming words, 'I'll talk to Cutter about that when I come in tomorrow.'

'You're coming in?'

There is an edge to Morales's question that she doesn't pick up on. She tells him that her car is at Kennedy airport, racking up parking charges, and she's still got the Hertz car that she needs to drop off and, yes, she's planning on coming to the office and, 'I should be there around noon.'

Another loaded silence which once again Flint is forced to break. 'What's wrong, Rocco?'

'Listen, this is none of my business and I heard it second-hand but the word is, Cutter doesn't want you in the office.'

'Says who?'

'Grace, don't.'

'*Rocco!*'

Morales sighs. 'Mr Stark said that Cutter wanted you kept out of the building and out of the city, at least for now. They think you're out of control.' He pauses and then he adds, 'Grace, the word is your access pass, your swipe card, it's been cancelled.'

His revelations are so astonishing that for a moment she cannot breathe. She feels bruised, as though she has been kicked, and she drops the phone and hurries out on to the balcony where she grabs the rail to stop herself from falling. She takes deep gulps of air to get oxygen back into her lungs and then forces herself to count slowly to ten. Only marginally recovered, she returns to the room and stares at the phone lying on the bed, hearing Rocco's tinny voice coming from the handset: 'Grace? Grace, are you still there?'

Her voice is unnaturally calm when she finally picks up the phone and speaks to him.

'Rocco, are you saying I've been suspended?'

'No, I don't think so. They just want you out of the way.' He does not repeat Nathan Stark's addendum: *where she can do no more harm.*

'Thanks for the heads-up,' says Flint. 'I'll deal with it.'

'Leave my name out of it, would you?'

'Sure, of course I will. Listen, I better let you go. I'll see you, Rocco.'

But like a faithless lover trying to soften the blow he is reluctant to leave her on this sour note and on the pretext of professional thoroughness he asks her to describe in more detail what she found at Customs Wharf. She does so mechanically, without the aid of notes.

'A locked door at the top of fifteen stairs with a shiny brass plate on it and the initials MAS; no indication what that's supposed to mean. Two rooms inside, each about fifteen feet by ten with an interconnecting door. Two metal desks, colour grey. Two swivel chairs, also grey. A four-drawer filing cabinet, empty, also grey. Fitted wooden bookshelves along the far wall of the inner room, painted white, also empty. Wood flooring, recently washed. Overhead fluorescent lighting. Oh,' she adds without changing her flat tone, 'and a signed confession from Ben.'

'One more thing,' says Morales, ignoring her poor joke, 'if the door was locked, how did you get in?'

She is about to tell him that she levered the door open with a tyre iron when she remembers his warning: *They think you're out of control.*

'How do you think, Rocco?' she dissimulates. 'I found the key.'

# twenty-two

Early afternoon at Miller's Reach and Flint has opened wide every window and door, admitting the fair breeze that is coming from the pond, as though she is trying to rid the house of a stubborn stench – which in a way she is.

She has not been to Kennedy airport to collect her car or return the rental, nor has she been to the Marscheider building to establish if it is true that should the Joint Assistant Director (Operations) attempt to use her FSF access card at the security checkpoint the light will flash red, not green, and the gate will not open to admit her. And should the JAD/O attempt to use her suspended card a second time a wailing alarm will be triggered and the guards will come running to escort her to the pavement, and nothing she can say will prevent or divert them.

Nor has she talked to Cutter – though she has tried, twice driving into Essex this morning to call him from a payphone only to be told that he is 'unavailable' and 'in meetings'; that he's left strict instruction that he'll take no calls.

It was on her return from the second futile journey – when, with time to kill, she was cleaning the kitchen – that she noticed the picture was missing.

Beneath the window, on a beechwood shelf that she was about to polish, claiming just a bit of spare territory from Ben's ubiquitous carved birds, there should have been – always had been – a picture of the two of them, taken outside the chapel on Hayman Island after their marriage had been blessed. *Steady*, she told herself as the implications of the empty space on the shelf yanked at her emotions like a ferocious rip-tide.

Because she knew with absolute certainty that when she was last here – before she left Miller's Reach to travel to Miami six days before (even if it now feels more like six years) – the picture was

there. Under it was the first of the usual places where she had
looked for the note that Ben had neglected to leave her.

'Oh, this is just too fucking much,' she'd said aloud, the storm
building in her mind as she'd run to her den and found the
cardboard box where most of her photographs were stored and
found them missing. Not all of them – just every one in which Ben
had appeared.

And then she'd searched the house from top to bottom – pulling
open cupboards and drawers, spilling the contents on to the floor
like some manic, vindictive burglar – to discover that every
photograph of Ben had gone; and the package of every letter and
note he'd ever written her, taken from its safe place in her underwear
drawer; and every other piece of paper that contained his handwriting.

She knew what they had done and why they'd done it. It was the
mechanics of the violation that eluded her.

*How?* she'd thought. *How did they get in?* – and she'd begun
examining the doors and the windows looking for the telltale signs
of forcible entry until it had dawned on her that they hadn't needed
to use force.

*Because they had Ben's key.*

And the tamper-proof security system she had insisted was
installed, despite Ben's gentle mocking – a state-of-the-art system of
the kind that silently detects any intruder, and alerts a monitoring
centre that is forever vigilant and dispatches burly armed men with
fearsome dogs to your home inside fifteen minutes, guaranteed or
your money back – had not deterred them.

*Because Ben gave them the code to disarm it.*

And then – *dear God* – another sickening possibility had occurred
to her: that it was Ben himself who had unlocked the door and
turned off the alarm and allowed them to come sneaking into the
house to search among her private things and remove every intimate
trace of her life with him.

There is one photograph of Ben they didn't get – the one
she keeps in her wallet that he probably doesn't even know
about.

She has it before her now, propped against a half-drunk glass of
white wine that sits on her desk alongside the picture of the mother
she barely remembers – as she barely remembers Ben, for almost
every certainty she held about him has vanished.

*How could you be so bloody stupid – you of all people? You spend your life chasing creeps, you know all about creeps, you think you can spot them a mile away and yet you allow the biggest creep of all into your life, into your bed. How could you be so naïve?*

It is her second glass of wine, or maybe her third, for alcohol calms her – and Ben's temperance propaganda now rings as hollow as everything else he's said.

She is determined to nail another of Ben's lies when she dials the home number of Inspector Gilles Bourdonnec of the *Brigade Criminelle* in France. As always when she calls Paris, the image that she sees is of Gilles walking towards her along Rue Tiquetonne stiff-legged like an old man – or, when he's too exhausted, in a wheelchair pushed by Dominique, his wife – and Flint feels the usual rush of guilt because she and Gilles both know it's her fault that he's crippled, whatever he might pretend.

He answers on the second ring and begins to greet her with his customary warmth, and even though the pleasure of that is like balm on the wound, she interrupts to tell him that the phone line is *very* insecure.

Bourdonnec goes quiet as she explains that she needs to trace a man whose phone number she no longer trusts – because Ben gave her the number, and *said* it was his father's number, and it has occurred to her in the last few hours that this may have been another of his deceptions. Just because she has called the number in the past, just because she has spoken to a man on this number who *said* he was her father-in-law, doesn't make it true.

'This man,' says Bourdonnec, 'he is in the south?'

'Yes,' says Flint, surprised.

'Then you are not alone. Cutter called, asking for the same information.'

'When?'

'Yesterday – no, Saturday. In the evening, my time.'

*Christ!*

'Wait a moment. I'll get it for you.'

And soon she has both an address and a telephone number – a different telephone number – for Joseph Gates, Emeritus Professor of McGill University, presently residing in Saint-Paul-de-Vence, and she has said a hurried goodbye to Gilles, and she has dialled France once more and now she's listening to a man's voice she does not recognise saying, 'Hello, hello.'

'Professor Gates?'

'Yes. Who is this?'

There is a pause and then, 'Joe, it's Grace.'

'Who?'

'Grace. Ben's wife.' Your daughter-in-law, she might have added.

There is too much silence on the line and it swells like an echo on the satellite link. Then comes a voice spitting fire: 'How dare you? How dare you do this?'

'Sir, I need to ask you some questions.'

'I've already told the police. I don't have a son. My son died when he was six.'

Even though she was half-expecting something like this she feels her heart squeezed as though by a giant's fist and she can't stop herself from saying. 'Ben *died*?'

'Stop this! Stop this at once! Don't you ever call here again.'

And the line goes dead.

Flint on the phone again, calling the Marscheider building – and she no longer gives a damn about who may be listening on the line.

For the third time today she receives the deflecting mantra from Cutter's secretary and so she demands to speak to Nathan Stark, and he too is unavailable, she is told: tied up in meetings, impossible to disturb. In this context, getting Jarrett Crawford on the phone seems to Flint like a significant achievement.

'Crawdaddy, what the hell's going on?'

'Meaning?' he says warily.

'Oh, come on, don't screw with me. I can't get in the building, I can't talk to Cutter, I can't even talk to bloody Nathan Stark. I've been put in limbo, Jarrett, and while I'm there I find out that my husband has burgled my house – except he hasn't because my husband died when he was six. And Cutter knows that, and so do you, I wouldn't be surprised, and what I want to know is this: Who stole my fucking life? Can you tell me that, please? Am I getting through to you, *Jarrett*?'

'Grace, Cutter's got a problem,' says Crawford.

'Believe it,' says Flint.

'No, listen. There's a couple of OPR guys from Justice with Cutter right now. They're looking for a fall guy for Ruth's murder and as things stand you're it, and Cutter's trying to dig you out of the hole. That's the only reason he doesn't want you around.'

'Terrific! Crawdaddy, do me a favour. Tell Cutter,' she begins and then she breaks off because through the window she has glimpsed movement at the head of the drive to Miller's Reach.

'Wait one,' she says, getting up from the desk and going out on to the deck to get a better view. Somebody has opened the gate and two dark sedans are heading in slow procession towards the house.

'I've got to go,' she tells Crawford hurriedly. 'Visitors coming.'

Friends of Ben, she believes.

# twenty-three

There are four of them, three men and a woman, and Flint doesn't need to see their credentials to know they are some kind of law enforcement. Their cheap suits and their bad haircuts give them away and there is a part of her that wants to say, 'Why do you people dress so badly?' Just to wind them up. Just to give herself a small edge.

'Grace Flint?' asks the tallest of the men who is the senior agent by the look of him. He is coming towards the porch on which she stands while the others hold back beside the cars. He reaches the bottom of the steps and shows her the open wallet he is holding in his left hand. 'Special Agent Mike Pritchard, INS, Criminal Investigations.'

'Congratulations,' says Flint.

His mouth turns up in a tired smile, making him handsome in a melancholic sort of way. 'Do you mind if we come in? I need to see your passport.'

'Not if you have a warrant I don't.'

He doesn't find this so funny and his mouth turns down. 'I don't need a warrant, ma'am, but I do need to see your passport and I do need to see it now.'

What Flint can see is that Special Agent Pritchard has it in mind to climb the three steps and reach her level but he's hesitating because she's standing at the top of them, nicely balanced with her legs apart and her knees slightly bent in what Quantico calls the ready position, and she shows no sign of moving, and there's no way he can get past her and reach the porch without using – or maybe meeting – force.

'You said you're a criminal investigator, Agent Pritchard.'

'That's what I said, ma'am.'

'So this is a *criminal* investigation that's brought you on to private property without the warrant you say you don't need but I say that's bullshit. Now, when all this comes out in the wash, I hope you can show you had probable cause that a crime had been committed, Agent Pritchard.'

He sighs and shakes his head as if he's heard this all too many times and then he slips into a routine he's learnt by rote, reminding her of his authority to investigate *possible* violations of criminal *and administrative* provisions of the Immigration and Nationality Act, citing the relevant statutes under the US Code.

'You're still not coming into my house,' she says.

'Then *fetch* your passport, Miss Flint.'

'Who are they?' she asks, turning her head to glance at the threesome by the cars but still not budging one inch.

'DEOs,' says Pritchard without bothering to explain what that means.

'What, all of them? Wait here – and keep your feet off my porch.'

She goes inside the house and closes the door and leans her back against it as her bravura shatters.

DEOs, she knows perfectly well, are Detention Enforcement Officers who are trained in, among other things, trauma management – managing the trauma they induce when they take a woman like Nina at Kennedy airport, and haul her away in shackles, and put her in an INS cell with the kind of scum Flint hopes her father never gets to meet. *Or a woman like me.*

Quickly, urgently, Flint rethinks her strategy. She can only guess at what's going on but *her* imminent detention seems very much on the cards and alienating her would-be custodians is not, she now thinks, the smartest thing to do.

She pulls open the door and calls, 'All right, I've changed my mind. Come on up.'

She meant Agent Pritchard but Flint does not object when the four of them come trooping into the house – warily, as though half-expecting a trap. The two other men are nondescript and they nod to her in a neutral way but the woman is another story. She has a hatchet face and bad skin and the disgruntled air of someone who is not comfortable with the body in which she is obliged to live. Resentful, Flint thinks, is the word that best describes her.

Flint leads the way to the living room where they do not accept her invitation to sit down. Instead they separate and navigate the room until they have casually surrounded her, and watch with careful eyes as she rummages in her bag to find her passport.

She hands it to Agent Pritchard who flicks carelessly through the pages, barely bothering to glance at them.

'Miss Flint,' he begins the speech he has so obviously prepared, 'you were permitted to enter the United States on the basis of a non-immigrant H-1B visa that entitled you to take up employment with the Financial Strike Force. Since, as we understand it, your employment with the FSF has now been suspended, the visa is no longer valid and it has been cancelled. Are you with me so far?'

*Suspended!*

Flint doesn't trust herself to speak. Carefully she inclines her head to indicate that she has understood.

'That being the case,' Pritchard presses on, 'your entitlement to remain here has also been suspended and, under the law, you are required to leave the United States immediately, and we are required to remove you from within these borders.

'Now, I'm obliged to tell you that, under the law, you have certain rights and choices. You can voluntarily withdraw your application to enter the United States, and agree to leave on the earliest possible flight, in which event any future applications you may make will not be automatically jeopardised. And, if you choose that course, and if your suspension of employment is lifted at some time in the future, you may apply for the visa to be reissued. And,' Pritchard says, slipping now into a friendlier tone, 'I personally don't see any reason why that application would be refused.'

There are thoughts forming in her mind but she can't yet turn them into words.

'You also have the right, under the law,' Pritchard continues, reverting to stiff formality, 'to appeal this decision to an immigration judge. In that case, if that's what you decide, you will now be detained and taken to an INS facility, or a facility contracted out by the INS, and held in custody until a hearing can be arranged.' He pauses to let that sink in and then, 'That could take a few days.'

Flint's thoughts are now of Nina, threatened with renewed INS detention, sobbing like a child.

'There's one more thing I should tell you. If you do not agree to leave the United States voluntarily and immediately, and if you appeal against the cancellation of your visa, and if your appeal is denied, you will be deported. In that eventuality, under the law, you will become an *excludable person*' – and Pritchard finds a way of giving that phrase a resonance that implies she will have committed a shameful act. 'That means . . . well, let's not go there.' He pulls his mouth into a lopsided grin. 'Believe me, you don't want to go there, Miss Flint.'

*This is absurd! I am the Joint Assistant Director—*

'You're booked on a British Airways flight that leaves JFK in four hours,' says Hatchet Face, her first words. 'We can do this in a civilised way, or I've got leg irons in the trunk of my car. Your call.'

'She knows the smart thing to do,' says Agent Pritchard.

'So, Tyler works for you, does he?' says Flint, proving him wrong. 'Or are you just lackeys clearing up somebody else's mess?'

'Step away from the table, ma'am' – and from somewhere within her baggy navy jacket Hatchet Face has produced a gun. 'Put your hands on your head and turn around.'

'We don't want any stupid accidents,' Pritchard says.

'Get down on your knees.'

But before she can comply – while Flint is still deciding what to do – one of the nondescript men sees something he doesn't like behind her and he says, 'Holy shit!' and points over her shoulder and she turns and there is Sirius standing in the open doorway – about 135 pounds of open-jawed black menace, a rumble like thunder forming in his throat.

'Easy, boy,' warns Agent Pritchard, sounding distinctly uneasy himself. 'Ma'am, is that your dog?'

'Sirius,' she says, not answering the question.

'Put him on a leash. Do it now, or we'll be forced to shoot him.'

And then a series of events begins that is so fast and confused, each reaction seemingly overtaking its cause, that afterwards Flint will have difficulty reconstructing the order of what happens. Her only certainty will be that it starts with a snarl from Sirius that grows into ferocious barking and the dog gathers on its haunches as though it is about to leap, and she sees Hatchet Face swing the gun around and up into the firing position and instinctively, without a second's thought, Flint twists her body and bends at the waist and pivots on one leg and kicks with the other – a high kick that catches Hatchet Face on the shoulder and sends her sprawling headfirst into the table, and the gun discharges.

Then Flint turns and sees Agent Pritchard going for his gun and she is about to kick again when she senses rather than sees a black wind hurtling across the room and Sirius smashes into his chest and he goes down, the snarling dog on top of him, searching for his throat.

Now Agent Pritchard is fighting for his life and there is a revolver in his hand and he's trying to cock the trigger and Flint is stamping on his wrist with the heel of her shoe and she hears him scream – though whether she is the main cause of his pain she cannot say. In any event, he lets go of the gun and Flint kicks it clear and she turns just in time to see one of the nondescripts lunging towards her, swinging a fist at her head, leaving himself wide open. She drops under the blow and comes up fast and hard, driving her knee into his groin and she feels a stab of pain – but nothing to what he feels, judging by the wail he makes as the breath leaves his body.

Three down, one to go and she can't see where he is. But she can see her bag lying on the floor by the table and she scrambles for it and reaches inside and now she has a gun and she works the slide and fires one shot into the ceiling and in the dinning echo she yells, 'Freeze!' – and even Sirius goes quiet.

'Come here, boy,' she calls and he looks at her with eager expectation and she calls again and now he comes loping towards her like a wolf, and Agent Pritchard lies awfully still.

So, too, does the fourth one for she can see him now on the floor beside Ben's favourite chair. He is curled on his side and there is a small pool of blood seeping from beneath the sleeve of his jacket.

She gets to her feet and surveys what she has done.

'You don't shoot dogs,' she tells them, vet's daughter that she is.

# twenty-four

It has taken Rocco Morales a little more than two hours to discreetly establish that the Immigration and Naturalization Service has no plans to cancel Grace Flint's non-immigrant visa or expel her from the United States; that it is not aware of any possibility that she might be suspended from the FSF (though listening to Rocco's cagey answers to her questions on this subject, Flint has the distinct impression that the word going around the Marscheider building says such a possibility does exist).

Morales has also established that, while there is indeed an INS criminal investigator named Mike Pritchard, he is presently in California, working on an undercover investigation, and he bears little physical resemblance to Special Agent Pritchard who now lies prone on Flint's deck, bloodied and patched up but not as seriously hurt as he might have been – although the puncture wounds in his neck and chin, inflicted by Sirius's teeth, may now be causing him some concern.

'I'm hoping the dog's up-to-date on his rabies shots,' Flint has told him. 'But I doubt it.'

Pritchard's official ID, though superficially impressive, is as fake as he is, as are the credentials of the three DEOs who were not sent by the INS to take Grace Flint into custody but who did, nevertheless, come equipped with chains and ankle irons that Flint has found in the boot of one of their cars.

The chains now bind them to each other and to Pritchard as they lie side by side on the deck under Sirius's watchful gaze.

Mutt – as Flint has christened one of the nondescripts – has a flesh wound in his upper right arm, a tear inflicted by the bullet discharged from Hatchet Face's gun as Flint's savage kick dislocated her shoulder. Hatchet Face also has a ripe bruise on her temple that struck the edge of the table as she went down.

As for Jeff – the name Flint has inevitably given to Mutt's colleague – he has no evident injury but his face is pale and he has been the least responsive, the least abusive, of Flint's prisoners.

'On your feet,' she says, coming out on to the deck, entering this surreal arena that is part casualty station after a battle, part slave galley. 'Come on, boy,' she says to Sirius, 'round them up, let's get them moving.'

Sirius growls and rises to his feet and they struggle to theirs, handicapped by the chains that are looped through the handcuffs that each of them wears; handcuffs they also brought to Miller's Reach. They look unnerved, as well they might, for Flint has not asked them a single question about their real identities.

Armed with another piece of intelligence rapidly obtained by the ever-efficient Rocco – that she was indeed booked on a British Airways flight to London, as Hatchet Face had claimed – she has asked only this: 'So, who is it who wants me out of the country so badly?'

And when they hadn't answered, staring their defiance, she had said, 'Okay, we'll talk about it in the morning. You'll feel more like talking then.'

Like a prison chain gang, urged on by Sirius growling at their heels, they hobble and stumble towards Flint's red barn until she stops them at the door.

'And now,' she says, whispering to emphasise her point, 'listen to me. You must be very, very quiet. Once you're inside, don't make a sound. Whatever you do, don't scream – not unless you feel like waking up about a hundred thousand bats.'

She lifts the bar and squeezes open the door and ushers them in, into the dark.

The house is full of ghosts. As Flint also waits in the dark, waiting for the phone to ring, waiting for Cutter to call, she can hear their sighs drifting through the roof spaces like a desolate wind.

The living room is wrecked. There is blood on the floor and plaster from the bullet hole in the ceiling, and a leg of the table was snapped and somehow a window got broken and so did a chair – and she doesn't care. She sits amidst the debris aware of it but only in a disconnected way. She dared to feel happy here and now that the happiness is as dead as the ghosts moaning in the roof she feels no further attachment to Miller's Reach.

She is as alone as she has ever been, dead-alive. She wishes that Sirius was here, but he lies by the barn door, the eternal guard, refusing to move.

Lying in Ben's favourite chair she half-sleeps until Cutter's call snaps her into consciousness.

Except it is not Cutter who calls.

'Miss Flint? Miss Grace Flint?'

A British voice, cautious and pedantic – and, also cautious, she allows that she might just be the owner of that name.

'This is Sergeant Manning of the Oxfordshire Constabulary. I'm calling about your father.'

Her stomach drops as he continues, 'Dr John Flint, that is your father, isn't it?'

Isn't *he*, she wants to say, but she's made these kinds of calls herself and she knows how your mouth goes dry and you get the words wrong.

'What's happened?' – all of her caution gone now, no further suspicion of a trick.

'I'm afraid he's been . . . injured. Rather badly injured.'

'How?'

'Well, that's not certain, Miss Flint. It *appears* that he was the victim of an assault, a rather vicious assault as it happens. In his house. Although he was actually found in his surgery. In, er . . . in a dog cage.'

She wants to scream but she can't make any sound.

'In any event, he was found this evening and taken to Horton General Hospital in Banbury where he's now in intensive care. I'm afraid I don't know the full extent of his injuries but he is in a coma and the doctors thought that you should know that . . . Well, put it this way, the prognosis is uncertain and you might want to make arrangements to get here as soon as you can.'

Sergeant Manning is relieved to have unburdened himself of that piece of news; she can hear it in his voice.

'I'm leaving now,' says Flint, a statement of fact.

'Well, perhaps you would just like to take down my telephone number,' Manning says, speaking to himself.

\* \* \*

The driveway leading away from Miller's Reach climbs a gradual rise and when it reaches the gate at the summit the elevation is well above the house and the barn beyond so that they seem set in a bowl, a natural arena.

Tonight – after Flint has left, taking a reluctant Sirius with her as far as the gate – the arena glows with red and orange light that flickers and rolls and intensifies, breaking through the roof in shooting columns of flame that seem to dance on the surface of the pond. Above that mirror image, panicked ravens dance and scream.

Gradually their screams are absorbed in a cacophony of approaching emergency sirens and, surely, the night is on fire.

# New York City

# twenty-five

Aldus Cutter in his apartment dressed only in his boxer shorts, catching up on his mail, opens a letter from Kenneth Trent, his personal attorney. 'My Dear Aldus,' Trent has begun, for their rapport extends far beyond a regular attorney-client relationship,

This afternoon I met with Eleanor and her attorney, Eli Brillings, in an attempt to clear the logjam and advance towards a final settlement. Eli lives in the real world and his counter-proposals to our offer are, I think, not unreasonable. Under separate cover I will send you a first draft of a provisional agreement that still needs some work, but we're getting there.

So far so good, as you would say. However, after the meeting I had a drink with Eleanor 'for old times' sake' and I'm sorry to tell you that she remains extremely hostile towards you. Normally I wouldn't bother you with this but during our chat she made a number of threats against you. As both your lawyer and your friend, I'm sure I have a duty to warn you as to what she said and what she intends.

Eleanor is convinced that for a number of years leading to the break-up of your marriage you conducted an adulterous relationship with Grace Flint.

Cutter glances at the clock on the living-room mantelpiece and notes that it is fast approaching 8 p.m. He has visitors coming and he takes Trent's letter to the bathroom and props it on the shelf beneath the mirror to continue reading while he shaves.

Eleanor told me that 'the affair' began sometime in 1997, after Flint was posted to Miami to liaise with your task force,

and that it became 'evident to everyone' at a party you jointly
hosted at your house that New Year's Eve (a party which, you
may remember, Sandra and I had the pleasure to attend, if
only briefly). Eleanor claimed that you 'pawed' Flint throughout the evening (though certainly not in my presence) and that
afterwards she confronted you, and that you tacitly admitted
the relationship.

'Horseshit,' says Cutter, stripping off his shorts and stepping
into the shower. His recall of that evening is very different, very
clear.

Young Flint, as he'd thought of her – and she was just about
young enough to be his daughter – had arrived in Miami from
London with an implicit FRAGILE warning stamped on her face.
For she had been stamped on, repeatedly, by a crooked lawyer
named Clayton Buller in the course of a high-profile undercover
operation gone wrong, and there was a general consensus at
Scotland Yard that Buller had shattered her confidence and her
courage as well as her jaw, her nose, her cheek bones and her teeth.
Surgeons had repaired the physical damage and given her an
ethereal beauty – *And yes, Eleanor, I do think she's one fine-
looking woman*, Cutter had once admitted to his wife, perhaps
unwisely – but the scuttlebutt said she was done, finished; that she
could never, would never, work undercover again – a conviction
Flint apparently shared.

But as he'd got to know her and recognised a spunk in her he
had rarely seen in other agents, Cutter had not believed that she
was done. And although her official function in Miami was to act
as Scotland Yard's liaison to the Federal Crimes Joint Task Force
that Cutter then ran – pushing paper from behind a safe desk at the
British Consulate, as far away as possible from the front line –
Cutter had asked her for suggestions on how to infiltrate a
prostitution racket being run out of Fort Lauderdale and seen in
her proposal a particular art for deception, and one that in the
event had worked brilliantly. So Cutter had set out to seduce her;
not into his bed but back into active operations.

Inviting Flint to the party – Aldus and Eleanor Cutter's New
Year Shindig, an annual event of some renown in local law
enforcement circles – had been part of the process, for Cutter
calculated that when she found herself on a patio loud with the

camaraderie of agents and detectives and prosecutors all telling her their war stories, bullshitting for all they were worth, she would get bitten by the bug again; that itch to be a part of the action.

And it had worked, more or less. Within three months Flint had found herself working undercover once more, pretending to be Aldus Cutter's wife, sitting in a plush hotel suite in Coconut Grove with a bunch of Russian mobsters; sitting on a couch in a skimpy jumpsuit, allowing Cutter's fingers to trace idle patterns on her thigh.

But it was not true that Cutter had 'pawed' her at the party, not according to his recollection. Touched her bare arm once or twice, maybe. Put a wrap around her shoulders when it got cold. Kissed her goodnight on the cheek.

'Like I would my daughter, Eleanor – if we had a daughter,' Cutter had rebuked his wife when she'd turned on him in the party's aftermath, the focus of her eyes uncertain from too many frozen mint daiquiris.

'Are you screwing her, Aldus, you sonofabitch?'

'Oh, come on, Eleanor! Act your goddamn age, can't you?'

Hardly an admission, tacit or otherwise, Cutter thinks.

Stepping out of the shower, he towels himself dry and rubs a cream into his face to take away the razor's sting and fetches a clean shirt from the closet, and only then does he return to the mirror to continue reading Trent's letter.

In order to continue 'screwing the bitch' (Eleanor's words, Aldus, not mine) she said you then involved Flint in task force undercover operations, even getting her to pose as your wife so that she could stay with you in the same hotel room.

Sure, thinks Cutter, a hotel room stuffed with concealed cameras and hidden microphones and half the task force monitoring the action from the floor below.

Eleanor claimed that after Flint returned to England in July of 1999 you came up with a 'bullshit excuse' to travel to London and during that trip the two of you spent four nights together in Paris where you stayed at the Hotel Westminster. Apparently Eleanor has obtained 'proof' of that from the hotel and although she conceded to me that you booked separate rooms she believes that you spent the entire time 'sneaking along the corridors'; that getting two rooms was nothing more than a 'lame attempt to give themselves an alibi'.

*Cute choice of words, Eleanor*, thinks Cutter, for he and Flint had gone to Paris to see Inspector Gilles Bourdonnec who was indeed lame, his legs shredded by flying glass from a bomb explosion while he was assisting a task force operation. Flint had insisted on the trip, practically dragging Cutter to the airport, for she wanted him to see with his own eyes what they had 'done' to Gilles. 'He helped us, Mr Cutter, far more than he needed to, far more than we had any right to expect, and he very nearly paid for it with his life. In a way he *has* paid with his life. We owe him, Mr Cutter.'

But owe him what? Cutter had thought as he'd followed Flint up the 137 steps of winding staircase that led to the Bourdonnecs' small flat at the very top of number 38 Rue Tiquetonne and found Gilles in his wheelchair with his unruly hair and his boy's face and his fragile body. Gilles had insisted on struggling to his feet for the formal introduction to Cutter and limped painfully across the room, leading the way to the couch, and there were unmistakable tears in Flint's eyes when she'd hugged him.

To her exasperation, Gilles had refused to play the victim's role, fetching them something to drink, getting up from the couch to answer the telephone, getting up again to greet each of the three Bourdonnec children as they came home from school, growing stronger with each new event. When Dominique, his wife, came home it was Gilles who prepared the supper, telling Flint to 'sit, sit' every time she tried to help.

'You think I am an invalid?' he'd bawled at her in mock anger when she'd insisted that she and not he should carry the meal to the table.

Things weren't so bad, he'd said as they ate. He was on medical leave and full pay for as long as it took and he was getting stronger almost by the day and when he was fit enough to return to work they would find him a desk job commensurate with his rank.

'But, Gilles, how are you going to *get* to work?' Flint had protested. 'How do you get down the stairs?'

Well, yes, Gilles had conceded, the stairs were a problem but he and Dominique were looking for somewhere else to live, somewhere nearer to his office, somewhere on the ground floor – as if such places grew on trees in Paris, not bothering to mention to Cutter that this had been his parents' flat and where he was born and where he had lived his entire life.

'Quite a guy,' Cutter had said as very late that night he and Flint had made their way to the Hotel Westminster, and Flint had not trusted herself to reply.

*Oh, yes, Eleanor*, Cutter thinks now, *Grace came sneaking down the corridor all right, at three o'clock in the morning, banging on my door like the hotel was on fire. And she stayed in my room for the rest of the night, and you know what we did? We argued.*

'Aldus, I've got it,' she'd said, pushing past him into the room, her eyes on fire.

'Got what?'

'What we can do for Gilles. What we *have* to do.'

'Which is?'

And she had grinned like a Cheshire cat and announced her revelation as though it was the recipe for world peace. 'We buy him a lift.'

'A what?'

'An elevator. We pay for an elevator to be installed in his building, one big enough for his wheelchair. So he's not trapped. Don't you see?'

'Are you out of your frigging mind?' Cutter had asked.

But Flint in that kind of mood was not easily denied and she and Cutter had spent the remainder of their time in Paris 'exploring the possibilities' – her words – and it turned out that it was *technically feasible* to run an elevator shaft up through the stairwell of number 38 Rue Tiquetonne, and the owners of the building were *not necessarily* opposed to the idea, and the municipal authorities *might well* grant the necessary permissions – and the only problem that remained was how to raise the 850,000 francs it would cost.

'How much is that in dollars?' Cutter had asked and Flint had done the calculation and told him it was about $140,000, more or less, and he'd raised his eyebrows into incredulous arcs and looked at the sky and whistled, and she'd said, 'Come on, Mr Cutter, how hard can it be?'

Very hard.

You might have thought that somewhere within the multitudinous coffers of the US federal government there would have

existed a budget from which Cutter could have extracted the means
to free Gilles Bourdonnec from his virtual prison, in grateful thanks
for what he'd done for the task force – but Cutter never found it.
The $50,000 he eventually raised for the elevator fund came from
a private foundation he had never heard of and to which he was
referred by a Justice Department lawyer – by coincidence or not –
only after he'd finally agreed to become the director of the new
Financial Strike Force.

And Flint had found no sympathetic ear in London until, despite
Cutter's misgivings and with some trepidation, she had taken herself
off to Thames House, the headquarters of the British Security
Service, to remind the deputy director that Gilles was actively
assisting his service when the bomb exploded *and* that it was rogue
elements within the service who had caused the bomb to be planted
– facts well known to the deputy director but not in the public
domain.

'What did A.J. say?' Cutter asked, referring to A.J. Devereaux,
the deputy director of the service, when Flint had called him at
home in New York to report on what had happened.

'He was still reading me the Official Secrets Act when I walked
out. And this morning I got a banker's draft through the post
for £75,000 from the Inter-Global Marketing Partnership, whatever that may be. Which, when you think about it, is a little scary
– that I got him that spooked, I mean. Aldus,' she'd continued
after a moment's hesitation, 'I think you better get me out of
here.'

'You read my mind,' said Cutter.

Which is how Grace Flint came to apply for the position of Joint
Assistant Director (Operations) of the Financial Strike Force – and
given Cutter's ringing endorsement of her undercover expertise,
and his back-me-or-sack-me position, she was always a shoo-in for
the job.

Mrs Cutter sees things differently, apparently.

After the Paris trip, Eleanor said, she hoped that you had got
over your 'pathetic infatuation' with Flint and when you
accepted the job with the FSF she hoped that the move to New
York would provide the opportunity for a 'fresh start'. She
said that she put her 'heart and soul' into decorating and
furnishing the new apartment and was very much looking

forward to living there with you. So imagine her 'horror' when she learned (and not from you, Aldus, apparently) that you had made 'that slut' your deputy; that you were bringing her to New York to continue your 'affair'.

Now of course I challenged Eleanor, saying I was absolutely certain you would never do such a thing. I also pointed out to her that, even if her allegations were true, they would make no possible difference to the terms of the divorce settlement.

But, Aldus, it is not an improved settlement that Eleanor seeks to extract from you. What she wants, she said, is 'revenge'.

In the bedroom now, Trent's letter lying on the dresser, Cutter selects a dark blue wool suit from his wardrobe, and a maroon tie that is patterned with tiny replicas of the crest of the FSF, and a pair of soft leather Bruno Magli loafers – a gift pressed on him by Flint, as it happens, to celebrate the inaugural descent of the Bourdonnec elevator. He dresses in front of a full-length mirror and recalls that glorious day, and Flint's radiant face, as they waited with Dominique and the children in the ground-floor vestibule; waiting for Gilles to emerge from the elevator car with his triumphant, roaring cry of '*Liberté! Liberté!*'

It was in Joe Allen's restaurant where Cutter had taken them all for a celebratory lunch – and where half the cops in Paris, it seemed, had arrived in ones and twos to drink a toast to Gilles – that Flint had first told Cutter about Ben Gates and a six-month relationship with him that was moving like a blue streak.

'Well, you sure kept that quiet,' Cutter said – and he will not deny that he had felt just the slightest pang of something; if not jealousy exactly, then disappointment. 'You gonna marry him?'

'Maybe,' she'd said coyly. 'It is within the bounds of possibility, but he doesn't know that yet.'

Ready for his guests, Cutter takes the letter back into the living room to read the final passages.

What has set her on this course, she said, the 'final sickening straw' is her discovery that your 'affair' has continued since Flint's own marriage last year; a marriage that Eleanor believes is 'a sham, as phoney as she is' and designed to hide the fact that 'Aldus is the one she's really screwing'. She said she had 'proof' that Flint regularly visits your apartment 'at all hours of the day and night' and that she intends to take her evidence to your superiors.

Now, Aldus, your personal life is nobody's business (and, if it becomes necessary, that is the position I will vigorously maintain on your behalf). However, I am bound to say that most employers, including yours, would look askance at a sexual relationship with a subordinate, not least because of a possible claim of sexual harassment by the subordinate should the relationship ever sour.

If you are in a sexual relationship with Flint then I would urge you to end it, or at least conduct it with far greater discretion. Eleanor's 'proof' of Flint's visits to your apartment comes, I gather, from the doorman.

The telephone rings and a voice every bit as Irish as it was when its owner arrived in New York thirty years ago says, 'Pat here, Mr Cutter. Visitors for yer.'

'Send 'em up,' says Cutter.

# twenty-six

This is fence-mending time and, despite his reputation for irascibility, Cutter can schmooze with the best of them when the need demands. To Dr Otto Schnell, a senior director of the *Bundesnachrichtendienst* (the German intelligence service more conveniently known as the BND) – a small, compact man who perches on the edge of Cutter's couch like an attentive bird – Cutter offers his warmest smile and says, 'I hope you didn't mind meeting here instead of my office?'

'On the contrary,' says Dr Schnell, who speaks English with no discernible accent, 'since my visit is of course private I appreciate your discretion, Mr Cutter.'

'Thank you. And call me Aldus, please.'

Dr Schnell gives a slight bow to acknowledge the offer, nothing more.

'I'm sure Felix has already told you this' – and Cutter glances towards the chair where Felix Hartmann is untidily sprawled – 'but I want to make it clear that the decision to keep the BND out of the loop on Operation Pentecost was mine, not his, and if that was a mistake – and in view of what's happened it clearly was a mistake – then the blame is also mine.'

'Ah, then you don't fully understand Felix, if I may say so. You see, our young friend' – Dr Schnell speaking of Hartmann as though he wasn't there – 'is one of those Germans who thinks it is his patriotic duty to be hard on himself. Taking blame is his prerogative.'

'Nevertheless, Dr Schnell, I apologise.'

'And nevertheless, Mr Cutter – because I cannot call you Aldus unless you call me Otto – I accept your apology. Whether others in Pullach will be quite as forgiving, I cannot say.'

'The view in Pullach,' Hartmann says laconically, speaking of the headquarters of the BND, 'is that the level of our cooperation – or, rather, our total lack of cooperation – was not *korrekt*. That was the word the president used – several times, as a matter of fact.' Hartmann runs the fingers of one hand through light brown hair that is long for a former army officer. 'Many, many times,' he adds.

'He's pissed at us,' says Cutter.

'That's exactly what he is,' Dr Schnell agrees.

'How pissed, Otto? Are you going to be able to help us with Gröber?'

Dr Schnell leans forward, reaching for the briefcase that sits between his legs. 'Aldus, I did not fly all the way to New York to waste my time – or yours, I trust.' He brings the briefcase to his knees and opens it and draws out three folders of different colours. 'These are Gröber's files,' he says showing Cutter ones that are coloured green and red. Then he opens a grey folder and continues, 'First, if I may, a short history lesson. How much do you know about General Erich Mielke and the *Staatssicherheit* – the Stasi, Aldus?'

'Not nearly enough,' says Cutter.

They have adjourned to a steakhouse on 3rd Avenue where Cutter has arranged a private room. In Cutter's view the prime rib is as good as it gets outside Texas and the general conviviality of the surroundings is supposed to relax Dr Schnell – but it's not working, for he is anything but relaxed. Since they arrived at the restaurant Dr Schnell has become reserved, monosyllabic, and he keeps glancing at the wood-panelled walls, and Cutter guesses why.

'Otto, you think this place is bugged? You think I'm trying to burn you?'

Dr Schnell does not reply.

'Okay, well, you're entitled to be suspicious and short of pulling the panels off the wall, and taking the legs off the table, and ripping up the floorboards, and taking off my clothes and getting Felix to strip, and the Lord knows what else, I don't have any way of proving to you that there are no microphones, no wires. So, let me try this. I'm gonna tell you something – and, Felix, close your ears – that I would sooner die than have recorded. Okay?'

Dr Schnell still does not reply but there is interest in his eyes.

'I found out tonight that my wife thinks I'm screwing my deputy director, a woman name of Grace Flint. She, my wife, is going to try and make a federal case out of it and she won't succeed because it isn't true. But, strictly between you and me' – and Cutter glowers at Felix Hartmann – 'now the subject has come up, and I've been obliged to give it a little thought, I recognise where this idea has come from. The deep-down truth, Otto, is that subconsciously I wish I *was* screwing Flint, and – God help me – if she gave me the slightest encouragement I'd be the first cab off the rank, and, that being the case, I'm gonna have to fire her, for my own protection.

'Now, what I've just told you, if that was on tape, that would be enough to get *me* fired, faster than you can think, and there's no way in hell I could suppress it. Okay' – Cutter grins – 'maybe you think that right now the tape is turned off; that nobody's listening; that I've arranged for the tape to start running when *you* start talking. So, here's what I'll do.'

Cutter takes a pen from his pocket and reaches for a paper cocktail napkin. 'I'm going to write you a signed confession that I'm about to fire Grace Flint for the worst possible reason – and Felix here is your witness. Okay? If I try to burn you, you burn me – and I'm the one who's going up in flames.'

Dr Schnell waves Cutter's offer away with a dismissive hand. 'Shall we order?' he enquires.


Awaiting the arrival of their meal, sharing a bottle of fine Bordeaux, Dr Schnell continues his revisionist account of the final days of the infamous Ministry for State Security of the wholly-misnamed German Democratic Republic.

'Now, Aldus, there was chaos. In theory the Stasi had been castrated. General Mielke had been forced to resign as minister, together with the entire Politburo, and his monstrous machine had been reduced by the new regime to a mere office, a benign shadow of its former self. But all of this was nothing more than an illusion, a trick. The Communists, they were simply buying time. Not to re-group – it was far too late for that – but to destroy the evidence of what they had achieved. Remember what the Stasi's mission had been, as defined by Mielke: "To know *everything*" – and record it, write it down. The files, Aldus, the files! You would not believe what the Stasi had achieved.

'I crossed over to the East in December of '89, about a month after the Berlin Wall had crumbled. At the BND we knew from intercepts that at the end of November the regime had issued a secret order to all of the Stasi regional and district offices, all 234 of them: "Destroy the files! Immediately!" Imagine, Aldus, for almost forty years they had "known everything" and written it down – and now they must destroy it all immediately. What a bonfire that would have made! But, of course, we had to prevent it if we could.'

'How?' asks Cutter.

'Encouragement, a touch of incitement here and there.' Dr Schnell raises his sparrow's shoulders. 'It was not difficult, Aldus. Here were seventeen million people who had believed for all or most of their lives that the state was infallible – and, if not that, omnipotent – and suddenly the entire apparatus of the state was in total disarray. Still dangerous, to be sure, a wounded animal, but floundering and suddenly incompetent and all that was required was some . . .' – there is a breath of hesitation – 'persuasion. Given the context, the logic of the argument was unassailable: the GDR was The People's state and therefore the files belonged to The People – who else? – and the Stasi had no right to destroy them. With or without our encouragement, "citizens' committees" emerged from the shadows into the light, to stand up and be counted and demand The People's rights. There were some confrontations, a few stand-offs – many tense days to be sure – and then, in the middle of December, some fifty thousand Stasi agents melted into the night as though they had never existed.' The memory sends a glimmer of a smile across Dr Schnell's face. 'Except in East Berlin.'

'The Stasi HQ was something else,' Hartmann interjects, 'a fortress designed by a truly paranoid mind. During General Mielke's time it was practically impregnable – to any kind of penetration, human or electronic, and you can be sure that we tried – and even after he was gone, and the rest of East Berlin was in a shambles, his ethos survived.'

Dr Schnell is impatient to continue. 'Normannenstrasse, number 22, the heart of Mielke's empire – and what an empire, Aldus! The street number was just a talisman, a token address, for within the Stasi's walls the headquarters' buildings sprawled for six city blocks and still they could not accommodate all the men and women Mielke had working for him: thirty thousand staff in Berlin alone, all with military rank, down to and including the secretaries; even the cleaners and the caretakers, even the cooks. And I have not included a single *Mitarbeiter* – the Stasi "co-workers", Mielke's ears and eyes. In every power plant in the land, Aldus; in every factory, government department, post office, bank, police station and prison; in every university, school, library, hospital and church; at every border checkpoint, airport, subway station, port, railway terminus, gas station, army barracks – *everywhere*, Mielke had his spies.' Dr Schnell slowly shakes his head to indicate his wonder at the sheer scale of the folly. 'One hundred and eighty thousand spies, Aldus.'

'That we know about,' Hartmann adds quickly. 'And that's not counting the informers, the people who spied on their neighbours, their friends, even their own partners.'

'Even their own children,' Dr Schnell whispers, as though this truth is too dreadful to be spoken too loud. 'Even their own parents.'

'Mielke was mad, of course,' he continues after a short hiatus, 'a megalomaniac. But there is also compelling evidence that he suffered from an obsessive-compulsive personality disorder similar to Dzerzhinsky, the founder of the All-Russian Cheka. Remember "Iron Feliks", Aldus, architect of the Bolsheviks' "Red Terror"?' – and Cutter nods his head to say that he does. 'Well, Mielke's personal quarters at Normannenstrasse were filled with mementoes of Comrade Dzerzhinsky: busts, wall plaques, pictures, quotations from his published texts – every room was practically a shrine to Dzerzhinsky, and Mielke was a true believer in the Cheka's doctrine of control through terror. Now, admittedly, his Stasi did not see fit to murder two hundred thousand people, as the Cheka did, but Mielke worked for thirty-two years – compulsively, day and night, the same as Dzerzhinsky – to create around Normannenstrasse an aura of absolute, merciless power that survived even his departure. Or,' adds Dr Schnell, 'that is the best explanation I have for you.'

Cutter looks puzzled until Hartmann says, 'To explain why the Stasi HQ survived intact until the night of January 15.'

'Nine weeks and four days after the Wall came down. Don't you find that incredible, Aldus?' Dr Schnell has vivid blue eyes that seem to reflect his astonishment. 'It was over, finished, the police and the border guards had flowers in their rifle barrels – and yet at Normannenstrasse, the Ministry of Fear, it was business as usual! Or, rather, not as usual for now the Stasi's business was to rewrite its history.'

'Destroy the files?' asks Cutter.

'Destroy them,' Dr Schnell tentatively agrees. 'Or fillet them. Alter them.' With slender fingers he plays a pianist's riff on the green file that is lying on the table. 'Create them.'

* * *

'Gröber, Karl Martin, born Leipzig, GDR, 28 June 1951,' says Dr
Schnell, briefly reading from the green file before lifting his head to
pose a question. 'Have you been to Leipzig, Aldus?' he asks, and
Cutter shakes his head to say that he has not. 'In some ways it is a
sad town,' Dr Schnell continues. 'Under the Communists entire
streets were practically destroyed by acid rain, from the refining of
brown coal. The sulphur, you see, it ate into the fabric of the
buildings until they became ... Well, the Party had a euphemism
for it: *ausgewohnt*, which means "too lived-in". They are still
there, many of those buildings, abandoned like old tombstones,
boarded up, awaiting demolition – if and when there is someone
who can pay the bill. In one sense you might say that the
*ausgewohnt* were a catalyst for the revolution. By 1989 the city's
decline was all too apparent and the people – students, mainly, and
priests – began to protest on Monday afternoons, carrying a coffin
into the centre of town to represent the death of Leipzig. Just a few
hundred the first time, then a few thousand, then *twenty* thousand,
then – who knows? A sea of people, Aldus, a tide.'

Dr Schnell beams and Cutter cannot resist chuckling. 'With a
little encouragement, I suppose. Just a "touch of incitement" was
there, Otto?'

'No, no,' says Schnell quickly. 'Believe me, we did nothing in
Leipzig. You know what *they* did, Aldus? They marched to the
offices of the Stasi! They stood on the very steps of the Stasi, in
front of the Stasi's surveillance cameras, and unfurled their banners
and shouted their defiance. These kids, Aldus, kids and priests,
they challenged the Stasi to use its power, something that Mielke
believed would never happen – *could* never happen. Incredible!
There was nothing for us to do except watch in awe.'

Hartmann coughs and Dr Schnell returns his attention to the
file.

'Gröber's father was Wilhelm, a professor of economics at Karl
Marx University. Mother, Eva, an obstetrician at the Staedi
gynaecological clinic. By GDR standards the family was relatively
well off. They lived on Karl-Heine-Strasse, in a house with a garden,
which was very much not the norm. There were – there are – very
few private gardens in Leipzig. For some, the privileged few,
the Party assigned' – Dr Schnell pauses to savour the word –
'*Schrebergärten*; allotments, Aldus, vegetable patches. But young

Karl Martin had his own garden to play in and, after four years, a
sister to play with. They called her Ilse. A pretty name, don't you
think? – and such a pretty child, and Karl, we read, was devoted to
her ... But, Aldus' – he removes his reading glasses and smiles an
apology – 'I am wasting your time. You are completely familiar
with Gröber's supposed antecedents, of course.'

'Am I?' says Cutter, instantly on guard.

'Aldus, let us be frank with each other, please. It is well known
that many of the more interesting Stasi files found their way to
Moscow where they were sold to operatives of your CIA; one of
the first positive assertions of capitalism in the post-Cold War era,
I believe. This' – Dr Schnell's fingers perform another riff – 'was
among the files the CIA bought, so I am assuming—'

'Then you need to understand something, Otto,' Cutter interrupts. 'The agency and us, we rarely have the same agenda. And if
and when we do, we're in competition and, on a good day, Langley
wouldn't give us shit – and if they did, I wouldn't believe a word of
it. Most of the background we have on Gröber comes from the
Brits and—'

'Really? Which agency, if you do not mind me asking?'

'Specifically, the National Criminal Intelligence Service. Flint's
former boss runs it.'

'And they would have got their information from where, Aldus?
The British Secret Intelligence Service, perhaps – or do they still call
themselves MI6? I get confused.'

'So do they,' says Cutter. 'And, I know where you're going.'

Dr Schnell's eyes sparkle with pleasure. 'Do you, Aldus? Then let
us play a game. You tell me what you think you know about young
Karl Martin Gröber and I will tell you if it derives from this file.
And then Felix will tell you what is in *this* file' – and Dr Schnell
momentarily holds up the red file before sliding it across the table
to Hartmann – 'which was *not* available for purchase in Moscow,
and then, perhaps, we can separate some of the myths from the
realities.' Cutter wants to know where the red file came from but as
he is about to ask Dr Schnell adds, 'Humour me, Aldus. Please.'

Cutter nods. The information on Gröber that Flint had brought
back from London was in the form of a written summary. Playing
Schnell's game for now, Cutter begins to recite what he remembers.

'Nothing exceptional about his childhood, so far as we know.
Stayed out of trouble and academically he was pretty bright. And

then when he was almost eighteen and about to do his military
service, the wheels came off. Ilse, who would have been around
thirteen or fourteen at the time, got sick; some form of leukaemia
that kids are especially prone to, as I recall. Anyway, she ended up
needing a bone marrow transplant and when it came to a matching
donor Karl was the only game in town, and something went wrong
during the procedure, and *he* got pretty sick. And somewhere in
the middle of all of this the parents were killed in a car wreck.'

'July 27, 1969 – a Sunday, I think,' says Dr Schnell. 'Your
summary is entirely consistent with the file, Aldus. Do you happen
to know where the Gröbers were killed?'

'No.'

'No, well that piece of information is not in my file either. Felix'
– Dr Schnell points to the red file – 'enlighten us, if you will.'

'One and a half kilometres north of Vacha,' says Hartmann
without needing to consult the file.

'Which is where, Felix? Or rather, which *was* where?'

'On the border with the Federal Republic – West Germany –
approximately two hundred kilometres southwest of Leipzig.'

'A long way from home, then, Felix. And do you know where
the Gröbers were heading late on that Sunday night when the
unfortunate accident occurred?'

'Directly towards the frontier on a forest track – and it was no
accident.'

'Ah,' says Dr Schnell, as if this comes as news to him.

'They were shot, by border guards,' Hartmann continues as
though he is following a script, speaking one more of his lines.

Schnell takes the merest sip of wine to moisten his mouth. 'You
see, Aldus, Ilse's treatment was not working, or so the Gröbers
thought. They wanted to take her to the West and, had it been a
few months earlier, that might have been allowed; despite the Wall,
travel to the West was not altogether impossible. But in 1968, the
Party tightened its grip' – he squeezes his small hands into tight
fists – 'and Ulbricht, the general secretary – remember him, Aldus?
the Bolshevik shit – Ulbricht was a firm believer in Stalinist methods
of dealing with any form of dissent: crush, grind, eradicate.

'When the Gröbers tried to reach the West, attempting to cross
the border for *any* reason – and there was their pretty Ilse lying in
a blanket on the back seat of the car – was practically a treasonable
offence. If your escape plan was not perfect, if you were unlucky

enough to run into the guards, you were very likely to be shot.' Dr Schnell presses his tongue against the roof of his mouth to reproduce the sound of two gunshots ringing out in the night. 'So' – he turns towards Hartmann – 'the Gröbers were unlucky. Is that correct, Felix?'

'No,' Hartmann says. 'Luck had nothing to do with it. The guards knew they were coming.'

'Because, Aldus my friend' – and Dr Schnell reaches out to lay one hand on Cutter's arm – 'they had been denounced to the Stasi. Betrayed.' He holds Cutter's eyes with his. 'By Karl. By their son.'

A knock on the door announces the arrival of their food.

'Just a second,' calls out Cutter. 'What happened to Ilse?' he asks Dr Schnell.

'She was never in danger because the guards had orders not to fire on the car. They simply forced it to stop and took the parents out and shot them in the back of the head. Ilse was returned to Leipzig and her treatment resumed as though nothing had happened. And the truth – the irony, Aldus – is that the medical facilities in the GDR were as good as we could have provided.' A thin smile as Dr Schnell adds, 'It was our propaganda that was better. Ilse was cured.'

'Come ahead,' says Cutter, calling to the door.

As if by an unspoken agreement they have not mentioned Karl Martin Gröber during the meal, but now that the table has been cleared and coffee and brandy have been placed before them, and Cutter and Schnell are each enjoying Havana cigars that the doctor has thoughtfully provided, and the door has been closed and they are alone again, Dr Schnell takes us back to Leipzig; specifically to a building known as *Runde Ecke* – Round Corner – at number 24 Dittrichring, the imposing, red-roofed citadel of the Stasi.

'It was Normannenstrasse in miniature with discrete departments to monitor the phones, open the mail, scan the radio waves for illicit broadcasts, forge documents, construct surveillance equipment, create disguises, conduct investigations and interrogations, analyse information. Above all else,' says Dr Schnell, 'to maintain the files.'

'Too many files, as it turned out,' says Hartmann. 'There were two thousand four hundred full-time Stasi personnel in Leipzig, not to mention ten thousand "co-workers", all of them generating paper. They had no computers at *Runde Ecke* so it all had to be typed or written down in files and on index cards.'

'Aldus, you cannot possibly comprehend the depth of their obsession.' Dr Schnell blows a plume of cigar smoke and watches it drift towards the ceiling. 'On an average day in Leipzig they opened and read and copied one thousand five hundred letters. All of the telephone cables in the city ran through a listening centre at *Runde Ecke* that recorded up to three hundred conversations at a time, and anything "suspicious" was transcribed for the files. A copy of every telegram received in Leipzig was instantly sent to the Stasi. From any "suspicious" letter, they collected and filed fingerprints and samples of saliva and handwriting. Aldus, if you had been a target of the Stasi they would have done their level best to obtain for your file samples of your body scent, your semen, your pubic hair.'

Cutter fidgets in his chair.

'Much of the paperwork was generated by the "co-workers" – the spies,' says Hartmann, taking up the story. 'Each one was assigned a case officer and the Stasi maintained "safe" apartments in Leipzig where debriefings took place; where the "co-workers" either handed over their written reports or the sessions were tape-recorded and then transcribed.' Hartmann dips one finger in his brandy glass as though it is an ink well and uses the liquid to write a number on the tabletop.

'There were six *hundred* "safe" apartments, Aldus,' says Dr Schnell. 'Six *hundred* factories producing yet more information for the files.'

'And what about Gröber's file, Otto?' asks Cutter. 'The red file – which I gather is the real one?'

Schnell sighs like a man who is reluctantly reaching the end of a journey. 'Who watches the watchers, Aldus? – that eternal conundrum. Since the Stasi trusted no-one it could not logically trust itself. So, under Mielke's orders, every Stasi officer maintained files on his subordinates, just as his superior maintained a file on him. And so it went, all the way up the chain of command in every Stasi region and district.

'But now there is another question: Who watches the commanders? Mielke's answer, in the case of Leipzig, was Gröber – for a man like Mielke could not fail to be impressed by a young recruit who had effectively signed his own parents' death warrant, and

Gröber became one of Mielke's favoured prodigies. Not that Mielke *trusted* Gröber, you understand, Aldus. He simply ensured that even after Gröber was transferred to the Berlin headquarters in 1980, he regularly returned to Leipzig on "special assignments" that enabled him to spy on the district commander. At the same time, naturally, the district commander was required by Mielke to compile and maintain a comprehensive dossier on Gröber. He was a lieutenant-general by the name of Kessel. This' – Schnell nods towards the red file – 'is the original of what he compiled: the closest we will ever come, I am sure, to the truth about Karl Martin Gröber.'

Hartmann says, 'It should and probably would have been destroyed. In late November of '89 a pulping machine the size of a large concrete mixer was installed in *Runde Ecke* and the systematic destruction of the files began. But on the night of December 4 – much sooner than anyone could have expected – the demonstrators occupied the building to preserve what was left.'

'And what was left,' chips in Dr Schnell, 'in a city of five hundred thousand people, was 3.7 *million* index cards and files that, lined up in a row, would have stretched for ten kilometres. What would that mean in terms of Manhattan, Aldus? Wall Street to the Upper West Side?'

'Close,' says Cutter. 'Maybe Midtown. But, Otto, getting back to the file, am I missing something here?' The expression on Cutter's face suggests the opposite. 'As I recall, all of the Stasi files that survived were handed over to an independent federal commission that was set up to examine them. The Gauck Commission, right? Run by some pastor out of Rostock?'

'Mmm,' says Dr Schnell.

'So, how come you have what you say is the *original* of Gröber's file?'

'I could tell you it was sent to us. In the mail. Anonymously.'

'Uh-huh,' says Cutter.

'It might have been found on a public garbage dump,' suggests Hartmann. 'Many of the Leipzig files were dumped.'

'Uh-huh,' repeats Cutter.

'Gröber had established many enemies inside the Stasi,' says Dr Schnell, his tone now growing a trifle tetchy. 'The fact that some senior officers took advantage of the delay in Berlin to doctor the files in Normannenstrasse – to create more sympathetic accounts of their careers – was well known within the Stasi. I think we can safely assume that somebody in Leipzig who knew the truth about Gröber wanted to set the record straight.'

'Uh-huh,' Cutter says for the third time.

'Aldus, what is the problem? Why do you care?'

'Otto, I'm not asking for your sources. I just don't want to find myself at the end of another blind alley so, please, tell me a couple of things: that you know where the file came from, and that you know for sure it's genuine.'

Dr Schnell looks grave and Felix Hartmann looks at the tabletop, his gaze locked on the file. 'First,' says Schnell, reaching for the brandy bottle and recharging their glasses, 'we should drink a toast. To General Kessel, perhaps, who may yet enable your Operation Pentecost to reach a successful conclusion.'

Solemnly they raise their glasses and drink and Dr Schnell wipes his lips and leans towards Cutter and softly says, 'Every document in Kessel's dossier has been analysed and forensically examined in order to answer a number of questions that I posed. Do the types of paper precisely match what was available in the GDR when each document was supposedly created? Yes, they do. Are the inks correct? Yes, they are. If a document was handwritten, do we have another contemporaneous sample of the author's handwriting and, if so, do they match? Yes, we do – and, yes, they match. Where we have more than one document supposedly written by the same author, does text analysis show a consistency in syntax and spelling? Yes, it does. Is it possible to retrieve fingerprints from any of the documents and, if so, do any of those prints match those of the supposed author? Yes and yes. With regard to those typewritten documents supposedly compiled by General Kessel, is it possible to establish if they came from his personal typewriter at the *Runde Ecke*? Yes, it is. And how do we know that? Because we have his typewriter.

'Aldus' – Dr Schnell leans back in his chair – 'in our line of business there are very few certainties, but this, I think, is one of them.'

'Thank you,' says Cutter. 'And you know where the file came from?'

'I do. From the archives of the Gauck Commission. We stole it,' adds Dr Schnell.

# twenty-seven

They have returned to Cutter's apartment where, pleading jetlag, Dr Schnell has removed his jacket and his shoes and stretched out on the couch in the living room. He has declined Cutter's offer of his bed, insisting that the couch suits him perfectly well – as indeed it does, his small body fitting comfortably between the armrests. In repose, Cutter thinks, with a handkerchief covering his face and his arms folded across his chest, he looks no bigger than a boy.

'This is Gröber's initial, informal application to join the Stasi,' says Hartmann, handing Cutter a protective plastic folder that contains a one-sentence letter written in an adolescent, uncertain hand. 'He was fifteen at the time.'

'Christ!' says Cutter. '*Fifteen?*'

'It was not unusual. Secondary school teachers had orders to encourage "suitable" pupils to consider an "interesting" career with the Stasi. Those who took the bait were required to write a letter like this – it only says, "Dear Miss David," who would have been his teacher, "I wish to serve my country in the Ministry for State Security" – and this went straight to the *Runde Ecke*, and they would have started doing background checks.'

'Fifteen!' Cutter says again, as though he still can't believe it.

'And this,' says Hartmann, handing Cutter a second plastic folder, 'is Gröber's formal application, written when he was sixteen. It was supposed to be countersigned by his parents but, as you can clearly see, their signatures were forged.'

*Wilhelm Gröber* and *Eva Gröber*, shakily traced, not signed.

'But the Stasi would have known that?'

'Of course,' says Hartmann. 'And this was the consequence. Note the date on the letter – 28 June 1967, Gröber's sixteenth birthday – now look at this.' The third folder that Hartmann produces contains a white index card covered on both sides with tightly-written entries in several different hands. 'The first entry is dated two days later, which is when Wilhelm and Eva Gröber formally came under the suspicion of the Stasi.'

'*They* came under suspicion? I don't get it,' says Cutter.

'Because, my friend,' says Dr Schnell from his horizontal position on the couch, 'you cannot think like the Stasi thought. In order to serve his country the boy has to forge his parents' signatures – so there must be something wrong with the parents, not the boy. Why could he not ask them to sign? Why would they not want him to join the Stasi? You see, Aldus, it is perfectly logical.'

Cutter grunts.

'At seventeen,' continues Hartmann, 'Gröber attended a "defence camp" – as all children in the GDR were required to do, whether or not they wished to join the Stasi. But, naturally, special attention was paid to those who had applied to join and this' – Hartmann pulls another plastic folder from the red file – 'is the instructors' assessment of Gröber's performance. In a word, they thought him "promising". Ulbricht had just sent East German troops into Czechoslovakia to help the Soviets crush the Prague uprising and that, and the new restrictions on travel to the West, had tested the loyalty of even some Party members. But in the debates held at the camp each evening, Gröber was an unswerving supporter of the Ulbricht line – which did his future prospects in the Stasi no harm at all.

'He also scored well in the practical aspects of the course, which was basic military training. He was big for his age and strong, and the instructors noted that during unarmed combat he would use his strength not merely to defeat his opponent but to inflict pain. They said he possessed an "aggressive streak", and that was not meant as a criticism.'

From Cutter's bedroom comes the soft warble of a telephone ringing twice before the answering machine picks up the call.

'Now we come to Gröber's eighteenth birthday,' Hartmann continues, 'and his third and final application to join the Stasi.'

'Just a second,' Cutter interjects. 'Before then Ilse got sick and needed her transplant, right? And Gröber was the donor and *he* got sick and—'

Hartmann, shaking his head, interrupts to say, 'There is nothing in the file about that. Not yet. We have to wait twenty years until General Kessel tells us what really happened.'

From beneath the handkerchief covering his face Dr Schnell sniggers. 'Don't tease, Felix. It is not polite.'

'So?' demands Cutter and Hartmann digs deep into the red file, to almost the very end of it, and produces a folder that contains perhaps forty pages, densely typed.

'You're right, Mr Cutter. In late 1968 Ilse was diagnosed with acute lymphocytic leukaemia that eventually required stem cell transplantation and her brother was the donor and he became very ill as a result of the procedure.' Hartmann creates a tense pause by scanning the first page of Kessel's report as though he needs to remind himself of the outcome. 'In fact,' he says, 'her brother died.'

Now there is a silence that hangs in Cutter's living room like the moment after death. Cutter will not break the silence. He sits motionless, giving his full attention to Hartmann's long, pale face as though he is memorising the contours.

'Don't tease, Felix,' whispers Dr Schnell.

'The Gröbers had *three* children' – Hartmann is no longer faking any need to consult the general's report – 'the second, the middle child, a boy, Heinz Frank, born May 6, 1953. When Ilse relapsed after a course of chemotherapy both of her brothers were tested for suitability as immunologically-matched donors. Karl was the closer match but he declined to be the donor. In his place Heinz volunteered, even though he was prone to infections. During or immediately after the procedure Heinz developed acute septicaemia complicated by viral pneumonia. He died without leaving the hospital on 5 May 1969, one day before his sixteenth birthday.' Hartmann pushes pointlessly with his hand at the mop of hair that constantly falls across his forehead. 'Karl did not attend his brother's funeral.'

The telephone rings for a second time, and the call is duly answered by the machine and for a moment it seems that Cutter is ready to listen to the messages. He gets up from his chair and walks slowly towards the bedroom and then he appears to lose his way, stopping and turning, heading now towards the kitchen, now stopping once more.

'Get you fellers something?' he asks in an absent-minded way.

'Water,' says Hartmann. From Dr Schnell on the couch comes only a gentle snore.

\* \* \*

'The final requirement to join the Stasi – the third act of enlightenment, so to speak – was a letter to be written on or about the
candidate's eighteenth birthday.' Hartmann and Cutter have moved
to the kitchen where they sit side-by-side perched on stools at the
breakfast bar, where the light is better and where their conversation
will not disturb Dr Schnell. Hartmann has produced a fifth
protective folder containing a six-page letter in Gröber's handwriting that is now more assured.

'The third letter was different in that the candidates were required
to reveal to the Stasi the most intimate details about themselves,
their family, their friends. For example, did the candidate masturbate, how often, where? What were their sexual fantasies? Had
they had love affairs, with whom, and when? – and do not neglect
to describe the precise nature of the sexual acts. What did they
know of their parents' sex lives and *their* affairs? The same for
their siblings and their friends. And, anyway, who were their friends
and what did the candidate know about their political views, their
weaknesses, their crimes, their fears? Who did they know who used
illicit drugs or alcohol – and what and how much and when and
where? Who had too little money, or too much?

'In the eyes of the Stasi there was no betrayal too trivial or too
banal.' Hartmann's voice has taken on a weary, defeated tone but
Cutter senses something dangerous lurking at the edges, like a bare
electrical wire waiting to be touched. 'Even so, Candidate Gröber
excelled in his treachery. In this letter' – Hartmann holding up the
folder – 'he provides compromising information on thirteen of his
friends, and on the parents of five of them; three of his teachers,
including Fräulein David, his initial recruiter; a neighbour of the
Gröbers who had made disparaging remarks about the Party; even
his sister.'

'For Christ's sake!' says Cutter.

'Oh, yes, sir, believe me, even Ilse is not spared.' Roughly,
Hartmann pulls the letter from the protection of the folder and flips
over the pages until he finds the paragraph he needs. Translating on
the fly he says, 'I myself do not masturbate since I consider sexual
self-gratification to be an act of weakness. I encourage others to also
resist. However, I regret to say that I have twice observed my sister,
Ilse, masturbating in the bathroom. How did he "observe" her, Mr
Cutter. Did he walk in on her? Spy on her through the keyhole?'

Cutter can think of nothing to say.

'And finally, and most of all, he betrays his parents.' Hartmann turns to the final page of Karl Gröber's letter. 'My sister's illness' – Hartmann translating once more – 'is obviously of great concern to our family. By the way,' he tells Cutter, 'nowhere in the letter is there mention of his late brother, Heinz.' Reading again, Hartmann says, 'I believe that the doctors of the Democratic Republic are providing Ilse with the best possible treatment but I am ashamed to say this is an opinion my parents do not share. They have been deceived by the propaganda of the Western Imperialists – he means us,' Hartmann explains – 'into believing that Ilse could receive superior treatment in their capitalist hospitals. I have argued with my parents about this on several occasions. Lately they have refused to discuss the matter with me or in my presence. I believe it is possible they are conspiring to remove my sister from the GDR, and that could seriously endanger her health.' Hartmann drops the letter on to the breakfast bar as though it is soiled. 'Whether Gröber subsequently discovered how and when his parents intended to escape, the file does not say. It scarcely matters. As soon as this poison reached *Runde Ecke*, the Gröbers would have been placed under twenty-four-hour surveillance. They did not stand a chance.' Hartmann gets down from the stool and stretches his back. 'He might as well have shot them himself.'

Cutter picks up the letter and flicks slowly through the pages, scrutinising words he cannot comprehend – as he cannot comprehend the self-loving hate that caused them to be written. 'What a piece of stinking shit,' he says, referring to Karl Gröber.

'There is a coda to this episode, Mr Cutter,' Hartmann says, speaking quietly. 'Gröber was formally accepted into the Stasi five days after his mother and father were murdered but first he was required to perform military service. Do you know where the Stasi sent him? To the border guards. To Vacha. To the same unit that shot his parents. For the next eighteen months, *their* killers were *his* comrades.

'And do you know what he did in Vacha? He spied on his comrades for the Stasi. Weekly written reports for *Runde Ecke*.' Hartmann reaches into the red file once more and pulls out the thickest folder Cutter has seen so far. 'Meticulous, toxic reports.'

'You know, Felix, what I tell my people all the time is that it's never personal. That's the golden rule – you *never* let the assholes get under your skin.'

Hartmann nods as though he's heard this homily before.
'Well, guess what? That rule just got changed.'

A forty-minute catnap and Dr Schnell is fully restored. It is getting
close to midnight, six a.m. German time, and that makes it almost
twenty-four hours since he and Hartmann left Pullach on their
journey to New York. Hartmann's fading but Dr Schnell comes
into the kitchen pin-bright, asking for coffee and rich with ideas.

'Now, Aldus, my friend, can I suggest what we might do next?'
And hardly waiting for Cutter's response Dr Schnell continues,
'Which is take you through General Kessel's account of Gröber's
career in the Stasi. Because, Aldus, you will find it interesting, I
think, to compare what Kessel has to say with what is in the other
file – let us call it, for convenience, "the Moscow file" – and what
is also in the summary you received from the British.'

'Fine,' says Cutter.

'In broad terms the Moscow file is accurate but there are gaps;
rather large and very interesting gaps. For example, there is no
mention in the file, or in your summary, I suspect' – an apologetic
smile from Dr Schnell – 'of Gröber's numerous assignments outside
the GDR: Cuba, the first time in 1978 and then again in 1983;
Africa – specifically Angola, Mozambique – in 1978 and 1979;
Paraguay in 1978 and again in 1983; Iran in late 1979; Turkey in
1982; Libya in 1984 and 1987.' Dr Schnell is counting off the
countries on the fingers of both hands and running out of digits he
simply adds, 'Czechoslovakia, Nicaragua, Iraq, South Yemen, the
Sudan. There were other foreign assignments. Many more.'

'You're saying Gröber was a spy?' asks Cutter.

'Not in the conventional sense. Foreign espionage was the
responsibility of the HVA, the *Hauptverwaltung Aufklärung*, which
means' – Dr Schnell pulls a wry face – 'Main Administration for
Enlightenment. No, Gröber was more of an adviser, sometimes a
provocateur, sometimes . . .' Dr Schnell raises a hand in the fashion
of a gun that he points at Cutter's head. 'An assassin.'

Cutter feels as though he has lost any capacity to experience
surprise. Flatly he asks, 'Now you're telling me Gröber killed for
the Stasi?'

'A killer, Aldus – but, no, not for the Stasi. For Moscow, the
KGB. That at least was General Kessel's conclusion, based on
analysis that I think you will find persuasive.

'When Gröber returned from Vacha to Leipzig he was first assigned to Department M – "Post Control" – where his job was to obtain a copy of the ID card of every person who sent letters abroad. Then, within a year he was reassigned to Department Ten, which liaised with the other Warsaw Pact intelligence services; in Gröber's case, the KGB, which maintained an office in Leipzig right up until the end. Initially he was no more than a messenger boy, delivering packages from *Runde Ecke*. But Kessel convincingly describes how Gröber ingratiated himself with his new Russian friends. He began socialising with them, sometimes inviting them to his home for dinner.'

'He would require Ilse to cook for them,' says Hartmann – and Cutter discovers that he has not, after all, lost the capacity to be surprised.

'You're kidding me? After what he'd done, she *lived* with him?'

'In their parents' house on Karl-Heine-Strasse. For almost twenty years.' It seems to Cutter that a shadow passes over Hartmann's face before he adds, 'Like a couple.'

It is Dr Schnell who breaks the resulting silence. 'Felix, you look exhausted. You should rest.'

Cutter agrees and since Hartmann is far too tall – far too long – to stretch out on the couch, Cutter is adamant that he take the bedroom. Grumbling his objections, Hartmann retires. When Cutter goes to check that Hartmann has everything he needs, the lanky German is lying prone on the bed, dead to the world.

On the breakfast bar Cutter has before him a legal pad and a pen, ready to record specific details of Karl Gröber's activities and friends, details that were excluded from the Moscow file, and also from what Cutter now sees as the worthless summary obtained by Flint in London. Worse than worthless – misleading. A deliberate plant? In the back of Cutter's mind a dark thought is stirring, like something suspicious disturbed in the undergrowth.

Dr Schnell has before him the report of General Kessel open at the relevant page, but he is not yet quite ready to begin its dissection because first he wants to sing the general's praises.

'His report was compiled during the early months of 1989, when he had the benefit of hindsight. By then everybody – even Mielke, Aldus, even he knew that they were reaching the end; that the entire Eastern Bloc would crumble. But what Kessel recognised, what he discerned from Gröber's file, was that Karl Martin was a visionary: that he had *always* known it would end and that his entire career in the Stasi was designed to prepare the ground, his ground, for *afterwards.*

'You know, in Leipzig they have a joke. Why do former agents of the Stasi make the best taxi drivers? Because you just give them your name and they know where you live.' A forlorn smile from Dr Schnell.

'But Karl Martin Gröber was never going to drive a taxi, Aldus. He saw that when the end came, when sooner or later the capitalist system achieved its inevitable victory, the Eastern Bloc would require entrepreneurs to embrace the exciting new opportunities: organised prostitution, drug trafficking, arms dealing, extortion rackets, bank fraud, wholesale tax evasion. Oh, Aldus, he saw so many opportunities! And who could be better placed to run these new enterprises than the people who had – to a great extent – suppressed those opportunities during the Communist years. His Russian friends, of course, and the similar friends he had cultivated in Prague and Warsaw and Sofia and Tirana and Budapest – everywhere in the Warsaw Pact.

'And here is the clever part, Aldus; here is Karl Gröber's genius. What he foresaw all those years ago, what he knew would happen, was that when these bustling new enterprises were underway, when his friends were shipping their girls and their drugs and their guns to the West, when they were skimming ten cents off every dollar of foreign aid, when they were extorting their protection money from every new legitimate business they could squeeze, then they would need assistance to get their profits to the West, to launder them through a banking system they did not understand.

'They would need Karl Gröber's assistance, for he *did* understand the system.' Dr Schnell puts on his reading glasses. 'Let me quote you one short passage from Kessel's chronology of Gröber's assignments. He writes, "In February 1984, while formally assigned to headquarters Department Twenty-One" – also known as ZAIG, Aldus, the Central Group of Analysis and Information – "*Oberleutnant* Gröber" – first lieutenant; curiously, he never advanced beyond that rank – "received permission from the Minister" – Mielke, of course – "to set up and supervise a subgroup to study the Western banking system. The pretext was to establish the most secure method of disguising the source of operational funds sent overseas. The sub-group continued its work for three years" – the general underlined that, Aldus; *three years* – "without producing any recommendations or a final report. The information it obtained was seen only by Gröber." ' Dr Schnell removes his glasses and pinches the bridge of his nose. 'Three years, Aldus; a virtual degree course in money laundering.'

'Tell me something, Otto. Is there anything in there' – Cutter nods at Kessel's report – 'that's going to show us how to find this asshole?'

'I think so,' says Dr Schnell. 'But, first, I have a question. Our young friend, Felix, is very fulsome in his praise of your deputy director Flint. He says she has an intuitive grasp of covert operations unlike anyone he has ever known. Now, I do not necessarily trust Felix's judgement on this matter for it may not be entirely professional. He is, I think, a little . . . What is the word, Aldus: taken, yes? I think that Felix is a little taken with Miss Flint.'

'He wouldn't be the first,' says Cutter.

'So my question is this: Is she really that good?'

Cutter hesitates. His innate loyalty to Flint wrestles with his instinct to be objective – and then there is the small matter of the guilt he feels over what he knows he must do to her career.

'As an operational supervisor, in light of what happened to Pentecost, I have my doubts. She got burned, and I got a dead agent to bury as a result. Frankly, I think she fucked up. But as a covert *operator*, Otto, she's second to none.'

'Why?' asks Dr Schnell.

'Because she has this knack of becoming the person she's supposed to be. She doesn't just live her cover, she *is* her cover. She's like the best actress you've ever seen – and then some, because Flint's got an edge. It's her face, you see, it's a mask.'

'Ah, yes. Felix told me she was badly beaten.'

'More than that, Otto. Her faced was pulped, and they had to reconstruct it, and they took about a year, and you can't tell. Wait a second.'

Cutter goes to his living room and Dr Schnell hears the sounds of a lock being turned and of a drawer being opened, and then Cutter returns bearing a leather portfolio that he opens and places on the breakfast counter. There are two photographs inside, set side-by-side. 'Before and after,' says Cutter.

Even Dr Schnell blanches. He does not require his glasses to register the hideous aspects of the photograph on the left-hand side of the portfolio. It is of a barely recognisable face that might have been found on a corpse; one of those tortured corpses pulled from a mass grave.

Quickly he shifts his gaze to the other photograph, the one that shows Flint's 'after' face.

She is full-on to the camera, her head tilted very slightly to the right, looking directly into the lens. Her hair appears to be dark brown or even black though the strands that fall over the left side of her high, flawless forehead have caught the light and shimmer like gossamer. Her eyebrows are pronounced and arched and the eyes beneath them, the shape of laurel leaves, are set wide apart, amber pools of light. Her cheek bones are high and perfectly matched. Her nose is pert with small nostrils that are slightly flared. The philtrum, the space between the base of the nose and the upper lip, is unusually deep which gives the impression that her mouth is floating free, fractionally off-centre in that heart-shaped face that ends in a strong chin set above a bare throat. The lips are closed in a neutral expression but Dr Schnell can see the character in her mouth. He has not the remotest idea what she is thinking.

'A face you would never forget, right, Otto?'

'I would think not.'

Cutter grins and shakes his head. 'Wrong. She's got another edge because she can be two, even three people at the same time. I've seen her in the morning as some hot-shot lawyer you'd want on your side and, that night, as a high-class hooker you'd sell your soul for. And if you had hired her that morning and tried to buy her that night, you'd never know it was the same woman.'

'A mistress of disguise,' says Dr Schnell in a teasing tone.

'Not really. Oh, she'll do something with her hair, play around with some makeup, maybe change the colour of her eyes – but that's not what does it, Otto. It's the way she changes her voice patterns and her body language: the way she walks, the set of her head, the way you *think* she's feeling – except you can't tell what she's really feeling because of that mask of hers. The point is, for as long as she needs to be, she *is* that banker or that hooker or anything else she damn well wants to be. She's not just good, Otto, she's uncanny.'

'Then, Aldus, I am very sure that you should not fire your deputy director,' says Dr Schnell, and his tone is grave. 'Send her undercover once again. Send her to Leipzig.'

'Leipzig? Why?'

'Because if there is one person in the world who knows where Gröber can be found, it is Ilse. She still lives in the house on Karl-Heine-Strasse but now she is alone and it is much too large for her, and her health is not good. She is looking for paying guests, Aldus, some company, someone to share.'

Cutter is still, watchful as a cat.

'Ilse would prefer that they are a respectable couple, not too young but not too old either. A couple in their thirties, perhaps? Felix and Grace, perhaps?' Dr Schnell smiles. 'I think Ilse might enjoy the company of an uncanny woman. I know Felix will.'

# twenty-eight

Jarrett Crawford in the lobby of Cutter's building, on the brink of losing his Celtic temper; Pat, the doorman, in protective mode, barring his way.

'Goddamnit, I *have* to see him,' says Crawford.

'I've told you, I have strict orders from Mr Cutter: no more visitors tonight. Now, go on with you. Get out of here.'

Crawford has already shown the doorman his credentials. He is on the point of showing him his gun when the doors of the lift open and out step Aldus Cutter and Felix Hartmann and a third man who is dwarfed by them.

'Mr Cutter!' calls Crawford over the doorman's shoulder, causing them to stop in their tracks, causing the small man to duck his head and turn his back as though he has heard the crack of gunfire.

'Crawford! What in hell's name are you doing here?' roars Cutter, striding across the lobby, using his body to block Crawford's view of the companions he has left behind.

'I told him, Mr Cutter,' says Pat who looks as if he's ready to brawl.

So, for that matter, does Cutter, now standing toe-to-toe with Crawford, livid anger in his face. 'Well?'

'I've been trying to reach you.'

'Well, now you have, what do you want?'

'It's about Flint, sir.' Crawford leans forward and lowers his voice to a near-whisper. 'She's gone crazy, Mr Cutter, totally fucking berserk.'

'I see,' says Cutter as though Crawford has told him nothing remotely alarming. He puts one arm on Crawford's shoulder and turns him around and walks him towards the entrance door. 'Jerry, you got a car here?'

'Yes, sir.'

'Where is it?'

Crawford nods to his right. 'Halfway down the block.'

'Well, go and sit in it and wait for me, and Jerry' – they're on the pavement now, Cutter turning back towards the building – 'who I've been seeing is none of your frigging business so, while you're waiting, keep your eyes closed.'

Crawford walks smiling along East 63rd Street, recalling a conversation with Felix Hartmann. They were on a plane to somewhere, telling war stories to pass the time, and Hartmann had a good one about his former boss at the BND: a Dr Otto Something-or-other, as Crawford recalls, but Hartmann said they called him The Gnome.

'Shoot,' says Cutter, settling himself into the front passenger seat of Crawford's car.

'She's burnt down the house and she's damned near killed four people and now she's gone AWOL. And her father's in a coma, maybe dying.'

'Whoa!' says Cutter. 'One step at a time.'

'Okay, this afternoon Grace called Rocco Morales from Connecticut, asking him to check out the IDs of four INS people. She didn't say why but Rocco got the impression they had turned up at her place. Anyway, the IDs were fake – nothing to do with INS – and Rocco called her back and asked if she needed any help, and she said no, she could handle it.

'Next thing, she gets a call from some cop in England telling her—'

'Whoa again,' says Cutter. 'How do you know she got a call?'

'Because we're listening to her phone.'

'We are?'

'Sure,' says Crawford – but he says it tentatively, as if he's not so sure.

'On whose say-so?'

'Yours.'

The cold look on Cutter's face tells him this may not be true.

'Mr Stark told Rocco you'd authorised it. Because you were worried she was out of control.'

'Did he?' Cutter's staring straight ahead now, talking to the windshield. 'And when did Nathan Stark tell Rocco to listen to Flint's phone?'

'First thing Monday morning. I was down in Rocco's room when Nathan . . . Oh, fuck!' says Crawford as the truth becomes all too clear.

'Crawdaddy, this conversation we're having, this is just between you and me. You mention this to a living soul and I'll—'

'I've got it, sir.'

Now Cutter turns to look at him, demanding eye contact. 'You sure?'

'I'm sure, Mr Cutter.'

Cutter resumes staring at the windshield. 'Go ahead. The call from England.'

'Right. Well, this guy from the Oxfordshire Constabulary says Flint's daddy has been attacked in his home but they'd found him in a dog pen and—'

'A what?'

'A cage – one of the dog cages he keeps in his surgery.'

'Go on.'

'The cop didn't say who or what hit him, but Dr Flint's in a local hospital, in intensive care, and the cop says that Grace should get over there pretty damn quick because he might not make it, or that's what he implied.'

'And she said?'

'On her way. And then,' adds Crawford, 'she sets her house on fire.'

'One step at a time,' Cutter reminds him.

'Rocco heard her make a 911 call reporting a fire. She gave a fake name and said she could see it from the road. The local fire service got there within twelve minutes and the place was already an inferno, and they said the stench of heating oil was unbelievable. She had a tank of the stuff, one thousand gallons, out in the garage.'

'Heating oil doesn't burn all that well,' says Cutter conversationally.

'It does if you mix it with gasoline,' Crawford replies, and Cutter nods.

'The house was gone. They couldn't do shit to save it. And the barn was about to go because some of the embers from the house had gotten into the roof and the whole place was smoking. Anyway, the fire fighters, they douse that and then they open up the barn and they find four guys – actually, three guys and a woman – trussed up like a bunch of turkeys, except they're in chains.'

'The phoney INS people?'

'We're assuming so but as soon as the chains were off those four were out of there before anybody could stop them. The local cops put out an All Points for them but—' Crawford pulls a face that says he's not holding his breath. 'They've also put out a bulletin for Flint.'

'Who's on her way to the UK?' Cutter supposes.

'Not on any plane that's left tonight,' says Crawford. 'Leastways, not under her own name.'

'Oh, come on, Jerry, you think Grace doesn't have some fake IDs stashed away? Just for a rainy day?'

'No one matching her description,' Crawford insists.

'Jerry! This is *Flint* we're talking about.'

'What do you want me to do? Call London, have her picked up at the airport?'

'God forbid. Anyway, we know where she's headed, don't we? Give me a second.' Cutter drums his fingers on the dashboard while he considers what to do. Then, 'You got any gasoline in this thing?'

'Sure,' says Crawford, half-surprised.

'And you know where Felix lives?'

'Yeah,' says Crawford, trying to put two and two together.

'Then drive me there. Felix has got a plane to catch.'

From a payphone in the cavernous lobby of Grand Central Station, Deputy Director Nathan Stark dials a London number. It is early in the morning UK time and he is prepared to be patient but Nigel Ridout is an early riser, evidently, for he answers on the second ring.

'Yes,' says the deputy head of the East European Controllerate of the Secret Intelligence Service, otherwise known as MI6.

'It didn't work out because the hired help screwed up. But your girlfriend's on her way to you anyway, on her way home. Virgin Atlantic, Kennedy to Heathrow.' Stark checks his watch. 'Should be with you in about four hours.'

'Splendid,' says Ridout. 'Mission accomplished, then' – but Stark has already cut the line.

# twenty-nine

For her small, rainy-day collection of fake IDs, the ones she keeps for extreme emergencies, Grace Flint relies on the private sector where no records are kept; where there is no paper trail leading back to a likeness in any corresponding file. In the southern French city of Marseilles, in the crooked alleyways of the Quartier du Panier that stands high above the Old Port, Flint found a forger – a master craftsman – who, for twenty thousand French francs and no questions asked, prepared a passport, a *carte d'identité* and press credentials in the name of Katia Portelli, freelance photographer. Flint has never used the Portelli identity – until now.

Tanned, henna-haired and green-eyed, snappily dressed in an olive green linen shirt that is open over a black halter top and tight black leather pants, Katia Portelli stubbornly occupies a row of three seats on a Boeing 747 that took off from Kennedy airport, and that is now edging across the time zones of the Atlantic towards the beckoning pinkish-yellow glow of an earlier new dawn. She needs to be stubborn because although the economy cabin is no more than half-full, the spare seats next to Katia have, apparently, irresistible appeal. 'This seat free?' and 'Do you mind?' and 'Don't I know you?' and, the boldest yet, 'Fancy some company?' – and Flint has reached into her repertoire to meet each enquiry with the look that Frenchwomen in particular have mastered to deal with unwanted attention; a look of disdain that is cold enough to chill wine.

The luckless lotharios are leaving her alone for now and she is sprawled across the three seats, her back propped against the bulkhead, taking frequent sips from an oversized bottle of Evian water. Despite the instructions of the cabin crew, her window blind is cracked open a few inches so that she can measure the Boeing's lumbering progress towards the distant light. The captain says they have an exceptionally strong tail wind in their favour yet, it seems to Flint, they do no more than inch across the still-black sky.

She feels suspended in time – and her feelings about her father are suspended, on hold. In the Boeing's womb she will not permit herself to imagine the scene in the intensive care unit of Horton General Hospital, nor will she contemplate the possibility that he is dying, that he might already be dead. For now she keeps him safe by holding in the corner of her mind a single vivid image of him: John Flint in his surgery, roaring his delight every time he first catches sight of his visiting daughter, his face transformed, alive.

It helps that her consciousness is largely absorbed with thoughts of her husband. The act of setting fire to her house – burning it to the ground, she hopes – has achieved its purpose of detachment: of severing her from the illusion that anything real ever happened at Miller's Reach. The effect on Flint has been cathartic. With her deceiving sanctuary in ruins, she now feels free to poke among the ashes of her marriage.

But not alone – not yet.

Visiting the truth about herself requires a self-protective technique that she developed long ago to cope with – or at least to soften – the havoc caused by unbearable pain.

*So, let me get this straight. You were married once before to another shit just like Ben and you learned nothing – nothing at all?*

This is Flint, the cynical inquisitor, the role she's played countless times in hard cop–soft cop situations.

*No, not like Ben. Jamie was nothing like Ben.*

This is Grace, the accused, who will not be led easily to her confession.

*Really? You don't see any similarities? Their liquid eyes, their easy smiles? What about their hands, Grace, those lovely long, graceful fingers that you wanted to feel on your skin?*

*That's crap. You're just talking about superficial things that weren't important.*

*All right. Let's do it your way* – the hard way, Flint, the inquisitor, implies.

*How long had you known Jamie when you married him?*

*Eight, nine months. Something like that.*

*And how much did you know about him – really know about him when you married?*

*That he was clever, full of curiosity, funny, gentle, kind—*
*Facts, Grace, give me facts. His antecedents.*

Grace, the accused, is aware that, for a cop, she was strangely uninterested in the 'facts' about her first husband.

*He was born in Cornwall – St Ives, I think. His father was some kind of banker. I'm not sure what his mother did – Jamie was estranged from his parents by the time I met him. He had a sister, Nicky, living in Zambia – or maybe it was Tanzania—*

*Maybe it was Tanzania? You think? You're not sure?*

*I wasn't marrying his bloody family*, Grace says defensively.

*What were you sure about, Grace?*

*That I loved him. That he loved me – or so I thought. That he fancied me, certainly.*

The fuselage of the Boeing trembles, disturbed by turbulence.

*How long had you known Ben when you married him?*

*Eight months. Almost.*

*And how much did you know about his antecedents?*

*Quite a lot, actually.* Grace feels her first footing on surer ground.

*How did you know? Because he told you?*

*Because I had him checked out.*

Flint knows this is a hollow truth. *Really? And why did you do that?*

*It was a mistake*, Grace admits, *a misunderstanding. I'd met him once, in a bar in Miami – I was down there talent-spotting for the FSF – and we'd chatted for a while and I liked him – nothing more than that. But then a couple of weeks later I had to go back to Miami and I thought maybe we could have a drink or something, and since all I knew was his name and vaguely what he did for a living I asked a friend at Metro-Dade PD to run a trace. I was really only looking for a telephone number or an address but my friend jumped to the conclusion that Ben was a suspect or a potential informant and he ran a full check. Came up with his DOB, Social Security number, driver's licence, pilot's licence, employment record, credit history – which wasn't that great – two speeding tickets, the works. The second time I met Ben, and we started talking about ourselves, I knew most of what he was going to say before he opened his mouth.*

Another pocket of turbulence and this time the Boeing bucks. The seat belt light comes on and a couple of cabin attendants begin moving down the darkened aisles checking to see that their dozing charges are secured.

*And did what he told you about himself tally with what you thought you knew?*

*I never asked him about his debts or the speeding tickets, if that's what you mean.* Perps, when they are nervous, often make evasive replies.

*Let's go back to the first time you met Ben. You say you met him in a bar?*

*Tobacco Road in downtown Miami, close to the river. On Friday evenings it's a hang-out, a watering hole for some law enforcement people: cops, DEA agents, prosecutors from the US Attorney's office. I used to go there most Fridays when I was based in Miami.*

*But you were no longer based in Miami, were you, Grace? Why did you go back to Tobacco Road? Not for old times' sake, surely?*

*I went there with Ruth Apple.* Grace spits this out, the way you do when truth has a sour taste. *I was talking to her about joining the FSF, coming to New York.*

*But Ruth didn't want to move, did she, Grace? Ruth didn't want to join the FSF?*

*Nope. Not at that point. She was still wedded to the DEA.*

*And Florida, Grace? Didn't Ruth just love being in Florida? She was fine, doing well at DEA, happy that her folks were just up the coast in Boca Raton? But you wouldn't take no for an answer, would you, Grace? You knew that she was a good undercover, could be a great undercover, and that's what you wanted, wasn't it? Someone in your own image? Someone you could mould?*

*Shut up!*

The Boeing drops abruptly and the synergy of the event makes Flint's blood jump. For a ghastly moment all she can think of is Ruth falling like a stone. Ruth hadn't made a sound when she was thrown from Karl Gröber's helicopter but all around her Flint hears muted cries of alarm.

*Let's concentrate on Ben. Would that be easier for you? Please.*

*So you went with Ruth to Tobacco Road and Ben was there—*

*No, he wasn't there, not when we arrived. The place gets pretty crowded on Friday nights but Ruth and I had bagged this table in the corner of the courtyard, and we'd chatted for about an hour, and she was leaving because she was driving up to Boca, and we'd just said goodbye and suddenly Ben was standing there.*

*Standing there?*

*Wanting to take Ruth's seat.*

*Do you remember what he said?*

*'Do you mind?'*

*And you didn't mind?*

*Not really.*

Flint, the inquisitor, uses silence like a knife.

*No, I didn't mind. Ruth had been . . . well, difficult, coming up with all kinds of objections about the FSF and New York and, frankly, I'd had enough of cop talk for one day. He looked like a nice guy and he wasn't coming on to me, or not much, and I thought . . . No, I didn't mind.*

*How did you know he wasn't a cop?*

*I always know.*

*You've never dated a cop, have you, not for a long time? Not since you first joined the Met? Never had a relationship with a fellow officer? Why is that, Grace?*

*Oh, let's not go there.*

Flint would like to go there, for Grace's aversion to personal relationships with cops of the male species is an interesting paradox and fertile ground. Another time, Flint decides.

*So?*

*So, he sat down and we started chatting about this and that: Miami, the weather – nothing of any consequence. We got on to jazz because that's what they play at Tobacco Road. I remember that he liked Pat Metheny and Keith Jarrett but that Bach was much more his thing. He said that Bach was the only composer whose music pierced the membrane between our world and whatever lies beyond it.*

*Did he ask what you did?*

*Not that I recall, but I wouldn't have told him if he did. 'Investment banking' is what I would have said, like always.*

*But he told you what he did for a living?*

*Yes, he said he watched birds, just like that, 'I watch birds' – and for a moment I thought he was hitting on me, 'Oh, Christ, here we go'. Then he told me he had a temporary assignment flying a small plane over the Everglades, photographing migratory patterns. That was it. Once he got on to the subject of birds, I thought he'd never stop.*

*And you stayed?*

*For a couple of hours.*

*That long?*

*There was nothing else I particularly wanted to do.*

How do the wings stay on? When an airplane weighing some three hundred tons flies into violently twisting winds that resemble the funnel of a tornado tipped on its side; when the plane drops one hundred feet or more, and then recovers, and then drops again, why aren't the wings ripped from the fuselage? Flint holds an explanation but it is one that came breezily from Ben and anything that Ben told her is now fatally compromised; assumed false until proved otherwise.

This is clear-air turbulence the Boeing has encountered, the kind that doesn't show up on weather radar, and since the flight crew can't see it they can't avoid it and there is nothing else to do except ride it out. A terse announcement from the flight deck has sent the flight attendants hurrying to their seats. Above Flint's head a panel has opened and three emergency oxygen masks hang like empty nooses dangling from a gallows.

*Let's concentrate on what we're doing, shall we?*

*Please.*

*Could Ben have known you would be at Tobacco Road that night?*

*No way. It was a last-minute thing. Ruth and I were just passing by on the way to my hotel when we decided to stop for a drink.*

*Could Ben have followed you there?*

*Why would he?*

*Maybe he was in Miami to get close to you. Maybe that was the whole point.*

This possibility has been lingering in Grace's subconscious for several days, hanging like a black cloud. She has chosen not to confront it, until now.

*Thank you very fucking much! What are you saying? That it was all a lie right from the very start? Well, you're wrong.*

*Am I?*

*Think about it. When I met Ben, Operation Pentecost didn't exist. Karl Gröber didn't exist, so far as we knew. I had known Ben*

*for months, we were about to get married, when Gröber and his
creeps first came into the frame.*

*Who said anything about Pentecost?*

*Well, that's the operation he's bloody compromised, isn't it?*

*Oh, I see. The little bit of hope you're clinging to is that Ben
became a rat after you got married. Then somebody, something,
with an interest in Pentecost came along and said, 'Hey, we know
a guy who can get his hands on the operational file.' And they had
some hold over Ben because of his past – and he's surely got a past
with all that fake history, hasn't he, Grace? So Ben was forced to
betray you. Is that it? Is that what you're clinging to?*

*It's possible.*

*Really?*

In Flint's experience there is a critical moment in most interrogations when it pays to close the last escape hatch. You let the perp
run for a while, let them twist and turn looking for a way out,
allowing them to fool themselves that there just *might* be a way
out, and then you tell them: No. Just when they think it can't get
any worse, it does.

*Shall I tell you what I think, Grace, what I know? From the very
first moment you saw him – from long before you first saw him –
Ben Gates was a mole. Invented, created, for one reason and one
reason only: to penetrate the FSF by penetrating you.*

*You don't* know *that.*

*Yes I do, and so do you, and I'll tell you why. The Metro-Dade
PD do a full background check on Ben and because it's a favour to
you they do it properly, and what they find is copper-bottomed.
Ben Gates exists because there are countless documents that say he
exists, right down to the speeding tickets. And when this all comes
out in the wash, I know and you know that every bit of the legend
that was created will be supported by corresponding documents on
file at the relevant agency. Ben isn't a paper hanger who bought
some fake ID, Grace. Ben is real – except he's not. Who can do
that, Grace? Who in America can make a phantom real?*

*US Marshal's Witness Protection for sure. The CIA, I suppose,
the IRS. Maybe the Feebs, maybe DEA.*

*Exactly, Grace, only a federal government agency. Now, do you
really think they would go to all that trouble to create Ben Gates
on the off-chance that he might meet and marry somebody useful,
somebody who just happens to work for an organisation they*

*might want to infiltrate? I don't think so and if you're honest with
yourself, nor do you – and do be honest with yourself, Grace,
because you've got to come to terms with this. Face it: Ben Gates
was created specifically to stalk you, charm you, seduce you and
fuck you in more ways than one.*

They're through the turbulence now. The captain is saying he's
sorry if it got a little bumpy back there.

*He didn't seduce me. I thought he'd never make a move so I
jumped him.*

Grace, the accused, clinging to her last bit of hope.

# England

# thirty

In the ornate dining room of the Reform Club on London's Pall Mall (that is, curiously, called the Coffee Room), Nigel Ridout of MI6 and A.J. Devereaux of MI5 enjoy an early breakfast. On several levels there is a debilitating rivalry between Britain's spies and counter-spies but Ridout and Devereaux consider themselves above that fray. They were both cut from elegant cloth, they attended similar privileged schools and the same Oxford college. Although Devereaux is the senior in rank, and eight years older, they share attitudes and some acquaintances and a taste for vibrant women. Watching them together you might even think they were friends.

'I'm aware that she's dangerous when cornered, Alan' – this is Ridout speaking of Flint – 'but can she hunt?'

'Oh, I'll say.' Devereaux seems enthusiastic, almost amused. 'She hunted one chap in particular as though he was a fox, a fellow by the name of Frank Harling. Picked up his scent in the Caribbean and tracked him from Italy to France to Cyprus – and then she shot him, would you believe? It was supposed to be in self-defence but, frankly, I rather doubt it.'

'And this was on her own initiative? I mean, her pursuit of Harling, it was never officially sanctioned?'

'Well, the Caribbean part was; a joint operation against some phoney bank with Aldus Cutter's cowboys and Scotland Yard that happened to stumble across Harling's trail. After that, when she got back to London, she was supposed to take sick leave and leave Harling to the grown-ups, instead of which she slipped out of the UK on a false passport and went hunting alone.'

Ridout sips weak Earl Grey tea, no milk or lemon, and nibbles on unbuttered toast; an ascetic's breakfast and all that he needs.

'So, after the Caribbean, she had no access to official resources?'

'Ah,' says Devereaux, who is feasting on a plate of kedgeree, 'not entirely true. No *official* access to official resources, but Flint is rather good at pinching the silver while one's back is turned. She beguiled a *flic* in Paris, one Inspector Bourdonnec, into helping her far more than he should have done – strictly off the books, of course – and Cutter also fed her information, I wouldn't be surprised.'

Ridout frowns, not entirely pleased with these revelations, it seems. Devereaux, who wishes to be helpful, seeks to reassure him.

'But I have no doubt she would have found Harling in any event, sooner or later. Bloody-minded is the best way to describe her, Nigel; irredeemably bloody-minded.'

Ridout has not disclosed the reason for MI6's interest in Flint and Devereaux will not ask. And Devereaux has not disclosed that Harling was an asset for MI5, nor that it was because of him that a bomb exploded in the centre of Paris, shredding the legs of Inspector Bourdonnec. Ridout has heard a whisper of these embarrassments but he will not mention them. When it suits them, the spy and the counter-spy exchange information about their own failings but never indiscretions.

But it crosses Devereaux's mind that the last time he saw Flint was when she came to Thames House as bold as brass to say she might not keep her silence about Frank Harling unless MI5 made a donation – a very generous donation – to the Gilles Bourdonnec lift fund. He recalls her standing in his office in her flat shoes and her sober suit, those striking eyes signalling her contempt as he tried to counter-bluff by reading aloud some of the more stringent sanctions of the Official Secrets Act.

Still wishing to be helpful, Devereaux adds, 'And she's got the balls of an elephant.'

Nigel Ridout nods his thanks.

Passing quickly through the lobby of Ceauşescu Towers, Ridout takes the corridor that leads to the library and, beyond it, a steel door that guards nothing more secret than the MI6 staff gymnasium where an underdressed Stephanie Cooper-Cole is bench-pressing weights. She does not hear him arrive and he remains mute, admiring the firmness of her breasts and the strength of her arms.

'Ah, there you are, Stephanie,' he calls the moment she senses his presence, as if he doesn't know where she is to be found at eight thirty on almost any weekday morning.

'Where else would I be, Nigel?' she says crabbily, wondering how long he's been watching.

'Need a word,' says Ridout. 'See you by the pool' – his small joke for, despite the aspirations of its planners, the headquarters of the Secret Intelligence Service does not contain a swimming pool; an extravagance too far its masters decided, rather late in the day.

Denied their pool, the planners substituted a badminton court, which is where Ridout waits while Cooper-Cole makes herself decent. He paces small circles around the service line, replaying in his mind A.J. Devereaux's parting advice delivered while they stood on the steps of the Reform: 'If you're thinking of using Flint for something, do bear in mind that she's a tad less controllable than an unstable bomb. If you decide to light the fuse you will keep your head down, won't you, old chap?'

Sound advice, no doubt, and Ridout will heed it. Keeping his head down well describes the strategy he has in mind.

In a better mood now, dressed in a tracksuit, a towel around her neck, her hair still wet from the shower, Cooper-Cole arrives with a jaunty challenge: 'Fancy a game, Nigel?'

'I fancy you on your bike, young Stephanie,' says Ridout. 'Heathrow, terminal two, a greeting party for Flint. She's flying Virgin, not BA. Take the wretched Fellowes with you.' He checks his watch. 'You've got two hours.'

'And what exactly do you want us to do after we've "greeted" her, Nigel?'

'Don't be so literal, Stephanie. You don't "greet" her – of course you don't. You *observe* her, follow her, keep her under surveillance. Make sure she gets home safely and gets to see her Pa, should he live that long.'

A grimace from Cooper-Cole, for Ridout is picking at an open wound.

'Christ! Look at that,' Fellowes had said when they had finished searching Dr Flint's empty house and returned to the barn to find the door no longer locked.

John Flint stuffed into a cage looking like a rag doll, the hair on the back of his head matted with blood.

Gingerly Cooper-Cole had opened the cage door and felt the pulse on his neck. It was sluggish and his breathing was shallow but she had made an instant decision not to call for medical assistance; not immediately. Instead they had searched the barn for Mandrake until they were satisfied he had slipped away – and then she and Fellowes also slipped away, leaving Dr Flint in his cage, closing the barn door behind them, and it was not until they reached Oxford that she'd told Fellowes to make an anonymous call to the police.

'Quite right, too!' Ridout had said, approving of her decision. 'Always keep the bigger picture in mind, Stephanie.'

But Cooper-Cole knows that Dr Flint's condition could only have worsened during the delay she caused and she feels, if not exactly guilt, then regret. Nigel being Nigel, he scratches at her vulnerability.

'Do you suppose he'll live?' Ridout asks. 'Any news, is there?'

'He's critical but stable,' Cooper-Cole says flatly, refusing to rise to his bait, relaying what the hospital had told her when she'd called an hour ago claiming to be Dr Flint's daughter.

'Well, it doesn't really matter either way, does it?'

Ridout watches her expressionless face.

'Dead or alive, it makes no difference.'

She still won't react.

'Not in operational terms. Just so long as Grace knows.'

Cooper-Cole swallows and asks, 'Knows what, Nigel?'

'That it was Mandrake, her Ben, who clobbered her poor Pa. Put him in the hospital – and perhaps, God forbid, the cemetery.'

That blow scores and she feels her jaw quiver.

'And then what?'

'And then she'll look for him, won't she? She's good at that, I'm told. One whiff of Mandrake's fetid odour is all she needs and she'll follow him, hound him, root him out from wherever he's hiding.'

Cooper-Cole takes the towel from around her neck and rubs at her hair. 'Very clever, Nigel, very neat. There's just one tiny flaw.'

'Mmm?' Ridout seems to doubt the possibility of any imperfection in his scheme.

'If it's just Fellowes and me, we can't possibly maintain covert surveillance on a moving target, can we? I'm going to need five teams of four watchers, minimum, more unless she gets very lucky – and I don't know where you think you're going to find them.'

'To do what, for heaven's sake?'

'To follow her to Mandrake. That's the point, isn't it? You want Flint to lead us to Mandrake?'

Nigel Ridout's bland features rarely show emotion but now his face is a picture of incredulity. 'Good God! You don't get it, do you? I don't want Flint to lead you anywhere *near* Mandrake. I want *her* to find Mandrake and when she does – when she holds her Ben to account for what he's done – I don't want you or anyone from the firm within a hundred miles of them.' Ridout takes her arm. 'Am I getting through to you, Stephanie? Is the cold light dawning on you, *Stephanie?*'

It is, and Cooper-Cole involuntarily shivers.

Ridout at his desk, gazing at a computer monitor, reading his email on the internal secure messaging system. Cooper-Cole halfway out of the door with the hulking Fellowes following in her wake.

She stops and turns to pose an afterthought: 'What if he can't tell her it was Mandrake? What if . . .' She was prepared to say, *What if John Flint dies?* but the words stick in her throat. 'What if he doesn't come out of the coma?'

'Then you'll have to find some other way to tell her, won't you?' says Ridout, keeping his eyes on the screen.

# thirty-one

In one corner of her father's hospital room Grace Flint stirs, drawn from half-sleep by a perception that something has changed. She holds her breath so that she may hear better the clicks and sighs of the apparatus that is keeping John Flint alive. Her eyes race to the screen of a black box positioned above the bed on which green lines register his heartbeat and respiratory function and, seeing that the waves are regular and ceaseless, she feels a flutter of relief in her chest.

She gets up stiffly from a chair that is just large enough to curl up in and goes to his bedside, careful not to disturb the mass of tubes and wires and IVs attached to his body. In the glow of the bed-light his face seems skeletal, the colour of parchment; an old man's face she barely recognises, and her admission of that makes her ashamed. His forehead feels clammy and cold to her touch. Were it not for the machines, she could easily believe she was looking at a corpse.

A polite cough disturbs her bleak reflections and a male voice says, 'Excuse me – Miss Flint?' She looks up from her father's face to see a backlit figure looming in the doorway, another hovering behind. 'Detective Inspector Flint?' A rush of absurd vanity urges her to reply, *Actually it's Deputy Director Flint*, but she merely nods to acknowledge her former rank in the Metropolitan police force to which she no longer belongs. Come to think of it, she knows it is very likely that she no longer belongs to the FSF either.

'DI Drake, Banbury CID. Might we have a word?'

Flint will go into the corridor and stand with her back against the half-open door but no further. 'We won't disturb him, Inspector,' she says coldly. 'I wish we could. I wish he'd wake up now and tell us to bloody shut up, but he won't.' She knows it's not their fault but right now no one is safe from her anger.

'Detective Constable Bastable,' says Drake, nodding towards his companion whose bright, insolent eyes flick over Flint, taking in the henna hair, the fake tan, the halter top, the tight leather pants. He's not the first today to have silently implied that her Katia Portelli disguise is not wholly appropriate for a death-watch. *Sod you, DC Bastable.*

'So,' she says to Drake, 'who did this to my father?'

'We don't know. We were hoping you might have some ideas.'

*Oh, great! It's the plod brigade.* Turnip-tops, her father would call them.

'I was three thousand miles away when it happened, Inspector. I *live* in America.'

Drake has calm eyes and an air of infinite patience. 'We know that, Miss Flint,' he says, stripping away her courtesy police rank as casually as he endowed it, 'but you still might know who did it. Your father certainly knew them.'

'What?'

'No forced entry, two glasses in the kitchen sink that had contained whisky, according to the analysis. Two beds slept in: your father's and the bed in what I believe to be your room; the room he keeps for you when you come home.'

*My room? The pond-slime who did this slept in my bed?*

'Prints?' she asks, keeping her thoughts to herself.

'No, the glasses had been wiped. The assailant also wiped the table lamp in your father's study, which is what he used as a weapon.'

*Sweet Jesus!* The base of the lamp was made of cast-iron and must have weighed twenty pounds.

'There is another reason why we think you know the man who did this.' Drake pauses because Flint has turned to stare into her father's room. She is thinking of her childhood, of the untroubled days before her mother vanished. Of lying in bed listening to the sound of her father's typewriter tapping out the murder mysteries that he wrote as a diversion. Of, more than once, creeping downstairs, careful to avoid the parts of the treads that squeaked. Of slipping into the study behind her father's back. Of climbing on to the low table where the lamp sat, ready to launch herself at her father's unsuspecting neck. Of his sudden, thwarting cry of 'Muppet!' – for he always knew she was there. Of him turning and sweeping her from the table into his arms, tickling her small body until she was made helpless by fits of giggles.

'I'm sorry,' Flint says vaguely, turning to face Drake. 'You were saying?'

'You haven't been to the house yet, have you, Miss Flint?'

'No, I came straight here.'

'Well, it's exactly as we found it – apart from the mess in the study where the attack took place, which I've had cleaned up.' He waits for Flint's wan smile of thanks. 'And when you do go home, what you'll see is that the house wasn't ransacked or even searched. There's no sign of any disturbance. Except' – Drake checks the corridor with his eyes as though to make sure he cannot be overheard – 'in your bedroom. What you'll find there is, your bed's been moved to one side and a section of floorboard that was under the bed has been lifted, pulled up. That tells us something, doesn't it, Miss Flint?'

'Does it?' she says. 'What?'

'Helps us to narrow the field?'

DC Bastable maintains his stolid silence but he folds his chubby arms to add emphasis to what sounds to Flint more like an accusation than a question.

'Go on, Inspector.'

'I think we can safely surmise that at some point in time something was placed, secreted, as it were, in the cavity under that floorboard by somebody who had access to your bedroom. And, two nights ago, that same person, in all likelihood – somebody your father knew, somebody he would share a drink with, somebody he would offer a bed for the night; not one of the beds in the spare room but *your* bed – returned to the house to retrieve it. Now, I don't mean to be disrespectful, Miss Flint, but how many men have had access to your bedroom at Glebe Farm?'

One, she thinks. *Fucking Ben.*

She feels bruised, beaten up, as though DC Bastable has worked her over with his farm-boy's fists. Instead he has found them plastic chairs to sit on and coffee in plastic cups. There is a sour taste to the coffee but it is scalding hot – fresh out of the microwave, she suspects – and she hopes it may thaw her frozen insides. On her bare arms she can see goose pimples showing through the fake tan.

'Are you cold, Grace?' asks Inspector Drake, moving to the

familiar, as all coppers will inevitably do in the course of their interrogations.

Flint would like to have her shirt; she would like one of them to fetch it, but the shirt hangs on the chair in her father's room and she will not permit them to go in there.

'No.' She shakes her head. 'I'm fine.'

She has not yet answered Drake's question about the visitors to her bedroom, and he is shrewd enough not to have pressed her. He waits, watching her face, presumably believing that he can learn something from that mask.

'Inspector, when I was twelve I went to boarding school, Tudor Hall. I only rarely came home at weekends and I spent most of the holidays in London, staying at the home of my best friend. When I was sixteen – sixteen and a half – I became ill. I was in hospital for a while and then I went to live in Paris until I was eighteen. What I'm trying to explain to you is that the boyfriends I had were not from around here and never came here; never came to Glebe Farm.'

It is part of Flint's tradecraft that she builds her lies on solid foundations of truth.

'After Paris I moved to London where I eventually joined the Met. That was very difficult for my father because he did not have a high opinion of police officers.'

Flint falters and Drake says, 'I know, Grace, I've read his file.'

'Have you?' She allows herself to show just a flash of surprise; nothing too melodramatic. 'All right, then you probably know that when I was sixteen I had a sort of breakdown. I started having dreams that my father had killed my mother and I was eventually persuaded they were real; suppressed memories coming back as dreams. I went to the police and accused him of murder, and they believed me, and he was given a very bad time. By your force, Inspector. Frankly, you lot were bastards, way out of line.'

Drake nods his understanding.

'The point is that after that he hated coppers, except me, and since I dated a couple of coppers when I first joined the Met I *never* brought them home. Then I met Jamie, my first husband, who wasn't a copper but he was allergic to the countryside. I mean really allergic: two miles out of London and he'd start sneezing. So, he never came to Glebe Farm either. And then, after we split up, I was sent to the States and I've been there or on other overseas assignments ever since, pretty much.'

'I see what you're saying, Grace.' Drake rests his elbows on his knees and leans forward in a confidential manner. 'Basically you're saying that no man's had access to your bedroom at Glebe Farm, to your knowledge?'

'Not quite.' Drake looks confused, as he is meant to. 'In America I met my second husband, Ben, who is also not a copper. After our honeymoon we came to stay with Dad for a few days and, yes, he did have' – for the first time since Drake's set eyes on her she smiles – 'access to my bedroom. Well, he would, wouldn't he?'

There is no response from Drake; no answering smile, nothing in the eyes. 'And this Ben, your husband, he's American is he?'

'Canadian.'

'But he's in America now?'

'Africa, actually, for the past couple of weeks. He's an ornithologist. He's watching birds in Tanzania.'

'Spoken to him, have you?'

'He's in the middle of the bush. With twenty other people.'

Drake leans back in his chair and stretches his arms. 'Bastable, fetch Miss Flint another coffee, would you?'

Flint knows better than to break the silence that endures. He's testing her, waiting for her to embellish her story, as liars are prone to do.

'I'll tell you what's intriguing, Grace,' Drake eventually says. 'We know from the forensics – the blood splatter and so on – that when your father was attacked he was sitting at his desk trying to make a phone call. He had his address book open to the page on which he kept all of your numbers – and only your numbers – so it's a fair bet that it was you he was trying to call. Only he couldn't, because the phone line had been cut. You see?'

Drake holds up two fingers and brings them together like the blades of a pair of wire-cutters.

'Now, what gets my imagination racing is this: Who would want to stop your father calling you? What was he going to tell you that was so important? Or, perhaps it wasn't important to him – not to your father. Perhaps he just wanted you to know that so-and-so had turned up safely. Who could that be, Grace? Who wouldn't want you to know he was at Glebe Farm, pulling up the floorboards in your bedroom, and not where he was supposed to be? Who would smash your father's skull to stop him from telling you?'

'He couldn't have told me anything,' counters Flint. 'You said the line was cut.'

'Ah, yes. But what if your father had discovered that? What if, he's trying to call you with his news and he gets no dial tone and he goes outside and finds the line hanging down the wall like a piece of useless string? That's going to get him thinking, isn't it? Get him asking questions?'

Flint takes it back about the plod brigade, the turnip-tops.

'Your husband's fingerprints, they'll be on record somewhere, I suppose?' This is DC Bastable, coming off the substitutes' bench, standing in for Drake while the inspector makes a call.

'I can't think why they would be,' says Flint, 'but he'll be home in a day or so.'

'That would be Connecticut?'

'That's where we live.'

'So, we could ask the FBI to print him for us?'

'I would imagine so.'

'Just to eliminate him from our inquiries, of course.'

'Of course,' Flint says.

*But you've got no prints to compare them with have you, Constable Bastable? Because he wiped the glasses, and the table lamp.*

'Then you'll call us as soon as he's back, as soon as you've spoken to him?'

*Actually, no, DC Bastable, because he's not coming back and I'm the last person he's going to speak to. Until I find him.*

'Of course I'll call you,' Flint lies.

She gets up from her chair and crosses the corridor to peer into the room; to reassure herself that the green waves still cross the screen in orderly procession, the only evidence of life.

# thirty-two

In her father's room – his real bedroom, where the bed is not unnaturally high, where there are no sighing life-support machines and intravenous drips – two large suitcases lie open on the floor. They contain clothes and the few personal possessions Flint removed from Miller's Reach before setting it on fire; the few possessions that, in her mind, are not irredeemably contaminated by association with Ben Gates.

She has found her mother's photograph in its silver frame and placed it on the bedside table, on what used to be her mother's side of the bed. This is where Flint will sleep tonight, if she sleeps at all.

There is also a mobile telephone on the bedside table, awaiting the call that the night nurse has sworn she will make if there is the *slightest* change in John Flint's condition – sworn it on her own father's life. Nothing less than a sacred promise would have persuaded Flint to leave the hospital.

And propped against the table is her father's shotgun that she has taken from the cabinet in his study and checked and loaded with two twelve-gauge cartridges, one for each barrel.

'There's always the possibility that the assailant might come back,' DI Drake had warned, offering to post DC Bastable and his car in the driveway for the night as her sentinel – an offer she had firmly declined.

*Please God.*

She has opened her father's address book, seen the page splattered with his blood that has now turned a dirty brown. She has looked into the barn, seen the cage where her father was confined like a dog.

*Please God Ben comes back.*

She has washed the henna dye from her hair and scrubbed the fake tan from her skin. She wears a tracksuit and soft-soled shoes that will not make a noise. She lies in the dark on her mother's side of the bed, the shotgun within easy reach, recalling from her childhood the treads on the stairs that squeak.

'You've been through a lot,' the nurse had said, not knowing the half of it. 'Frankly, if you ask me, you don't look too good. I think you should see a doctor, dear.'

*Oh, really? And what should I tell the doctor? That I married a man who doesn't exist – that my husband is a phantom of some bastard's twisted imagination, a ghost? No, not a ghost because ghosts don't rape and that's what he did – over and over again. He raped me because you can't consent to sex with someone who doesn't exist, can you? It's not consensual if they blind you with lies, tie you up with their stinking deceptions.*

*You know what Ben did, doctor? He* impersonated *my husband. Every time he stuck his dick into me he was* pretending *to be the man I thought I'd married. And do you know – do you have any idea – how degraded that makes me feel; how used, how dirty, how stupid?*

*Got a cure for that, have you, doc? Got a pill I can take three times a day after meals? Or, maybe there's a procedure that can fix it? Maybe you can cut out the humiliation, zap it with some radiotherapy?*

*How about a little rape victim counselling? How about I sit down with somebody and try and explain how it feels to have been fucked by a ghost?*

She knows she needs to cry – to howl and wail and scream – but her cold rage won't let her.

*Please God he comes back.*

Dry-eyed despite herself, Flint waits in the dark, listening to the restless sounds of the night.

Ben Gates lies naked on his side. His naked wife – his utterly deceived wife – has her back towards him, her buttocks pressed into his groin, feeling the stirring of his erection. With one hand he cups a breast, holding it gently. With the fingers of his other hand, he strokes the down on the nape of her neck. 'Hold me,' she says, which is Flint's code on those occasions when she does not yet want to make love. To her repeated surprise, Ben's libido usually obeys Grace's wishes in these matters. They are both drifting in the no-man's-land between wakefulness and sleep. They lie quietly in the half-light of the dawn like two conspirators, listening to the timbers of Miller's Reach shift and creak in the wind.

A discordant sound snaps her awake. It takes a moment for the clarity of the dream to fade, for Flint to grasp that she is alone and not at Miller's Reach. Sunlight is flooding through the windows, so nor is it dawn. She lies motionless, waiting for a repetition of the noise that disturbed her.

There it is again – the scrape of stone on stone, footsteps on the gravel.

The windows of her father's bedroom look out over Glebe Meadow and offer no view of the driveway or the barn. To see who is prowling around she must move quickly to her own room, the last known place where Ben lay down on a bed and the last place she wants to go. *Get a grip!* Lifting the shotgun, feeling its comforting weight and the polished smoothness of the stock, she slips from her father's bed and hurries towards the hallway.

Her bedroom is beyond the master bathroom, beyond her bathroom, three doors down the hallway on the right. For the first time she notices the faint traces of fingerprint powder that the crime scene technicians have left on the handles, the door panels and the doorframes – latent evidence of their diligence. Her bedroom door is slightly ajar. She pushes it fully open with the twin barrels of the gun.

*Here's a joke for you, doc, this'll make you laugh. Know what happened the first night Ben and I spent at Glebe Farm, after supper when we came upstairs to bed? He said he wanted to carry me across the threshold of my bedroom like it was a rite of passage: you know, girl about to become true woman, for she's about to get royally fucked in her childhood bed? And I let him do it.*

The bed is pushed hard up against the wall, the covers dishevelled. The flooring that has been exposed is light oak painted grey and the missing section of board gapes like an open wound. The cavity is three feet long, eighteen inches deep, and you could break an ankle falling into it.

Flint steps over the cavity heading for the window where the curtains are only half-drawn. Through the gap she sees a metallic-grey car parked close to the barn door, which is not closed as it should be; not locked as she is sure it was when she left the barn last night.

Quickly she leaves her room and runs along the hallway to the top of the stairs and only then does she obey her training to always open the breech of a loaded shotgun so that it cannot accidentally discharge. The stairs are taken recklessly, two at a time, Flint clinging to the banister with her spare hand to keep her balance; Flint ricocheting from the bottom step into the study where she fills the pockets of her tracksuit with extra cartridges of shot.

Now she's moving through the kitchen, unlocking the back door, crossing the terrace and slithering down the grass bank that is hidden from the barn. At the bottom of the bank and still in cover she pauses until the noise of her breathing subsides and then in a crouch, her body bent below the level of the windows, she approaches the side of the barn, keeping to the grass, keeping off the gravel.

Now she squats beneath a window debating the risk–reward ratio of sneaking a look through the glass and possibly being seen. The intruder is unlikely to be armed so she has the advantage but the shotgun is at least a hundred years old, a Flint family heirloom, and she doubts it has been fired for a quarter of a century. So, how old are the cartridges and how unstable? One way to find out – *Do it. Move!*

She closes the breech and comes off her haunches until her eyes are just a couple of inches above the bottom of the window pane and she can see into the reception area with its few wooden chairs and a table strewn with old copies of *Country Life* magazine. No one there. To the right she can just see the line of cages where Dr Flint's patients recover from surgery – and where Dr Flint himself was recently caged and left to die. No-one there either. Beyond that she cannot see, not without going inside.

*MOVE!*

Now she's edging towards the corner of the barn, coming around it, coming up on the open door, going in low, swivelling to one side to get out of the backlight, dropping down on to her belly, lying prone on the floor with the shotgun to her shoulder in the firing position, looking down the barrels, pulling back the ancient hammers and hearing them lock, two fingers on two triggers taking up the slack.

She senses rather than sees movement, imagines that she hears a sound.

'Grace?' – a voice calling to her from beyond the thick curtain that hides her father's operating room.

She does not mean to fire – not yet – but she has misjudged the pressure required to trip the hammers. With a deafening explosion the gun kicks into her shoulder like the hoof of a mule and the curtain billows and shreds, and for a moment there is perfect silence that is broken by an enraged, primeval howl.

Flint has opened the breech and emptied the chambers; she is reaching into her pocket for two fresh cartridges; she is on her feet seeking a new firing position when she is stopped in her tracks by a flow – a veritable torrent – of the crudest obscenities she has ever had directed at her in the German language.

Felix Hartmann lies on Dr Flint's operating table, his shirt removed, Grace Flint picking at the pellets in his arm and chest with a pair of tweezers. She's apologised what feels like a million times for firing the shotgun but he won't be placated and she's grown tired of it and now they squabble.

'That *hurts*!'

'For God's sake, Felix, keep still. It only stings.'

'Stings? You could have killed me.'

'Not with that gun at that range through that curtain.' Flint succeeds in extracting a fourth pellet and drops it with a clang into a metal dish. 'Anyway, I missed you – mostly. And these are *flesh* wounds, Felix. The pellets barely broke your skin.'

'I cannot believe that you would fire at a target you could not see.'

'I've told you, the gun went off accidentally – sort of. And you shouldn't have been sneaking around my barn. You shouldn't have broken in.'

'For the third time, I did *not* break in. The door was *not* locked.'

'Yes it was.'

'*It was not!*'

'Well, locked or not, it's still called breaking and entering in my book. Why' – she swabs another puncture wound with rubbing alcohol – 'why on earth didn't you call first?'

'Because you have no phone. Because your line is out of order.'

'You could have called my mobile.'

'Oh, yes. And tell me, Grace, please, when exactly did you give me the number of your English mobile phone?'

Hartmann and Flint will continue along this quarrelsome path until she has finished her primitive surgery and cleaned and dressed his wounds.

And even when she has taken him up to the house and sat him down in the kitchen – while she brews a pot of coffee and pokes around in her father's fridge for something to eat – Hartmann will continue to complain, and she will parry and banter, until they reach the question of what he is doing at Glebe Farm.

'Anyway, why are you here?'

'You and me, we are to go to Leipzig.'

'*Leipzig?*'

'To find Gröber. We have a lead.'

Flint slams the fridge door, no longer interested in food.

'Excuse me?'

'We are to get close to Gröber's sister, Ilse. Cutter's orders.'

'No, Felix. Maybe you're going to schmooze with Gröber's sister but I'm staying here.' There is no longer any trace of banter in Flint's tone. 'In case you've forgotten, my father's *in a coma.*'

'Cutter says—'

'Screw Cutter.'

'Grace, listen, there is nothing you can do to help your father – not yet, not now. And Cutter says . . .'

Flint is not listening. She has left the kitchen, marched out on to the terrace where she now stands on the edge above the bank, staring out over the valley at the horizon, seeing nothing. Hartmann joins her, hands in his pockets, waiting for his opening.

Eventually, 'What?' – and Flint's challenging glare.

'Okay, Grace, screw Cutter. Screw Leipzig, screw Gröber, screw Ruth, screw me, screw your job and everything you are supposed to be. Screw it all. Just answer me one question, please.'

Nothing. No response from Flint.

Hartmann holds her blazing eyes and asks his question regardless: 'If we do not go to Leipzig, if we do not get a lead on Gröber, if we do not find him, how will you do it, Grace?'

She knows what he means but he says it anyway: 'How will you find your husband?'

# thirty-three

Liverpool airport, a little after noon, and Mandrake waits in line with his habitual traveller's edginess. There are no immigration officials waiting to examine his passport, no customs checks to pass, but Mandrake has more than one hundred thousand dollars in cash in his carry-on bag and he is not entirely convinced it will be invisible to the security X-ray. He knows it will certainly be discovered by even the most cursory of hand searches.

Will they care? Will they ask where he got it?

*From under my wife's bed* would be the truthful answer but he can't tell them that without the risk of serious complications: of police inquiries being made at Glebe Farm, leading to his arrest for criminal assault or even attempted homicide. Even actual homicide, perhaps, for Mandrake has no way of knowing if Dr Flint survived. He regrets that, regrets that the arrival of Ridout's people forced him to flee, regrets that he was obliged to hurt Grace's father in the first place. Come to that, he regrets ever becoming part of Ridout's operation, though not entirely. He does not regret Grace.

Thinking of her, Mandrake smiles and to calm himself he plays music in his head, even hums an accompaniment – not a piece of Bach for once but Edith Piaf's '*Non, je ne regrette rien*'.

No, he has no regrets about Grace.

'Do I know you?'

The money man has a face that does not match his billing: crumpled, creased with lines that both cross the forehead and descend from it like vertical scars between heavily-hooded eyes. The sign on his door describes him as an Expert Consultant in Offshore Financial Services, but with his premature jowliness, his sensuous mouth, a shadow of grey stubble on his chin, the red silk scarf looped loosely around his neck, he looks to Mandrake more like a dissolute artist, a painter or sculptor out of some Paris café of the 1950s.

'Not yet,' says Mandrake. 'We have a mutual acquaintance, one of your clients.'

The office does not fit the bill either – one small room set above a chemist's shop in the main town of Douglas. But then, Mandrake supposes, few if any of the money man's clients ever come to this small island set in the middle of the Irish Sea, an island that is the safe haven for some fifty billion dollars in offshore funds. Grace has done the math and she says that equates to six hundred and sixty thousand largely unaccountable dollars for every man, woman and child who resides on the Isle of Man. If the FSF had its way, she told Ben, they would bomb the Isle of Man.

'And that would be?' asks Patrick Archer, seeking the name of his client.

'Gröber. Karl Gröber.'

A frown, a shake of a head that is crowned by wild, chaotic curls of salt-and-pepper hair. 'I don't think so. You're confusing me with somebody else.'

As if he hasn't heard, Mandrake is removing from his carry-on bag packets of fifty-dollar bills – one hundred to a packet, ten packets in all – which he places in a line across Archer's desk.

'I would like to open an account, make a deposit.'

'I'm afraid that's quite impossible.' Archer's tone is laconic. 'You see, despite what people may think – despite what *you* may think – we have very strict requirements on the island. To begin with, I am required to know both the *proven* identity of each of my clients and the source of their funds. In particular' – Archer nods at the small wall of currency that confronts him – 'liquid funds. And in this case' – a pained smile of regret – 'I don't.'

'Of course, this is not the deposit,' Mandrake says. 'This is your initial fee. There may be other charges, expenses, that I'll be happy to meet. After Herr Gröber has transferred funds to my new account. Five million US dollars.'

'I wish I could help you.'

'I'm sure you do. Tell Herr Gröber that I have no wish to see his stay on the island disturbed by uninvited visitors; visitors from London or New York, say. Particularly New York, particularly friends of Ruth. Tell him exactly that: Friends of Ruth will be coming to the island unless I receive my fee of five million dollars. Tell him he has twenty-four hours to make the transfer.'

'Sadly ...' Archer lifts his hands palms up to testify to his inadequacy.

'I'll call you tomorrow.'

Mandrake is heading for the door.

'I didn't catch your name,' says Archer.

'He'll know,' says Mandrake.

# Leipzig

# thirty-four

Johann Sebastian Bach stands before a church in a picturesque square in Old Leipzig, magnificent in stone but stony broke. Seffner, the sculptor, carved the left pocket of the frock coat hanging inside out to illustrate the relative penury in which Bach died – his genius unrecognised by the burghers of Leipzig and his music no longer in fashion – and it is Flint's understanding, gained from Ben, that he was buried in an unmarked grave. So, she wants to know, how come the old bones interred inside the church two hundred years after Bach's death are claimed with certainty to be those of the master? Ben told her that the provenance of the remains was established beyond any doubt but, personally, given who that assurance came from, she'd like to see the DNA.

And here's another mocking coincidence – *and you'll like this one, doc.* The church to which Bach's faithful pilgrims come in their droves, and the former churchyard where Flint sits glumly at a café table toying with a cup of coffee she doesn't really want, are both named in honour of – *wait for it, doc* – Thomas, as in *Thomaskirche* and *Thomaskirchhof*. It was the doubting apostle, Thomas, whom Leipzig had in mind but Flint's thoughts are inexorably drawn to a Thomas in Maine with his expensive new toys; the Thomas who lied to her through his teeth and spoke jocularly of *federales*.

'Tyler's off the hook,' Jarrett Crawford had told her, calling her room on the second floor of the Holiday Inn, located next to Leipzig's clattering tram terminus.

'Hang on, I can't hear you. I need to close the window . . .' And when she had, 'What did you say about Tyler?'

'I said he's in the clear.'

'Not in my book, he isn't.'

But Thomas Tyler, Crawford had insisted, was guilty of nothing more than gullibility; of taking on trust the word of a false friend.

'September of '99, Tyler was in Washington at some conference when he runs into an old pal, a Brit name of Hudson; they were at college in England together, apparently.'

Flint was only half-listening, distracted by the memory that September 1999 was the month she first set eyes on Ben.

'Hudson used to work for the British Foreign Office, but now, he says, he's living in Virginia running a charitable foundation and Tyler, who's always looking to raise money for Audubon, starts hitting on him for a grant. Hudson says, "Come out to my place for the weekend and we'll talk about it," so that's what Tyler does and – wouldn't you know it? – there's some other guy there, some friend of Hudson's he wants Tyler to meet.'

'Crawdaddy, where's this coming from? Did Tyler just call you up?'

A brittle laugh from Crawford. 'No, his lawyer called. He wanted an assurance that you weren't going to turn up at Tyler's house with a SWAT team and slaughter his wife and kids. I said I could guarantee it, so long as Tyler came in and talked to us. Which is what he did, last night.'

'And you believed him?'

'Yeah, I believed him, mostly. Grace, listen, you scared the crap out of the guy but you also got him to see the light. You made him realise he's been used and screwed and he's madder than hell. And, by the way, he *has* just inherited a chunk of money from his aunt. I checked it out.'

'Terrific.' Getting to Leipzig from Mid Compton – via London and Berlin – had taken the better part of the previous day, and she hadn't arrived until nearly midnight, and Flint was feeling distinctly jaded, her damaged knee still giving her pain. There was no message waiting for her at the hotel from Felix Hartmann as there should have been. The news from the hospital, both last night and this morning, said her father's condition was unchanged.

'Don't knock it. Hudson's friend could be the best lead we've got.'

'So, who is he, Jerry? The suspense,' she added, irony in her tone, 'is killing me.'

'First name Sherman, no second name – that's the way Hudson set it up: "Thomas, I'd like you to meet Sherman, he works for the American government." It never got any more specific than that.

Tyler says the guy had an aura about him, like he was used to people saying "yes" to him; like he was doing you a favour just by asking for one.'

Flint had watched the trams arriving in a steady stream beneath her window. She saw Felix Hartmann alight from one of them and had the window still been open she would have called out to him. Puzzled, she watched him turn his back on the hotel and cross the road towards the railway station.

'Anyway,' Crawford had continued, 'this Sherman guy, he didn't rush it. Waited until after lunch on the Sunday when Hudson made some bullshit excuse and left them alone. Then Sherman pops the question: "Thomas, if I told you that our meeting this weekend is no accident, that I asked Hudson to arrange it because you are in a position to do something important for the government, for America, what would your reaction be?" See, he flatters him, wraps him up in the flag – and what's Tyler supposed to say?'

Now Flint was distracted by the sight of Felix Hartmann standing near the side entrance to the railway station, directly opposite the hotel, in the company of a much smaller man who wore a brown fedora with the brim turned down. 'I don't know, Jerry,' she had said. 'Screw the government might have been the smart call.' Hartmann was leaning over at the waist, his head cocked to one side, as though he was paying careful attention to the words of a child. 'What did Tyler say?'

'He says, "Of course I'll help, if I can." Then he adds, because he's nobody's fool, "So long as it's nothing illegal." And Sherman tells him, "On the contrary, Thomas. What we want you to do for your country is help us to uphold the law." Classic bait.'

What Flint was hearing had perplexed her almost as much as the scene she watched through her window; Hartmann now receiving an envelope from the small man that he slips into his pocket like a bribe. 'Jerry, does this sound like a WITSEC operation to you?' Flint had asked, referring to the Witness Security Programme run by the US Marshals Service.

'Nope. For one thing, from what Tyler says, this guy Sherman is not like any marshal I've ever heard of. And, number two, WITSEC's got a whole bunch of tame corporations that provide references or jobs for people in the programme. So, why would WITSEC need Tyler to provide cover for Ben? – because that's what Sherman was after. Not that he gave Tyler any details, not then. He just said they needed to provide a, quote, viable fairy tale, unquote, for some guy who was doing important work for the government.'

Hartmann and his diminutive companion were done with their business, going their separate ways, Hartmann striding away from the railway station in the direction of the old city. Flint had felt a sudden need to know where he was going and she was about to turn away from the window when she saw a woman – thirty-something, baseball cap, dressed like a tourist – lose all interest in the guidebook she had been studying. The woman gave a barely-perceptible nod to somebody who was out of Flint's line of vision and set off in Hartmann's wake, matching his pace. Moments later a man with a weightlifter's build – also thirty-something, short hair, also dressed like a tourist – had joined the procession.

'Crawdaddy, I've got to run,' Flint had said, hunting for her bag.

'Just tell me one thing. Did Tyler ever meet Ben?'

'Twice, initially. Once at the Mayflower Hotel in Washington where Sherman introduced them, the second time when Ben came to Tyler's house in Portland for an all-day briefing on what the Maine Audubon Society did: who worked there, the office routine, that kind of thing.'

'And?'

'Tyler liked him. Said he was smart, a quick study. Said that, for an amateur, he seemed to know a fair amount about ornithology. Since then, Ben's been round to Tyler's place several times for dinner and Tyler says they generally talked about birds.'

Running down the stairs Flint thought, *So, not every word was a lie. At least Ben didn't lie about the birds.*

Old Leipzig, the part containing the precious few baroque buildings that survived the area bombing raids of the Second World War, is no more than a handful of alleyways and squares that Flint had thoroughly explored in less than an hour.

No sign of Felix Hartmann and no sign of his tails, and now her puzzlement as to what he could be up to and why he's being followed has turned to pique. She doesn't want to be here, doesn't want to pose as Felix's wife, doesn't want to live with him in Ilse Gröber's probably gloomy house on Karl-Heine-Strasse. Most of all, she doesn't want to waste time on what she regards as the very long shot that Ilse will lead them to her brother – and the even longer shot that Karl Gröber will lead her to Ben.

'Gröber is, of course, our principal target,' Hartmann had said stiffly when she'd voiced her doubts.

*Hello, Felix, are we living on the same planet?*

In the end she'd said she would give Leipzig and the hunt for Gröber five days. Well, Felix's already wasted half of one of them, she thinks, getting up from the café table, giving Bach's statue a hostile parting glare.

Drifting back towards the hotel in apparently aimless fashion, Flint stops at a bookshop to buy a detailed map of Leipzig and its surroundings, one that shows where the tramway lines run. She locates Karl-Heine-Strasse to the west of the city centre, notes that a tram runs along its entire length and decides that, in Felix's continued absence, she has nothing better to do; that, in the words of the old adage, time spent on reconnaissance is seldom wasted. Taking a short diversion to the railway station where she instinctively employs her countermeasures against covert surveillance, checking for tails and finding none, Flint heads for Ilse's house.

# thirty-five

Peering through iron railings that are taller than she is, Flint gawps. The edifice that confronts her is five storeys high and topped by multiple mansard roofs and from her trespassing position she can see at least thirty windows set in pilasters. In almost any setting, Ilse's house would stand out. In this dull suburb of Leipzig, where only strident graffiti brightens the ubiquitous concrete walls, it seems like a mansion, the more so because it is set in its own – albeit overgrown – grounds.

But what rivets Flint's attention are the garden gnomes – scores, maybe hundreds of brightly-painted gnomes standing half-hidden by the undergrowth, entwined by creepers. No two that she can see are alike. One of them, she is sure, is meant to be female.

*Female gnomes?*

She does not hear the approach of Ilse's wheelchair.

*'Sind Sie wegen der Wohnung hier?'*

'What?' Two feet away inside the railings, at the height of her waist, Flint sees a face so pale it is almost translucent. The ears with huge distended lobes are set flat against the skull. The eyes are also out of proportion to the head, spreading puddles of intense blue that hold Flint's startled gaze unwaveringly. *'Bitte?'* says Flint, buying time while she recovers her composure.

*'Warum sind Sie hier? Wie heißen Sie?'*

Flint's German is rusty, nowhere near as good as her French and she flounders for a moment. Why is she there? What does she want? *I'm fascinated by your gnomes* she might say, but what is the German word for gnomes?

Ilse is growing impatient. *'Wer sind Sie? Wie heissen Sie?'*

Who is she? Flint takes a leap into the dark – *'Mein Name ist Frau Hartmann'* – and, to her relief, Ilse's glower softens from one

of stark suspicion to mere impatience. Why didn't you say so? she
demands. Where is your husband?

'*Mein Ehemann?*' Falling back on the literal truth, Flint says
she has no idea. She is a stranger to Leipzig, she explains, and, as
must be very obvious to Frau Gröber – it is Frau Gröber, isn't it?
– she has only a passing acquaintance with the German language
and—

'*Sind Sie aus Amerika?*' Ilse demands, suddenly hostile once
more.

No, not American. '*Nein, ich bin Engländerin,*' Flint replies.
English and careless, for she has lost her husband, she admits. She
was supposed to meet him at the hotel but she got confused
wandering around the Old City and was late for their rendezvous
and he was gone, and she does not know where to find him. She
has come to Karl-Heine-Strasse in the hope that he might be here
discussing with Frau Gröber the possibility of renting her apartment. She is, she says, extremely sorry for any alarm she may have
caused.

Ilse's wheelchair on which she sits side-saddle is state-of-the-art,
resembling a motorised scooter with any number of gadgets and
dials attached to the handlebars. She lifts an arm that is pencil-thin
and points to one of them – a clock, apparently. Herr Doktor is at
work, of course. Where else would a professional man be in the
middle of the afternoon?

*Herr Doktor* Hartmann? Doctor of what? Flint wonders, trying
to guess what notional profession her fictional spouse has adopted
for Ilse's benefit. Wisely, she decides not to speculate until she has
more clues. Yes, she agrees, it is more than likely that her husband
is at work.

*He said you would come at six o'clock.*

*Then I am far too early.*

*And that he would bring the references. I require excellent
references.*

*Of course.*

Ilse adjusts the swivel seat so that she is facing the handlebars.
She turns the ignition and flicks the throttle to execute a nifty turn.
She slowly and overtly examines Frau Hartmann from head to toe,
taking in her hair that is tidily held in a knot, her wire-rimmed
spectacles that give her face an owlish expression – a face that is
pale and bears not a trace of makeup. She sees that her woollen

cardigan is modestly buttoned to the neck and that her skirt falls to
mid-calf, that she wears no jewellery except for a plain wedding
ring, that her bag is unpretentious, her shoes sensible. Frau Gröber
nods what may be her approval or simply goodbye and sets off
towards the house, steering a bumpy, erratic path between the
legions of gnomes.

'*Kommen Sie, ich zeige Ihnen die Wohnung,*' she calls.

Come, I will show you.

From outside Ilse's house had seem tired, worn out by grime – at
first sight, even abandoned, like many of the buildings Flint had
observed on her tram ride. Inside – Flint trotting to keep up with
Frau Gröber as she powered her way up the ramp to the *piano
nobile* – it was fantastic: an exuberant, even playful paradigm of
rococo style. In the drawing room, where Flint now sits on an
exquisite if worn chair, the windows overlooking the garden are at
least twelve feet tall, allowing in a flood of light to reflect off
panelled walls and a ceiling painted in iridescent pastels to represent
the sky.

*And will you also work at the university?* Ilse enquires.

*Not yet*, Flint replies, now better able to guess the legend that
Felix has chosen for himself. First, she says, she must improve her
German. She is hoping to find a private tutor to practise conversa-
tion with. Perhaps Frau Gröber knows of someone?

A tutor is not necessary; an unnecessary expense. Diligence is
what is required. Frau Hartmann must never speak English. She
must learn five new phrases a day. She must listen to the radio,
though not at excessive volume. She must read German newspapers
and German books. Frau Gröber has many books. It might be
possible for Frau Hartmann to borrow a book or two from time to
time.

*You're most kind.*

*If, that is, Herr Doktor Hartmann's references are satisfactory,
of course.*

*Of course.*

There is a large red button on the handlebars of the scooter that,
without warning, Ilse jabs with the palm of one hand, causing a
horn to blare so loudly that Flint is momentarily stunned. Ilse does
not remove her hand from the button, and the dinning racket does
not cease, until a man appears in the doorway of the room and

comes no further; a round man with bow legs and a peasant's wrinkled face.

Ilse shouts at him in a language that sounds to Flint like Turkish and, wordlessly, the man goes away.

*We will take tea,* Ilse explains. *Each afternoon we will take tea and I will set a topic for our conversation. Are you familiar with the works of Schiller?*

Alas, Flint says, she is not.

*Then we will begin with Schiller, 'The Death of Wallenstein', perhaps. Each morning you will read a passage and in the afternoon we shall discuss it, and that is how you will improve your German.*

*You are very, very kind,* says Flint.

Only after tea has been served by the silent Turk, only after Flint has received more instruction as to how she will improve her German, only then does Ilse provide an opening, the first opportunity for Flint to plant a seed that in time – *quickly, please God* – will flower into a discussion about Frau Gröber's personal circumstances.

*And your parents, they live in England?*

*My father does,* says Flint, not mentioning his current tenuous grip on life. *My mother died when I was very young.*

Ilse's eyes appear to shimmer.

*How young?*

*I was six,* Flint says truthfully. *She was murdered* – a probable truth, though the body of Flint's mother was never found.

*She was shot,* she pretends. *In the head* – an outright lie.

Even if Flint had not read a translation of General Kessel's report, devouring every word of it on the plane to Berlin; even if she had not known the precise circumstances in which Ilse's parents were betrayed by brother Karl and summarily executed in a forest near Vacha; even without that knowledge, she would have recognised the intense pain in Frau Gröber's face. What little life remains in her features vanishes, as though it has been snuffed out. Her eyes fade and she does not breathe. For the moment she is a young girl lying on the back seat of a Trabant ambushed by border guards on a forest track on a Sunday night more than thirty years ago. Despite the interval, Ilse hears the shots as if they had just been fired and her body jerks.

Is Frau Gröber unwell? Flint reaches out to touch her hand. Is there anything Frau Hartmann can do for her?

*Who killed your mother?* The words come from Ilse's throat in a croak.

*We don't know, my father and I. We will probably never know. That is the worst thing about it. Not knowing is an almost intolerable burden.*

*You think it would help if you knew?*

*Yes,* says Flint firmly – an unvarnished truth.

Sometimes, says Ilse, speaking mainly to herself, it is better not to know.

*Bingo!* There it is: an open invitation that suggests Ilse is willing to divulge that as a child she also experienced a unique, enduring loss. Though Flint is aware of the risk that she is pushing matters too fast and too far she does not hesitate to grasp the opportunity. She frames her questions carefully. Her sly words have barely left Frau Hartmann's mouth when she knows she has made a colossal blunder.

Did Frau Gröber suffer a similar loss in childhood? Did her mother also die, perhaps?

'*Was erlauben Sie sich?*' – How dare you? Ilse's challenge is so volcanic, so venomous, that Flint recoils as though she has been whipped.

*How dare you be so impertinent?*

Frau Gröber's slight body trembles with fury.

*Forgive me,* stutters Frau Hartmann.

*You have no right.*

*I know. I did not—*

*You are a guest, a total stranger, in my house and yet you pry? You dare to ask me personal questions?*

*You cannot forgive me because what I did was unforgivable.*

Frau Hartmann rises from her chair, clutching her bag to her stomach in both hands, giving the impression – Flint hopes – that she knows she must take her leave.

*I did not mean to pry. I simply hoped that you would understand what it is like to—*

'*Setzen Sie sich!*'

Frau Hartmann sits. She looks wretched. It is possible she is on the brink of tears.

They wait in loaded silence while Ilse studies Frau Hartmann's pinched face, examining the evidence of what she has achieved. Satisfied, apparently, she throws off her anger like a cloak.

Does Frau Hartmann have a brother? The question is gentle and floats like a lure.

*Sadly, no.*

*Did your brother also die?*

*No, Frau Gröber, I am an only child.*

I had a brother, Frau Gröber says. He died.

*Say nothing, Flint – not one bloody word.*

Frau Hartmann keeps her silence, staring at the floor, her hands in her lap knotted into fists.

*We will talk more of this, about your mother.*

*I would like that.*

*You should see the apartment.*

*Please, if I may.*

*The servant will show you.*

In the sleeve of her baggy cardigan, Ilse finds a handkerchief that she hands to Frau Hartmann so that she may remove from her cheeks the faintest evidence of tears.

The first floor of Ilse's house is reached by a curving staircase that rapidly ascends into shabbiness. Beyond the first curve the stair carpet is threadbare, the paint on the wall nicotine-yellow with age. The stair light is no brighter than a candle and it flickers like one, causing Flint to wonder about the state of the electrical wiring. The Turk who leads the way, pulling on the banister, wheezes from the effort.

As though the house has shrunk, the ceilings are lower on the first floor and the windows are smaller; no splendid shafts of light to penetrate the gloom. Only one door is open, at the end of a long corridor, leading to a suite of three rooms.

There is a living room furnished with a meagre two-seater couch and matching chair covered in worn maroon-coloured damask, a scratched low table, a dresser affair with a faux-marble top bearing at its edges the stains of cigarette burns, two skimpy rugs on a bare wooden floor. At the far end of the room there is an improvised kitchen. Flint pretends to take an interest in a garish framed print that hangs above the dresser and is the only decoration to be seen: a landscape of sorts.

The Turk looks at her enquiringly and Flint says, 'Very nice.'

The bedroom is next, a windowless room about twelve feet square. There is a chest of drawers varnished with a lacquer that has a burnt-orange tinge, a tall standing mirror that is mottled where the silver nitrate backing has faded away. Instead of a wardrobe, Flint supposes, there is a sagging clothes rail suspended in an alcove and concealed by a curtain, and there are two wooden chairs that might serve as night tables. The bedstead is made of iron and is just about wide enough to be called a double.

*So, where will you be sleeping, Felix?*

Flint tests the mattress and finds it mostly firm, except in those places where the bedsprings have broken.

She barely bothers to notice the fittings in the bathroom. She stands at the window looking down on a patch of waste ground at the rear of Ilse's house that is littered with debris and green plastic garbage sacks. A scavenging dog is tugging at one of the sacks – come to think of it, the first dog she has seen in Leipzig.

Flint cannot stay – would never stay – in this dismal place, a virtual prisoner of the monstrous Frau Gröber.

But Frau Hartmann can. She will bring her simple clothes and hang them from the bent rail in the alcove. She will arrange her cleansing cream and her other toiletries on the surround of the cracked washbasin. She will buy a small radio and listen to the news in German at moderate volume while she heats her husband's frozen quick-fix supper in the toaster-oven. In the mornings, when he has left for the day, she will read Schiller, taking one of the wooden chairs to the bathroom window where the light is better. At noon she will go downstairs and make herself useful to Frau Gröber; offer to run errands, to shop, to clean, whatever. And in the afternoons they will talk – and not just about the works of Schiller.

*For how long will you stay?* Flint asks, appalled by the prospect.

*For as long as it takes*, Frau Hartmann replies.

# thirty-six

A longside the Holiday Inn, in the abandoned annexe of the vast but equally-abandoned Hotel Astoria, Stephanie Cooper-Cole waits, seething with impatience, for her mobile phone to ring. Thymus – as in *Thymus vulgaris* which grows in abundance in Nigel's English garden – is safely wrapped up in his hotel on Richard-Wagner-Strasse with Fellowes camped out in the lobby and two more watchers in the street maintaining observation on the side and rear entrances. Through her binoculars, trained across the small park where a cluster of junkies is gathered, Cooper-Cole can see one of Fellowes's team lounging in his black leather chaps at a café table close to where his motorbike is parked. But where is Catmint? – Catmint as in *Nepeta mussinii* of the *Labiatae* family; handsome in a muted way, grey leaves and blooming spikes of purple flowers. And how in God's name could four of them lose her?

For the umpteenth time in the last forty-eight hours, Cooper-Cole entertains ungenerous thoughts about Nigel Ridout.

'Very well, Stephanie,' he'd said crossly in response to her alarming news that Catmint was bound for Leipzig, 'you may have your watchers but use locals.'

'*Locals?*'

'For reasons of economy.'

'Nigel, you can't be—'

'*Stephanie*, we are in a recession. We live in a time of budget cuts and miserly bookkeepers. They rule the roost at Ceauşescu Towers, as you know perfectly well. So, you will use locals, a maximum of four.'

'*Four?*'

'Six. And that's my final word.'

Locals in Leipzig meant the left-overs from the Cold War: freelancers used by MI6 in GDR times, their loyalty bought with

paltry retainers and always made questionable by the suspicion
they might also work for the Stasi – which, as it turned out, many
of them did. Paradoxically, of course, and as Nigel pointed out,
that meant – 'ipso facto,' he said – they had considerable experience
of surveillance operations.

But as Cooper-Cole now knows – and will loudly tell Nigel
when they're next face to face – maintaining covert surveillance on
a subject in a police state where almost every phone is tapped,
where the target can't spot the tail vehicles because almost every car
is an identical Trabant, where there are tens of thousands of pairs
of watchful eyes to call on, is not the same as trying to keep tabs on
an experienced undercover agent in an open city with none of
those advantages.

They had lost Catmint in the railway station, they said. One
minute she was there – wandering along one of the shopping
arcades, drifting into the food court, drifting out again, killing
time, or so they thought – and then she was gone.

'Gone?'

Vanished, they said, swallowed up in the vastness of the largest
railway terminus in Europe. Did Cooper-Cole have any idea how
many levels there were, how many platforms?

'You searched the platforms?'

'Of course. And every train.'

'You thought Catmint went there to catch a bloody train?'

She had sent them back to their motorbikes, glowering and
resentful, with orders to split up and comb the city in four
quadrants, quadrants that will become ever-larger as they work
their way out from the centre to the suburbs, looking for the
proverbial needle in a haystack. Rashly she had offered a bonus:
one thousand US dollars for the first one who calls in to report a
sighting of Catmint, even a glimpse. Still her phone does not ring.

Cooper-Cole knows full well that their chances of finding
Catmint are somewhere between slight and none. They will not
pick her up again until she makes contact with Thymus or returns
to the Holiday Inn – if she returns to the Holiday Inn; if she has not
already found Gröber's scent and followed it.

'She is not supposed to be hunting Gröber,' Ridout had complained. 'She is *supposed* to be hunting Mandrake, her Ben.'

'Perhaps she thinks that Gröber can lead her to Mandrake,'
Cooper-Cole had suggested.

'But Stephanie, my *dear*' – Nigel at his most patronising – 'Karl Gröber is not in Leipzig, has not been within five hundred miles of Leipzig for ten years.'

'I know that.'

'So, why' – Ridout had slapped his fingers on the desk to punctuate his question – 'is ... Catmint ... going ... to ... Leipzig?'

'I don't know that.'

'To ... see ... whom?'

'I'll find out.'

'Please do.' And then Ridout had stroked the desk with his fingers, as though to heals its wounds, and said, 'You know, Stephanie, I do see many similarities between you and Flint. You are both bright in a street-smart sort of way, you have similar intuitive skills, remarkable tenacity, a certain – how shall I put this? – disregard for authority? Someone recently described Flint as "irredeemably bloody-minded" and I thought instantly of you. You are even rather attractive in the same aloof way, which is most endearing.'

*Fuck you, Nigel*, she thought.

'All of which is to say that you do make interesting, worthy opponents, but I *really would* like you to make absolutely sure that you win.'

For a price that will turn Nigel's face white when he learns of it, Cooper-Cole has a key to the Astoria's abandoned annexe and carte blanche to come and go as she pleases. There are no furnishings or facilities in her observation post – no provisions, no electrical power, no working toilet – but she is damned if she will leave it until Catmint is found.

Dr Otto Schnell wishes to leave a note for Miss Grace Flint with the receptionist at the Holiday Inn. It is most urgent, he says, and please make sure she receives it the moment she returns. He is exceedingly polite; he would be most, *most* grateful.

Rest assured it will be done, the receptionist says.

Dr Schnell doffs his fedora and takes his leave of the hotel. He walks twenty yards along the street and turns left into a passageway that leads to the hotel's parking lot and the rear service entrance. He pockets his hat, slips inside and, careful to remain out of sight of the reception desk, takes the stairs to the second floor. A copy of the maid's pass key gains him entry to Flint's room.

Since he is not here to search her room, he notes with approval the telltales she has left: thin strips of almost invisible tape that will break if he attempts to open the closet or any of the drawers.

It is a small room but ingeniously designed to accommodate two large single beds that are pushed together. From the clutter of her things on the nightstand he assumes that she sleeps in the one nearest the window. Removing his shoes he takes the other bed and settles in comfortably to wait.

Alighting from a tram, Flint removes Frau Hartmann's unflattering spectacles and the clip that holds her hair in a knot, shaking her head to set it free. She undoes the top two buttons of her cardigan and abandons the posture that implies the timidity of a woman who would rather not be noticed. Watching the transformation through binoculars from her post in the Astoria annexe, Stephanie Cooper-Cole grudgingly concedes that Flint does have a chameleon's skills.

Out of instinct, Flint does not go directly to the Holiday Inn. Instead she returns once more to the railway station and dissolves into the crowds in the shopping complex, working her way slowly to the top mezzanine, apparently window shopping. In reality she uses the windows to watch the reflections of those about her.

When she is satisfied there are no tails, she leaves the terminus but not by the entrance directly opposite the Holiday Inn – and not one, as it happens, that can be observed from the Astoria annexe. She heads south towards the Old City and then turns west and walks for six blocks, then north towards the hotel but on a parallel street, passing behind it. Then east, then south again, and having completed her wide deceptive circle, she reaches the Holiday Inn unseen by – and invisible to – Stephanie Cooper-Cole.

If Flint's hearing was as acute as her instincts, she might have heard a room in the Astoria annexe fairly shaking with frustration.

'Good evening, Miss Flint, there is a message for you.'

Felix, at last, she assumes, but the handwriting on the envelope is copperplate, nothing like Hartmann's untidy scrawl. 'MOST URGENT: Please open immediately,' it says. She drifts into a quiet corner of the lobby to read the message inside.

My name is Otto Schnell. I am from Pullach, a colleague of Felix Hartmann. Felix cannot make contact with you because he is under constant surveillance by hostile forces. I am waiting for you in your room. Please do not be alarmed to find me.

Under Flint's alert gaze, Dr Schnell gets up from the bed and fussily straightens the duvet on which he has been resting. Even minus the fedora he is instantly recognisable to her as Felix's companion, because of his height.

'Schnell,' he says giving a small bow. 'Dr Otto Schnell.'

'How did you get in here?'

'A bribe, I regret to say.' Dr Schnell notes with satisfaction that Flint's eyes are checking out her telltales and finding them intact. 'I bought a copy of the pass key.'

'Who's watching Felix?'

'A team of three. They picked him up at the airport as soon as he arrived. Two of them are locals, from Leipzig, and the third is British, we think.'

'You think?'

Dr Schnell is putting on his shoes, adding two inches to his height. 'We have not asked him – yet. But he is using an apartment that, in the GDR days, was favoured by your MI6 because of its proximity to the Stasi headquarters.' Flint doesn't get it and Dr Schnell adds, 'It had an excellent view of the Stasi headquarters.' With his hands he mimics the operation of a long-lens camera.

'Am I under surveillance?'

'You were, by a team of four who picked you up here at the hotel. But then you lost them at the railway station – very skilfully, I thought.' Dr Schnell rewards her competence with an impish smile. 'Just before you paid your visit to Frau Gröber.'

'Then I didn't lose you, apparently.'

'We are playing at home, Miss Flint – Grace, if I may. We have the home-field advantage. We also had an excellent idea of where you would go. How is Ilse, by the way?'

'Creepy,' says Flint. 'Otto, if that really is your name, what the hell's going on? Why are there reptiles crawling all over my patch?'

'Reptiles?'

'Snakes, spies, spooks – whatever you want to call them. Sorry, but the inhabitants of the espionage world are not my favourite species, present company excepted, perhaps. Do you know what they're up to?'

Dr Schnell looks wise. 'No, but I think we can assume that
British intelligence has an interest in Karl Gröber; either to protect
him, for whatever reason, or to find him through you. And, Grace,
clever as you are at avoiding surveillance, I think it would be
prudent if we moved you to another hotel, somewhere quieter. I
happen to know of just such an hotel, in the country but not far
from Leipzig, which has an excellent restaurant where, if you will
allow me the honour, we might have dinner together tonight. Where
I can guarantee we will not be disturbed – where there are no
microphones, no inquisitive eyes. And if you will give me one hour,
I will arrange for a small diversion to take place so that Felix may
join us, and then the three of us can consider why there are reptiles
other than me' – a broad smile from Dr Schnell – 'crawling on your
patch. Is that acceptable to you?'

Flint appears to consider the offer. 'What was in the envelope
you gave Felix this morning?'

'Envelope? What envelope?'

Silence from Flint who watches his face.

'Ah . . . Very good. *Very* good.' He chuckles and shakes his head
to cover his embarrassment. 'You were also watching. Excellent!
And you have reminded me of something I should not have
forgotten. The envelope contained references that Ilse is demanding
– the very best references Pullach could forge for Herr Doktor
Hartmann and his charming wife – and Felix is supposed to take
them to her tonight. He will have to go—'

'There's no need,' says Flint.

'No?'

Flint puts down the small can of Mace she has been concealing
in her hand and reaches into her bag. What she has in her hand
now, what she shows to Dr Schnell with just a hint of smugness,
are the keys to Ilse's house.

# The Irish Sea

# thirty-seven

Mandrake on the Dublin ferry, bracing to keep his balance on the forward deck, watches the bow rising precipitously to meet the next swell. The weather is worsening, the sea now a dirty grey and spitting spume that stings his face like nettles. He would go below to one of the salons but if Ridout has put out an alert for Mandrake, and if his hunters are on board, the salons are where they will prowl – and a shaved head and five days of stubble is unlikely to deceive them. Mandrake has done what he can to alter his appearance but there's nothing he can do about his height. At 6ft 3ins he towers over most of the other passengers on the boat and the girl with an urchin's face and a sewer for a mouth barely comes up to his shoulders. Obscenities have stained almost every sentence she's spoken since she came on deck with her sullen boyfriend and then driven him away with her spiteful hostility.

'Fookin' 'ell!' she yells as bow spray douses the cigarette that is cupped in the palm of her hand. To Mandrake, in response to his smile of understanding, she demands, 'What yuse fookin' lookin' at?'

He turns away and in the shelter of the bulkhead he lights a replacement cigarette that he silently offers to her.

'Fook yuse,' she says, declining to take it.

Mandrake shows his indifference. He does not care about her insolence or her foul mouth just so long as she remains with him on the foredeck. She serves as his camouflage for he knows that a couple is somehow less apparent, less likely to be noticed, than a lone male would be.

And it is not only Ridout's hunters that concern him. Karl Gröber will also have scouts out looking for Mandrake, he is certain, for Gröber's response to his demand for hush money was almost exactly what he had expected.

'Yes and no,' the money man said when Mandrake had called to ask him if the transfer had been made.

'No games,' said Mandrake.

'The client is understandably concerned that even if he pays your fee in full he has no guarantee he will not receive a visit from Ruth's friends.'

'He has my word,' Mandrake said – and heard only a scornful silence on the line. 'So,' he had continued, 'what does the client propose?'

'Payment by instalments, weekly instalments that will only continue so long as the island remains . . . peaceful.'

*Or until he finds me*, Mandrake knew.

'I already hold a deposit of ten per cent that I have authority to transfer to anywhere you wish. The balance is payable over four weeks, which is how long the client requires to arrange his relocation.'

*And much less time than he thinks he needs to trace me through the transfers.*

'He could relocate today,' Mandrake had said.

'He could indeed, in which case your information would be worthless. He prefers to make more orderly arrangements and he's not opposed to paying for your . . . services. He's buying time and, naturally, he wishes to ensure that he receives full value for money.'

*Buying time to hunt Mandrake.*

A rogue swell, this one much steeper than its forerunners, breaks over the bow, causing the ferry to stagger and lurch violently to starboard. With one hand Mandrake grabs the guard rail and with the other hand the girl, clinging on to her arm as a torrent of water deluges the foredeck. She screams and fights to free herself from Mandrake's grasp until she feels the force of the water sucking at her like a rip tide and now she's got her arms around his neck holding on to him for dear life.

Another monstrous wave breaks over them and Mandrake turns to seize the guard rail with both hands, swinging the girl round so that she is wedged tightly between his bulk and the superstructure, and it occurs to him in an abstract sort of way that he should feel a sense of satisfaction that he has saved her life. But Mandrake feels nothing more than the press of her body. He knows that he grabbed the girl instinctively only because she serves his temporary purpose; that, except for that and when he no longer needs her, he is utterly indifferent as to whether she lives or dies.

She means as little to him as another skinny girl with blue-tinged skin whose body he had once lifted from his bed and wrapped in a blanket and laid – half-in, half-out of the water – on the bank of the River Thames.

# The Marscheider Building

# thirty-eight

Of Grace Flint's supposed father-in-law – the impostor who attended her wedding – Jarrett Crawford has this to say: 'He's a flake, an out-of-work actor, most of the time. Name of Defoe, first name Pierre. They found him working behind a bar in Montreal and offered him fifteen hundred bucks US and all expenses paid to stand in for Joe Gates.'

'They?'

'Well, Ben for one, Mr Cutter. Defoe picked him out from a picture line-up. The other guy, Defoe only saw him that one time in the bar and his description is pretty vague.'

The weather has turned unseasonably hot. It's eighty degrees inside the Marscheider building and Cutter has a portable air-cooler running that makes the papers on his desk curl and flutter. Crawford catches glimpses of the first page of Nathan Stark's personnel file and he tries not to squirm in his chair.

'When you say they found Defoe—'

'I should have said they sought him out, sir. When Defoe's not acting or tending bar he runs an outfit called Phone Fantasies. You pay him fifty bucks and he calls up your best friend, your boss, whoever you like, and pretends to be the cops, the IRS, your wife's divorce lawyer, whatever.'

Cutter looks puzzled. 'Why would he do that?'

'It's meant to be a joke, sir. Anyway, that's how they found him. They said, "Since you're into fantasies, how about this?" Ben claimed that his real father had been fired from the university in Montreal for hitting on some of his female students, and not for the first time, and that he'd turned into a drunk. Said that if his old man turned up at the wedding he'd probably hit on the bride and she'd throw a fit. They said Defoe wouldn't have to be a witness or anything, so there was nothing illegal to it. Just turn up and behave himself and bullshit about Montreal, his sick wife, his retirement, going to live in France, and so forth.'

Cutter is very good at giving his full attention. He's doing it now, listening to Crawford as though every word has a deeper meaning. Crawford can feel the sweat in his moustache. He resists the urge to wipe it.

'That was it?' Cutter demands to know.

'Not quite. After the wedding when Ben paid Defoe the balance he owed him – a thousand dollars – he also gave him a cellphone with a French number. Said it was just in case Grace decided to call her father-in-law; she'd have no way of knowing he wasn't in France. Said that if he did get a call he was to let Ben know, and Ben would send him a hundred bucks. Well, it happened a few times, Grace would call to say hello, and Defoe always got his hundred bucks. Then, one time when he was short of cash, Defoe tried to rip Ben off, saying Grace had called when she hadn't. Two days later a guy he'd never seen before walks into the bar and tells Defoe that if he tries that stunt again he's going to wake up with his throat cut. Scared him half to death. After that, Defoe says, he threw the phone away.'

To Crawford's relief Cutter's gaze loses its intensity as he seems to lose interest in Pierre Defoe.

'Canadians still holding him?' he asks.

'Yeah, they're talking to him about a couple of other things – impersonating a cop for some of his Fantasy clients for one. They're happy to play ball. Put him in jail for a while if we want.'

'Be a waste of space wouldn't it, Jerry?'

'I think so.'

'So?'

'So what, sir?'

'So when are you gonna tell me what's really on your mind?'

Crawford has come to Cutter's office knowing this moment would very likely come, but he's still not sure how to play it so he prevaricates.

'Flint wants me to pick up Regal.'

'Who?'

'Vincent Regal, the original CI on Pentecost. The guy who works for the agency that set up all of Gröber's Delaware companies.'

Rightly suspecting this is another of Crawford's diversions, Cutter merely nods.

'The thing is – and it's been bugging her for more than a year – the night she debriefed Regal he let slip, accidentally on purpose, that he knew she was getting married. He even knew Ben's name.'

'So?'

'So how did an asshole like Regal know her private business? It wasn't like she'd taken out an ad in the *Times*. Grace says that only a handful of people knew. The question is, which one of them told Regal?'

'Ask him,' says Cutter. 'And, Jerry, are we there now? Are you finally gonna tell me what's really bugging you?'

Crawford nods his head but he's looking at his shoes. 'The Hudson guy, the one who introduced Mr Tyler to Sherman,' he begins tentatively.

'What about him?'

'I'm due to go down to Virginia tonight so that I can roust Hudson at his house in the morning, nice and early before his lawyer's awake.'

'Good.'

'Even so, Mr Cutter, I don't think he's the type who will fold. He was a pretty senior diplomat for the Brits and he's been around, got posted to some major hotspots in his time. I don't think he's going to tell us who this Sherman guy is whether his lawyer's there or not.'

'And?'

'And the minute I leave there, sir – because I don't have probable cause to pull him in – he's going to be making a phone call to someone, to Sherman I would think, telling him that Mr Tyler is talking to us, and I don't think that's a good idea. If it's all right with you, Mr Cutter, I'd just as soon leave Hudson alone for now and try and ID Sherman some other way.'

'And, *Jerry*?'

'So, hoping you would agree, I've got Mr Tyler downstairs right now working with Rocco, trying to come up with a computer image of Sherman's face. Trouble is, Mr Tyler's not what you would call the most observant witness. He's great at describing birds – if I let him he'd describe every damn bird he saw in Hudson's garden down to the length of its beak – but when it comes to human faces they just don't register. He's sitting with Rocco, been there three hours, and I tell him to close his eyes and describe Rocco's face. He couldn't do it – didn't come close. And ... I really don't know where to go with this, Mr Cutter.'

'Jerry, quit waltzing with me, I'm getting dizzy. Just spit it out.'

'Look, sir, this business with Mr Stark, him telling Rocco to listen to Grace's phone on your say-so. I know you told me not to mention it to a living soul, and I swear I haven't, but . . .'

Cutter's eyes are suddenly like laser beams fixed on Crawford's face.

'Okay, Rocco says he's gonna try a different approach, he's gonna show Mr Tyler real photos of real people a bit at a time, starting with the hairline and working down. The idea is, Rocco keeps showing him hairlines on the screen with the rest of the face masked until he gets one that's more or less right, and then he shows him the forehead and, "no that's not right", so he shows him more foreheads from other photos until he gets a near match. Then he shows him the eyes and if they're not right he shows him some more eyes, and so on. He's trying to build a composite, you see?'

'I get the picture,' says Cutter without a trace of a smile.

'Only he doesn't – Rocco doesn't have to build a composite, Mr Cutter. Tyler sees a hairline that's not right but then Rocco shows him the forehead from the same picture and Tyler says, "Yes", and then the eyes, same thing, and then—'

'Why did he do it, Jerry?'

'Do what, sir?'

'Why did Rocco put Nathan Stark's picture on the screen?'

Crawford swallows. 'Because I told him to. I didn't say why.'

'But you are going to tell me why, aren't you, Jerry?'

'Last Saturday afternoon Tyler got a call from Sherman. First time he'd heard from him in a couple of months. There was a bit of bullshit back and forth and then Sherman warned Tyler that a couple of agents from the FSF were on their way to Portland; that we'd be banging on his door, asking a lot of questions about Gates; that the FSF wasn't in the loop and that he, Tyler, should keep his mouth shut – just deny he'd ever heard of Gates. I was still trying to figure out how Sherman could have known that – how anybody outside of this building could have known that Flint and me were on our way to Portland – when Mr Tyler said something else. He said we didn't need a computer; what we really needed was one of those machines that detects odours. He was joking but I asked him what he meant. He said he thought Sherman had a problem with bad breath because he used a really strong mouthwash, and that he would recognise that smell anywhere. Mr Cutter, he said the smell reminded him of quince.'

Rocco Morales at his bench in the basement of the Marscheider building seething, the air thick with his undetonated anger.

Thomas Tyler has been trying to pass the time with polite conversation but Morales has heard barely a word. His sister, Rosetta, says that Rocco's temper will be his undoing and right now he's about to prove her right.

Jerry Crawford, avoiding Rocco's icy glare, says, 'Mr Tyler, this is Director Cutter and he'd like to shake your hand.'

'What you've done for us,' says Cutter with grave sincerity, 'is profoundly important, Mr Tyler.' He takes Tyler's hand and does not release it. 'Now I need you to do one more thing. I need you to go upstairs to my office with Agent Crawford and call your wife. Tell her to pack a couple of bags, sufficient for the two of you and your children for, say, four or five days. If the kids aren't home right now, she needs to locate them immediately. If she needs assistance in doing that, tell Agent Crawford. Do you understand?'

Tyler, his face drained of colour, looks as though he may be on the brink of a seizure.

'In about five minutes there's going to be a mess of police cars parked outside your house,' Cutter continues. 'They will remain there until the hostage rescue unit arrives. In plain language, that's a SWAT team in an unmarked vehicle that will extract your family from the house and take them to a place of safety. Later on today, I hope, or tomorrow at the latest, you will be reunited with your family and you will be protected for as long as there is any risk.'

Tyler manages to say, 'My God, what have I done?'

'You've done the right thing, Mr Tyler. Now, please' – Cutter releases his grip – 'go with Agent Crawford and make that call.'

In the silence, as Tyler is led away too stunned to resist, Rocco Morales hesitates and under his breath he begins to count slowly to ten, like he knows you are supposed to do when you're contemplating doing something extremely stupid. He gets to ten and then he explodes.

'Fuck it, Mr Cutter. Can you please tell me, sir, what the *fuck* is going on?'

Cutter says calmly, 'You listening to Flint's phone, that wasn't on my say-so. Stark lied to you.'

'And Crawford knew that? How long has he known that?'

'Since Monday night.'

Morales kicks at his chair, sends it skidding across the room. 'Five days! He's known for five days and he never said a fucking word. This is fucking unbelievable.'

'I ordered him not to tell you, Rocco. My call. You want to get mad with somebody, get mad with me.' Cutter's tone is still calm but there is a warning blush on his face that suggests his patience is being tested.

'Why, Mr Cutter? In God's name why wouldn't you want me to know that my ops director is dirty?'

'I didn't know he was dirty, Rocco – not then. All I knew was that he'd given you an order I didn't authorise, and that he lied to you about it. I wanted to know why he did that without alerting him – and you would have alerted him, Rocco, because you can't help yourself. I was working on it, going through his file looking for some things I might have missed. I might have got there in the end but' – Cutter beams his gap-toothed smile – 'you beat me to it.' He nods at the blank computer screen on Morales's bench. 'You want to show me what you came up with?'

'Fucking Jerry,' Morales says but his anger is deflating like air from a punctured tyre.

'Rocco, one more time: it was my call. It's what I get paid to do.'

Hunched with resignation, Morales goes to his bench and types in the code that brings the screen alive, and Nathan Stark's gaunt face, all bones and sharp angles, comes into view. It is unmistakably Stark's photograph – the one contained in his personnel file that currently sits on Cutter's desk – but Morales has added a pair of spectacles and a full head of wavy hair swept back from the forehead.

'When Tyler met him at Hudson's place he was wearing a rug, a hairpiece,' Morales explains. 'Had us fooled for a while. When I showed Tyler this' – Morales removes the hairpiece with a flick of his mouse and masks the picture so that only Stark's bristled hairline is showing – 'he said "No", it wasn't him. But then Crawford insisted that I show him this' – and the mask descends to reveal the deep brow – 'and Tyler got all excited and suddenly we were in business.'

'You got any doubts, Rocco? You think Tyler's identification is solid?'

'Well, Tyler's pretty sure but I wouldn't want to see him tested in court, not on the basis of this picture. Unless he can pick Stark out of a line-up, I think any good defence attorney could shake him.'

'What if Tyler heard Nathan's voice? What if he saw him in action?'

'Yeah, well, that would help but I don't see how you're going . . . Oh Christ, yes I do.' The glum look that Morales has been wearing vanishes from his face. 'You mean show him the Pentecost tape?'

'Can't hurt, can it?'

Morales is rummaging in a drawer, finding the DVD on to which he has transferred the finished version of the tape that shows all-too-vividly the scale of the disaster that Operation Pentecost became. He inserts it into his computer and waits for the media player to load.

He does a chapter search and then, *Nathan, take the desk*, Flint is yelling, her voice tinny over the computer's speakers, and here is Nathan Stark coming into frame.

*He's put a fucking gun in her mouth* – Crawford's voice loaded with rage.

*Take him down*, says Stark, caught by the camera as though he is staring at his fate.

'Can you rig better sound, Rocco?' asks Cutter.

'Sure. I've got a pair of Bose speakers I can run it through.'

'Then show it to Tyler when he's finished with his phone call,' says Cutter. 'Show him as much as he wants to see, until he's absolutely sure that he' – Cutter points to Stark's frozen image on the screen – 'and Sherman are one and the same. And after that, not a word, Rocco, not a word to a living soul. You, me and Crawford need to know – and that's it.'

Cutter turns to leave.

'And then what, Mr Cutter?'

'Like the man said, Rocco, we take him down.'

# thirty-nine

The next day and Cutter in his office studies that part of Nathan Stark's personnel file that lists the highlights of his previous career with the FBI. Stark himself hangs from the wall, not yet taken down – on the contrary, he appears flourishing, even buoyant.

One floor above Cutter's office the troops are gathering in the main conference room that the young terriers now insist on calling ZAIG Command, a joking reference to the Stasi department that Karl Gröber employed to acquire his considerable knowledge about the loopholes in the Western banking system. Though Cutter gripes about their frivolity he tolerates it, for the terriers have truly lived up to their name: their pursuit of the paper trail left by the Gröber organisation has been nothing if not dogged.

Most of the estimated two billion dollars that should have been the prize of Operation Pentecost – 'dirty money' that would have been seized by the FSF had the cover of Agent Ruth Apple not been comprehensively blown – has vanished like mist from the pipeline. But the terriers believe there is still a few million to be found and they have gathered evidence that, on Monday morning, will enable FSF agents to conduct simultaneous raids on twenty-three banks in Boston, New York, Wilmington and Chicago.

And, on what will be Monday afternoon in Europe, nine banks in Geneva, London and Douglas, Isle of Man will also be simultaneously raided by detectives brandishing court orders empowering them to seize documents and computer records, to freeze accounts. And on both sides of the Atlantic there are lawyers and accountants and other facilitators of the money-laundering trade who, before Monday is out, will be rudely disturbed in their homes or their offices by stony-faced men and women carrying warrants for their arrest.

In all, the terriers have identified forty-nine premises to be raided
and 118 individuals to be taken into custody in what will be the
largest operation ever coordinated by the Financial Strike Force.
Almost every FSF investigator has been co-opted but there are
fewer than two hundred of them so Cutter has called in favours to
ensure that special agents from the FBI, the DEA and the Criminal
Investigation department of the IRS will also take part in the raids.
Their representatives are part of the audience crowded into the
conference room where an elaborate wall chart compiled by the
terriers describes the labyrinth through which the Gröber organisation launders its funds.

The briefing is being broadcast to similar gatherings in four
American cities as well as London and Geneva, and Nathan Stark
stands at the podium waiting for confirmation from Rocco Morales
that the video links are live. Unknown to Stark, Morales has rigged
an extra feed to Cutter's office, which is why the gaunt face of the
Joint Assistant Director (Operations) looks down on Cutter from
the flat screen hanging on his wall.

While setting up his equipment, Morales has also bugged ZAIG
Command with hidden, sensitive microphones and one of them
relays a whispered conversation to Cutter.

'Is Nathan waiting for Godot, Kate?' says one of the more
irreverent terriers, evidently speaking to Kate Barrymore, the team
leader.

'What?'

'If he had hair he'd be an absolute ringer for Samuel Beckett. Get
it?'

Cutter grins despite himself, despite the anger that burns his
insides like indigestion. His loathing of internal corruption is part
of his legend within law enforcement. He has boasted that there are
no dirty players on his team because they'd have to be dumber than
dirt not to know what he'd do to them – and Aldus Cutter does not
hire dumb people. Stark's treachery has shattered this self-belief
and provoked Cutter into one of his rare and never-welcome bouts
of self-examination.

Why did he hire Nathan Stark, woo him away from the FBI?

Studying the personnel file on his desk Cutter can see that part
of Stark's attraction was the manner in which he had risen to the
rank of an assistant director at the Bureau; a career marked by
steady achievement rather than flashy success and one that had left

Stark largely unscathed by a series of FBI fiascos. Despite his position in the FBI's hierarchy, Stark attracted no blame for the unnecessary killings at Ruby Ridge, the firestorm at Waco, the rush to judgement over the bombing at the Atlanta Olympics. Stark was sound, Cutter had decided, plodding, by-the-book – the antithesis of Flint and therefore her perfect counterweight.

A sharp rap on the podium captures Cutter's attention.

'People,' says Stark, speaking to Cutter from the screen on the wall. 'Let me have your attention. It is now 1200 hours Eastern Standard time on Saturday April 28 – and to you gentlemen and ladies in Europe, good evening. Operation Payback will commence at exactly 0900 on Monday April 30, which means we have forty-five hours to go, and a great many logistical matters we need to resolve and accomplish.'

From ZAIG Command and six other rooms come murmurs of all-too-ready agreement. Stark waits for the grumbles to subside.

'First off, let me say that Director Cutter would have been here this afternoon but for other matters that need his urgent attention.'

*Damn right, Nathan*, thinks Cutter.

'In his absence he wants me to remind you that the objective of Payback is to inflict the maximum possible damage on what is a truly evil empire. Keep in mind, please, that people, even children, are enslaved in prostitution to earn the money that Gröber and his facilitators launder. Every single day miscreants in Europe and the United States OD on the narcotics that Gröber's clients supply. People – many of them entirely innocent people – are murdered by the weapons and explosives which Gröber's friends supply to gangsters and terrorists. Come Monday, you're going to be knocking on the doors of some pretty comfortable folks who don't associate themselves or what they do with any of that misery. But they *are* associated. Whether they know it or not, whether they care or not, every rotten dollar they've taken came to them from merchants of slavery and death.'

Stark's voice has taken on a messianic tone.

'And if Director Cutter was here he would want to remind you, every single one you, of one more thing' – Stark leaning on the podium as though it is a bully pulpit. 'Because of *their* greed, because they and bloodsuckers like them exist, a law enforcement officer – one of ours, one of us – lost her life.'

Stark turns from the podium to face the wall chart which, with a flick of a switch, Rocco Morales transforms into a screen. On it appears the grainy image of a helicopter rising above a cloud of smoke, of a black underbelly, of a body spilling out of the cockpit; of Flint sprinting across the plaza of The World's Greatest Emporium, reaching out her arms; of the collision of two bodies that sends Flint sprawling. Morales has doctored the soundtrack to extend the length of Jarrett Crawford's animal howl. It ends abruptly with the enhanced sound of Ruth Apple hitting the ground.

In ZAIG Command – and six other centres – there is absolute silence until Stark breaks it.

'As a matter of fact, and probably in law, Karl Gröber acted alone when he threw Special Agent Apple to her death. But we all know that a fact taken out of context doesn't tell the whole truth. In the next couple of days when the logistics of Operation Payback seem overwhelming; when everything that can go wrong does just that; when you get to thinking "to hell with it", that this is just another case, I want you to remember that everyone who works for Gröber, everyone who profits by him, had a hand in that.'

Stark is pointing to the screen where Ruth Apple's twisted body lies on the paving stones of the World Emporium in freeze-frame.

But what Cutter sees on his screen – what he imagines – are much earlier sequences from Rocco's tape: Stark standing behind Flint's chair, urging her: *Call it off*; Stark taking the chair next to Flint, telling her: *Grace, you have to pull the plug*; Stark leaning so close to Flint that she must have smelt the quince on his breath, pleading: *Grace, listen to me . . . They can do what the hell they like . . .*

Now Cutter has closed his eyes to concentrate on what he is trying to recall and what is not on Rocco's tape – the phone call he'd received at Ronald Reagan National airport as he was stepping off the Washington shuttle.

Stark had said, *Aldus, you have to stop her, you have to close this down* – something like that.

*Why?*

Stark had presented a litany of reasons: because the back-up was not in place; because the weather was bad; because there was no Plan B; because Ruth Apple was too inexperienced. *Flint could handle this, she can't.*

And when Cutter had dismissed his concerns – *Grace knows what she's doing* – what had Stark said?

Cutter can recall it now, practically word for word: 'Aldus, please, I'm begging you, tell her to stop. Close it down. However good Flint may be, I have a feeling in my gut that if you don't do something this is going to end in disaster.'

Cutter opens his eyes and stares at the screen on which Assistant Director Nathan Stark is describing the logistics of Operation Payback. Now he understands intuitively.

*You knew, didn't you, you sonofabitch? You knew what Gröber was going to do.*

'I need a favour' – Saturday afternoon and Cutter is on the phone to the Maryland home of his mentor at the Department of Justice in Washington DC.

'When don't you need a favour, Aldus?'

'This is a real favour because this is going to cost.'

'Go on.'

'I need you to find a reason to pull every case file that Nathan Stark signed off on during his last fifteen years with the Bureau.'

'Jesus!'

'I need them first thing on Monday morning, earlier if you can, and whatever reason you come up with, Nathan mustn't know.'

'Whatever reason? Aldus, this is absurd. What am I supposed to tell them?'

'Not them, sir, him – the Director, and only him.'

Silence on the line.

'Is this bad, Aldus? I mean, is this bad bad?'

Cutter says, 'About as bad as it gets.'

# Leipzig

# forty

It is only the Hartmanns' first day as Frau Gröber's tenants and already Grace Hartmann has turned out to be a poor companion. During tea, taken in the garden and served by Felix – since this is a Saturday and the servant's day off – she complained of a headache: not yet a migraine but she was prone to them, she explained, and it seemed sensible to take precautions. If Frau Gröber would excuse her, she said, she would retire to her room and take one of her Inderal tablets. Then, after an hour or two of rest, she hoped she would be well enough to join them for the supper that Felix – *thank God* – had volunteered to prepare. Only partly mollified by Felix's assurance that he would remain to keep her company, Frau Gröber gave her permission with a curt nod.

Free to investigate, Flint is working her way along the gloomy corridor on the first floor intrigued by a small mystery: Where are the stairs leading to the upper floors? She is sure they must be concealed behind one of the locked doors but she has opened the four most likely candidates to find only darkened empty rooms. Now she's probing with a pick at the simple mortise lock of a fifth door, willing the bolt to turn.

The lock yields but the door is stuck in its frame and Flint needs to use her shoulder to open it. A rush of stale air, sickly-sweet with the stench of mildew, makes her want to gag. She is standing in a void in utter darkness, breathing through her mouth, berating herself for not having had the foresight to bring a torch or even a box of matches to Ilse's house.

'You silly cow.'

Flint listens to her own voice resonate and deduces that the void is narrow. She raises one arm to shoulder height and takes a sideways step to the left and then another, and now her fingers find the rough plaster of a wall. She repeats the process, taking three, then four sidesteps to her right with the same result. So, she calculates, the walls are about five feet apart, suggesting a passageway rather than a room. Feeling slightly ridiculous, now with her arms stretched out in front of her, now to the side, now to the front, as though she is performing an exaggerated breast-stroke, she edges forward into darkness, waiting to collide with something solid.

It is her right foot that makes contact with a solid obstacle, and made of wood judging by the sound of the impact. She raises her foot to confirm that she has found the stairs and now she gropes for a banister that is not there. Crawling on her hands and knees she climbs the stairs one by one, following the curve, trying to ignore the soft objects that brush her face, consoling herself with the thought that whatever they are at least they do not flutter like bats.

She knows she has reached the summit when she crawls head-first into a second door. This one feels more sturdy and her searching fingers discover that it is secured by a latch and also metal clasps that are held together by a hefty padlock that is rough with rust to her touch. *Terrific!* Flint takes the pick from its safe place in her hair and goes to work on the lock, half-expecting that it will not open, until it comes apart in her hands.

Beyond the door there is only blackness. Flint slides her hand along the wall searching for a light switch that logically should be there and finds instead two brittle wires protruding from a hole. For a while she stays where she is, considering the possibility that if she moves too far from here and does not find some source of light, if she becomes even a little disoriented, she might not easily find her way back to the stairs.

*There has to be light – a window, something. Find it!*

She assumes she is in a corridor that mirrors the one on the first floor, and if that is the case there should be a room more or less opposite where she is standing. Pushing off from the wall, swimming with her arms, she tiptoes across wooden floorboards that creak and seem to give alarmingly under her weight.

*Bingo!* There is a door where she expected to find it and it is not locked and beyond it Flint sees a horizontal shard of light slipping through what must surely be a window. She stands in the doorway waiting for her night vision to kick in and form some impression of this room; watching as colourless, amorphous shapes vaguely emerge from the gloom.

Now that she can see sufficiently to navigate a safe passage she goes to the window, squeezing past a large dresser, intending to crack open the blind just a couple of inches, only to discover that it is not a blind blocking the light but a hardwood board nailed tightly to the window frame. She turns to the dresser hoping to find something that she can use to ease the board away from the frame and her hand strikes an object, knocking it over, sending it crashing to the floor with the sound of breaking glass. *Shit!* Flint crouches down and warily feels the remains of what seems to be a large vase – and then her fingers find what is unmistakably the stub of a fat pillar candle. Immediately she knows that she has broken what in France is called a *photophore* – a decorative hurricane shade – that, generally speaking, come in pairs. Carefully now, she searches the top of the dresser, locating the second of the pair and – *Halleluiah!* – a box of matches.

The first match breaks, the second splutters and dies, the third provides only a paltry flame but it is enough to ignite the candle.

Behind the dresser what was an invisible wall is now bathed in a ghostly light. It is covered with dark red fabric and dominated by a wooden crucifix that Flint is sure must be six feet tall. On either side of the cross hangs a portrait, each held in a silver frame: to her right, a photograph of a man's striking face with penetrating eyes, a broad forehead and almost flawless skin; to her left, a three-quarter profile of a once-handsome woman who looks worn down by cares. The way the woman's picture is positioned, she appears to be gazing down at Christ's impaled feet where, hanging from the nail, is a third photograph, this one of an impish girl with a white bow tied in her hair, posing coquettishly for the camera.

A pound to a penny the girl is Ilse, Flint believes, and this is Ilse's shrine to her murdered parents; their bedroom, preserved much as it was more than thirty years ago.

On top of the dresser beneath the crucifix there is a narrow display shelf containing two dozen or more votive candles set in small glass jars and there is a taper with which Flint lights them. Now the wall glows a deep crimson and Flint has a clearer view of Ilse's picture and she can see that the girl is not alone; that in the background, behind her right shoulder, there is the pale face of a young boy with flaxen hair flopping over his forehead who grins shyly into the lens. Brother Karl? Given the context, Flint thinks it is unlikely.

And now she sees that the backdrop behind Ilse's left shoulder has been crudely doctored – that whatever, or whoever, was there has been obliterated with black crayon. Cautiously taking down the picture, Flint removes the glass from the frame and scratches at the crayon with her fingernail until another face emerges: that of an unsmiling older boy who even then showed traces of Karl Gröber's distinctive widow's peak.

Flint turns her attention to the rest of the room. It is rectangular in shape, with a large canopy bed set in deep shadow against the far wall. Between the two windows to Flint's right there is an armoire with an overhanging cornice and elaborately-carved double doors and, alongside it, a simple desk and chair. To Flint's left, between the doorway and the bed, there is a wooden bench that looks as though it may once have served as a choir stall, furnished with two red cushions matching the faded fabric that covers all of the walls. Not much to search then, Flint decides.

She begins with the dresser, opening the three drawers from the bottom one up, smelling the faint scent of camphor, finding sweaters and cardigans, half a dozen folded shirts, underwear and hosiery in the top drawer, nothing hidden within the layers. Now she carries the surviving *photophore* to the table where there is a hand mirror, a hairbrush, a pair of tweezers and a jewellery box containing a few cheap trinkets. Flint finds no concealed compartments in the box. She does find human hair in the bristles of the brush and using the tweezers she extracts a few strands. The desk drawer is empty but it is lined with paper and Flint tears off a section to make an improvised envelope for the hair samples – samples that may contain the DNA of Karl Gröber's mother that could be matched with his DNA, should Gröber's identity ever become an issue.

*If you ever find bloody Karl Gröber, that is*, says the whining voice in Flint's head, the part of her subconscious that wants to leave this ghoulish room.

*Shuddup!*

*What's the point? What do you hope to find? Ilse's a cripple. She hasn't been up here for years.*

*SHUT UP!*

Next to the armoire, which is cavernous inside and divided unequally into 'his' and 'hers'. There are only two cotton dresses for Ilse's mother, three skirts, three blouses and a shawl; no pants, no belts, no hats, no shoes. Ilse's father's wardrobe is much more extensive. There are six suits – two brown, two blue, two grey – a green corduroy jacket and another made of fake Harris tweed, eight pairs of trousers in various colours, three leather belts, three pairs of heavy brogues and, on a shelf at the top of the armoire, a black fedora similar to the one that Dr Schnell wears.

Taking down Herr Gröber's hat to search the lining, Flint is struck by a morbid thought: Was Wilhelm Gröber wearing it the night they killed him in the forest? Did they make him take it off before they shot him in the head?

Item by item Flint plunders the clothes of the dead, taking them from their hangers, rummaging through the pockets, piling her booty on the table: a few coins, several scraps of paper bearing words she cannot decipher, a couple of tram tickets, a small key contained in a velvet pouch – *a key to what?* She is running out of hope of finding anything that clearly matters when a beam of light falls across her shoulder and her heart almost stops.

She drops the jacket she is searching and whirls around and sees that the light is steady and coming from the corridor. For a moment she is paralysed, her mind a commotion of questions and uncertainty.

*It must be Felix. So where is he now? Where did he find a light switch? How did he know I was here?*

*WHAT IF IT'S NOT FELIX?*

Flint hurries to the door and peers into the corridor which is filled with light but otherwise empty. She is about to call Felix's name when from her left, from the direction where the corridor makes a right-angled turn, she hears a high-pitched whine that she instantly recognises – the fast approach of Ilse's scooter.

There is no time to put back the clothes that are scattered on the floor, no time to pick up the debris of the shattered *photophore* or blow out the candles. Flint can only close the door on the chaos she has caused, dash across the corridor to the head of the stairs, pull that door closed behind her and hide in the dark.

While she waits for all hell to break loose she considers what is now obvious: there has to be some other way up to the second floor – a ramp, some kind of elevator or chairlift.

*Why didn't you check?*

*In the pitch dark?*

*Why didn't you wait until you had a torch? Why did it have to be today? Why are you always in such a goddamned hurry?*

*Because. Because there is no time.*

She has no better answer.

Through the door she listens to the approach of Ilse's scooter and waits for the moment when it will stop, about six feet from where she is hiding, and the moment when Ilse will discover the invasion of her parents' shrine.

*And then what?*

But the scooter does not stop. The whine of the motor grows into a crescendo and then gradually fades as Ilse continues along the corridor at what sounds to Flint like full throttle.

She cannot help herself. Blind to risk, she counts to ten and eases open the door to steal a look, just in time to see Ilse executing a fast three-point turn into the very last room on the left.

Now the reprieved Flint is re-crossing the corridor, slipping back into the shrine, wedging the door with a chair; re-hanging the clothes in the armoire, picking up pieces of broken glass, blowing out the candles.

Only the *photophore* is still alight when, out of a copper's instinctive habit, she decides to check the bed. She pulls back the canopy and sees on each pillow a single blood-red rose.

# forty-one

'*Ihre Frau ist sehr empfindlich*' – Your wife is very delicate, Ilse says.

She is certainly very pale, Felix Hartmann responds, speaking of his supposed wife as though she wasn't there. It is the migraines, he offers. They drain her.

He has served pan-fried calves' livers in a delicate mustard sauce with crisp *haricots verts* and new potatoes. Frau Gröber has eaten heartily and she continues to accept refills of her wine glass. Pale Frau Hartmann, on the other hand, plays with her food and drinks only water.

*I refer to the fragility of her mental health*, says Frau Gröber.

Felix manages to look both uncomfortable and uncomprehending.

Frau Gröber presses the point.

*You are surely aware that your wife has failed to come to terms with the death of her mother? After so long it is not healthy, not natural, to continue to grieve for a lost parent.*

*Bitte*, Frau Hartmann pleads.

Felix stiffens. *I'm sorry, Frau Gröber, as you can see this is not a subject that my wife cares to discuss.*

*Why?*

*Because that is her choice.*

*Why?* – Ilse animated, her insistence fuelled by wine.

*Bitte, bitte*, says Frau Hartmann. Please, *please* stop this now.

Abiding by her instructions – *If she even hints at talking about my mother, get out of there*, Flint had said – Felix excuses himself, claiming to have urgent business in the kitchen; a soufflé that will collapse unless he attends to it immediately. The women wait until he is out of earshot.

*Why don't you talk to your husband about your mother's murder?*

*Because he can never understand.*

*He seems to be a sympathetic man.*

*He is a caring, kind, wonderful person. But, as you say, Frau Gröber, he is a man.*

*So?*

*Do you think a man can ever really understand what a woman feels?*

*What does he say?*

*He offers platitudes. He talks about 'coming to terms', about 'closure'. What is 'closure', Frau Gröber? What does 'closure' mean to you?*

*A zip fastener.*

*Exactly.*

Ilse is torn between caution and curiosity but the wine makes her brazen.

'*Sagen Sie mir*' – Tell me, Ilse says. Tell me about your mother.

*I was six years old. My father was – is – a country vet and sometimes he would take me on his rounds. This was a Saturday in October. We came home in the early evening and there was no sign of my mother. Her name was Marie-Madeleine but everyone called her Mad.*

They are sitting at a long table in the formal dining room where Frau Gröber has manoeuvred her scooter so that she is now very close to Flint, close enough to rest her skinny fingers on Flint's arm.

*I had a dog, a Labrador called Hector. He wasn't at home either and my father assumed that Mad had taken him for a walk. He went to look for her – we went to look for her – and we found Hector in a lane not far from the house, lying in a ditch, all bloody. I was sitting on my father's shoulders and I slipped and fell and he caught me and I was hanging upside down looking at that poor puppy. My father said he'd been beaten with an iron bar. There was no sign of my mother.*

All of this is true and the memory of it never fails to induce in Flint a profound sadness that seems to diminish her, to make her physically smaller. What she is about to tell Ilse is not true – for her mother was never found, alive or dead – but she believes that so long as she clings to the image of her dog's bloodied head she can make her lie thoroughly convincing.

*The police found my mother's body several days later – I don't remember how long exactly. She was in a clearing, in a forest near to where we lived, just lying there, there had been no attempt to bury her. I never saw the body of course but my father told me she looked very peaceful. I don't believe that, Frau Gröber. How can someone be peaceful when they're abducted, taken away, shot in the back of the head? I mean, you might not see the gun but you'd know, wouldn't you? You'd know you were about to die?*

Ilse is staring intently at Flint's face as though she is mesmerised.

*That was almost thirty years ago and I still think about it every single day. Felix would tell you I'm obsessed by a question that can never be answered: What was she thinking just before she died?*

'*Möglicherweise dachte sie an Sie?*' suggests Frau Gröber.

*Thinking of me?* Flint risks a smile. *Wouldn't that be something.*

Felix is returning bearing the soufflé, telling Flint with his eyes *I stayed away as long as I could.*

Frau Gröber prepares to resume her position at the head of the table but before she leaves Flint's side she has one more thing to say.

'*Meine Mutter dachte an mich.*'

My mother thought of me.

Grace and Felix in their apartment preparing for bed. Flint usually sleeps naked but tonight she wears a plain flannel gown with a high neck that is a part of the wardrobe she bought for Frau Hartmann. She is sitting on the bed applying cleansing cream to her skin, listening to Felix take a shower, wondering how much to tell him about her rash exploration of the second floor and its nearly-disastrous consequences.

*Not a lot*, she decides. *Just the essentials.*

He comes out of the bathroom wearing a robe, rubbing at his hair with a towel and Flint says, 'This afternoon I went upstairs to the second floor to take a look around.'

Hartmann grins. 'Really? And all the time I imagined that you were lying in the dark nursing your headache.'

'It was dark' – a repentant smile from Flint – 'I forgot to bring a flashlight.'

'And what did you find in the Gröbers' apartment?'

'Apartment?'

'Sure. In the GDR days the house was divided into apartments. The Gröbers had five rooms on the second floor.'

'Ilse told you that?'

'Ilse told me many things,' says Hartmann in a teasing tone. 'I think she likes me. She even flirted with me a little bit.'

'Lucky you. Maybe she'll show you her parents' bedroom. Believe me, it's something else. The point is, I used the stairs but there's got to be some other way for Ilse to get up there, some kind of ramp or—'

'There is a small elevator,' Hartmann interrupts. 'It's in the hallway between the dining room and the kitchen, purpose-built for Ilse's scooter, I would think. So, Grace' – he pretends to look solemn – 'did Ilse almost catch you up there while you were snooping?'

'Not even close,' says Flint. Then, 'I wonder who stumped up the cash for Ilse's elevator fund?'

'Please?'

'Who paid for it, Felix? Come to that, who bought the house for her, and that bloody scooter? Who pays for the servant? How does she live?'

'Karl?' suggests Hartmann.

'Let's hope so. And, if he is funding her, let's hope there's a decent paper trail.'

Flint gets up from the bed and goes to the bathroom to put away her cream and brush her hair. 'I have to go back up there,' she calls to Hartmann through the open door.

'Tonight?' He sounds alarmed by the possibility.

'No, because I need a flashlight and you need to find some way of making sure she doesn't come up there while I'm looking around. Do you think Otto will help?'

'With the flashlight, certainly.' Hartmann comes to the doorway and watches Flint's reflection in the mirror. 'With the elevator, I do not see how.'

'I was thinking of a temporary power failure to stop the elevator working. There must be some way of cutting off the electricity supply to the house for a couple of hours.'

Hartmann pulls a doubting face. 'I do not think Dr Schnell would sanction interference with a public utility.'

'Oh, really? And what about the stunt he pulled last night?

Don't you think that having half a dozen emergency vehicles at your hotel to deal with a totally non-existent fire might qualify as "interfering with a public utility"?'

'That was different.'

'Yes?' Flint turns to face him. 'How?'

'I was hungry' – a sheepish grin. 'It was necessary that I joined you for dinner.'

'Go to bed, Felix – or rather, not to bed. Take your blanket and your pillow, please, and let me go to sleep.'

Felix Hartmann retires to the living room where he attempts to make himself comfortable on a two-seater couch that is nowhere near as long as he is tall. Flint turns out the bathroom light – and in a car parked on Karl-Heine-Strasse some fifty yards from Ilse's house one of the watchers makes a note of the time in his log.

# forty-two

After the reunification of Germany they built a new terminal at Leipzig-Halle airport that did not come close to meeting the surge in passenger traffic. Now, belatedly, a replacement terminal is being constructed and the frantic building work has seriously reduced the number of spaces in the car park and, having circled in growing frustration looking for an empty bay, Stephanie Cooper-Cole abandons her rental car in a strictly *verboten* no-parking zone. Given the choice between a stiff fine and being on the receiving end of Nigel Ridout's acid temper, she is certain she would rather take the fine.

She is late even so. Ridout leans against a wall in the arrivals hall impatiently flicking through the pages of a Sunday magazine supplement.

'Ah, Stephanie, *there* you are,' he says, making an exaggerated show of tossing away the magazine and looking at his watch. 'I was beginning to think you'd lost yourself as well as sight of your objectives.' When she bristles he continues, 'Found Catmint, have we? No, I thought not. Shall we go? You *do* have a car, I suppose.'

They drive along the autobahn towards Leipzig in silence until Ridout says, 'The fellow who turned up at Dr Flint's house is with the FSF but not *of* them, if you get my meaning, Stephanie.'

'No, actually, I don't, Nigel,' Cooper-Cole says frostily, eyes firmly on the road, still smarting from his jibe.

'His name is Hartmann, Felix Hartmann, and he's on secondment to the Americans from the German federal police – officially, that is. Actually, his masters are in Pullach. He works for Otto Schnell.'

'Oh, Christ,' she says and Ridout chuckles.

'No, Otto only thinks he is, Stephanie, but the BND's involvement does explain Friday night's events, doesn't it? All those sirens, all that excitement, all that *confusion* – and, doubtless, Herr

Hartmann slipping unnoticed through the back door. Otto would have enjoyed his little diversion. In the circumstances, I don't think you should be quite so hard on the wretched Fellowes.'

'*Me?*' It was not Cooper-Cole who, thirty-six hours ago, had called Fellowes a moron and half a dozen synonyms; not Cooper-Cole who had threatened to fire Fellowes on the spot for gross incompetence.

'Speaking of which, of *whom*,' says Ridout, 'where is the wretched Fellowes?'

'Where he's been since it happened, riding a tram. They all are.'

'A tram? I don't think we're going to find Otto's boy, or Catmint, on a tram, are we, Stephanie?'

'They're scouring the city, Nigel,' she says. 'You see more from a tram. Apparently,' she adds.

*Runde Ecke*, which was for forty years the Leipzig district head-quarters of the Stasi, stands alongside a small park at approximately a forty-five-degree angle to the apartment building on the other side of the ring road where Nigel Ridout spies out the land from a fourth-floor window.

Part of *Runde Ecke* is now a museum that preserves in replica the way it was in the Stasi days, down to the grand marbled entrance hall and the cracked linoleum on the floors; a permanent reminder of the folly. The museum is closed to the public on Sundays but private tours can be arranged and Ridout watches as a dozen or so middle-aged men gather on the steps, greeting each other like old friends.

'Former *Mitarbeiters*, I wouldn't be surprised,' he tells Cooper-Cole. 'Old Stasi comrades come to wallow in a little nostalgia.'

*They're not alone in their nostalgia*, she thinks, for it is evident that Nigel knows the apartment well. 'Been here before?' she asks but he only smiles at her, running his hands in a familiar way along the back of the leather couch, picking up objects as though he's pleased to find them still here.

Ridout drifts back to the window to stare at *Runde Ecke* and asks, 'Does it look to you like a monument to evil?'

'No. Actually it looks like a bank.'

'Ah, very good, Stephanie, though it was *actually* built for an insurance company. But before the Stasi – before you were born, my dear – it was the headquarters of an outfit known as K5, as nasty a bunch of goose-stepping goons as you could wish to meet. And before that, if you were taken up those steps then you were a guest of the Soviet NKVD, which taught the KGB a thing or two about interrogation methods.'

Cooper-Cole, who is aware that Nigel shares Dr Schnell's fondness for convoluted diversions, waits patiently for him to reach his point.

'Mind you, before that, at the end of the War, it served as the headquarters of the American army. And, speaking of our cousins,' says Ridout, effortlessly changing tack as she knew he would, 'you don't suppose that Langley is holding out on us, do you?'

'Meaning?'

'Gröber's file – not exactly complete, is it?'

'It's all they have, or so they say.'

'No mention of any family, is there – no kith and kin for Karl? Looked in the phone book, have we?'

'Yes, Nigel, and do you want to know how many Gröbers there are in Leipzig?'

'Many, I expect, *columns* of them, I would have thought. So, you'll be needing help to find Catmint, won't you, Stephanie? Reinforcements?'

'Are you serious?'

Ridout winks.

'Locals?'

'Hardly,' Ridout says in a tone suggesting that the very idea is preposterous.

'When?'

'Very soon, I expect. They're on their way from Berlin as we speak.'

Cooper-Cole's relief is transparent and so is her exasperation. 'Nigel, if only you'd allowed me proper help in the first place, this would never—'

Ridout isn't listening. 'Can't have you playing away from home against Otto's boys without a decent team, can we, Stephanie?'

# forty-three

D r Schnell, perched three hundred feet above the ground and master of all he surveys, considers Flint's startling demand to cut the electricity supply to Ilse's house. Could she not simply pull a fuse, he suggests? Flint, who did not sleep well last night because of Felix's restlessness, rolls her eyes in frustration.

'There's an electrical shop practically next door to the house,' she says breathlessly – still out of breath because Dr Schnell has insisted that she and Hartmann climb with him the five hundred steps to the summit of the *Völkerschlachtdenkmal*, the mountainous monument to the 100,000 soldiers who were slaughtered in the Battle of Leipzig in 1813. Far below their vantage point, six of Dr Schnell's men mingle among the sightseers strolling in the grounds.

'Sod's law says they'll have someone round to the house in five minutes,' continues Flint, 'and the first thing they'll do is check the fuse box. It has to be a problem that no electrician can fix.'

'I see that,' says Dr Schnell, 'but any electrician will surely be suspicious if Ilse's house is the only one without power?'

'Then black out the street, the whole area, the whole city if you have to, Otto. All I need is an hour.'

'I am afraid that you overestimate my powers.'

'Okay, what about emergency road works right outside Ilse's house?' Flint is now pacing the viewing platform, reminding Dr Schnell of a caged animal; a tigress, he thinks. 'They cut through the cable and one of your people goes to see Ilse and explains what's happened?'

'Even assuming we could find the cable, I do not think so, Grace.'

*Why is this so difficult?*

'They don't have to cut the cable, or even find it,' Flint says, failing to keep the irritation out of her voice. 'That's just the pretext, the explanation for why she has no electricity. They don't even have to dig up the road. They just put up a workman's tent and a couple of signs and make it *look* as though they're digging up the road. Honestly, Otto, this isn't rocket science we're talking about.'

Felix Hartmann, who has fallen into one of his characteristic brooding silences, looks at Flint as though he thinks she has gone mad.

'What?' – a challenging glare from Flint.

'Grace, tell me, please: what is it that you think you will find on the second floor?'

'Felix, think about it. Ilse loathes Karl for what he did to her parents and for what he did to her afterwards. She is obsessed by what happened because it defines her, which is why she keeps her parents' bedroom exactly as it was. But she's still in touch with Karl, taking money from him, perhaps *extorting* money from him – she has to be – and somewhere in that house I'm betting she preserves Karl in some way, just as she preserves her parents.'

Hartmann seems inclined to argue but Dr Schnell intervenes. 'Assuming it is possible to interrupt the power supply, when should that happen, do you think?'

'Tomorrow afternoon, around four, after Ilse and I have had tea. I'll get another of my headaches – an hour of talking about the works of Schiller should do it – and tell her I'm going upstairs to rest.'

'No,' says Hartmann sharply.

'Why?'

'I have to be there, in case something goes wrong. What if you are caught?'

'How, Felix? Who's going to catch me?' Flint feels as though she is swimming through mud.

'What if she sends the servant upstairs to find you, to see how you are, to tell you that the power has failed – and you are not in your room? What if he comes—'

'Then I'll have to kill him, won't I?' says Flint straight-faced, trying to get a rise. 'Oh, *come on*, Felix, he's about a hundred years old, he can barely make it up the stairs. Look' – turning now to appeal to Dr Schnell – 'the worst that can happen is that I'll blow my cover, and then at least I won't have to read bloody Schiller any more. Otto, I know it's a long shot but I also know we've got virtually nothing to lose.'

Dr Schnell, who stares at the distant skyline of Leipzig, seems not be listening, as though he's already made up his mind.

A mile or so from Ilse's house, where Dr Schnell has ordered his driver to stop the car, an old Russian-built turboprop airliner sits on the roof of a squat grey building as though it has landed there in error. It is painted red and white in the livery of Interflug, the defunct East German airline, and Dr Schnell says that although its purpose is to advertise a cabaret club he sees it as a metaphor for the fate of the whole GDR and its institutions. 'In America people might say they ran out of gas.'

Flint, who shares the back seat of the car with a morose Hartmann, smiles politely at the simile but her attention is focused on the messages coming over the radio. Dr Schnell's watchers have spotted a Mercedes with Berlin plates prowling suspiciously in the neighbourhood, making too many passes by Ilse's house. Now four teams of Otto's watchers are playing tag, covertly following the car wherever it goes and reporting in.

'It was bound to happen sooner or later.'

'The Wall?' asks Flint, misunderstanding.

'Yes, that too, but what I meant is that they were bound to find Ilse.'

'If it is them.'

'Oh, I think we can safely make that assumption,' Dr Schnell says, nodding to indicate the radio that is now reporting the Mercedes has turned around and is once more westbound on Karl-Heine-Strasse, proceeding slowly towards Ilse's house. 'I think it is entirely clear that Ridout's cavalry has arrived.'

'Excuse me?'

Half-turning in his seat to watch Flint's face Dr Schnell explains, 'Nigel Ridout – one of your reptiles, Grace. He flew into Leipzig via Frankfurt this morning, not travelling under his own name of course, but Mr Ridout is well known to us. Our paths have crossed on many occasions.'

The corners of Dr Schnell's mouth turn down to suggest that his long acquaintanceship with Nigel Ridout has brought him little pleasure.

'He works for MI6, as does the woman who met him at the

airport this morning. You may remember her, perhaps? About your height and build, about your age? Pale complexion, distinctive red hair?'

Flint, puzzled, shakes her head.

'She sat two rows behind you on your flight from London to Berlin but I expect that took precautions to avoid being noticed. No matter,' says Dr Schnell. Affecting not to notice Flint's blush of embarrassment he continues, 'She is travelling under the name of Fitzroy but I doubt that is her real name. Ridout has an assistant whom we know by her MI6 codename of Firefly – perhaps because of the luminescence of her hair – and I expect we will discover that Firefly and Fitzroy are one and the same.'

Dr Schnell chuckles. 'Ridout does so enjoy inventing his code-names. Usually he chooses the names of plants, plants that he grows in his garden. It is one of his tics. Yours, by the way, is Catmint, which seems a dull choice. I must confess that I would have selected something more exotic.'

'Why are they here?'

'Looking for you.'

'Why?'

Dr Schnell wrinkles his eyes. 'A good question. Do you want to ask them, Grace? I could easily arrange for that to happen.'

Part of Flint wants to leap at the offer. Part of her wants to see Schnell's men rounding up the reptiles, tracking them to their lairs with Teutonic efficiency. And she definitely wants to be there when the questioning begins for she has reason to know that spooks fear nothing more than their own exposure. But the other part of her is now fixated on her conviction that there is something to be found on the second floor of Ilse's house that will lead her to Karl Gröber and – *please God, if there is a God* – to Ben. 'Not until after tomorrow,' she says. 'Please, Otto.'

'*Das Auto hat gegenüber vom Haus angehalten*,' says a voice on the radio – the Mercedes has stopped opposite the house. Two occupants, just sitting there, watching, waiting.

They will also wait, Dr Schnell announces, and the driver pulls off the road into a car park set beneath the turboprop's tail. Flint excuses herself and gets out of the car, taking her mobile phone to call Horton General Hospital for the second time today, to be told, for the second time today, that there is no change in her father's condition.

Dr Flint is 'stable', the nurse says – about the only thing in my world that is, Flint thinks.

The late April sun has lost its strength and it's getting cold out here and Flint turns up the collar of Frau Hartmann's thin woollen coat, stuffing her hands into the pockets, wandering aimlessly across the lot. She kicks at a stone and watches it bounce and she follows its path to kick at it again like some bored urchin, aiming casually at the faint traces of a soccer goal painted with whitewash on a brick wall. She scores and kicks a second stone and scores again and she lines up a third, telling herself that if she achieves a hat-trick, three in a row, then it means her father will live.

The third stone misses the goal – and Flint is suddenly over-whelmed by a sense of utter helplessness.

*Don't you dare die on me*, she silently implores her father. *Don't you dare bloody die.*

Staring at the wall, her back to the car, Flint finally manages to cry.

# forty-four

*Where is your husband?*

That question again, and once more the truthful answer would be that Flint has no idea – but that is not the answer she provides.

There has been an emergency, Frau Hartmann tells Ilse Gröber. One of Doktor Hartmann's students, a young woman, is in trouble and requires his immediate attention. He received the call on his mobile phone while they were out walking and went straight to the university. Frau Hartmann does not know when her husband will return.

From her scooter Frau Gröber stares at Flint with rank suspicion.

*A young woman? What kind of trouble?*

A crisis, says Frau Hartmann. An *emotional* crisis, she believes.

By emphasising *emotional* she hopes to imply that this is delicate territory that should not be further explored, but Ilse's inquisitiveness is not so easily deflected. Is Dr Hartmann equipped to deal with a *young woman's* crisis, an *emotional* crisis? What training does he have? Surely a psychiatrist is required? Or a doctor of medicine? – and on and on she goes, probing and pushing, until even meek Frau Hartmann's patience snaps.

*Genug!* Enough!

Given her normal timidity her vehemence is shocking and it provokes in Ilse a stony, offended silence that will endure, she makes clear, until Frau Hartmann comes to her senses.

Eventually: It is late and she is very tired, Frau Hartmann admits in her most placatory tone. She is sorry for her impatience and her rudeness. Perhaps she should prepare supper? What would Frau Gröber like to eat?

Eat? At this hour? And risk indigestion, a night of painful discomfort and insomnia? Does Frau Hartmann – by insinuation the extremely selfish Frau Hartmann – not understand the inconvenience she has caused by the lateness of her return? And, come to that, why was she so late in returning? Where has she been since her husband went to deal with the crisis?

*Actually, Ilse dear, freezing my butt off in some bloody car park while Otto figured out a way to get Ridout's goons away from your house.*

'A small diversion is required,' Dr Schnell had said after giving Flint time to pull herself together, coming over to the corner of the lot where she leaned against the wall, pretending not to register the blotches on her cheeks. 'Felix will be the bait. Felix and you, my dear, if you will allow me to arrange an illusion.'

It has taken forever to set it up, for Dr Schnell to acquire from the state police the services of a female detective who, dour and silent, had pulled into the car park in a small VW and looked Flint up and down as though she was comparing her appearance to the circulated description of some wanted miscreant. Then she had removed the makeup from her face and the jewellery from her ears and neck, and pulled her hair into a knot, and produced a pair of spectacles, and demanded that she and Flint exchange coats, and when she was done Dr Schnell had nodded his approval. Glimpsed through the window of a passing car, he said, she could easily pass for Flint.

She has been walking, says Frau Hartmann in reply to Frau Gröber's question – walking all the way from the *Völkerschlacht-denkmal*, which is where they were when her husband received the call; on the viewing platform at the very top of the *Völkerschlacht-denkmal*, she adds, to give her fiction a veneer of truth. Felix told her to take a taxi home but in the haste of his departure – in his concern for his *emotional* student – he neglected to leave her any money before racing down the stairs. When he emerged at the bottom of the monument she had called to him from the platform but he had not heard. Frau Hartmann sighs. It was not his fault. How could he hear from such a distance?

'Felix' – Flint calling to Hartmann as her impostor was about to drive him away towards Ilse's house where an accident with a van awaited them, courtesy of Dr Schnell. Nothing too serious: a minor shunt at the traffic lights fifty metres shy of the house that would cause Felix to leap from the car to inspect the damage and remonstrate with the other driver. If all went to plan, Ridout's watchers were bound to see him, bound to catch a glimpse of a woman they would assume was Flint, bound to take the bait and follow their targets away from Ilse's house.

'Listen, watch yourself, will you?' Flint had said, remembering a bomb planted in Paris that had shredded the legs of Inspector Gilles Bourdonnec. 'Reptiles play by different rules. Don't put anything past them.'

'No, *you* be careful,' Hartmann had replied. 'If it comes to it, we know how to deal with Ridout's men. Ilse, I think, is far more dangerous.'

Shrivelled, aged beyond her years, she hardly looks dangerous but Flint will admit that watching those blue eyes that watch her intently she feels a suggestion of alarm. She no longer thinks it ridiculous that, out of Dr Schnell's sight, Felix slipped a small-calibre pistol into the pocket of her replacement coat.

*You were a fool not to have taken money of your own*, says Frau Gröber. *Why do you expect your husband to take care of your every need when he has so many other concerns?*

*You're right, of course*, says Frau Hartmann.

*You are very demanding and very selfish.*

*I don't mean to be.*

*You think only of yourself.*

*I'm sorry.*

*You think that because your mother was murdered you have the right to be a pathetic creature for the rest of your life. You behave like a child. You think you are the only one who has suffered? Well, you are not and some have suffered far more than you. Shall I tell you, Frau Hartmann, shall I tell you what real suffering is?*

Flint does not say a word. Knowing it is time, she gets up from her chair and goes to the dresser where a bottle of plum brandy sits on a silver tray. She brings the tray to the dining table and pours a large measure into a crystal glass that she warms with cupped hands until she is satisfied that the temperature of the brandy is correct. Still mute, she passes the glass to Frau Gröber and pours a smaller measure for herself.

Frau Hartmann has taken on an air of infinite patience. By her bearing she wishes to indicate that she will wait until Frau Gröber is ready to begin. They have all night if needs be. No reason to hasten, no need at all.

\*    \*    \*

*My father was a gentle man but strong, so very strong. I had been
in hospital and I was still too weak to walk and they had acquired
a wheelchair for me but he preferred me in his arms. He would
carry me for hours, for kilometres, and never tire. It was as though
he was trying to give me strength, his magnificent warm strength
flowing from his arms.*

The gentle light from a candelabrum softens Ilse's face. She
suddenly seems much younger and her voice has taken on an almost
childlike quality.

*That night, the night it happened, he carried me from my bed
while I was still half-asleep. I had no idea what was happening
because my parents had not prepared me. He said I must be very
quiet; not a sound, not a word. It was dark but I was not afraid. I
was never afraid in my father's arms.*

*In those days this house was divided into many apartments.
Ours was the largest because of my parents' professional status
but it was on the second floor and he had to be very careful
coming down the stairs in case anyone should hear. There were so
many spies, you have to understand. Informers for the secret
police, they were everywhere. You never knew who you could
trust so you trusted no-one.* Ilse gulps at the brandy. *No-one at
all.*

*The front door used to squeak when it was opened, but not that
night. It didn't make a sound. I wondered about that. Had my
father fixed it, done something to the hinges? And wouldn't that
have alerted the spies? Wouldn't they have asked themselves, 'Why
has Dr Gröber silenced the door?' and wouldn't they have told the
Stasi? For a long time afterwards that is what I thought must have
happened, how they knew we were coming. I was very naïve, you
see. It never occurred to me to suspect him.* She drinks again. *Not
Karl. Not my brother.*

Flint is motionless, she barely breathes. She has angled her
chair so that her face is in shadow and unreadable to Ilse. She is
like the audience in a darkened theatre – present but essentially
invisible.

*My mother was waiting in the car. She was wearing a hat.
I'd never seen her in a hat before and I laughed. She told me
to be quiet but not in an unkind way; my mother was never
unkind, not to me. She had a blanket for me and a pillow, and
my father laid me down on the back seat. They told me to sleep and*

*that when I woke up we would be at the start of a great adventure, but I was much too excited to sleep. I asked them if Karl was coming. They said no; that the adventure was just for me.*

*We drove for a long, long time. Occasionally I heard my parents murmuring to each other but not what they said. They seemed very calm as if we were simply on an outing, going to the mountains or the lake as we sometimes used to do before I got ill. Except that Karl wasn't there, or Heinz. Well, Heinz couldn't be there, could he? Because Heinz was dead.*

*I must have fallen asleep eventually. When I woke up we had stopped on the side of the road; not a road exactly, more like a track, a track in the forest. I was cold. I told my mother, 'Mama, I'm cold' but she told me to shush. Now they were very tense. I could feel it.*

Ilse's glass is empty. Flint, gliding ghostlike from her chair, refills it almost to the brim.

*They were waiting for a sign, I think – a signal that it was safe to cross. It was a clear night, crystal clear, filled with moonlight and utterly silent. I could hear my heart beating. I sat up to look out of the window but my father said I must stay down. 'Just for a little longer, Liebling,' he said. I was always his Liebling – his favourite. Anyway, I did as I was told so I don't know what the signal was. I just heard my father say, 'There it is,' and he started the engine. He drove very slowly, very carefully because the track was rutted. I suppose we had travelled only two or three hundred metres when suddenly my mother screamed. Like this.*

Her eyes closed, Ilse attempts to scream in imitation of her mother but what comes out of her throat is a low moan as haunting as the night wind. Her face tilted towards the flickering light is now a picture of misery.

*My father cursed; filthy, filthy words. I'd never heard him use such language before and I remember being shocked – frightened because he was frightened. He turned around, trying to reverse the car, and I saw the fear in his face. Then we hit something, or something hit us, and I was thrown from the seat, and I heard shouting and whistles being blown and the barking of a dog. Then the door was pulled open, my door, and I was lying on the floor looking up at this man in uniform, a soldier or a guard, and he grabbed me by the hair and pulled me out of the car on to the ground. I saw him raise his boot and I thought he was going to kick me in the face, but he didn't. He put his boot on my throat to hold me there, to keep me still.*

*My mother was yelling, 'Leave her alone, leave her alone!' I heard glass breaking and my mother screaming again and then the sound of . . . I don't know – slaps, punches? No, not punches – blows. Now my father was shouting and the car was rocking and I heard more blows, and cries. And then suddenly it went very quiet. All I could hear was people panting, out of breath as though they'd been running. The man who was pressing on my throat with his boot pointed a gun at my face and did something to it that made a sharp metallic sound.*

Not all of Flint is in this room with Ilse. Part of her is miles away – years away – lying broken and bloody in a London stairwell, listening to the slide of a nine-millimetre Browning being worked as Clayton Buller prepares to kill her.

*Of course I understand now that he was preparing the gun, preparing to shoot me but I didn't really understand at the time. My mind was frozen, you see, in shock, I suppose. I had nearly died once before in hospital and I remember experiencing the same feeling of unreality, as though I was remote, disconnected from the events going on around me. It was very strange. I was lying in mud and I was wearing only my nightdress and yet I didn't feel cold or afraid. Just numb.*

*A man said, 'Get them on their feet,' but he didn't mean me. 'Not her.' I remained pinned to the ground and I couldn't move my head, couldn't see what was going on. I could only hear. I heard my parents being half-carried, half-dragged away from the car – but not very far. I heard my mother say, 'Ilse' as though she was trying to comfort me. Then, two shots: bang, bang. I heard the bodies fall. Nothing more. Nobody spoke.*

Ilse also sinks into silence as though she has run out of words, or the will to speak them. Her glass is empty once more but Flint does not reach for the bottle to replenish it – not yet. She waits for what seems like an eternity until she judges that it is time for Frau Hartmann to speak.

*And Karl did this?*

*Did what?*

*Killed your parents.*

*No. I told you, the guards killed them.*

*No, the guards only fired the shots. Karl did this, didn't he? Karl betrayed your parents, betrayed you?*
Yes.
*Where is he now, Ilse? Where is Karl?*
Ilse Gröber raises a skinny arm to point towards the ceiling.

# forty-five

In MI6's safe but compromised apartment overlooking *Runde Ecke* Stephanie Cooper-Cole puts down the telephone and, as if the possibility has only just occurred to her, asks Nigel Ridout, 'You don't think they're making it just a little too easy for us, do you?'

Ridout, who sits before a baize-covered table on which he is building a house of cards, rewards her with a broad smile. 'Very good, Stephanie. Marvellous, *splendid*, congratulations. Now' – and abruptly there is no longer any trace of levity in his tone – 'tell me why you think that – *finally*.'

She should know better than to be surprised, and better still than to show it, but she can't help herself from reacting. 'You *bastard*, Nigel.'

'Language,' says Ridout, as though he is correcting a child.

'It's a charade, isn't it, another of Schnell's bloody diversions – and you've known all along?'

'Not strictly true, not *all* along, Steff.' Failing to look at her, he concentrates on completing a pyramid with only one tier to go. 'But when you tell me – when you told me – that Catmint and Thymus are holed up in a building that has a single exit, a building to which you followed them with only the minimum of difficulty; when I consider how extremely fortunate you were to pick up their scent in the first place; when you tell me that Otto's boys are conspicuous by their absence, nowhere to be seen, then, yes, I do indeed – did indeed – smell another one of Otto's deceptions.' Ridout flicks at the corner of his edifice and watches the cards collapse. 'Thymus being nicely visible, is he? Helpful glimpses of him at the window, are there – and he stays visible just long enough for us to be absolutely sure it's him?'

Cooper-Cole answers Ridout with a furious look.

'Ah, but Stephanie, not too many glimpses of Catmint, are there? What are we seeing through the window? An occasional silhouette? The back of her head? It could well be Catmint's head but on the other hand . . . Stephanie, what are you doing?'

She has picked up the phone and is brutally punching in a number, taking out her frustration on the keys.

'*Stephanie?*'

'Calling Fellowes. Calling them off.'

Ridout comes out of his chair with remarkable speed to cross the room and take the phone from her hand. 'You will do no such thing.'

'Why, Nigel? What's the point?'

'The *point is*, young Stephanie, that just because Fellowes tells you there is no sign of Otto's boys does *not* mean they're not there. They *are* there, invisible to Fellowes, no doubt, but do not, for one moment, doubt Otto's resources nor his cunning – and if you end surveillance, if you pull out, Otto will instantly know you're on to him. Maintain the watch, *intensify* the watch, go there yourself if you wish, but do not – do *not* – fall into Otto's trap. Do you understand?'

He's standing very close to her.

'Where's Catmint?' she asks.

'Think, Stephanie, think – and then you tell me.'

'The house on Karl-Heine-Strasse. Where we found them – or, rather, where they found us. From where they led us away like bloody sheep.'

'Very good, Stephanie, *very* good.' Ridout beams.

# La Rochelle
# France

# forty-six

Mandrake rides a yellow bicycle along the Quai du Bout Blanc, shading his eyes against the brilliant light to search the yacht basin for the slip where he has been told his prize lies. The last time he was here was with Grace, at the tail end of their honeymoon, and they'd stood on the edge of the quay, bundled up inside his parka against the sharp Atlantic wind, watching the wheeling gannets escort the fishing boats back into harbour. Grace had the kind of skin that the sun turns quickly from office-white to copper-bronze and after two weeks on Hayman Island that flawless face of hers had positively glowed. He'd stood behind her, holding her very close, nuzzling her neck, and promised her that she was the most beautiful thing he'd ever seen – which as far as women go was the unvarnished truth. He'd also promised that he would never, ever leave her – never, ever let her down – which was anything but the truth, though a detached part of him wished that it could have been.

*Never forget what she is, Mandrake,* they'd said during the final briefing at Fort Monkton. *Never forget she's a cipher, a lever, the means to your end. When you're holding her, when you're fucking her, just remember that's all she is – somebody you're fucking with to get what we need. Never, ever, let your emotions become involved.*

And Nigel Ridout, who just happened to be passing through Monkton on that day – or so he said – had laughed as though it was the funniest thing he'd ever heard. 'Emotions? Dear Lord! You think that Mandrake has *emotions*?'

In Mandrake's MI6 file there is a report that records his remarkable autonomic responses to loaded visual and auditory stimuli: Sadistically violent and sometimes pornographic images, interspersed with sunsets and pastoral landscapes, flashed on to a screen; shrieks of unbearable agony punctuating a Brahms lullaby and played to him through earphones. He was at the time hooked up to machines that monitored his blink rate and the electrical conductance of his skin – and no matter what Mandrake was shown, or what he heard, the needles did not move. His non-response was so marked that the examiners concluded he was entirely cut off from his instinctive feelings and, having seen nothing like it before, they concluded that the ventromedial region of his brain – the part that regulates all of our emotional responses – must have been damaged.

Had Mandrake sustained head injuries in, say, a car accident, they asked? Ridout's cynical response – his small joke – was that Mandrake's only accident was the one that had led to his birth.

But while it is true that Mandrake is a virtual stranger to the constraining feelings of guilt or remorse or shame – that, as Ridout says, he is close to being a sociopath – it is not true to say that he has no feelings. There are stimuli that could make the needles move: almost any birdsong, for example, and almost anything by Bach; the shape and the feel of Grace's body; the smell and the sound of the sea.

He feels a small jolt of pleasure now as he gets his first sight of the *Lady Jane* and knows instantly that she is right for him; that before very long she will be bearing him away from land and away from those who hunt him. She is eleven metres long with a full set of sails and a sturdy diesel engine and you could circumnavigate the world in her – and perhaps Mandrake will.

She is his for a mere fifty thousand dollars of Karl Gröber's money.

# New York

# forty-seven

There are no detention facilities in the Marscheider building, no holding cells or interview rooms with doors that lock from the outside. So obstreperous Vincent Regal is sitting on the floor in the basement – his left wrist handcuffed to Rocco Morales's stout metal bench – where, he has been told, he can holler until his lungs give out and no-one will hear.

This is not entirely true. Pacing the pavement outside the building, smoking the last of the five cigarettes that he allows himself on weekends, Jarrett Crawford can hear an unending if muted wail of obscenities coming from the air vents. Flint warned him that Regal had a foul mouth and now it's getting on Crawford's nerves.

Reluctantly he finishes the cigarette and uses his swipe card to re-enter the building and takes the stairs down to the basement – the caterwauling growing ever louder – and, coming up silently on Regal's blindside, he picks up a Manhattan telephone directory, swinging it with both hands like a baseball bat at the back of Regal's head, sending him sprawling. It is more the shock than the violence of the impact that stuns the little man into incredulous silence.

'Now look what you've made me do,' says Crawford calmly. 'First time in twenty years I've assaulted a prisoner. But, Vincent, listen to me. If you say fuck or fucking or fucker or motherfucker or any other kind of fucker one more time, I'm going to make you eat this.'

By 'this' Crawford means the telephone directory that he still holds like a bat, lining it up on Regal's head. 'Are we clear on that, Vincent?'

'On April 26, 2000 – no, strike that.' Crawford corrects himself for the benefit of the cassette tape recorder that he has placed between them on the bench. 'On April 27 – repeat, *twenty-seven* – at

approximately 1 a.m., you met at your request with Deputy Director
Flint in the parking lot of the River Café in Brooklyn. Remember
that, Vincent? Also present, but not at your request, was Special
Agent Ruth Apple – and you better remember that, Vincent,
because, as you well know, Agent Apple was subsequently killed
and this is, among other things, a homicide investigation and right
now, as things stand, you're in the frame as a possible accessary to
that homicide, so your memory needs to be very clear. Do you
recall that meeting, Vincent?'

There is a red light glowing on the machine indicating that it is
recording – though it isn't because Rocco Morales has reversed the
circuits, but Regal has no way of knowing about this deception. No
longer handcuffed to the bench he is nevertheless restrained, perched
on a stool, frozen into submission by Crawford's air of menace, his
superior bulk, the telephone directory that he keeps close to hand.

'Vincent, one more time: do you recall that meeting?'

'Yes,' says Regal tightly, as though the admission is costing him
money he can ill-afford to spend.

Crawford feigns to refer to a copy of the Pentecost file.

'In the course of that meeting you informed on your employer by
divulging confidential information relating to clients, information
that may very likely lead to a number of indictments being handed
down, multiple-count indictments with major penalties attached.
Now, Vincent' – Crawford reaches out to press a switch on the
machine and extinguish the red light, and now, conversely, it *is*
recording – 'between you and me, when that happens there are going
to be a lot of mightily pissed people trying to figure out who ratted
on them so the question is, who else knows you're a stoolie, a fink?'

Regal scowls but he is immune to insults and empty threats. He
waits in sullen silence to hear what Crawford really wants.

'You see, Vincent, here at the FSF we're very protective of our
CIs, which is what you are – a CI. To anybody except your handlers
you're not a name, just a number. See?' Crawford offers him a
glimpse of the Pentecost file, opened to the page that begins Flint's
narrative summary of her interview with 'Confidential Informant
#00217'. Regal looks away.

'Only three people in this building knew that CI217 and Vincent
Lowell Regal were one and the same – and one of them is dead. So
it's just me and Deputy Director Flint who know, and that's how
we protect you.' Crawford turns two or three pages of the file as

though he is seeking something specific in Flint's summary. 'But we can't protect you from yourself, can we Vincent? There's nothing we can do if you go around telling the world you're a fink.'

'That's bullshit,' says Regal.

'Oh, really? What are you saying, Vincent, that you didn't tell anybody? That nobody else here knows that Vincent Regal informs on his friends, his associates?' There is derision in Crawford's voice. 'Now, *that's* bull. That's a pile of shit a mile high.' With the fingers of one hand he jabs at the page in front of him. 'What about Ben Gates?'

'What about him?'

'Who is he, Vincent?'

'You know who he is.'

Crawford chuckles as though Regal has told a joke. Then he leans forward on his elbows and says quietly, 'I surely do. My question is, how did you know, Vincent? Who was your informant? Who told you?'

They watch each other while Regal's quick brain explores the implications of Crawford's question, the process showing in his eyes. Not expecting this line of interrogation and not yet sure of all the angles, he stalls. 'Who cares?'

'The Deputy Director cares,' Crawford replies evenly. 'She wants to know which of her colleagues, which of her friends, would tell a slimeball like you her private business – and she wants to know why. And' – Crawford coming to his feet, picking up the telephone directory in both hands – 'I care, Vincent, because I also want to know who's been speaking out of turn, and there's something you need to understand. It's like they say: the first time you break the rules is the hardest. After that . . .' He takes a step back, gearing up for a practice swing.

Regal is fast, ducking off the stool, keeping low to avoid any blow that Crawford might aim at him. He drives his head into Crawford's gut, sending him bellowing to his knees, and keeps on moving, still in a crouch, heading for the door that leads to the stairs.

The door is secured and it takes Regal a moment to find and release the catch. Then he's free and clear, running up the stairs, taking them two at a time, pausing at the first turn to yell to Crawford, to shriek at him with all the force he can muster, '*Motherfucker!*'

# forty-eight

A little before seven o'clock on Sunday evening Nathan Stark prepares to leave his home on Staten Island, counting out three hundred dollars from his wallet and countersigning five blank checks on the Starks' joint account, reminding his wife that if she really needs to use them she must record the details in the ledger. He also pedantically reminds her that her car is due for service, that the sprinkler in the yard needs fixing, that she should cancel dinner with the Carpenters, that Nathan Junior has an appointment with his orthodontist, that on weekday evenings eight o'clock is the cut-off hour when the boy must cease his relentless surfing of the Internet. (He's turned sixteen but Nathan Junior remains 'the boy' to his father.)

'Yes, yes,' Melinda Stark says impatiently, anxious to be done with the exasperating ritual that precedes each one of her husband's business trips. As is his habit, he has not said where he is going or when he will return but she notes that it is the mid-sized Samsonite rather than his overnight bag that sits in the hallway. Several days, then; with luck, a week or even more.

Stark goes to his study and closes the door. From a wall vault that is concealed by one of the many framed certificates of Achievement, Appreciation and Award he removes his Glock 23 semi-automatic pistol and two spare magazines, two US passports, neither of which is in Stark's name, and a leather portfolio that contains, among other things, what Stark thinks of as his emergency travelling fund: Swiss banknotes bearing the portrait of the philosopher Jacob Burckhardt; ninety of them, each worth more than six hundred dollars. For the last two weeks, since – despite his best efforts – Operation Pentecost imploded, Stark has travelled everywhere with his emergency fund, for he now has reason to share Burckhardt's notion that history is an ever-accelerating process: that seismic developments that you would have expected to take years can now occur in a matter of days.

The vault is sturdy and guarded by a combination lock but Stark knows that if the worst happens it will not prove much of a challenge to the safecrackers of the FBI – or, for that matter, to Rocco Morales, should he get there first. Whoever opens the vault will find inside only two letters. One, short and to the point though not without affection, is addressed to Melinda; more an apology than an explanation. The second is addressed to Aldus Cutter and it runs to five closely-typed pages and it explains – in Stark's view, justifies – why Nathan Stark betrayed both the Financial Strike Force and his country.

Nathan Junior, glued to the computer screen in the family room, responds robotically when his father comes in to say goodbye. Stark has mixed feelings about his son's obsession with the Internet, for the boy employs its vast resources to track criminals, taking names and descriptions from the 'Wanted' sites posted by law enforcement agencies and searching for matches in online direc-tories, newspaper libraries, property registers, military records and the like. Using a software program called Net Detective he has twice succeeded in locating fugitives and on the second occasion he received a reward of five thousand dollars from the grateful state of Florida for providing information that led directly to the capture of an escaped prisoner. 'Chip Off The Block,' said the headline in the *Tampa Tribune*, comparing young Nathan's crime-busting ways to those of his 'veteran Fed' father. Well, only up to a point, Stark knows, for what the newspaper called his son's 'zealous pursuit of Justice' is driven purely by avarice, the bounty hunter's creed – whereas Stark's motive, as he insists in his exculpatory letter to Aldus Cutter, was never *just* money.

Nathan Junior's stated ambition is to make 'serious dollars' by claiming the reward for one of the FBI's Ten Most Wanted. Driving to the ferry terminal, aware that he may never retrace his route, Stark reflects on the irony that he could soon be on the FBI's list with, say, a million-dollar price tag on his head. If that day arrives he has little doubt that he will then become the subject of his own son's most zealous pursuit.

Stark banishes the thought to that compartment of his mind that he keeps locked for most of the time. Operation Payback is due to commence in little more than twelve hours and there is much detail to occupy him. He intends to spend the night in the Marscheider building going over the operational plan, finding and correcting the flaws that he knows will be there. If this is to be Deputy Director Nathan Stark's last hurrah he is determined it will also be his finest hour.

He has reached the ferry terminal, is waiting in the boarding line, when his firm intention turns into a fantasy. His mobile phone rings and without a thought he answers it to hear the frantic, whining voice of Vincent Regal calling him 'Mr Stark', babbling about Flint, cursing Jarrett Crawford with spectacular profanity, alternately threatening and pleading, demanding an immediate meeting.

Stark cuts the line without responding. Getting out of the car he walks to the water's edge and drops the phone into Upper Bay.

For all the good that will do. Abandoning his plan to go to the office, pulling out of the line, heading now for the Verrazano Bridge, Stark imagines Crawford – or perhaps it will be Rocco Morales – turning off the tape of the intercept, punching the air, reaching for the phone to report to the Director that Regal has fallen into the trap and the set-up has worked. 'Got him,' they will say, meaning Nathan Stark.

Only up to a point, thinks Stark.

# Ilse's House

# forty-nine

There is a storm tonight, one of those black storms that seems to have come out of nowhere, borne across the high plains of Belarus, perhaps, gathering strength as it races across Europe to hurl itself against the northeast side of Ilse's house. The gusts are periodic, and each time Flint hears the pitch of the wind building from a low moan towards a whistling shriek she pauses her careful progress along the corridor on the second floor and waits until the gust's ferocity is spent.

*Ilse, I want you to know that we are sisters, that I have also been betrayed. Betrayal is something else we have in common.*

The torch provided by Dr Schnell is heavy, quality-made, with an adjustable halogen beam that can illuminate much of the corridor or focus on a single spot with the precision of a laser. Flint has it on a setting that gives her just enough light to work with as she edges towards Karl Gröber's room, the last door on the left.

*Karl's here? In the house? Upstairs?*

Ilse, sodden with brandy and about to pass out, had merely nodded.

Flint knows she should have called Schnell or slipped out of the house to alert one of the watchers; that creeping along this corridor at two o'clock in the morning without back-up, armed with nothing more than a can of Mace and the pistol Felix gave her – a weapon with almost no stopping power – is absurdly foolish. There could be, should be, a dozen armed officers surrounding the house and a SWAT team going in, but then Karl Gröber would very likely die. And he cannot die – she will not let him die – until he answers the only question she presently cares about: *Where's Ben?*

She is well-enough armed, she has rashly decided. If Gröber is not cowed by the sight of her puny gun, and the Mace does not stop him, she will use the high-intensity beam of the torch to temporarily blind him and the torch itself as a baton.

But part of her brain – the snivelling part – is recalling Cutter's summary of General Kessel's report: 'Kessel says that between 1976 and 1987 Gröber was frequently sent on overseas assignments for the KGB. He went as an adviser, sometimes a provocateur, sometimes an assassin.'

*An assassin? And you're going to fight him with a torch?*

*Shuddup!*

The storm is intensifying, the wind tearing at the roof tiles searching for weak points. Pressed against the corridor wall, Flint waits for the night madness to abate; until she can hear herself think; until she can listen for sounds of movement beyond Karl Gröber's door.

To avoid being too obvious, Dr Schnell's watchers are stationed in pairs in two cars parked on Karl-Heine-Strasse some five hundred metres to the east and to the west of Ilse's house. To compensate for that sensible precaution, they are equipped with night-vision goggles that enable them to see, in ghastly-green relief, a human figure up to twice that distance away. That, at least, is the theory.

But at long range – beyond the range of ancillary infrared illumination – night-vision technology depends solely on the amplification of available light and tonight that is only intermittently provided by the occasional passing car. There is a power blackout that has not been engineered by Dr Schnell, and, in the presence of this vast storm, no moonlight, no assistance from the stars.

So the watchers do not observe the passage of the black-clad shape that, emerging from the cover of a bank doorway, takes advantage of a sudden squall of lashing rain to cross Karl-Heine-Strasse and climb the fence of Ilse's garden.

A lull. Not a total abatement of the storm's clamour but a lessening, a pause for regeneration before the next assault.

*Do it and do it now. Kill the light. Remove your shoes and slide your feet along the boards and, nevertheless, hear them creak under your weight – and pray that he attributes what he hears to some trick of the wind. Gun on the right hip, safety on; mace in the left pocket of your jeans. Ten feet to go.*

Waiting in her bedroom, standing before the mottled mirror, she had practised her quick-draw, snapping the pistol from the holster, bringing it up with two hands, arms extended, to just below the sight line. 'Freeze,' she'd mouthed, regardless of the parody. But that was before the power failed and the lights went out; before she knew that to see her target she'd need one hand free for the torch.

*Left hand for the torch, right hand for the door handle. Release the latch then kick open the door. What if it's locked? Shoot the lock? Fat chance with a gun that wouldn't stop a rabbit. It won't be locked – why would he lock it? – but remember that: you've got no stopping power. Despite what they taught you at Quantico, aim for the head because a head shot is the only chance you've got of putting him down. Breathe. Take deep breaths through your mouth and get your heart rate going. Get the adrenalin going until you can taste its coppery bitterness on your tongue.*

*Release, kick, draw, torch on, fix him in the beam and warn. Freeze! Now, down on your knees, keep your hands where I can see them. Move, Gröber! Do it now!*

The fingers of Flint's right hand that are feeling their way along the plaster wall encounter the edge of the doorframe and now the door itself. She eases into position and presses one ear to the cold wood, listening for sounds beyond the door. Nothing. Gingerly her right hand tests the door handle and feels it give. Not locked.

*Move, Flint! Do it now!*

Like a diver about to submerge she takes a gulp of air and tells herself this is no different to a hard-entry training exercise at Quantico, one that she's been through a dozen times. *Sure.* Then she banishes everything from her mind except the rote and she is pressing on the handle, kicking at the door; bringing up the gun, safety catch off; two steps forward, the beam of the torch searching the room; the beam raking Karl Gröber's hideously-distorted face, the uniform, the peaked cap he wears; the truth dawning on her, mocking her; the command 'Freeze!' dying in her throat.

Flint giggles. She cannot help herself. As the fear evaporates, replaced by a surge of relief that is mixed with anger at her own stupidity, her laughter escalates, growing uncontrollably until she feels as though she is on the verge of a cataplectic attack. She goes down on her knees and now her stomach is in spasm and the laughter is becoming hysterical, convulsive sobs that threaten to suffocate her. She leans forward on her hands, fighting for breath, waiting for the spasms to subside and as they do it suddenly strikes her that she must look like some supplicant paying homage to Karl Gröber – or, rather, not Karl Gröber but this ridiculous representation of him – and the convulsions start again.

Now she lies on the floor, her head close to the leather boots of a gnome: a devil-gnome like the one in Fuseli's *The Nightmare* – except this crouching gnome would stand four feet tall, dressed in a Stasi uniform, the fly buttons of the trousers undone, a dried blood-sausage poking out to depict the shrivelled stump of a severed penis.

# fifty

Who did this? Who filled this room with Stasi memorabilia (uniforms, medals, helmets, gas masks, knives, bayonets, truncheons, two Kalashnikov automatic rifles; blank ID cards, a magistrate's official stamp, false beards, wigs, a grotesque false stomach; a camera concealed in a briefcase, a tape recorder hidden in a box; a hard, narrow cot that looks as though it has come from a detention cell; handcuffs, shackles, chains, hoods), creating a sort of black museum?

And if it was Karl Gröber – as Flint assumes it must have been – who despoiled his collection with symbols of another despotic era?

Flint, drained by the convulsions but otherwise recovered, sits on the cot training the torch's beam on smaller gnomes that crouch behind Karl, their right arms raised in the fascist salute. There are six of them, all wearing Stasi ceremonial uniforms that are daubed with crude Nazi swastikas painted the colour of blood. Their painted faces have black hollows instead of eyes. Their gaping mouths are set in the posture of eternal screams.

Two more swastikas, these painted black and rendered like lightning bolts, adorn the far wall on either side of a portrait of General Mielke, the Stasi's chief architect, who would look as forbidding as his reputation were it not for the Hitler-like moustache that has been crudely painted on his upper lip. By Ilse, Flint assumes, extracting her revenge.

The wall to the right of the cot is papered with ageing newspaper and magazine cuttings that report charges brought in reunified Germany against General Mielke for the murder of those who were shot while trying to cross the border. The cuttings that record the collapse of Mielke's trial on the grounds of his senility, and his peaceful old man's death in a hospital bed, are ringed in angry red crayon. There is a list of his victims that Flint sees does not include the names of Wilhelm and Eva Gröber. Alongside the list the same red crayon has been used to scrawl a despairing question: *Warum?* – Why?

Now Flint notes a grouping of much more recent cuttings that report a contemporary murder in New York. Most of them are brief factual accounts of the events at the World's Greatest Emporium and the issue of an international arrest warrant for one Karl Gröber, but some of the tabloids have uncovered Gröber's Stasi past. *Bildzeitung* even has a picture of Karl, standing belligerently on the steps of *Runde Ecke* before a militant crowd on what the caption describes as 'The Last Stand: Final days of the Stasi terror'. He's in civilian clothes and apparently unarmed, but at his shoulder there is a phalanx of uniformed men holding automatic weapons, rather as a phalanx of uniformed gnomes stand with Karl in this room. They are not identified in the caption. Two of the faces, however, are ringed with crayon and someone – Ilse? – has written their names in capital letters: DANNECKER. KROL.

Flint removes the cutting from the wall and reads the racy text. No mention of Dannecker or Krol. But there is a morsel of information that gets Flint's juices flowing: 'According to well-informed underworld sources, Gröber owns a luxurious villa somewhere on the Adriatic coast in what used to be Yugoslavia where, it is believed, he was recently visited by two former Stasi officers from Leipzig.'

Journalistic bullshit? Probably. Nevertheless, Flint pockets the cutting and, squeezing past the gnomes, surveys the furniture she must now search: a scratched wooden desk that is set beneath Mielke's portrait, a trunk with a carved lid, a three-drawer filing cabinet painted institutional green. Selecting the torch's widest beam she props it on the desk so that it acts as a lamp and begins with the trunk, kneeling on the floor, lifting the lid warily, an inch or so at a time, as though she half-expects to find something unpleasant inside. Smelling mustiness, nothing worse, she heaves open the lid to be confronted by the severed head of a wild boar with fearsome curved tusks that must be a foot long. The tusks are yellowing with age, as are the reams of paper they seem to guard: the contents of old Stasi files, Flint guesses, plundered from *Runde Ecke* – but why? She extracts a handful of the pages from beneath the boar's head and takes them close to the light and struggles to make sense of the text. She understands some of the words, the odd phrase here and there, but the syntax is so convoluted that the meaning is impenetrable.

To replace the papers in some semblance of order she has first to remove the boar's head, lifting it by the tusks, surprised by its weight. As she does she sees that it was resting on a large book, one with a faux-antique cover that is embossed with gold lettering: *FotoAlbum*. Karl's album, apparently, recording a long period of his life, from childhood to middle age. Each picture has a caption written beneath it in black ink in a formal hand.

Here is chubby Karl, aged three, perching on a park bench, screwing up his eyes to shield them from the sun. Here is Karl, aged six, in swimming trunks, cherubic, at somewhere called Waren that is either a beach or a lakeshore. Karl, at ten, in Dresden, smiles shyly at the camera. Karl '*Berlin, Juli 1963*' – and therefore twelve – looks stiff and sullen, and Karl at fourteen, a studio portrait by the look of it, is positively disdainful, his mouth . . .

Flint lifts her head. The clamour of the storm has become familiar and the sound she has just half-heard, one that barely registered on her senses, was discordant; indefinable but definitely out of place. She dims the torch to its lowest setting and goes swiftly to the door. The gun is in her right hand, safety off, as she slips into the corridor. She crosses to the other side and moves to her left until she is beyond the reach of the soft glow coming from Karl's room. In virtual darkness she waits to see what or who may be attracted to the light.

And as she waits Flint considers the photographs that are missing from Karl's album, leaving telltale traces of glue and captions that have been obliterated so thoroughly as to leave holes in the pages. Pictures of Karl with Ilse, perhaps, or with his parents or his brother Heinz – pictures Ilse cannot abide to see. But then why would Ilse keep any of the pictures? Why not just destroy the album?

*Did Ben destroy the pictures he stole from Miller's Reach? Or is he looking at them now, showing them to his friends, laughing himself silly. 'Look at this one, this was our wedding night, after I'd fucked her. See that smile on her face?'*

*Bloody stop it! Bloody concentrate!*

She can hear the rain beating against the windows, the howl of the wind. Nothing else.

*I will find you, Ben.*

Her alter ego does not ask, *And then what?* For once the snivelling part of her has nothing to say.

Here is Karl as the smug-looking captain of the school soccer team, arms folded, one foot on the ball. Here's another group shot: Karl, the boy soldier, burlier than his pals and in his element, judging by the arrogant set of his shoulders, the assured look on his face.

Karl, the border guard, photographed at Vacha, location of his parents' execution.

Flint has closed the door of Karl's room and wedged it with a chair.

Karl with a young woman – a striking young woman – standing close behind her, arms wrapped possessively around her waist. Her name is Sabine, according to the caption, and the date is 1974. By which time Karl Gröber was living with his sister 'like a couple', according to General Kessel's report. 'Meaning?' Flint had asked Dr Schnell over dinner on the night he spirited her away from the Holiday Inn. 'That he slept with his sister, or they were like the Odd Couple?' she'd asked, but Dr Schnell had no opinion. Either way it now strikes Flint as peculiar that the photograph of Sabine has survived for, surely, Ilse would have hated Sabine: either seen Sabine as a rival who might take Karl away – or, conversely, if she was locked miserably into an incestuous relationship, blamed Sabine for *not* taking Karl away?

Evidently not, for as Flint flicks through the album she finds many more pictures of Sabine, usually entwined with Karl but sometimes on her own – here in Havana in September 1978, for example, reclining beside a swimming pool, vamping it up – that suggest an intimate and enduring relationship.

Now it's the early Eighties and Karl and Sabine are still together, a distinctly handsome couple: he coming more and more to resemble his father; she filling out, her figure growing voluptuous. The spring of 1982 finds them arm-in-arm in Prague, that winter in Istanbul and then in Damascus, where they pose with a minaret as the backdrop, wrapped up against the cold. In 1983 they are in Havana once more and also Asunción, the next year in Tripoli – and with a jolt, as though she has received a small electric shock, Flint recognises the symmetry between their travels and Dr Schnell's description of Gröber's foreign assignments for the KGB: Cuba,

Czechoslovakia, Turkey, Syria, Cuba again and Paraguay,
Tripoli . . .

*So, what were you, Sabine? Pleasure mixed with business – or
were you part of it, part of Karl's assignments? And where are you
now?*

Using her fingernails Flint eases the Tripoli picture from the
page.

There is a gap, no more pictures of Sabine, until the last page;
until December of 1988, less than a year before the Wall came
down. She is sitting at Karl's side at the head of a long table
crowded with food and bottles of wine, four other couples turned
sideways in their chairs, smiling for the camera. Sabine is still a
handsome woman with frank eyes and long auburn hair that falls
to her bare shoulders, but Flint sees something pained in her
expression, a forced joviality. The caption says, *Das Letzte
Abendessen* – The Last Supper.

Flint closes the album and then her eyes and calms herself and
concentrates on what it is she has seen that has triggered a niggling
flicker of recognition.

And then it comes to her that the man seated on Sabine's right,
the man whose hand is casually draped on her shoulder, also
appears in *Bildzeitung*'s picture of The Last Stand on the steps of
*Runde Ecke*: the man identified in red crayon capitals as KROL.
And next to him, on his right, is a woman whose startled face
appeared to Flint from behind the breakfast menu in Friendly's
restaurant at the Howard Johnson hotel in Portland, Maine.

'*Ich spreche kein Englisch.*'

The hell you don't, Frau Lender.

The filing cabinet is locked, Flint attempting to force open the top
drawer with a bayonet she has taken from one of Karl's phalanx of
gnomes. She does not care about the damage she is causing, twisting
the blade with increasing pressure until she hears the lock snap.

Inside the drawer are hanging files, each one neatly labelled:
telephone, utilities, insurance, guarantees and so forth; domestic
trivia of no interest to Flint. There is a section labelled 'medical'
and from it she removes several thick files that she takes to the desk
and quickly scans. The language of the reports is too technical for
her to make much sense of but many medical terms are universal
and there are sufficient clues to suggest the host of problems that

have reduced Ilse to a crippled skeleton: premature menopause due to autoimmune reaction; postmenopausal osteoporosis; osteo-sarcomas in both knee joints that have not responded to chemotherapy.

Surgery is recommended. Amputation above the joints.

*Oh, you poor cow.*

When Ilse finally passed out, Flint had guided the scooter along the passageway that led to her bedroom and lifted her body on to the bed and thought that Ilse weighed nothing, as though her bones were made of glass.

She replaces the medical files and continues her search of the top drawer until, with a frisson of anticipation, she comes to a section labelled *Bankverkehr*. Here are Ilse's bank statements and payment receipts going back five years that Flint eagerly examines, hoping – even expecting – to find evidence of transfers; large transfers of hush money from Karl. Aldus Cutter likes to say that Flint can get more information out of the average bank statement than he gets from the *New York Times*, but Ilse's statements tell only a meagre tale. Her income is modest and comes from the state and her account has never held more than a few thousand marks.

Picking up the bayonet, Flint goes to work on the lock of the second drawer.

The drawer is empty – totally, mockingly bare. *Terrific!* In her frustration Flint slams it closed. *Wait a minute.* Slowly she opens the drawer again, lifting it by the handle, testing its weight, feeling the way that it glides on the runners. Something is wrong – or rather, something's right, for this does not feel like an empty drawer. Guessing there is a false bottom she reaches inside and raps the metal with her knuckles, searches with her fingers for a hidden catch. Nothing. Now she is probing under the drawer, finding a recess, finding within it a button that she presses. She hears the satisfactory click of the release mechanism, sees the bottom of the drawer rise, revealing a compartment two inches deep and the white envelopes it contains. They are stacked in threes and there are six stacks; eighteen identical bulging envelopes addressed simply to 'Ilse', all of them unopened.

Flint picks one at random and breaks the seal and removes a sheet of notepaper that is folded around a wad of German banknotes that she quickly counts: twenty-five thousand marks – or, by Flint's calculation, a little over eleven thousand dollars.

*Is that the price of your silence, Ilse, and how often does Karl have to pay? Once a month, every week, every day?*

There is a hand-written note on the paper that Flint translates: 'As always, my dear Ilse, Karl sends you his warmest affection and his deep concern and wishes to be informed if there is anything else you need. Please let me know so that I can tell Karl. Ilse, please call.' It is signed 'Krol', and underneath his name there is written a telephone number.

Flint pockets the note, returns the banknotes to the envelope, selects the next one to open.

Once more she tells herself *I will find you, Ben* – and now, for the first time, she really does believe it.

# fifty-one

Nick Fellowes, obeying orders, continues his exploration of the darkened house on Karl-Heine-Strasse.

'Use your initiative,' Ridout had said. 'Just find out if Catmint's there – and, if she is, why. And, Fellowes,' Ridout had added as he was halfway out of the door, 'don't let anybody see you, and don't get bloody caught.'

Not obeying orders – indeed, in direct contravention of MI6 standing orders – Fellowes is armed. In a sheath strapped to his left ankle he carries a nine-inch throwing knife made from a single cut of black stainless steel, the double-edged blade honed to razor sharpness. Practising with the knife is Fellowes's only hobby, other than keeping his body in shape which is more a mission than a pastime. Hunting at night in the fields behind his mother's cottage in Sussex is what he does for fun. Nine times out of ten he can hit a moving target as small as a rabbit from thirty feet.

Like Schnell's watchers, the morons he has so easily evaded, Fellowes is equipped with night-vision goggles but he is working well within a range where the invisible beam of his infrared light perfectly illuminates everything he wants to see. The light is mounted above the goggles and he directs the beam by simply moving his head from side to side, or up and down.

Down now to see the contours of the legs beneath the covers, lifting his head an inch or so to run the beam up over the buttocks, a little more to see the shape of the upper torso, her bare neck, her head resting on the pillow. Down again to the foot of the bed to repeat the process, more slowly this time, the beam inching up her body like a caress, he feeling the exhilaration of the absolute power that he holds.

It would be so easy. In their catalogue the manufacturers of the knife boast that it cuts through animal hide like butter. Her throat would be like cream. One glide of the black blade is all that it would take and she wouldn't even know. They could tell the family that she died peacefully in her sleep and that for once would be the literal truth.

Fellowes suppresses these dark thoughts, as in the past he has concealed similar fantasies from MI6's psychological examiners.

He slips from the room and softly closes the door. The next room he will check is at the end of the passageway and four steps up to a half-landing. He moves towards it with the silence of a cat; a black cat since black is the colour of everything he wears.

Inside the room, his back to the door, the knife held in his hand like a dagger. This is poor accommodation compared to the woman's bedroom: cell-like in its dimensions, no window, a hanging rail for clothes, a washbasin screwed to the wall, a chair, a single bed. Whoever's sleeping in it snorts, like an apnea sufferer gasping for breath.

Fellowes sheathes the knife and moves to the bed and looks down on the crumpled face of an old man whose mouth is open, whose *eyes* are open, who stares up in terror at the presence he cannot possibly see.

If the old man does not move. If he just lies still and convinces himself that he has woken from a nightmare and imagined the presence. If he closes his eyes and goes back to sleep. If . . . But, no.

The old man lifts himself on to his elbows and roars.

Until Fellowes clamps his mouth shut, takes the pillow, pushes him down, presses the pillow on to his face, using one knee to increase the pressure, holding it there until the feeble struggling stops.

Obeying Ridout's orders to the letter: *Don't get bloody caught.*

The third drawer of the filing cabinet also contains a hidden compartment in which Flint has found twenty more unopened envelopes. Ilse's stash, duly counted, amounts to 900,000 marks – a little over $400,000. A small price to pay for Ilse's silence, Flint thinks, but an extravagant amount to leave untouched.

Eight of the envelopes had contained notes from Krol, all saying much the same: *Please call.*

*You've got Karl worried, haven't you, Ilse? Krol keeps pushing his envelopes through your letterbox and you don't respond. What is it that you know, Ilse? What is it that you want?*

Flint returns the envelopes to their compartments. It occurs to her that when all of this is over the money could be seized as the highly-probable proceeds of money laundering, but she will not be the one who causes that to happen. She will not mention Ilse's stash to Dr Schnell.

There is nothing in the desk to interest Flint. She leaves Karl's room as she found it, except for the broken locks on the filing cabinet, the cutting from *Bildzeitung* she has taken from the wall, the photographs of Tripoli and of the Last Supper, Krol's note.

As an afterthought, halfway along the corridor, she is tempted to go back for the bayonet which seems to her to be a more intimidating weapon than either Felix's pistol or the Mace. But why? she asks herself. What's the point?

Fellowes on the first floor in another bedroom, this one unoccupied, going through a woman's things, checking the labels of her panties to see where she does her shopping. Even the best undercovers can be careless about their underwear if they're fussy about what they put between their legs. Because they don't imagine that anyone's going to check.

## MARKS & SPENCER
### UK – Size 10

Catmint. Has to be. Fellowes imagines her nipping down to the Marble Arch branch of M&S every time she returns to London, stocking up on panties and bras.

So where is she? Why isn't she in her bed at three o'clock in the morning? Fellowes uses his knife to slice off one of the labels. Evidence for Ridout if this is all he finds. Then, for the hell of it, he slices through the crotch.

'A bit of a goer is she, a good fuck?' he'd asked Mandrake at the safe house, just killing time with a little friendly conversation.

'Oh, believe it, she's great in the sack.'

'How does she like it?'

'How *doesn't* she like it?' Mandrake had said giving sod-all away as per usual.

Thinking of Mandrake sets Fellowes on edge. He moves swiftly to and through the living room and stands in the doorway checking the corridor, shifting his head to run the beam along the walls. Empty.

But some instinct tells him to wait, to remain where he is and keep watching, and as he obeys the impulse he is rewarded by the sight of pin-pricks of light emerging from the wall to his left. No, not from the wall but from the cracks around one of the doors he'd passed, one of the doors that was locked.

Seen through his goggles, amplified three thousand times, the light is intensifying, growing like a stain until it is phosphorescent-bright. The source of the light is getting closer to the door and moving up and down and Fellowes is sure that what he's watching is a torch or a lantern being carried down the stairway from the second floor – the stairway he couldn't find.

Catmint. Has to be.

Fellowes retreats to her bedroom and conceals himself behind the curtain in the alcove where she hangs her clothes.

Feeling responsibility, even guilt, Flint checks on Ilse Gröber. Feeding her more than half a bottle of brandy, refilling her glass even when she was practically insensate, had seemed pretty reckless at the time. Now, in light of what Flint has learned about her medical condition – *and God knows what drugs she's taking, drugs that don't mix with alcohol* – it seems more like madness.

*What if you've poisoned her?*

*Don't.*

*What if you've killed her?*

*Shuddup!*

Shielding the torch's beam, leaning over the bed, Flint places one cheek close to Ilse's mouth and feels the feathery brush of her breath. It stinks of alcohol but it is warm and recurring and there is no smell of vomit, no sound of gurgling from the lungs.

'Ilse. Frau Gröber,' Flint says softly, touching her forehead, feeling the pulse in her neck. Her skin is just a little clammy, her pulse a little weak, but there's no movement of the eyelids so she's probably just going through one of the deeper stages of dreamless non-REM sleep when the heart rate slows and the body temperature drops.

*Or she's in a coma.*

*SHUT UP!*

Flint sits on the bed and strokes Ilse's face as though she is a child.

'*Frau Gröber, wachen Sie auf, bitte*' – Wake up, please – but Ilse barely stirs.

She thinks of her father lying in a hospital bed beneath the black boxes that provide the only evidence of life.

Flint is stroking the inside of Ilse's skinny wrist, now running her fingernails along the bulging vein.

*Wake up, goddamnit. You have to wake up.*

'*Sie müssen aufwachen,*' is what Fellowes hears Catmint say from his position in the passageway – words he doesn't understand.

He runs the infrared beam over Flint's body appreciating the shape of her thighs and the curve of her breasts and allows himself to indulge in another of the dark fantasies that he knows how to keep from the prying psychologists.

'How *doesn't* she like it?' Mandrake had said.

# fifty-two

White and green *Polizei* vans toting enough gear to quell a small riot block the westbound carriageway of Karl-Heine-Strasse, the reflection of their emergency lights dancing in the windows of Ilse's house. Felix Hartmann, the last to know, abandons his car on the pavement and runs towards the front door brandishing his BND credentials like a shield, unwilling to be delayed by the swarm of cops looking like soldiers with their camouflage trousers tucked into boots, their flak jackets, their belts bristling with weapons and equipment that stands in his way. They let him through reluctantly, as though they think a spy has no legitimate business at a murder scene.

They've rigged up three generators in the garden and there are cables snaking everywhere to feed the powerful spotlights that make the interior of the house look like a film set. Hartmann finds Dr Schnell pacing the living room, talking urgently to Pullach on his mobile phone. In this unforgiving light the doctor's face looks as though it has been bleached.

Hartmann sees the missing window pane and debris on the floor, evidence of a forced entry. Swathes of sticky tape on the glass and a single blow to break it – crude but effective. Then the intruder reached inside to slip the window catch and climbed on to the sill leaving a footprint that the crime scene boys haven't yet got around to preserving. Did Flint hear the window break and come running? Hartmann looks for traces of her blood on the carpet but there are none that he can see.

Dr Schnell, still on the phone, raises his eyebrows to Hartmann as if to say, 'Can you believe these people?' Whatever it is he wants from headquarters he's meeting obduracy, apparently. '*Nein, nein,*' he says emphatically. '*Überlassen Sie Ridout mir.*' Of course he wants them to leave Ridout to him. Dr Schnell has waited a long time to deliver Nigel Ridout his comeuppance.

They're bringing in a gurney now, two paramedics carefully negotiating the tight corner into the passageway that leads to Ilse's bedroom. They are not in any hurry; no point in damaging the paintwork when all that they're collecting is a corpse.

'Felix,' says Dr Schnell, covering the mouthpiece of the phone with his hand, 'I will be a while longer. Go to her, please. Upstairs.'

Grace Flint lies on the bed that is just about wide enough to be called a double. Her skin also looks bleached, washed out, but this has nothing to do with the emergency lighting. There is a brownish stain growing on the thick bandage on her left hand that says she is still losing blood. 'You need stitches, Grace, you need to go to the hospital,' says Hartmann but she only smiles wanly and pats the covers with the hand that doesn't hurt like hell and answers, 'Sit with me, please.'

She makes room for him on the bed.

'I thought I'd killed her.'

'Who?'

'Ilse. I'd been pouring brandy down her throat to get her talking and I thought I'd overdone it. She wouldn't wake up. I was going to call for an ambulance but the phone in her bedroom wasn't working. I was on the way up here to get my mobile when the bastard jumped me.'

Flint is speaking very quickly, running her words together.

'He grabbed me from behind, in the passageway, just outside her bedroom door. Grabbed my mouth, grabbed my breasts, tried to put his knee in the small of my back. So I bit him, bit his hand, made him yelp, twisted round, kicked him in the balls. Tried to kick him again but he got hold of my leg and pulled me down, came down on top of me. I tried to Mace him but I couldn't get the bloody can out of my pocket so I went for his eyes with my fingers except he was wearing goggles – night vision, which meant he could see and I couldn't because I'd dropped the flashlight when he grabbed me—'

'Grace,' Hartmann cuts in. 'Slow down.'

'Sorry. But I think you're right. About the hospital, I mean, and before I go you need to know what he said. About Ben.'

Her hand is throbbing, making her wince.

'Go on.'

'Where was I? Okay, on the floor, him on top of me, trying to get at his eyes but I couldn't. He got hold of my arms and pinned them

above my head with one hand – and, *Christ*, was he strong – and
then I got the message that he was excited – sexually, I mean,
because I could feel him – so I went slack like I was giving in and he
came down to kiss me, or whatever, and I got my teeth around his
mouth and . . .' Flint chomps her jaw, biting on thin air and grinds
and tugs at imaginary lips. 'He tried to shake me off, but I wouldn't
let go. I was like Sirius, tearing at his face—'

'Sirius?'

'A dog at Miller's Reach. When those fake INS people . . .' Flint
breaks off because now the pain is really getting to her and she
can't afford the time for this diversion. 'It doesn't matter. I'm just
like a wolfhound hanging on to his mouth for all I'm worth and
he's trying to stand up, taking me with him, and I'm trying to get
my gun – the pistol you gave me – except it isn't there, it must have
fallen out of the holster when I went down, and . . .' She pauses for
breath. 'Felix, Ben was working for bloody MI6.'

Hartmann studies her face, trying to fathom the source of her
startling revelation.

'He *told* me, taunted me with it. "Mandrake says you like to
fuck." That's what he said.'

*'You hitch, you ucking hitch.'*

*His words chasing her up the stairs, distorted because he can't
close his lips.*

*'Andrake says you like to uck ut you don't know wat ucking is.'*

*She, bouncing off the walls of the second-floor corridor because
she can't see where's she going. He, gaining on her, because he can.*

*'I'm going to uck you to death.'*

Hartmann shakes his head. 'Please, Grace, you're making no
sense. Who is Mandrake?'

*'Who's Mandrake?'*

*Now she's the one wearing the goggles and he's the one who's
blind. Lying on the floor of the corridor outside Karl Gröber's
room, his face black with blood in the eerie light, the tip of a rifle
barrel an inch away from his throat.*

*'Your ucking husand.'*

'Ben. It's his codename. Actually, he said "Andrake" because he
was having trouble with his Ms – as well as his Bs and his Fs – but
I knew he meant Mandrake. Bound to, wasn't he? Ridout chooses
plant names. As Otto said, it's one of his tics.'

'It is indeed,' says Dr Schnell, announcing his presence in the

doorway and, like the soldier he once was, Hartmann abruptly gets
to his feet. An apologetic smile from Dr Schnell. 'I could not help
from overhearing,' he explains. He motions Hartmann to resume
his place on the bed and takes the wooden chair for himself. 'How
are you feeling, my dear?'

'Not great,' Flint admits.

Dr Schnell nods. 'There is a doctor on his way.'

'How's Ilse?'

'Thoroughly confused.' Dr Schnell smiles. 'I think she has an
epic hangover but otherwise . . . The doctor will look at her, after
he's taken care of you. Now, Felix, you look as though you are also
thoroughly confused?'

'Bewildered,' says Hartmann. 'And deprived of information.'

'Then I will explain. Mandrake is a plant with a fetid odour,
which seems to make it a perfectly appropriate codename for Ben'
– he looks quickly at Flint – 'if you don't mind my saying so.'

Flint makes a sour face. 'Be my guest,' she says.

'But I wonder . . .' Dr Schnell taps his chin. 'I wonder if Ridout
was also amusing himself in other ways when he chose the name.
Grace, when was your marriage to Ben? The month? Was it May?'

'May 2000.'

'Yes. Well, if I remember correctly, in the United States the
mandrake plant is sometimes called the *may*apple. And Mandrake
is also the name of a play, *Mandragola* in Italian. Written by – who
else? – Machiavelli. Do you see what I'm suggesting?'

'Perfectly,' says Flint.

'*Please*, Grace,' says Hartmann. 'Can you *please* just tell me
what happened?'

'Happened? He threw a knife at me. I didn't see it but I heard it.
He missed because I tripped and fell over. I was trying to find it, in
the pitch dark, of course; trying get it out of the woodwork and
that's how I cut my . . .' She holds up her bandaged paw. 'Anyway,
Karl's room is like a Stasi armoury and—'

'Karl's room?'

'Up there.' She points at the ceiling.

'But you said you were *downstairs*.'

'Right. Okay, let's rewind the tape.'

Dr Schnell chuckles and says, 'I wish there was a tape, Grace. I
would like very much to have seen it. Perhaps your friends at
Quantico will stage a re-enactment for one of their training courses?

Though,' he adds, smiling mischievously at Hartmann, 'they may have some difficulty finding a volunteer to play the bad guy. Felix, you will volunteer, perhaps?'

The doctor is swimming in and out of focus and Flint begins to wonder if she's going into shock. Trying to clear the fug, she shakes her head and presses on.

'Okay, Felix, listen. I'm downstairs in the passageway just outside Ilse's bedroom. I was clinging to his face with my teeth and he was trying to punch me in the head but he couldn't; couldn't get a proper swing at me because I was too close to him, and I'm punching *his* head, and putting my knee in his groin.' She's babbling again, trying to get the story told. 'Anyway, he loses his balance and goes over backwards and I go with him and now I'm on top and I've got some leverage with my knee and I know that I'm hurting him because I can feel that he's not excited any more. Anything but.' The memory of it makes her think of the gnome in Karl's room with the unbuttoned fly and she breaks off her narrative to ask Dr Schnell, 'Did you see what Ilse did to Karl; what she wants to do to Karl?' and Schnell raises a hand to indicate that he did, and Hartmann looks even more exasperated. 'Sorry, Felix. You'll see when you get up there. Anyway . . .'

They wait while she gathers her thoughts.

'Anyway, my jaw was getting tired and I lost my grip on his mouth and suddenly he's screaming blue bloody murder, and he's spitting blood – and I can taste it – and I know it's time to get out of there. I tried to get his goggles so I could see and I managed to get them off his head, but then he grabbed my crotch and I had to fight him off and I dropped them. I kicked them away so he'd have to search for them, give myself a head start, and then I ran. I'm running into everything, hitting the walls, but I've got the advantage that I know the house better than he does, and I know where I'm going, which is Karl's room because, like I said, there are enough weapons up there to start a war. Or, if I don't make it that far, I'm trying to think of somewhere I can ambush him with the Mace.

'The problem is – was – that I'm not sure the Mace is going to stop him. He's already in pain, so the endorphins must be flowing of course, and he's madder than hell, yelling after me, calling me every name he can think of – which is fine by me because he's wasting breath, *and* it tells me how close he's getting.' Flint pauses as though she's lost the plot. Then, 'Too bloody close, as it happens.'

*Flint running blindly up the stairway to the second floor, his hail
of obscenities getting louder. She reaches the door at the top and
can't find the latch and she can hear him on the stairs behind her
and any instant now she expects to feel his hands wrenching at her
body, pulling her down, and if she can just think, if she can just put
aside her dread and think about what matters, she might remember
where the latch is.*

JUST BLOODY CONCENTRATE!

*And there it is and she's pulling open the door, passing through,
pulling it shut – which would have been a waste of time if she
didn't have a plan, a just-conceived desperate notion of how to
slow him down. She pivots, so that she is facing the door, an arm's
length away, and waits until she hears his fingers on the latch,
hears it open, and then, with all of the monstrous strength that
terror has given her, she kicks. She hears the door panel shatter
and, almost instantaneously, a second impact, a shriek that dies in
the throat, the sound of a body careering down stairs.*

*Now she's the one who is careering, down the corridor, feeling
her way along the wall, coming to the door of Karl's room, playing
blind man's buff with her arms outstretched until her hands find
the gnomes. Here's crouching Karl, but he's not the one she wants.
She edges past him, reaching for the next gnome and the next and
then the third, and now she's running her hands over its clay body,
exploring its contours like a lover, finding the strap on its shoulder,
following the webbing down until her fingers reach the cold metal
of a Kalashnikov – and, sweet Jesus, let it be loaded. She releases
the clip and it is loaded with ammunition and at this moment she is
willing to forgive Karl Gröber almost anything.*

'And then I got cocky or careless, or both,' Flint tells Felix
Hartmann, who watches her face with a fixed expression that she
can't read. 'I came charging out of the room assuming that he was
still lying at the bottom of the stairs – and you know what
assumptions are worth. He was waiting for me in the corridor. I
sensed rather than heard him, and tried to turn back, and that's
when I stumbled, thank God. Something went past me, thudded into
the door, and, like an idiot, I felt for it, got a hold of it, I'm tugging
on it . . .' With the hand that doesn't hurt like hell, Flint taps the side
of her head to indicate that it must be empty. 'This is the blade of a
knife that I'm fooling with, and it's double-edged, sharp enough to
etch glass. Why would I do that, Felix? Why didn't I just shoot him?

---

After all, I shot you,' she adds, 'and all you'd done was call my name' – and now it is Dr Schnell's turn to look perplexed.

It was nothing, Hartmann tells him. A minor accident.

'Anyway, then I did shoot him, or shot at him, roughly where I guessed he was. It was meant to be a warning shot but I'd never handled a Kalashnikov and I didn't realise it was set to full-automatic. I barely pulled the trigger, or so I thought, but I must have fired half the clip.'

'Magazine,' says Hartmann pedantically. 'With the Kalashnikov the clip is what you use to load the magazine.'

'Whatever. I know that when the gun went off it made a hell of a racket. Frightened me half to death – and him.'

'*Stop, stop,*' *he tries to say but he's having trouble with his Ps and it sounds to Flint more like,* '*Star, star.*'

'*Get down on your knees. Remove the goggles and throw them over here. Do it now, or I swear . . .*'

*Flint crouching, holding the rifle at waist level, aiming low, swinging the barrel from side to side to cover the width of the corridor, straining to hear the slightest sound.*

'*Two seconds, then I'm pulling the . . .*'

*She hears a rustle and then something hits the ground near her feet and she wants to reach for it with her injured left hand, keep her right finger on the trigger, but the left hand feels as though it is glued to the stock and she doesn't like the way the skin tightens when she tries to pull it free.*

'*Just stay where you are. Don't even think of moving.*'

'*I can't ucking oove. You roke I ucking leg.*'

*Flint doesn't believe him but she's only got two choices: either spray the corridor with the rest of the clip or risk taking her finger off the trigger. Do it! She goes down on her knees and begins searching the floor in front of her, stretching forward as far as she dare, now to her right side, now to the left – and this is tricky because she has to twist her body to achieve any kind of reach, and it would be a great deal easier if she could put the gun down, lean on her left hand, but she can't do either and . . .*

*Got them! The very tips of her fingers find the goggles and she lunges to retrieve them, puts them on her head, fumbles with the strap – and suddenly, magically, it is as though a spotlight has been turned on under water, bathing the corridor in a viridescent glow. She gives her eyes a moment to adjust and experiments on directing*

*the infrared beam by moving her head before fixing it on the figure
that half-lies on the floor no more than fifteen feet away from her,
his back wedged against the wall. She can't believe what her teeth
have done to his face. His right leg is twisted at an impossible
angle.*

'It must have been a ricochet off the wall,' says Flint speaking
slowly, as though she is reluctant to complete the story. 'Not a
direct hit because there wasn't that much blood but it shattered his
kneecap, and the joint.' Flippantly she adds, 'I guess he won't be
jogging for a while.'

She lapses into a silence that neither Hartmann nor Dr Schnell is
ready to break. They sit like priests waiting for the final part of her
confession.

'He was in a lot of pain; trying not to show it, of course, but I
knew.'

'*How much does it hurt?*' she'd said standing over him, feeling
not a shred of pity. '*Can you imagine it getting any worse?*'

'I didn't have much time, you see. Your people had heard the
gunfire, I supposed, because I could hear somebody trying to kick
down the front door. And I had to know, didn't I? About Ben?'

'*So, this Mandrake – my fucking husband, as you put it – how
do you know him? Does he work for you, for MI6?*'

'*Uck you.*'

'I had the gun pointed at his throat but he knew I wouldn't
shoot him. Well, I couldn't, could I? Not with your cavalry about
to arrive. Anyway, he couldn't tell me what I wanted to know if he
was dead so there was no point in threatening him with the
Kalashnikov. I had to think of some other way.'

'*If you don't tell me I will really hurt you.*'

She can hear his screams, him begging her to stop.

'I didn't have a choice. He didn't leave me any choice.'

Now she waits as silently as they do, as though she has told them
everything there is to tell.

'What?' – this to Hartmann who might have worked it out,
because he is looking at her in disbelief. 'What would you have
done? What else could I do?'

'What did you do, Grace?'

She seems puzzled that he needs to ask the question. It's obvious,
her tone implies. 'I stood on his knee.'

# Korcula Island
# Croatia

# fifty-three

Ilse's brother is restless tonight.

A sea fog is rolling across the Korcula Channel, obscuring the distant lights on the Peljesac Peninsula and even the searchlights on the jetty that is some two hundred feet directly beneath the bedroom balcony where Karl Gröber prowls, hearing the muted voices of the night watchmen he cannot see. He chain-smokes another cigarette and replays in his mind the conversation that has left him infuriated: Krol on an unsecured line from Leipzig, seeking to excuse his failures.

*They missed him. By an hour.*

*Missed him?*

*He left the hotel an hour before they got there.*

*But how is this possible, Krol? You assured me the hotel was under observation.*

*He used the fire escape, they think.*

*They think? And the fire escape was not under observation?*

*No. They say they had no reason to believe he was expecting visitors.*

Gröber tosses the cigarette butt over the balcony rail. Right now, if Krol were here, there is a very good chance he would also go over the rail.

*So, Krol, what now?*

*It is possible he has left Dublin for France.*

*Possible? Many things are* possible, *Krol.*

*More than possible. He has given instructions for the transfer to be made to a bank in Bordeaux. And our friends in Dublin have a sighting of someone matching his description on a ferry to Cherbourg that left Ireland on Saturday evening. I've called—*

*No names!*

*. . . I've called our other friends in France. They are looking for
him in Bordeaux.*

*And when they find him – if they find him – these other friends
of ours, will they know to watch the fire escapes?*

*I will see to it personally.*

*I hope so – and, Krol, what news of Ilse?*

*None. She has still not responded to my letters and I cannot call
the house because I am certain they are listening.*

*Then you must find another way.*

*What other way?*

*Find one, Krol. I pay you for results, or not at all.*

Gröber increasingly feels as though he is surrounded by fools.
Even Sabine has lost her edge. She drinks too much and falls into
bed each night incapable of conversation or anything else. When
he reprimands her, she blames him for her drinking, for condemning
her to the dreary boredom of life within the compound that she
says might as well be a prison. One, even two bottles of Korcula's
renowned white wine have become her daily ration and she snores
like a hog. He can hear her snoring now, even though the doors
leading to the bedroom are made of bullet-proof glass.

Just a few more days and they will leave the island, he has told
her. Korcula was never intended to be more than their temporary
sanctuary and, long before the shit Mandrake delivered his
demands, Gröber had made arrangements for him and Sabine to
assume new lives and identities in Brazil – lives free from pursuit
because the world will believe they are dead. Staging their deaths
convincingly is to be an elaborate deception to which Gröber has
devoted much thought and detailed planning. Though, if his present
dark mood persists, it is no longer a given that Sabine's death will
be a deception.

Whatever happens, Mandrake will die before Gröber leaves
Korcula. To him, it is simply unimaginable that Mandrake's
treachery should go unpunished. And if Gröber cannot rely on
Krol to get the job done, then he will make the arrangements
himself.

Now, he decides, sliding open the glass doors.

Most of the Villa Dora, which stands within a fenced compound
on a clifftop overlooking the Korcula Channel, is modern, built
in 1997, except for the cellar where Gröber has installed his

communications centre. The cellar and its foundations are medieval
– part of what was once a small fort – as is the tunnel cut into the
rock that leads to an escarpment camouflaged by pine trees. From
the escarpment there are roughly-cut steps down to a rocky cove
that is just a short boat ride away from the peninsula, and Gröber
assumes that the tunnel was built as an escape route in the days
when pirates preyed on the inhabitants of the island. Certainly it
will serve as Gröber's escape route when the time comes to leave
Korcula; when he primes the detonator for the explosion that will
pulverise the Villa Dora and everyone within it.

After he is certain that Mandrake is dead.

Gröber's hands are much too large for the cramped keyboard of
his laptop computer. He uses only one finger to write his message
and since Fabien, the recipient in Marseilles, does not understand
German, and Gröber has little French, he must write it in English,
which makes the task of composition even more cumbersome. It
takes him a good hour to complete the first draft and the best part
of another hour to edit and correct it. When he is finally satisfied
with what is literally a written contract on Mandrake's life –
complete with every possible lead to the target he can supply –
Gröber painstakingly attaches to the message file a series of digital
images: scans of all of the photographs of Ben Gates and his wife
that were removed by Krol's wife from Miller's Reach.

Now Gröber connects the laptop's modem to an encryption
device that is in turn connected to a satellite telephone that transmits
Mandrake's death sentence into the ether. Gröber expects it will be
the morning before he receives word from Marseilles that the
contract has been accepted but he has no doubt it will come.
Fabien's organisation generally kills with great efficiency for one
hundred thousand dollars. As a powerful inducement, the price
that Gröber has set for Mandrake's head is ten times that amount
– but still only a fraction of what Mandrake has attempted to
extort from him and therefore a bargain.

Still restless, Gröber unlocks a heavy wooden door in the cellar
and ducks into the entrance of the tunnel where the demolition
explosive – potent charges of RDX, TNT and plasticisers – is ready
to be detonated. He retrieves a torch from his escape kit and sets
off down the tunnel in a crouch. There are turns where the roof
drops so low he must crawl on his hands and knees, and others
where the tunnel narrows and he must twist his shoulders and suck

in his belly to squeeze between the walls. Even so, on his many practice runs it has taken him no more than five minutes to reach the escarpment and another two minutes to make it down to the cove, where a Zephyr inflatable is hidden under brushwood. All in all, allowing for minor mishaps and time to launch the boat, he has determined that a ten-minute delay on the detonator's timer will be more than sufficient.

Tonight, as on many previous nights, he goes no further than the escarpment, pushing his way through the pines to stand on the edge. The fog shrouds his view of the peninsula but it does not completely deaden the sounds coming from the mountain slopes of Peljesac. In the distance, drifting across the channel, he hears and is soothed by the cries of hunting jackals.

# Runde Ecke

# fifty-four

Nigel Ridout did not sound at all put out when Dr Schnell telephoned him at 5 a.m. to demand without explanation an urgent meeting. Always delighted to meet, said Ridout – so long as it's on neutral territory. So for their confrontation – their 'accounting', as Dr Schnell describes it – the doctor has used his influence to obtain the keys to the former Stasi headquarters where he now sits in a small office awaiting Ridout's arrival. Flint restlessly roams the halls of *Runde Ecke* examining the curious exhibits. The knife wound to her left hand has been treated, stitched and dressed, and it still hurts like hell.

Drifting into one of the rooms that is an exact replica of how things once were, she tries for size the wooden chair in which Stasi detainees were photographed under lights with an old plate camera, the seat made shiny by innumerable buttocks. Through an interconnecting door she can see the post room where a steam-powered contraption mechanised the business of opening and then re-sealing letters. She assumed that when Mandrake – she no longer thinks of him as Ben – opened her letters, he would have relied on steam from the kettle.

*What was his job?*

*To si on you* – Nick Fellowes, still having problems with his Ps.

*Why spy on me? What did Ridout want to know?*

*Everything.*

Everything. Which is what the maggots who occupied this building set out to know, of course – for all the good it did them – and Flint sees no distinction between the creeds of the Stasi and Ridout's dark forces, only a difference in scale. The Stasi may have forced husbands to spy on their wives but Ridout *created* a husband to spy on his wife; manufactured him, gave him a legend, sent him out to seduce her like a pimp sending out his hooker. That is how she sees Ridout: not as a spymaster but as Mandrake's pimp.

'Grace, you must guarantee one thing,' Dr Schnell had said before he would agree that she could be present. 'That you will behave. That, metaphorically speaking, you will not stand on Ridout's knee.'

She'd sworn to be as good as gold but now she's not sure she can keep that promise. When Otto comes to tell her, 'It's time, Ridout is arriving,' she remains in the detainee's chair. 'Perhaps it's better if I stay here.'

She can hear them through the thin wall, glad-handing in the adjoining room, going through the ritual *politesse* that attends their trade.

'Otto, dear chap, good to see you.'

'It has been a long time, Nigel.'

'What, three, four years? Vienna the last time, wasn't it?'

'Stockholm, I think.'

'You're probably right. So, Otto . . .'

Flint hears the sound of metal chairs scraping on a linoleum floor.

'Quite alone, are we?'

'No,' says Dr Schnell. 'I have a colleague with me, in the next room.'

'Ah, that explains it. Thought you might have company. Well, *my* girl's just having a look around – hope that's all right. Your girl, not *recording* is she? Not running a tape, not writing anything down?' Ridout raises his voice. 'Take a look would you, Stephanie? See what she's up to?'

The woman who casually appears in the doorway and studies Flint as though she is one of the exhibits has pale skin and a mass of rich red hair barely contained in a ponytail. Alias Fitzroy, codename Firefly – perhaps, Dr Schnell had said, because of the luminescence of her hair.

*I've seen you before*, thinks Flint. *Not on the plane, because I wasn't paying attention. Outside the railway station, baseball cap, losing interest in your guidebook, tailing Felix.*

'Nice jacket,' Flint says. It's black linen, cut to mid-thigh and loose enough to conceal a weapon.

'*Stephanie?*'

'It's cool, Nigel. Nothing for you to worry about.'

'Ah, but I do worry, Stephanie. Because when Otto Schnell calls us from our beds at such an indecent hour, when Otto *demands* a meet without so much as . . . Ouch! Good Lord!'

Flint supposes that Dr Schnell has slipped one of the Polaroids across the desk.

'What on earth happened to his face?' asks Ridout.

'He was bitten.'

'By a rabid dog, by the look of him. Stephanie' – Ridout stalling but also recovering fast – 'come and meet Otto. He's got some *charming* photographs to show you. Who is he, Otto?'

'He says he works for you.'

'Does he, indeed? Hear that, Stephanie? One of the hounds has slipped its leash, apparently. You should *definitely* come and take a look.'

She seems reluctant to leave her post but, after a moment's hesitation, a last warning look at Flint, she obeys Ridout's summons.

'Otto, meet Stephanie, who is in awe of your formidable reputation. Stephanie, this is Otto – Dr Schnell to you – who is under the impression that this unlovely wretch – don't flinch, Stephanie; don't be a girl – that this unlovely wretch is one of ours, because that's what *he* says. Is he of our kin, Stephanie?'

'No,' she says flatly.

'So, not one of ours?'

Again, 'No.'

There is a pause and then Flint hears Ridout say, 'Well, there we are, Otto. You seem to have a fantasist on your hands, one of those deluded chaps who thinks he's James Bond. Happens all the time, of course. They read Fleming's nonsense – or, more likely, see the movies – and they imagine we live lives sated by sex. If only that were true – and don't you glower at me, young Stephanie. So, Otto, sorry, not one of ours . . . Are we done? Are we through?'

There is no response from Dr Schnell.

'I suppose we could *try* and identify him for you,' Ridout says doubtfully. 'Do you have a name, Otto? Carrying any ID, was he?'

Still Dr Schnell does not respond and Flint, intrigued by his silence, slips out of the chair and goes quietly out into the hallway, positioning herself just shy of the doorway from where she has a partial view of the office.

Nigel Ridout faces Dr Schnell across a metal desk, lounging in his chair, theatrically relaxed with his legs crossed and his hands clasped behind his head. He is wearing a dark blue three-piece suit that was tailored for him, a light-blue cotton shirt, a maroon-coloured tie that Flint does not recognise as either old school or military. He is younger than she had expected, mid-forties, good bones, well-nourished and well-kept. With his expensive clothes, his broad Saxon face, hair that is swept back to fall just above his collar, he looks as though he might work in advertising, Mandrake's pimp.

Dr Schnell is leafing through a folder that he holds close to his chest, concealing the contents.

'All right for time are we, Stephanie?' says Ridout.

From her position in the hallway Flint cannot see Firefly but she imagines her making a play of looking at her watch before she replies, 'It's getting a bit tight.'

'Got a plane to catch, you see, Otto. So, if there is anything we can do for you . . .'

'The man you don't know,' says Dr Schnell, affecting to find what he's been looking for, placing a number of photographs face-down on the desk in a stack, picking up the first one and turning it over for Ridout's inspection, 'will be charged with murder, among other crimes. He killed an old man, suffocated him with a pillow. It was an unnecessarily violent assault. The victim's larynx was crushed.'

Ridout, leaning forward to glance at the photograph, entitled to expect a shot of a corpse, sees instead a street scene: Stephanie Cooper-Cole and the wretched Fellowes engaged in conversation on Richard-Wagner-Strasse not two feet apart. Ridout smiles at Dr Schnell and reclines in the chair. 'Nice shot of you, Stephanie, for what it's worth.'

'His name is Nicholas Fellowes, although he carried no papers in that or any other name.' As he speaks, Dr Schnell is turning over another photograph, holding it up for Ridout to see: Fellowes and Cooper-Cole together in the front seats of a car. Flint comes forward to stand in the doorway where Ridout cannot fail to notice her. She is also wearing a jacket that is loosely cut around the hips.

'He is under the illusion that he has immunity, that the charges against him will be quietly dropped because you and I will reach an arrangement, some kind of a deal. Or, rather,' Dr Schnell continues, 'he *was* under that illusion.' Now he is revealing the remaining photographs one by one, turning them over, holding them up.

A close-up of Fellowes and Cooper-Cole in conversation; Fellowes entering the apartment building opposite *Runde Ecke*; Fellowes and Ridout in the window of the apartment; Fellowes, Ridout and Cooper-Cole in the lobby of the apartment block – a grainy picture shot through the front door with a long lens but all of them eminently identifiable; Ridout, halfway out of the door, turning back to say something.

In the ensuing silence Flint enters the office because she needs to know where Firefly is standing, needs to watch what she does with her hands. Ridout nods and smiles broadly as though he is pleased to see her.

'Bravo, Otto,' he says. 'Got some *moving* pictures, have you? What about some sound? Tapes?'

Dr Schnell doesn't seem to have heard.

'Who did the wretch kill, Otto?'

'A Turk named Ciller. He was Ilse's housekeeper, her servant.'

'Ilse?'

'Ilse Gröber. Karl's sister.'

'*Ah*,' says Ridout, glancing at Flint then turning his head to look at Cooper-Cole. 'Hear that, Stephanie? Karl has a *sister*. No mention of that in the file, is there? I told you the Yanks had been holding out on us. So' – he turns back to look at Dr Schnell – 'what's it to be, Otto? Your girl and my girl, pistols at dawn? Winner takes all? Or they could wrestle each other, perhaps in mud. You'd enjoy that, Otto. Stephanie works out, don't you, Steff? She's *very* strong.'

He laughs, pleased with himself. His taunts are so assured, his lies so insufferably glib, that Flint fears that any moment now she's going to lose it; break her promise to behave herself. But before she can move Ridout snaps out of his careless, jocular pose and leans forward in the chair as if to stress the importance of what he's about to say.

'He said his name was Foster; some kind of mercenary, ex-Special Forces, or so he claimed. He called us, called the Firm in London, out of the blue. Said he knew where a certain Karl Gröber could be found and were we interested? Well, of course. After the debacle in New York ... What an utter cock-up that was' – a knowing glance at Flint – 'and any mite of confidence we had in

Operation Pentecost was entirely gone. So, of course we were bloody interested. Anyway . . .'

Ridout stands up and begins to pace the floor.

'No further details were forthcoming from Foster until, he said, we had discussed the matter of the reward he would be paid should he deliver Herr Gröber gagged and bound to our door. He wanted a meet in Leipzig. Seemed like a long shot but Stephanie had nothing planned for the weekend' – a quick smile for Cooper-Cole – 'and long shots are better than no damn shot at all. So, out she comes, meets Foster who drops a couple of gems that indicate he really *might* know something, and then he names his price: half a million dollars. "A bit steep," I told Stephanie when she called, but not totally out of the question, not if he *does* deliver Gröber into our eager hands. So, I came to Leipzig to dictate the terms: not a penny, not a *pfennig* does Foster get until I can *smell* Gröber's scent, I tell him. And then only a small down-payment – the balance of the bounty due when and if Gröber is sitting in one of my more uncomfortable chairs back in London under a very strong light, answering questions about where he's stashed his ill-gotten gains.'

There is a small vanity mirror hanging on the wall to the right of Dr Schnell's desk and Ridout pauses before it to examine the immaculate knot of his tie.

'Foster – or Fellowes, if that's what you say his name is – whinnies and whines and demands spending money to bring in some hired help; some former Stasi thugs he knows who are now in the mercenary game. Asks for ten thousand dollars and, generous soul that I am, I give it to him. Off he goes and he calls our apartment a time or two to report in, in somewhat cryptic terms, I might add – as you will know if you were listening to the phone. The last time was yesterday, early evening, since when . . .' Ridout turns from the mirror and holds up his hands. 'Precisely nothing. And that, Otto, is more or less all I can tell you. Of course, I had absolutely no idea he would *kill* some poor bloody Turk. Come to that, Otto, why on earth *did* he kill some poor bloody Turk?'

Dr Schnell is staring intently at the ceiling, as though he is absorbed in tracing the elaborate pattern of cracks in the plaster. 'Because you told him not to get caught,' he says.

'Oh, did I indeed?' Ridout puts his hands on the desk to lean over Dr Schnell. 'Got that on tape have you, Otto?' he says, shaking his head because he already knows the answer. 'I don't *think* so, Otto. Because we did check the apartment for any little toys you might have planted, you know – *and* we found them. Of course we did. Finding bugs is another of Stephanie's many talents.'

Firefly has put her hands behind her back where Flint can't see them.

'What I actually *said*, Otto' – more bluster now in Ridout's tone – 'was, "Don't do anything *illegal*." By which I meant no speeding, no running red lights, no breaking into houses, no snuffing the citizenry in their beds.' Ridout pauses and then continues, 'I would have called you, Otto, once we had Gröber, of course I would. But, after the farce in New York . . . No offence, Otto, but at least one of your boys was involved . . . Well, I'm sure you understand why we acted alone.'

There is a silence that Flint breaks, though she speaks so softly she might be talking to herself. 'How's Mandrake, Mr Ridout?'

He stands up and turns to look at her in puzzlement. 'What?'

Flint, hands in the pockets of her jacket, shuffles on her feet, getting closer to the desk – and closer to the edge. 'I asked you how Mandrake was.'

*Be very careful how you answer, Mr Ridout, because I've had it with your lies.*

'Mandrake?' he says as if the name means nothing to him but there is a smile dawning at the corners of his mouth.

'Ben, if you like,' she sighs. 'My husband, your whore.'

'My whore? Oh, *very* good. And what does that make you, my dear?' Ridout laughs and is still laughing when the Mace hits his face.

'Someone once said that it's like being blind and having an asthma attack and dipping your face into a deep fat fryer all at the same time but, honest to God, I've never seen it work on anybody like that, or that fast.'

Flint in disgrace, banished to the back seat of one of the many cars now parked outside *Runde Ecke*, minded by Felix Hartmann who is not quite as disapproving of her as he is trying to make out.

'Splat! One moment he's being the lying pompous prick that he is and the next he's on his knees screaming like a baby.' Flint shakes her head as though she still can't believe it. 'Then Firefly's coming at me as though she's Wonderwoman and, splat, she goes down as well. Maybe it wasn't just Mace? Do you think there might have been some pepper spray mixed in there?'

She begins searching her jacket, looking for the can so she can check the contents, and then she remembers that it was confiscated by Dr Schnell.

'Otto was livid, standing there bawling at me: "*You think you are a law unto yourself!*" Well, he's not the first one to say that. Cutter told me that when I was being hired by the FSF and my references came in from the Met some joker at the Yard had attached a note that said, "*Question: What's Flint's Law? Answer: Whatever she wants it to be.*" Meaning I don't always play by the rules. Oh, really? So how do you define Ridout's Law? As I said to Otto – when I could get a word in – bloody Ridout's the one who sabotaged Pentecost; he's the one who got Ruth killed; it's because of him and fucking Mandrake that my father's in a coma and he's the one hiring psychopathic mercenaries to kidnap Gröber – if you can believe a word he said, which I don't. "*Said his name was Foster. Called the Firm out of the blue.*" Bullshit. Almost every word he said was a lie. I'll bet my pension that Fellowes is a full-time thug for MI6, even if he is off the books and deniable.'

Hartmann says, 'Tell me, Grace, do you honestly think you will live long enough to receive your pension?' and that makes her smile.

# Staten Island

# fifty-five

Melinda Stark sits hunched on the very edge of the cherry wood rocking chair in her living room, clutching her knees, watching Aldus Cutter with vacant eyes and trying to comprehend the incomprehensible. Cutter speaks softly as though he is explaining a sudden death in the family, which in a way he is. She does not interrupt except to say from time to time, '*Nathan?*' in a startled tone that suggests that what Cutter is saying about her husband cannot possibly be true; that there is some ghastly mix-up, some error of identification.

She is not the dummy that Nathan takes her for, not the butterfly-brain that needs to be reminded of every little thing. But right now, under Cutter's unceasing assault, she's having trouble holding on to anything he tells her. For the second time – or is it the third? – she notices the jumble of cars in the street, the men in the driveway waiting silently like pallbearers for a funeral to end, and she doesn't understand what they're doing there and Cutter has to tell her again.

'Melinda, we need to search the house. It's going to take a while. It'll be better if you and Nathan Junior aren't here so you won't get any more upset. We're going to take you somewhere you can stay until it's over. Just for a few days.'

A few days? With a jolt of alarm she suddenly remembers that the Carpenters are coming for dinner tonight because she forgot to cancel and she hasn't been to the store and she's trying to recollect what she's got in the freezer. Probably nothing that will do and Nathan will roll his eyes and say '*Melinda*' in that weary what-else-did-I-expect voice of his and they'll have to serve pre-cooked from the gourmet counter which, as Nathan always says, is *ruinously* expensive.

Except Nathan won't have anything to say because Nathan is a fugitive. That's what Cutter called him. A *double-agent* working for a *foreign power* and now *a fugitive*. An image comes to her of Nathan trailing the mid-sized Samsonite across an airport terminal where all the signs are in a language she cannot read. She feels an urgent need to know where it is.

'Which foreign power?' she demands imperiously, interrupting Cutter's flow.

'The Brits,' says Cutter. 'The United Kingdom.'

The Carpenters are British and for an instant this symmetry seems to make sense to her. Then, 'But I thought they were on our side?'

'Not all of them,' says Cutter.

This enigma baffles her as much as anything she's heard and she puts it to one side. She wishes for the company of her son. She wants him sitting beside her on the couch, awkwardly holding her hand as he sometimes does when Nathan is away, trying to provide the comfort she rarely receives from her husband.

'Where's Nate?'

'In his room,' Cutter assures her – but Cutter is wrong.

Nathan Junior is in his father's study watching Rocco Morales working on the wall safe. It shouldn't be that hard to crack but Rocco's having trouble, evidently.

Quickly growing bored, Nathan asks in a superior way, 'Have you tried the combination? One, six, nine, four . . .'

'I expect, Aldus,' Nathan Stark's letter begins,

> that you will tear the house apart but, for the sake of Melinda and the boy, I hope you don't. There really is no point, nothing to find – except perhaps on the computer's hard drive, if my grasp of erasure algorithms is not all that it should be.

Cutter has taken Melinda's place in the rocking chair to read the letter for a second time; more slowly this time now that he's calming down. From Nathan's study he can hear the sounds of floorboards being pried up. From the hallway comes the murmur of Jarrett Crawford's voice talking on the phone.

> Every document I 'borrowed' from the Bureau was returned after I'd extracted the information I wanted. I 'borrowed'

nothing from the FSF because, as you will surely figure out, there was no need. And even if there had been a need, I would have hesitated. Truly, Aldus, the document security you devised for the Marscheider building was *much* superior to anything the Bureau ever had. If it hadn't been for Flint, I don't think that it would have been possible to deceive you. She was always your Achilles heel.

How many cases have I betrayed? None. All I ever did was share information with our allies, information they were entitled to but denied because of the Bureau's culture of secrecy. I realised long ago that, from the top down, the Bureau would rather see a perpetrator walk away than share information. I thought it would be different at the FSF, you *said* it would be different, but if anything it's worse. We had a chance to lead a global fight against crime and terrorism, to make international borders as irrelevant to law enforcement as they are to the opposition. But we never did that because, just like the Bureau, we'd never give information, we'd only take. Well, I gave, Aldus. I *shared*.

'No,' says Cutter to himself, 'you *sold*, Nathan, you sonofabitch.' It is Stark's attempts to sugar-coat his greed with pious motives that has Cutter's blood pressure once more rising towards dangerous levels. His head is throbbing with the warning signs.

I won't tell you how many times I shared – let's give the terriers something to do! But I will tell you about the first time. In 1984 the Bureau was running surveillance on a KSA named Kalinin who was operating under diplomatic cover at the Soviets' UN mission. Kalinin was a bag man servicing a dead-letter drop in Queens and we'd identified his contact – or thought we had – when a deputy military attaché from the British Embassy in Washington walked into the frame. His name was Manyon and on three consecutive Sundays he flew to New York and met with Kalinin, a Known Soviet Agent in a Known Soviet safe house, and we had it all documented and recorded – *and we would not tell the Brits!* Not then, not ever. The attaché returned to London to become something more important in their foreign office and there was every reason to think he could be a Soviet mole and we did not breathe a word. We didn't want to blow the Kalinin operation, you see. Director's orders.

Does that make any sense to you, Aldus? Well it made no sense to me. I told the Brits. That was the first but not the last time I thought we had a common interest that was not well-served by our obsession with secrecy and our arrogant assumption that nobody outside the Bureau could be trusted. I'll leave it to you to figure out the other times – if you can!

*We're way ahead of you, Nathan*, thinks Cutter.

Back at the Marscheider building, Kate Barrymore and her team of terriers is working its way through every case file that Nathan Stark signed off on during his last fifteen years with the FBI – files obtained by Cutter's mentor at Justice on heaven knows what pretext. The last time Barrymore called she told Cutter that, in addition to the Kalinin case, they had so far found nineteen files where Stark might have identified a 'common interest' with the Brits.

Crawford coughs from the doorway. 'Excuse me, Mr Cutter, but you'll want to know. I think we've got a sighting of Nathan.'

Cutter rubs at the pain in his head. 'Go ahead, Jerry.'

'Just before midnight a white male matching Stark's general description crossed into Canada at some place called Coburn Gore up in Maine. It's pretty remote, just a two-lane road, and there was only one INS guy on duty. He'd seen the APB on Stark but he didn't make the connection because it wasn't Stark's car, because he was using another passport – and because he wasn't alone.'

Cutter would raise an eyebrow but he thinks that moving any muscle in his forehead might increase the pain.

'He had a passenger,' Crawford continues. 'Not much of a description but a white female, twenty to twenty-five years old, same last name on the passport, which was Lacey. INS guy thought they might be father and daughter. Said she was pretty in a flashy sort of way.'

'So, Nathan has a girlfriend.' Cutter says this in a tone that suggests he would have thought it unlikely. 'How do you know it was him? The quince, right?'

'Yes, sir. The INS guy says the car stank of it. Late-model Ford, black or dark blue, Maine plates. The way I figure it, either she lives up there and it's her car and Stark took a plane to join her, or they flew up to Maine together and picked up a rental. We're checking the airports and the rental agencies.'

Cutter nods and instantly regrets it.

'You all right, sir?'

'No, Jerry,' says Cutter speaking slowly, feeling as though his head is about to explode. 'I don't believe I am.'

# fifty-six

The keening of the ambulance siren is fading when Crawford picks up the phone to call Flint in Leipzig, to tell her something else she won't want to hear. Crawford has received only sketchy details of her run-in with MI6 but he knows that Otto Schnell has allowed two of the three British agents to quietly leave Germany, no fuss, no charges – and that Grace, in Cutter's words, is 'climbing up the walls, spitting blood'.

'Was that before or after you told her about Nathan?' Crawford had asked.

'Oh, that was before. After she went *real* quiet.'

And she's still barely audible when she answers the phone and Crawford tells her that he has more bad news to impart.

'Christ,' she says faintly and nothing more.

'It's Cutter, Grace, he's had some kind of seizure, maybe a stroke. His blood pressure's through the roof. The paramedics have got him stabilised and he's on his way to the hospital but it's not looking great.'

He imagines she is thinking of her father.

'Where?' Flint asks. 'Where did it happen?'

'Here, at Nathan's house.'

'That figures,' she says. She sounds as though she is drugged. 'Did he say why he did it?'

'Nathan? Not really. There's a lot of self-justifying bullshit in the letter about sharing information to fight a global war on crime but the bottom line is the Brits paid him. They've been paying him for years. He's got himself an expensive girlfriend, apparently. They crossed over into Canada last night.'

There is a silence on the line that lingers until Crawford checks if she's still there. 'Grace?'

'What did he say about Mandrake?'

Crawford hesitates because he's not sure how much more bad news Flint can take. He asks, 'You sure you want to hear this right now?'

'I'm sure.'

'It was a set-up from day one. The Brits, meaning MI6, had known about Gröber since August 1999. They knew what he was up to, knew there could be at least a billion dollars in the pipeline ready for the taking but they didn't know exactly where and they didn't have the resources to find it, which is where we came in. They needed the FSF to do the legwork so they fed us Gröber. They got Nathan to lean on Vincent Regal to drop a couple of pointers in your lap and then you did all the running for them. They could just sit back and watch, because . . .' Crawford lets the sentence die.

'Go on, Jerry.'

'Because they'd already planted Mandrake on you. He was one of their illegals, a deniable deep-cover operator they've used before. Grace,' Crawford hurries on, 'I don't know if this helps but Nathan says it was never part of the plan that you two would get married. Mandrake was just meant to become your lover.'

'Lover?' Flint murmurs uncertainly as though the word is new to her. 'That's a pretty weird name for somebody so loveless, don't you think?' When there is no answer she continues, 'No, Jerry, it doesn't help. Getting married was my idea.'

'Right,' says Crawford, because he can think of no other reply.

'It gets worse, Grace. MI6 didn't just want to know what we were up to. They had to make sure that Pentecost imploded so that when it did they could pick up the pieces and go after Gröber's money for themselves. That was the other part of Mandrake's job: to contact Gröber and say he was in a position to spy on the FSF, to monitor every damn move we made.'

'Not quite every damn move, Jerry,' Flint says sullenly. 'Even I wasn't stupid enough to take home every Pentecost report.'

'Yeah, but besides what he saw in the Pentecost file, Mandrake was also getting the printouts of your reports from the Met computer at Scotland Yard. Remember Scratchwood and Peter?'

Flint says, 'I remember.'

'Okay, well it turns out that Peter was a spook. There was no bent cop at the Yard. It was MI6 that was hacking into the Met's computer and feeding the info back to Mandrake – and he was selling it to Gröber. Nathan says there was a real panic in London when the courier got stopped by INS because if you'd told the Met they might have been able to figure out who was getting into their system.'

'Oh, shit!'

'The fact you didn't tell the Met, because you didn't know who to trust, proves Nathan's point – or so he says. His point being, we don't share.'

While Flint silently absorbs the extent of her failure, Crawford turns the pages of Nathan Stark's vindicatory letter until he finds the passage that describes and mocks her culpability.

Flint was always meant to fail, of course. Gröber was never going to walk into the trap she set for him because he knew about it all along, and only God knows why he showed up for the meeting with Ruth Apple – and, believe me, Aldus, I wish to God that he hadn't. More of that in a moment. What I want to stress here is how *spectacularly* she failed because she is blinded by the reckless impulsiveness that you mistake as both courage and talent.

She is blind in so many ways. I asked you a few days ago how she could possibly be married to someone and not know who they are, and you gave me a cryptic reply. Now you know the truth, Aldus, perhaps you should reflect on that question again.

'And the fact that Ruth got thrown out of a helicopter' – Flint's voice now icy – 'was neither here or there, I suppose. Just a bit of collateral damage, a tick in the minus column. I mean, so long as the reptiles got to justify their existence and top up their slush fund, and Mandrake got his money and Nathan got to pay for his whore, what's an agent's life worth? Bugger all. What does he say about Ruth?'

'Not a lot,' says Crawford, being stingy with the truth. 'That Gröber was never meant to show up for the rendezvous. That when he did show up, Nathan bust a gut to get you to abort the operation.'

Actually, Nathan Stark has a good deal more than that to say about the murder of Ruth Apple.

Agent Apple's death was almost entirely Flint's responsibility. She should never have selected an undercover of Ruth's experience – or, I should say, *inexperience* – for an operation against a target as unpredictable and ruthless as Gröber, and I told her that when I begged her to abort. It's on the tape – 'You could do this, Ruth can't.' But, Aldus, you must share part of the blame. You wouldn't order her to call it off because you couldn't let go of your stubborn belief that Flint knows exactly what she's doing. She doesn't. She flies by instinct, a danger to herself and everyone around her, and I have to say that I've often wondered why you don't see that. You see more than anybody I know, Aldus. Why are you so blind to Flint?

'I've gotta go,' says Crawford.
'Go to the hospital, Jerry. Hold Cutter's hand for me.'
'I will, just as soon as I can. What about you?'
Flint says nothing much; just that she's on hold, awaiting developments, waiting for something to happen.
'Any leads on Mandrake?'
'Not really,' Flint replies, being stingy with the truth herself.

# Leipzig

# fifty-seven

Flint still wears Frau Hartmann's cheap woollen coat buttoned to the neck and her hair tied back but the body language has changed. There is nothing meek about the woman who pays off the taxi in the suburb of Grünau; who marches purposefully across a sodden patch of grassland towards the forest of high-rise apartment blocks where one-fifth of the population of Leipzig lives; who accosts a child to check the directions she has been given; who enters Block Five as though she belongs there and takes the lift to the tenth floor. At the door to apartment 107 she puts on a pair of wire-rimmed spectacles to inspect the nameplate beneath the bell push. 'KROL,' it says and – in a hurry, no time to waste – she jabs the button twice.

The eyes of the woman who opens the door a few inches register her suspicion as she studies Flint and tries to recall why she finds her face vaguely familiar. She is not allowed time to dwell on it.

*My name is Hartmann*, says Flint in her brusquest German. *We talked on the phone. I must speak with your husband immediately. About Frau Gröber.*

Frau Krol opens the door wider but she does not step aside to admit Flint. The blemish on her left temple is more vivid today than it was on the morning of their previous encounter. Definitely a birthmark, Flint decides.

*My husband is not here*, Frau Krol says, still regarding Flint with instinctive wariness. *He has been detained.*

You bet he has, thinks Flint, but not in the way you imagine.

Unknown to his wife, Manfred Krol is currently losing patience and his temper at police headquarters in Goethe-Strasse where he has been taken to answer entirely trumped-up allegations of criminal assault, courtesy of Dr Schnell.

*Then I must speak with you*, Flint insists, leaning forward, lowering her voice. *In private*, she whispers, as if it is a code.

Frau Krol's memory has failed her. As Flint breezily predicted to Dr Schnell, she does not make the connection between the cop who rousted her in Friendly's Restaurant and the woman who now furtively checks the corridor in both directions wishing to imply it is important that she not be seen kept waiting outside Frau Krol's front door.

'*Bitte*,' says Frau Krol, finally stepping aside.

This is not one apartment but two joined together, the dividing wall removed to produce a spacious living room. Scattered on polished wood floors are three exquisite Persian rugs of the kind that take a year or more to weave and cost a king's ransom, probably even more than the lush furnishings, the bank of state-of-the-art hi-fi equipment, the giant television screen hanging on the wall. The Krols may live in one of the dreariest apartment blocks that the brutalist architects of the GDR ever devised but they do not live shabbily.

Seated on a plump white leather couch, holding in her lap the cup of rich black coffee Frau Krol has served, Flint spins her web of lies.

*I am Hartmann*, she repeats. *Frau Gröber's live-in companion, her only companion, the only one she speaks to. Ilse is not well. She has malignant tumours in her knee joints that require surgery, radical surgery, but she will not speak of it. Increasingly she only speaks of what obsesses her – her brother, Karl. She hates Karl because of what he did to their parents, because of what he did to her. In his room, what used to be his room, she keeps an effigy of Karl that is grotesque. She has taken her revenge on Karl by mutilating him, by cutting off – and you must excuse my bluntness, Frau Krol – by cutting off his penis.*

Flint sips the coffee and returns Frau Krol's unblinking gaze.

*But, of course*, Flint concedes, *that revenge is not sufficient for Ilse because it is imaginary. Ilse knows that she is dying and what she wants before her end is true revenge. She wishes to hurt Karl in any way that she can and now she has found a way. She intends to betray Karl as he betrayed her. That is why I am here, Frau Krol. To warn you, to warn Herr Gröber. It is my hope – in fact, my expectation – that your husband and Herr Gröber will not be ungrateful for this warning. Once more* – Flint forces a tight smile – *you must excuse my bluntness.*

Until now Ilse has been persuaded not to make any rash decisions. *However, the progress of her illness is accelerating and she thinks that her time is running out and*, Flint adds gravely, *I fear she is correct. Two days ago, when she was particularly distressed, she asked me to make contact with the police to inform them that your husband knows the whereabouts of the murderer Karl Gröber. She said I should also give them proof. This proof.*

Flint is putting her coffee cup on the side table, taking an envelope from her bag.

*This is a note from Herr Krol in which he says that Karl is anxious for news of Ilse, anxious to know if there is anything she needs besides the money he sends her – money, Frau Krol, that Ilse will not touch.*

Now from her bag Flint produces a wad of banknotes that she places on the arm of the couch, then a second, then a third.

*Ilse calls it 'guilt money tainted by blood,'* Flint says, raising her eyes to suggest she thinks that Ilse overstates her case – eyes that today are an intense blue, a transformation achieved with contact lenses. Flint's hair has also been transformed, dyed a dirty blonde.

*The remainder of the money is intact*, Flint assures Frau Krol. *I have not taken a single mark, though I could easily have done so for every time your husband delivers one of his envelopes Ilse tells me to burn it. But I am not a thief, I do not steal. I only expect to be rewarded for the value of the information that I provide. How valuable that information is, I will leave you to decide. After I've told you the rest of Ilse's plan.*

Flint idly picks up one of the wads of banknotes and riffs it with her fingers like a pack of playing cards.

*When I talk to the police – if I talk to the police*, Flint says, suggesting that the matter is not yet decided – *I am to propose that they do not take immediate action against Herr Krol. That they do not, for example, demand to know the source of the funds he has delivered to Ilse.* Flint pauses and then she adds, *Considerable funds, Frau Krol. Almost one million marks!*

Frau Krol's eyes have drifted away from Flint's face to some point beyond her right shoulder.

*No, I am to suggest that they do nothing except tap your telephone, perhaps place hidden microphones here in your apartment.*

Flint glances around the room, her eyes suggesting the myriad places where listening devices might easily be concealed.

*And when that has been arranged,* she continues, *Ilse will call you on the telephone and demand to speak to your husband. She will tell him it is imperative that he makes contact with her brother immediately because she needs money, a great deal of money. To make her story convincing she will say what is true: that she is a sick woman in urgent need of an operation. But then she will say that she has no more faith in German doctors, that they are fools, that she must go immediately to the United States where there is a clinic and doctors who can save her life. 'Tell Karl I must have money now,' she will say. 'Tell Karl he owes me. Tell him that I am desperate enough to do anything.'*

*So . . .*

Flint waits until Frau Krol looks at her.

*You see the cunning of Ilse's plan. Had I not come to warn you, Herr Krol would doubtless have made the call providing the police with proof that he knows the whereabouts of the murderer Karl Gröber. And then what choice would your husband have had?*

Getting up from the couch, replacing the money on the arm, Flint wanders over to the bank of hi-fi equipment and holds up two fingers to indicate the poverty of his options.

*Either he must tell the authorities where Karl is to be found or he himself becomes an accomplice to murder. The Americans will demand his extradition and you, Frau Krol, I fear, will find yourself under the intense scrutiny of the fiscal police.*

Flint's fingers caress the satin dials and cover of an expensive stereo amplifier.

*You have so many nice things . . .*

The telephone rings, startling Frau Krol. She goes to answer it but before she can lift the handset the ringing stops.

Flint has twenty minutes to get out of here, the signal means. Manfred Krol has been released from police detention, is on his way.

*Fortunately,* says Flint, as though there has been no interruption, *I did come to warn you and it is possible I can be of further assistance. I could delay matters for several days. I could tell Ilse that I have been to the police and they are considering her plan. I could then say that they have agreed but that it will take some time – two more days, maybe three – to make the arrangements for the telephone to be tapped, for the microphones to be placed. Eventually I will have to do as she asks but by then, Frau Krol, if I may make a suggestion, you and your husband will have decided to take an extended vacation. To somewhere that is not in Germany. Not anywhere in the European Union, nor, of course, the United States.*

Flint has no set script. As always in these circumstances she flies by instinct, guided by the reaction she gets from the target. Frau Krol's reaction is one of extreme suspense. She seems to be holding her breath.

*I'm told,* Flint says casually – as though what she is about to reveal is neither here nor there – *that at this time of the year the Adriatic can be most pleasant.*

For a split second there is only astonishment in Frau Krol's eyes. *Got you!* thinks Flint.

'*Wer Sie sind?*' – the first words Frau Krol has spoken since her nightmare began.

Flint shows a puzzled face.

*I told you. I am Hartmann.*

*But who are you? You say you are Frau Gröber's companion but you are English, yes?*

Shaking her head Flint plucks an explanation for her accent out of thin air. *My mother is English,* she admits, *but my father is German. They were divorced when I was very young and I lived with her. Now I have returned home.*

*How do you know about . . . ?* Frau Krol begins, stopping herself only just in time. Now she poses another question: *What is it that you want?*

*Your gratitude, Frau Krol, and some recompense for my services. For it occurs to me that I can be of further service to you. When Ilse is dead – a tragedy that cannot be more than a few weeks away, two or three months at the most – the only evidence against your husband will be this note, and that is not explicit about the money. Indeed, in itself, it merely suggests that on one occasion Herr Krol was asked by his former comrade Karl Gröber to contact his sister and give her a few marks and, since the note is not dated, this may well have occurred before Herr Gröber was a murderer and*

*international fugitive. It is only when one reads Herr Krol's other
notes, some of which are dated, that the true nature of his* con-
tinuing *relationship with the murderer Karl Gröber becomes
apparent. Fortunately, I can assure you that those incriminating
notes are hidden somewhere that is very safe, very secure. That
leaves only the question of the money that the fiscal authorities
must not—*

Flint gets no further for Frau Krol has finally seen the light. '*Sie
sind ein extortionist,*' she screams.

Not at all, says Flint calmly. *You think I would be so foolish as
to try and extort money from a murderer? I will take only what
you say I may take. For my services.*

Frau Krol lunges and for a moment Flint thinks she may have to
fight her but it is the wads of money on the couch arm that Krol
seizes and holds out in a quivering hand.

*Take it*, she demands. *Take it and get out.*

*Thank you*, Flint says solemnly. *And the rest? Shall I keep it for
you until this unfortunate matter has passed?*

*Keep it. Keep it all. Now* GET OUT.

At the doorway Flint turns to say, *Remember, Frau Krol, be very
careful what you say on the phone.*

# fifty-eight

Flint striding through Grünau, heading for the tram stop, a blue and white panel truck with Deutsche Telekom markings a couple of hundred yards behind. It matches her pace, stops whenever she stops, and it's so bloody obvious what they're doing that she wonders why they don't just put out a sign. When she is certain there are no other tails she calls Hartmann on his mobile phone.

'Felix, it's cold out here. Why don't you just come and pick me up?'

It is not Hartmann's fault that Ridout and Cooper-Cole are free and clear and back in London, no doubt shrugging off the consequences of their sabotage of Pentecost and covering their traces – in particular, any connection between MI6 and Nicholas Fellowes. That was Dr Schnell's decision, his call, and not one that he had any intention of justifying to Flint.

'You've let them walk away?' she'd asked incredulously. 'After what he's done?'

Schnell was in the front passenger seat of the car and he wouldn't turn around to look at her.

'I know how you feel about Ridout, Grace, but there are broader considerations.'

'No, Otto, you don't know how I feel.' She'd gone very quiet until a thought had occurred to her. 'Does Cutter know?'

'It was his proposal,' Dr Schnell had said. 'Do not imagine that Ridout is entirely in the clear. There will be consequences, a price to pay.'

'You've got that right,' said Flint but in a whisper so that only Hartmann had heard.

Even so, there is an air of palpable tension in the back of the Telekom truck when Flint squeezes between the racks of listening equipment, nodding hello to the tech boy and then to Felix, unbuttoning the woollen coat and the top two buttons of her blouse, pulling the button microphone from its hiding place inside her bra.

Squatting down on an equipment box she asks, 'Did you get it?' meaning the transmission of her one-sided conversation with Frau Krol.

'Every word,' Hartmann says stiffly. 'More, perhaps, than you had intended?'

'And what's that supposed to mean?' By Flint's reckoning, Ruth Apple was killed precisely two weeks ago at this hour, give or take a few minutes, and she's in no mood for what she knows is coming.

'Considerable funds, Frau Krol,' he mocks in a fair imitation of Frau Hartmann's relentless voice. 'Is that right, Grace: almost one million marks?'

'I was just bullshitting, Felix, saying whatever came into my head.'

Hartmann looks at her as if to say, I don't think so.

'Does it matter?'

'Yes, I think one million marks matters.'

'Oh, come on, Felix, give her a bloody break!'

The eruption of Flint's anger is so seismic that the tech boy turns to watch her, open amazement on his shiny face.

'Ilse hasn't touched a cent of Karl's stinking money. But she's got cancer, she's dying, and when – please God – we take Gröber down, when the money tap's turned off, maybe it's not the worst thing in the world if she buys herself a little extra time or a bit of extra comfort. Maybe something that's not all bad can come out of this.'

Flint is reaching under the hem of her skirt, removing the transmitter from the inside of her thigh, snapping the tape from her skin without regard for the pain she is causing.

'If you want to seize her slush fund, claim your share of the bounty for the BND, fine, go ahead. But keep in mind that in my book Ilse's a victim, not a perp, so don't expect me to help you do it.'

'What we want, Grace,' says Hartmann, 'what Dr Schnell expects, is that you do not withhold information. Please. We are supposed to be partners.'

Open-mouthed, she stares at him until he has the grace to look away.

In the car park behind Block Five the Telekom truck with its satellite receiver mounted on the roof stands out like a neon sign. The high-definition camera concealed in the bulbous housing records that even Manfred Krol – preoccupied though he is by his encounter with the police and still in a foul mood, apparently – notes the presence of the truck, peering through the windscreen of his Mercedes, taking the long, hard look of an experienced Stasi hood and a veteran of who knows how many surveillance operations.

Flint studies his belligerent face on the screen. Peter, the tech boy, over whose shoulder she leans, is wearing earphones and through the cans Flint can hear faint strains of music coming from apartment 107. It is Bach's *Mass in B Minor* if she's not mistaken and she is struck by the irony that Frau Krol soothes her ragged nerves with one of Mandrake's favourite pieces.

*I will find you, Ben* – Flint's mantra running through her mind.

'No noise,' says Hartmann sharply.

Krol is out of the car, coming slowly towards the truck like a hunter stalking game. He passes out of the camera's range and they hear him trying the doors, imagine him cupping his hands to look into the darkened windows of the empty cab. There's no doubt he's spooked by the presence of an unattended truck parked outside his home. As he is meant to be.

*Run, rabbits, run,* Flint silently implores.

Krol now coming back into the frame, hurrying towards the rear entrance of the apartment block. In his haste he has neglected to lock the Mercedes – not that it matters because the vehicle locator is already installed, concealed inside the steering column. Hartmann said that with Krol detained in police HQ for as long as they needed, the tech boys had been spoilt for choice as to where to hide it.

The transmitter planted by Flint, on the other hand, is merely attached with a magnet to the back of the Krols' stereo amplifier and she has predicted that, unless he is a complete idiot, it should take him all of thirty seconds to find it. 'I practically made love to the damn thing,' she says. 'She can't have failed to notice.'

In the snug confines of the truck they wait in silence until Peter, pressing the cans to his ears, says 'Here we go' and activates the reel-to-reel recorder.

'Talk us through it,' Hartmann says.

'Okay, but they need to get closer to the mike . . . She's doing most of the talking but I can't make out what she's saying . . . Wait . . . Come on, come on . . . That's better . . . Okay, now it's him talking . . . Why did you let her in? She said she was Ilse's companion, blackmailing bitch, blah, blah . . . Seen her somewhere before . . . Where? Don't know . . . Describe her . . . Mousy, dyed hair, hard face' – a glance of apology to Flint – 'pretended she was half-German but terrible accent, could be American or English, blah, blah . . . Shut up. That's Krol, shouting – boy, he's really getting mad. Where was she? She doesn't understand what he means . . . Where did she go? Where did she sit? Here, on the couch . . . He's doing something, sounds like he's practically tearing it apart . . . Where else, woman? Where did she walk, what did she touch? She went over there. What are you looking for? Be quiet . . .'

Flint is timing him on her watch. It's been one minute and forty seconds and the clock's still running. Okay, she decides, he is a complete idiot.

'*Hell!*'

Peter recoils as though he has been punched and pulls the earphones from his head.

Flint was wrong about the music. It is Bach's *St Matthew Passion*, coming through the earphones' speakers at maximum volume, rising inexorably to its glorious crescendo.

Press, press, press, press – Flint is repeatedly ringing the doorbell of Apartment 107 and still getting no reply.

'Are you sure you want to go through with this?' Hartmann had asked.

Not really, would have been the truthful answer, but for her scheme to work somebody's got to scatter a little more confusion and Flint is the only plausible candidate.

*Frau Krol, it's Hartmann* – Flint pleading in an urgent whisper through the woodwork. *Are you there? I must speak with you.*

Absolute silence from the Krols, but Flint is pretty sure she can sense human presence on the other side of the door. Any moment now she half-expects it to fly open, one or both of them coming for her throat. She forces herself to stay where she is and raps on the panel with her knuckles.

*Listen to me. We have both been deceived.*

She speaks a little breathlessly, as though she has been running.

*When I got back to the house the police were there. Ilse must have called them. I don't know what she's told them but it may already be too late.*

She gives them a moment to ask themselves, Too late for what?

*I came back to warn you. You must look for microphones. Don't speak on the phone. Do you understand?*

So, not too late to run, perhaps? She wills them to understand her message that their only chance is to flee.

*I'm leaving now, leaving Leipzig. I won't return.*

A last word before she slips away. *Good luck to you, Frau Krol.*

Run, rabbits, run.

# fifty-nine

Flint knows that the type of vehicle locator concealed in the steering column of Manfred Krol's Mercedes uses GPS technology to continuously report its precise position anywhere on earth, more or less, within an accuracy of three hundred metres, if the satellites are working – knowledge that is no comfort at all since in the last seventeen hours Krol's car hasn't moved an inch. She can see its mocking presence in the car park from the window of her temporary sanctuary where Dr Schnell has suggested that she get some rest. In apartment 117, directly above the Krols' living room, an apartment borrowed by the BND from its astonished tenants on grounds of 'national security', she shares a child's bunk with an impressive collection of stuffed toys. Between her and the Krols, inserted into the ceiling void, are heat sensors that confirm the presence of two live bodies below, and fibre-optic microphones that have picked up occasional sounds of domestic activity, but not a single spoken word. Hartmann has unhelpfully speculated that the Krols are communicating with each other by means of written notes.

*Thanks, Felix! Saying what, exactly? Why don't they run? What are they waiting for?*

Twice in the night Frau Krol left the apartment. The first time, just after midnight, she was observed walking purposefully along the tenth-floor corridor past the lift and through the doorway leading to the stairs. Where she went after that, and whether she went up or down, is anybody's guess since, in the time allowed, even Dr Schnell's resources had not stretched to installing hidden cameras on any floor except the tenth. All that is certain is that Frau Krol did not leave the building by either of the entrances and that she returned to her apartment after thirty-five minutes.

And then, at a few minutes before 5 a.m., she had set out on a second journey, once more vanishing into the stairway. Just after five o'clock, one of the watchers posted on the roof of the apartment block to maintain surveillance on the car park had been forced to scramble for cover when Frau Krol had emerged from the skylight no more than twenty feet from his position.

She'd moved close to the edge of the roof and waited there, looking down, taking no more than a passing interest in the small van that was driven into the lot, that circled once and then departed. 'She just stood there like a statue,' the watcher had reported. 'There was no other activity, nobody else about.' After another five minutes she had gone inside and taken the stairs back to the tenth floor. The expression on her face, recorded by the hidden cameras, was entirely neutral.

'Okay, Felix, speculate some more,' Flint had said tetchily, the tension of the long wait getting on her nerves. 'What's your best guess?'

'I think that they have called for help, somebody to get them out of here. I think Krol has decided that they cannot use his car because he suspects it might be tagged and that they need alternative transport. So, the first time his wife went to see a friend, somebody she knows in the building, and asked to use the phone. The second time she went on to the roof expecting to receive some kind of signal from whoever it was that she called.'

'And?'

'Perhaps she did?' Hartmann had suggested. 'Perhaps the van was the signal that their transport is on its way? It made one circuit of the parking spaces, correct? Perhaps that meant that their friends will be coming for them in one hour?'

But that was almost six sleepless hours ago and still the Krols haven't moved. Flint is pretty sure that Hartmann is right, that they're waiting for somebody to pick them up, but how long can it take for Krol's friends to come up with a car?

*Not a car*, says a voice inside her head.

*What?*

*They're not waiting for a car.*

She closes her weary eyes and forces herself to concentrate.

*Of course they're bloody not* – and Flint could kick herself for being so slow.

She's tumbling out of the bunk, running from the room, searching the apartment for Dr Schnell, hearing him in the kitchen talking with Hartmann, bursting in on them as though the building is on fire.

'Wings!' she says breathlessly. 'The Krols, they're waiting for wings!'

Wagner on the stereo, his booming *Ride of the Valkyries*, which Flint always associates with swooping helicopters. An ironic up-yours gesture from Krol? she wonders. Unlikely, she decides, on the grounds that former Stasi hoods are probably not much into irony. The more likely explanation is that he's chosen it to mask the sounds of their departure from the apartment.

It is five minutes before 1 p.m. and Flint is now sure that the van's single circuit of the parking lot was intended to signal the departure time. The Krols are travelling light, apparently – an overnight bag for her, no more than a briefcase for him. They wear sensible overcoats, walking unhurriedly along the tenth-floor corridor past the lift and towards the stairs, looking for all the world like a bourgeois middle-aged couple off to visit their grandchildren.

There are no longer watchers on the roof. All of the surveillance units have been stood down by Dr Schnell and there is only a remote camera on top of the adjacent apartment block, transmitting a flickering black and white image to a monitor that sits on the kitchen table. Peter, the tech boy, fiddles with the controls, smiling apologetically at Flint as if to say 'It's the best I can do in the circumstances', and she nods her understanding. She's thinking of Rocco Morales trying to get her a picture of a boat moored in the East River yacht basin with something on its roof, something hidden under a tarp.

'Heads up,' she says, because the monitor now shows two small figures emerging on to the rooftop and Hartmann and Dr Schnell join her at the table. 'This is going to work, isn't it, Felix?' she adds quietly, but it's not really a question, more an expression of her anxiety.

One minute to go and the Krols are searching the skyline, and now he's pointing towards the southeast and his wife has got one hand to her forehead trying to shield out the sun. Hartmann hurries to open the kitchen window and all of them can hear the thwack of rotor blades growing louder, echoing and amplified within the man-made canyons of Grünau.

Now the monitor shows the black shadow of the helicopter crossing the rooftop and the Krols' sensible overcoats bellowing in the downdraught. Now the machine itself edges into view, also black, no markings, not even a tail number. The pilot is using cyclic pitch to make a sideways approach, manoeuvring between the central heating ducts and the TV aerials.

'What is it?' asks Dr Schnell as the landing gear touches down.

'A Robinson R44, I think, but I will check,' says Hartmann, reaching for his mobile phone.

Flint can see that only the pilot is on board and it occurs to her that if Otto could be certain it was Karl Gröber he would never have agreed to let him go; never agreed to her hare-brained scheme to attempt to track the route of a low-flying helicopter across Europe through air traffic control.

Two doors have opened in the fuselage and the Krols are in a crouching run, half-bent to stay beneath the blades, and – as though he's read her mind – Dr Schnell says, 'This could be the last we see of them, Grace.'

'Trust me, Otto.'

'That is precisely what I am doing.'

Hartmann finishes his call and says, 'That is confirmed, sir – it is an R44, also known as a Raven. The maximum range is about 600 kilometres, allowing for reserves, so if the Adriatic is their destination it won't be sufficient. They will have to refuel, probably in Austria . . .' – he goes to a map of Europe that he has pinned to the wall – '. . . somewhere around . . . Wolfsberg. Then they will fly over Slovenia and cross into Croatia and then' – Hartmann holds up his hands – 'who knows? The coastline is five hundred kilometres and there are more than one thousand islands . . .'

Flint is barely listening. The Krols are on board and the doors are closed and the black Raven is lifting from the roof – rising and wheeling like the ravens that danced above the flames at Miller's Reach.

# sixty

'Grace, it's me' – Aldus Cutter calling, which comes as a surprise to Flint because the last she'd heard he was strictly incommunicado on doctor's orders. Jerry Crawford said that Cutter was barely out of intensive care and still on a saline drip when a nurse caught him using the phone to call the Marscheider building. Crawford said they'd virtually strapped Cutter to his bed, read him the riot act, taken the phone out of his room.

But here is Cutter on the line, waking her up, not giving her time to collect her thoughts. 'We need to talk.'

'How are you?'

'Fine,' says Cutter. 'It was a false alarm – or maybe just a warning bell. Anyway, listen, I'm not calling about me. It's about your father, Grace.'

The room is dark and she can't find the light and her legs are tangled up in the sheet.

'I don't know how to do this any way that's going to make it easy so I'll just tell you. John didn't make it.'

'John?' She whispers her father's name as though it means nothing to her, because there is a part of her brain that refuses to make the connection.

'He's passed away, Grace. Pneumonia, they think. I haven't got the words to tell you how damn sorry I am.'

*This is not true! This cannot possibly be true! But in order to prove the lie she knows she has to get out of bed and she's thrashing her legs, tugging at the sheet, not taking any notice of what else Cutter is saying to her. Now she's halfway out of the bed, reaching for the floor with her outstretched hands but there's nothing there and then the sheet rips and her legs are free and she's falling headlong into a void . . .*

Flint wakes. The room is not in total darkness. She finds herself sitting on the floor, her back against the ladder of a child's bunk, her legs bent double and pressed against her chest. Her mobile phone, broken into two pieces, is on the floor beside her.

She thinks she must have fallen from the bunk and landed on her head; must have stunned herself because she can't remember why she's in a child's bedroom wearing only her underwear and a T-shirt that's too small for her. Nor can she remember where Felix is, or Otto, or why that matters – and then her stomach lurches as she vividly recalls the rest of what Cutter said.

'Grace, is Felix around, Felix or Otto? Because you're in shock and when you come out of it it's going to seem like you've had a bad dream, except you haven't, and I don't want you to be alone when that strikes home. Grace? Are you there? Grace, please, get Felix, put Felix on the line.'

*I can't. The phone's broken. I fell out of bed and broke my phone.*

*OH, JESUS!*

Now she's frantically trying to put the phone back together, trying to make it work, getting nowhere, hurling it against the wall. She's on her feet, running from the room, searching the apartment, finding no-one, yelling for Felix, yelling for Otto, getting no reply.

There is a landline phone in the hallway and she snatches at the handset and starts to dial but she can't remember the number and she's running back into the child's bedroom, searching for her bag, finding her address book, running back to the phone; dialling, misdialling, starting over, telling herself to slow down; getting it right this time, waiting for the connection, listening to the ringing tone, forcing herself to breathe.

*Oh, please, answer the—*

'Hello, Intensive Care.' A young woman's cheerful voice, one of the nurses, Flint assumes.

She takes a deep breath and then, 'This is Grace Flint. I'm calling about my father. Can you—'

'Oh, hello, Miss Flint' – like this is just a routine call, nothing important. 'I'll get Sister for you. Hold on.'

'*Wait!*' – but the nurse has gone. It is Flint who waits until there is a crackle of static on the line and a sharp click and for a moment she thinks she has been disconnected and then she hears not the Sister's voice but that of a man saying, 'Hello, are you there?'

'*Yes.*'

'Ah, good, it's Baxter here – sorry about the confusion. We've been trying to get in touch with you but there's been some problem with your phone, apparently, and—'

'Doctor, *for Christ's sake! Please ...*' Her voice is much too loud. She swallows and tries again, 'Please, doctor, just tell me, is my father still alive?'

'Alive? Oh, yes, I'll say so' – Baxter chuckles – 'very much alive. He came out of the coma just after midnight, snapped out of it as though he'd just woken up – quite startled the duty nurse. That's why we've been trying to get hold of you, of course, but we couldn't get through to your number. Now, I should say that your father's not entirely out of the woods. There's no paralysis but there is some aphasia and amnesia. For one thing, he's not entirely certain who he is, though he does remember you. Wants to know where the hell you are – his words, not mine. Otherwise, his memory loss is probably temporary but I should warn you that it's early days and there are tests we still need to do ...'

The neurologist's caveats are wasted on Flint because it feels as though her brain is melting and she can't take them in. She's biting her lower lip, tasting the blood, trying to prove to herself that this is not another deceiving part of the dream. The pain she inflicts makes her whimper and Baxter interrupts himself to ask, 'Hello? Miss Flint? Is something wrong?'

If she could speak she would tell him: Not any more.

But this is a rush to judgement delivered before she goes to the kitchen to quench her furious thirst and discovers on the table a package addressed to her in Dr Schnell's meticulous hand. It contains a cassette tape, no note, nothing more. She looks around the kitchen and sees no means of playing it.

Feeling a growing unease, Flint searches the apartment until in the child's bedroom she finds a boom box, one with a translucent purple plastic cover, and inserts the tape. She presses the Play button and Dr Schnell thunders 'Good evening, Grace' at a level of decibels that makes her jump. She pauses the tape and adjusts the volume and then allows him to continue.

'At least, I hope it is the evening because you badly needed to sleep, Grace. We are all agreed you have pushed yourself beyond endurance.'

It's flooding back to her now: After the departure of the Raven, Schnell and Hartmann doing a double act, outbidding each other with their estimates of how long it would take to reach its destination – eight to ten hours, Otto had said; more like twelve to fourteen, Felix had countered, because of the need to refuel and pilot fatigue. In any event, there was ample time for Flint to rest; nothing else to do except wait – and of course they would wake her when there was definitive news. Sleep, Otto had urged; I'll make you a hot drink, Felix had insisted – and she'd been too tired to resist.

*You bastard! You spiked the tea!*

With a barbiturate, no doubt, one of those to which she has an allergic reaction, and now she knows the reason for her furious thirst.

'The Adriatic coast – you were entirely right, of course,' Dr Schnell is saying. 'And the next time a newspaper tells me where a target might be found I shall not dismiss it out of hand – even if it is *Bildzeitung*. The flight was tracked with very little difficulty and the Croatian authorities have been both efficient and extremely cooperative. Thanks to you, we know precisely where Karl Gröber is. And, yes, Grace, once again you were right – Mandrake is with him. They are both caught like rats in the same trap.'

A telephone rings and for a moment Flint thinks it is the landline in the hallway but then it stops and she hears Hartmann answering the call. There is a click as the recording is cut off. When it resumes Dr Schnell speaks more quickly, as though he now has reason for haste.

'Grace, it is because Mandrake is there that we have left you to sleep. You cannot come with us to Croatia; you cannot be a part of the final act, because we are afraid of what you might do. This is something that Aldus and I agreed even before your . . .' – Schnell pauses to choose the right word – 'your contretemps with Ridout. This is too personal, Grace. It is because you have been so badly betrayed that you must leave us to deal with Mandrake. What was that?' – Schnell is asking the question because Hartmann is saying something to him, speaking in the background. 'Ah, yes, Felix reminds me to tell you that Cutter is making a remarkable recovery.'

*Sod Cutter, sod Felix, sod all of you!*

Flint is pulling on her clothes – Frau Hartmann's clothes – and running through a mental checklist of what she needs to accomplish:

Call a cab and get back to Ilse's house to collect her things; have the cab wait and take her to the airport; a flight to where? – probably Frankfurt then a connection to Zagreb; rent a car and get to the coast . . .

*And then what?*

'Crawford is on his way,' Schnell is saying, 'so the FSF will be represented at the dénouement, as it should be. Grace, listen to me. I know what you are thinking but it would be futile for you to try and follow us. And even if you could, even if you could somehow get to Mandrake, you would only succeed in doing precisely what Ridout wants you to do. Understand this, please. Ridout wants you to find and eliminate Mandrake because Mandrake knows too much. He knows *far* too much about the reptiles.'

Flint is only half-listening. She needs to get money from a cash machine. She needs to buy another mobile phone.

Dr Schnell sighs as if he knows he has been wasting his breath. 'Grace, there is a car waiting for you downstairs, and two men outside the door of the apartment. They have orders – the strictest orders – to take you to Berlin and arrange a flight to England for you. Only to England, Grace, nowhere else. By the time you get there it will all be over.'

*Two men, Otto? Only two?*

'Go home, Grace. Because your father needs you.'

# Korcula Island

# sixty-one

*It is Ilse who has betrayed you* – Krol's poisonous words spoken first on the phone and now repeated in person. He stands defiantly in the living room of the Villa Dora with his fists clenched, still wearing his overcoat, his face grey with fatigue from the shuddering journey but refusing to be cowed by Karl Gröber's glare.

*You must face the truth, Karl. Your sister has betrayed us both.*

*Enough.*

*She hates you, Karl, she always has—*

*ENOUGH!*

And without further warning, and with astonishing speed for a large man, Gröber steps forward to deliver a back-handed slap to Krol's face, a blow that sends him reeling, and before he can recover Gröber hits him again, driving him to his knees, and Krol's wife screams, and Sabine, who is slumped on the sofa, emerges from her stupor and yells to him to stop.

But Gröber does not stop. He brings up his knee and finds Krol's throat and now Krol is on his back and Gröber straddles his chest, pinning his arms to the floor, methodically raining blows to alternate sides of Krol's head – now with his left hand, now with his right; slap, slap, slap, slap, and still he continues – not even aware of the women's attempts to drag him off, not hearing their appeals. Only when his rage is vented, and Krol is unconscious and there is blood trickling from the lobe of each ear, does Gröber stand up, roughly pushing the women away, leaving the room without a word.

Blame Mandrake for Karl Gröber's explosive anger – or rather, Mandrake's failure to be found. But earlier today Fabien had promised Gröber that his hunters were very close, that they had picked up Mandrake's trail at the bank in Bordeaux from where he had made his first cash withdrawal, and followed it to the pleasure port of La Rochelle where Mandrake seeks to buy a boat, apparently. It was only a matter of time before they would have him, Fabien said; most likely, a matter of hours.

And when they have him they will play with him for a few days to teach him the error of his ways, and then they will kill him and dump his body in the Atlantic. Or, those were Gröber's orders.

Now there is to be a change of plan.

In the cellar that serves as his communications centre, feeling calm and the incident with Krol almost forgotten, Gröber composes an email to Fabien that revises his instructions.

Disable Mandrake but do not kill him, the message says. Keep him alive and still receptive to pain, and bring him immediately to Korcula. Charter the fastest helicopter you can find. Expense is not an issue.

Gröber sends the message and, while he waits for Fabien's acknowledgement, he unlocks the door that guards the entrance to the tunnel. The explosives are wrapped in black plastic and loaded around the stone columns that support the Villa Dora, and into the first batch Gröber now inserts a cylindrical charger attached to electrical wire. Because he distrusts timers of all types, the delay mechanism he has chosen to use is simply the length of the fuse, and it needs to be finely judged. Once, a long time ago, Gröber miscalculated and the bomb he had planted in a hotel in Managua exploded prematurely as he was leaving the lobby, and he was among those injured by flying glass. One legacy of that is a scar on his right forearm that is precisely six inches long, and now he uses that as his gauge to measure the length of fuse he requires.

When he is satisfied with the fuse he connects the end of the electrical wire to a controller box the size of a pack of playing cards that has two buttons on its side. Now he must test the box and although the routine is entirely familiar to him, and one that he's carried out at least a score of times before, he still feels a frisson of something – not fear exactly, but a heightened sense of danger – as he presses and holds the first button that is labelled 'charge' and waits for the indicator light to tell him that the electrical voltage has built to a sufficient level to ignite the fuse. He is very, very careful to keep his fingers away from the second button that is labelled 'fire'.

Everything is in order and Fabien has acknowledged the message. Now all that Gröber must do is find the patience to wait for Mandrake's arrival.

He will not sleep tonight, he decides. He takes the torch and heads along the tunnel towards the escarpment where he will remain among the pines and anticipate the moment when he will first hear the throb of an approaching helicopter.

# Mid Compton

# sixty-two

Grace Flint is working in her father's surgery, his unpaid locum, taking care of seven small emergencies. Dr Flint is not yet strong enough to resume his practice but a neighbour's collie bitch has rejected her litter and there are seven pups that need bottle feeding about a hundred times a day. Mindless work, Flint thinks, good for the soul.

'Grace, *Gracie*' – John Flint calling to his daughter in the barn from the high bank of Glebe Farm because he still can't work out how to use the intercom she's had installed. 'Darling, I'm going through the bills and I can't find my chequebook anywhere. I've no idea where I put it. Do you mind?'

For the umpteenth time in the last ten days Flint trudges from the barn to locate what he has mislaid or remind him of things he has forgotten. With a rueful smile he watches her climbing the steps. 'Am I being an absolute pest?'

'Totally,' she says.

'Driving you mad, I expect. I don't know how you put up with me.'

'Now you come to mention it, I think I'll have to have you put down.'

She reaches the top of the bank grinning hugely and links arms with her father to lead him back into the house. Through his jacket she can feel his ribs and his bony elbow, for he is painfully thin. In her eyes he has aged ten years and almost all of his faculties seem diminished; with shocking suddenness, he has become a forgetful old man.

Physically he will regain much of his strength and already the walks they take together each day are growing longer. But his mind has lost its sharp edge, clouded by confusion and absentmindedness, and Baxter, the neurologist, has warned Flint that this is as good as it's likely to get; that the capacity of his working memory may have been irrevocably reduced.

And while his amnesia has improved, there are gaps in his long-term memory, and one curious distortion. John Flint has detailed memories of the night when he believes he fell heavily and banged his head: of standing on the terrace with his son-in-law, of going inside for a drink; of talking late into the night about Ben's work, his mother's illness, their mutual delight in Grace. What is curious is that Dr Flint is quite certain that his daughter was also there that night. In his vivid recollection she played chess with him, and grumpily lost, and as a penance she made cheese on toast for supper. He has not the faintest idea that he was attacked by Ben – or rather, not by Ben since Ben never existed, another fact of which he is blissfully unaware since his daughter has not told him.

Nor does he know that his son-in-law is dead.

She must tell him soon, she has decided. After their walk this afternoon, perhaps.

'Darling, did you say that Ben was coming?' Dr Flint asks and not for the first time in the last few days.

'No, Dad, Ben's not coming.'

Standing in the kitchen she sees in his dull eyes the look of puzzlement that has become depressingly familiar. 'Mmm,' he says vaguely. 'Can't think why, but I could have sworn you said that he was.'

Early evening in the kitchen, after their walk across the fields and after he's taken a nap and a shower; the best part of the day because the combination of exercise and rest seems to refresh him, to make him as alert as he's likely to be. He's sitting at the table, working on a crossword puzzle, when Flint quietly takes her place opposite and waits for him to finish.

'There! Done!' he says, putting the cap back on his pen with a flourish. He's pleased with himself, but his smile dies when he sees the look on his daughter's frigid face. 'Is there something wrong?'

'This is very difficult,' she begins, speaking with unnatural calm. 'I have something to tell you, several things to tell you – things I've been keeping from you until you were strong enough to hear them. I need you to be strong now, Dad, as strong as you've ever been.'

Her father doesn't speak. Instead he reaches out across the table and takes her hands in his.

'It's about Ben. He deceived us. He always deceived us, from before the very first moment I met him. Everything he ever said to me, everything he told you, was a lie. Even his name was a lie. He set out to seduce me and then he married me for one reason only and that was to find out about my work, about a particular operation. He helped to sabotage that operation and one of my agents died. Then he ran away and came here because there was something he needed, something he'd hidden in my room, and you almost died. You didn't fall that night, Dad, he attacked you. He hit you on the head with the table lamp in your study and then he locked you in one of the cages in the surgery. You're only alive because somebody called the police and told them – and it wasn't him. I've been looking for him ever since and I would have killed him for what he did to you but somebody else got there first. He's dead, Dad. I know you don't want to hear me say this but I'm glad that he was killed. I only wish I had been there to watch him die.'

For half a minute or more John Flint watches his daughter as if he's become a statue made of stone, his eyes fixed, not a flicker of expression on his face. Then he releases her hands and gets up from the table and comes around to her side and lifts her effortlessly from the chair as though she is a child and holds her to him and she thinks of another father's embrace, and now she truly knows what Ilse meant.

*It was as though he was trying to give me strength, his magnificent warm strength flowing from his arms.*

It is much, much later and they are still in the kitchen, though Flint has lost all track of time. When her father said, 'Can you please begin at the beginning, darling?' she'd inwardly groaned, but telling the story to an entirely sympathetic audience, admitting to him things she had not admitted even to herself, has been cathartic for both of them. Flint feels unburdened, as though sharing the truth has made it less unbearable. Her father seems to grow stronger the more he takes on the load.

She has made no significant omissions – unless you count the moment when she dreamed that her father was dead.

'And that's about it,' she says. 'Otto's minders were both about ten feet tall and *very* attentive and I didn't really see how I could give them the slip, and by the time we got to Berlin I didn't see the point. Even if I managed to get to Zagreb, what was I going to do, how was I going to find them? Anyway' – Flint smiles – 'once they'd put me on the plane, all I could think about was seeing you. Good decision,' she adds. 'One of the very few.'

He dismisses her admission with a flick of his hand. 'And you know what happened in Croatia?' he asks.

'Some of it – but only Jerry Crawford's version. I'm not presently on speaking terms with Dr Schnell, or with Felix bloody Hartmann. I'll promise you one thing, one of these days I'm going to slip something into *his* drink that'll make him think he's dying of more than thirst.'

Her father laughs. 'I'm sure I can find you something suitable in the dispensary.'

'Something you might give to a severely bloated cow, for example?'

'Something like that. What did Jerry tell you?'

'Gröber and Co., including Mandrake, were holed up in a villa on one of the Dalmatian islands – an island called Korcula – that was about fifteen miles off the coast. The house was very isolated, apparently, and set on a cliff overlooking an inlet, so very hard to approach without being seen. By the time Jerry got there – there being Dubrovnik – the Croatian air force had done a high-altitude reconnaissance and spotted a compound behind the house with two helicopters and half a dozen vehicles and a bunch of guys wandering around who looked very much like armed guards. Big mistake. The guards, I mean.'

Flint, who, unlike her father, is running out of steam, stretches her arms and yawns. 'The police there are paramilitary and they're not known for their subtlety. Schnell had already told them about Gröber's background – and they knew what had happened in New York, of course – and once they heard about the guards, the Croats decided they were up against an entire army of Stasi thugs. So, it wasn't a police raid they mounted so much as a military invasion. They went in the next morning, just before dawn, with their own helicopters, fast patrol boats, all kinds of equipment. Jerry was on one of the navy boats and he said there was one hell of a firefight but it was clear from the outset that Gröber's lot didn't stand a chance.'

She stares into the middle distance and then continues, more slowly now. 'So they tried to make a run for it, or some of them did: Gröber, Mandrake, the Krols, three unidentified males and one female, also not yet identified although I'm pretty sure her first name was Sabine; Gröber's girlfriend. They made it as far as the two helicopters, even managed to take off. Climbed to a few hundred feet – and then there was this huge explosion. The house literally blew up and either the helicopters got hit by the debris or they collided. In any event, they came down in flames. Eight bodies, most of them burned to a crisp. Which, in Gröber's case, if you think about it, was sort of appropriate. That he should die in a helicopter crash, I mean. Poetic, even.'

John Flint asks, 'And how can they be sure that Ben – I'm sorry, Mandrake – how can they be sure that Mandrake was one of those who died?'

'Prints. Fingerprints. His corpse was the only one that still had skin.' She gets up from her chair. 'Let's have some tea.'

Going to the sink to fill the kettle she continues over her shoulder, 'And here's an irony for you, Dad. No law enforcement agency had Mandrake's prints on file and there were none found in his office because Frau Krol – or Lender as she was calling herself then – did a pretty good job wiping it clean, and I did an even better job at Miller's Reach by burning it down. So, guess where the prints came from?'

'I have no idea.'

'Bloody MI6.'

'Really?'

'Yes. Schnell knew that since Mandrake was one of theirs, MI6 was bound to have his prints and he *persuaded* – that's Jerry's word – persuaded Ridout to hand them over. Actually, it probably wasn't that difficult because Ridout would have been just as keen to know if Mandrake really was dead. Ties up one of the loose ends for him, doesn't it?'

Her father does not answer immediately and Flint busies herself getting cups and saucers from the cupboard, making up a tray.

'Gracie, I don't suppose there's any way that this Ridout fellow could have tricked Dr Schnell?'

'No, no,' Flint says quickly. 'Ridout wasn't involved in matching the prints to the corpse, wasn't allowed within a thousand miles of it. Schnell and Hartmann made the identification. Jerry was there.'

'I see.'

The kettle has boiled and she's filling the teapot when the revelation hits her like a body blow, as John Flint quietly says, 'The thing is, in one of my novels I once had the police faking a death and a set of fingerprints and then lying about it. They'd have no reason to lie, would they, Grace? No reason to *pretend* Mandrake was dead?'

# sixty-three

Flint on the phone to the Marscheider building, waiting for Jerry Crawford to finish his tirade.

'Grace, you're chasing ghosts! Ben is dead, Gröber's dead, they're all dead. I was there, remember? Look, I know you're pissed at Schnell and Hartmann and I don't blame you because if I was in your position ... well, never mind. But, Grace, this just doesn't make any sense, you know it doesn't. Why would the BND fake Ben's death? For what? This is just so fucking crazy...'

He runs out of words and Flint asks, 'Are you done?'

'Sure,' says Crawford wearily.

'There never was a Ben. We call him Mandrake. Now, one more time, just tell me what you saw.'

'I saw the choppers going up – well, heard more than saw, but I sure as hell saw them come down. The villa just blew, this gigantic explosion, and then one or both of them was on fire and they were locked together coming down like bricks, and when they hit the ground there was another explosion, a mini-fireball. By the time I got up there, just after first light, there wasn't much left other than the frames and the engines. Charred cadavers littered about, Kentucky fried, some worse than others. Mandrake had been thrown clear when the wreckage hit the ground, I guess, and we were able to get prints off him, but otherwise none of them was identifiable.'

'And where were Schnell and Hartmann?'

'When?'

'You tell me.'

Crawford says, 'Wait one,' and puts the line on hold. Flint wanders from the kitchen into the living room where her father lies dozing on the couch. With his help – his clever questions and his plain common sense – it had taken her a good two hours to work it out and by then she'd seen fatigue dulling his eyes and creasing his face – though not his spirit, apparently. No amount of her cajoling could persuade him to go to bed. 'Not on your life,' he'd said firmly. 'Not until I know the end of the story.'

'Sorry,' says Crawford. 'Had to take another call. Where were we?'

Flint returns to the kitchen before telling him, 'Schnell and Hartmann.'

'What about them?'

'*Jarrett!*' – a warning shot across his bows reminding him that, for all her sins, she is still Joint Assistant Director (Operations) of the FSF, even if she is on compassionate leave and three thousand miles away; even if her access card still won't get her into the Marscheider Building. Come to that, with Aldus Cutter still on forced convalescence and Nathan Stark still on the run and not coming back unless it's in chains, she's the acting head of the FSF, technically speaking.

*Until they get around to firing you.*

*Shuddup.*

'Okay,' says Crawford, 'I remember. During the attack Dr Schnell and Felix were on board one of the assault choppers and still airborne when the villa blew, lucky for them. When I got up to the compound around dawn they were sifting through the debris going through Gröber's things.'

'Things?'

'Bunch of stuff that didn't get burnt in the explosion and was tossed around like confetti. Files and papers – but no financial records, if that's what's on your mind.'

That is exactly what is on Flint's mind. 'How do you know?'

'Because they showed me what was there, what they'd be able to salvage. I went *through* what was there, every damn piece of it. Come on, Grace, you think I just went along for the ride?'

'Tell me what you found.'

'Nothing. Household trivia – bills, receipts, guarantees, that kind of stuff – mostly written in Croatian but I had a couple of local cops doing the translating. Bank statements, *local* banks, one in Split and one in Dubrovnik, and, Grace, we're talking here about a couple of hundred thousand dollars *total* – not a couple of billion. Some legal stuff: Gröber was in dispute with a neighbour who wasn't too keen on the choppers disturbing his tranquillity,

---

apparently ... Grace, there was *nothing* there, nothing that mattered.'

'Nothing that you saw,' says Flint.

'*Christ!*'

'Jerry, how long had Schnell and Hartmann been in the compound before you got there? How long did they have after the choppers went down? How long did they have to pick among the wreckage and the debris of the house – three, four, five hours?'

'No, nothing like that. After the explosion, after the choppers came down, the skipper of the boat I was on headed directly for the cove. We got there within thirty-five minutes, forty max. Then it took me maybe another ten to get up to the compound. And, Grace' – Crawford putting a little sarcasm into his voice – 'they couldn't have *picked among the wreckage*, not until at least a couple of hours after I got there. Because it was *too fucking hot.*'

'Tell me about the computer,' says Flint relentlessly.

'What computer?'

'Gröber's computer – his laptop, or whatever it was. Karl had to have one, didn't he? Stuck out there on some island but he was still moving his dirty dollars around the world, trying to stay one step ahead of the terriers, still keeping track of business. He wasn't doing that on an open phone was he, Jerry? He wasn't calling his washers in the Cayman Islands or the Isle of Man and saying "Move this here, move that there." He was doing it online, on the net, encrypted emails and all that jazz. So there must have been a computer, either in the house or else he took it with him on the Raven. Either way, it might have got badly burnt or blown to pieces, it might have melted, but it didn't *evaporate*, it didn't just *disappear*. You would still have found some trace of it when you looked – and I know that you did look, didn't you, Jerry?'

'Of course we looked. The Croats brought in earth movers and we were practically down on our hands and knees for three days going through that shit.'

'And?'

Crawford does not reply.

'So, if there was no trace of the computer what happened to it? Let's think about that, Jerry. If it was on one of the helicopters then maybe it was thrown clear in the crash? – like Mandrake's body, you said. Or, maybe Gröber left it in the house and it survived, like

some of his files?' Flint waits a beat and then, 'The one thing I'm
sure of, they found it – Schnell and Hartmann – before you got
there. They stole it from you, Jerry. They wanted Gröber's secrets;
they wanted to know where the money is – and whatever they
manage to find, whatever they seize or steal, they don't intend to
share with us.'

Now Flint needs a pause because she's pretty sure what's coming
next and she wants to be prepared; wants to bring some clarity to
the clutter of the now so-evident truths that are racing around in
her mind.

'Jerry, I'm going to call you back in a few minutes. I need to
check on my father.'

She finds him in deep, non-REM sleep, sleeping like a baby, and
that's an immensely cheering sign for he has complained of night-
time restlessness since coming home, which Dr Baxter said could
indicate damage to the neurons in the basal forebrain.

Whatever that means, thinks Flint.

Jerry Crawford back on the phone sounding less exasperated, and
a little less sure of his sceptical position.

'Okay, Grace, I see where you're coming from but I still don't get
it. If you're right about Schnell and Hartmann, why did they
cooperate with us in the first place? Why did Schnell give us the
Stasi file on Gröber – the real Stasi file? Why get Cutter to send you
to Leipzig?'

'They never cooperated with us, Jerry. They used us – or, rather,
me – just as much as Ridout used me, and for the same reason.
They were just better at it. After Pentecost blew up, after Gröber
got away and most of the money vanished from the pipeline, it
became open season: find Gröber, find the money, maybe – and
may the best man win because the bounty's up for grabs, and
we all need extra funding. But I didn't fit the picture because I
didn't care about the money. I only cared about Gröber for two
reasons: first, because of Ruth – because, whatever you say, it was
my fault she got killed; second, because of Mandrake – because
after what he did to my father I'm going to find him if it takes me
the rest of my life. Nobody's more motivated than I am, and
nobody cares less about the rules. I'll do whatever I have to do
because this is very, *very* personal, and Hartmann knows that as
well as you do.'

She pauses for breath and Crawford says, 'I've got no argument with you so far.'

'So, think about it. After Ruth was killed, Cutter sent Hartmann back to Pullach to tell the BND that we've been running this giant operation against a German national for almost a year, and not telling them a thing about it – and, even so, now that it's all gone wrong, we're saying, Can you please help us out? Sure they can because they've got the real Stasi file, but why should they? Why not just find Gröber for themselves and seize the assets for their slush funds – and fuck the FSF?' Flint is determined to stay calm but the anger she feels is eating at her like acid. 'Because they're not sure they can find Gröber, that's why, not on their own. They need me because I'm the one who's really motivated – or that's what Hartmann tells Schnell, and Otto gets that little twinkle in his eye. He's not going to get mad at us for keeping quiet about Pentecost, he's going to get even by *pretending* to cooperate. He feeds Cutter the Stasi report and suckers him into sending me to Leipzig where I was their runner, just like I had been Ridout's runner, and I was so focused on Mandrake I never saw it. I was totally blind.'

'Maybe you're still not seeing things too clearly,' suggests Crawford.

'Jerry, believe me, right now my vision is twenty–twenty. Hear me out. The only problem they faced was how to *stop* me running once I'd found Gröber for them and pointed the way. They knew it would be no good telling me that Gröber's dead and there's no sign of the money and expecting me to go home because they know I'm going to keep looking. When everybody else has called it a day and moved on to other cases, they know I'll still be looking under every Gröber rock because I might, just *might*, find a lead to Mandrake. And they also know that if I do that, sooner or later I am definitely going to find some of the accounts they've plundered, and there will be audit trails leading back to Pullach, and I will follow them, and I will expose them. But if Mandrake's dead, who cares about Gröber's missing dollars? There's plenty more dirty money to chase. That's what they thought, Schnell and Hartmann. With Gröber dead, Mandrake dead, where's Flint's motivation?'

'Grace, Mandrake *is* dead.' Crawford's exasperation is building again. 'Eight dead in the choppers, five more dead in the explosion. All the bad guys got killed and nobody walked away. I was *there!*'

'You were, Jerry. Mandrake wasn't,' Flint answers flatly. He's trying to protest when she continues, 'Who said that Mandrake was on Korcula in the first place, who identified him? The Croatians? How could they? Based on what? A photograph, witness ID, prints, a phone intercept, a blood sample, DNA? Hardly – because none of those existed. It was Schnell who *said* Mandrake was on the island, and when he first said that he was about a thousand kilometres away in a poky apartment in a suburb of Leipzig making damn sure I wasn't going to be around to *not* identify my husband at crunch time. Think about it, Jerry. How could Schnell have possibly known that Mandrake was on Korcula? The answer is, he didn't. He had no idea where Mandrake was and he didn't care. Mandrake was just a pawn in Dr Schnell's great game – like Mandrake's wife.'

'I have no idea how he knew, Grace, but you're wrong, because you're forgetting about the prints. Whatever happened in Leipzig, there *were* prints. Schnell got them from Ridout – and they match the prints from the one cadaver that still had skin. I was there when Felix took those prints. They're on my desk, alongside the prints Ridout sent out from London. I'm looking at them now and I'm telling you they match.'

'I'll bet they do' – a half-laugh from Flint – 'I'll bet they're the finest match you've ever seen, and do you know why? Because they printed the corpse *twice*, Jerry: once before you got there and once again when you were present and correct. Schnell didn't get any prints from Ridout, he just said he did. He pocketed the first set Hartmann took from the corpse, waited three days, and then, *hey presto!*, hot off the plane from London, he produces the perfect match, courtesy of MI6 – he *says*. You fell for it for the same reason I did: because it never occurred to you that we're not on the same side.'

She lets the silence linger until Crawford says, 'You're guessing.'

'Sure I am, some of it, and here's what you do to prove me wrong. Call Cutter now—'

'Grace, it's almost midnight—'

'I know what time it is and I want you to call Cutter now and tell him what I've said – everything I've said. Tell him that I think he should call Schnell at home, wake him up and tell him that we *know* what he's done. He should warn Schnell that unless he produces Gröber's computer, unless he shares, we're going to declare holy war: Pullach's going to be on the cover of *Der Spiegel* and the front page of *The Times*, and that's just the beginning: Senate hearings, diplomatic protests, trade embargoes, whatever it takes. If Cutter does that and sounds like he really means it, he'll know if I'm wrong. He'll know from Schnell's reaction because Aldus is the best poker player there is. But I'm not wrong, Jerry. Trust me.'

A subdued Crawford asks, 'Why don't you call Cutter?'

'Because he's got to hear it from you. You were there, I wasn't. You know they put you on a boat to keep you out of the way, to give themselves time. You know there should have been some trace of a computer to find, and there wasn't. You know that on the crucial points – Mandrake's ID, the matching prints – everything depends on what Schnell said, and that what he said doesn't square. Cutter's going to be asking a lot of questions, Jerry. He needs the answers first-hand from you.'

'What are you gonna do?'

'Sleep, until you call me back.'

Flint is about to hang up the phone when Crawford says, 'Hold it, I've got one more question. How did Schnell know there'd be an explosion? How did he know he'd have a corpse to print?'

'Oh, he knew, Jerry. Whatever happened, wherever it happened, there was always going to be at least one unrecognisable body that could still be identified. Dr Schnell was always going to give me Mandrake.'

# sixty-four

Dr John Flint has announced to his daughter that, for the first time since his release from hospital, he is returning to his surgery. Just for a couple of hours. Just to poke around, check the stock in the dispensary, check out those ravenous collie pups. Sitting on the edge of the terrace, warming her bare legs and feet in the brilliant May sun, Flint can hear him in the barn whistling something lively from Gilbert and Sullivan to match his mood.

It's been five hours and no call-back from Crawford yet and she's nursing the phone in her lap. Reviewing their conversation in the balmy light of day she's not totally sure that she convinced Crawford about Dr Schnell's duplicity but, whatever his reservations, he will have called Cutter because she made it an order – and Cutter will know that she's right because he trusts her instincts implicitly.

*Maybe.*

*And if he doesn't, what's Plan B?*

'Pilgrims, you gotta have a Plan B,' Flint says in her imitation of Cutter's drawl.

*Find Mandrake.*

*That's Plan A.*

*And B and C, and right on through the alphabet.*

But *how* she will find him is not yet coherently described in any of Flint's plans. All that she knows is that she will begin with Ridout, that she will find a way to force him to tell her who Mandrake is – or who he was before the creation of the mythical Ben Gates. *Yeah, right.*

Pushing aside these unsettling thoughts, she is getting to her feet, planning on making coffee, when at last the telephone rings. 'Jerry?'

But this is Cutter not Crawford on the line. Typical of Cutter, there is no preamble.

'Schnell will play ball. He's going to share – and there's a lot more on Gröber's laptop than just his bank account details.'

'You trust him, Mr Cutter?'

'About as far as you could throw me. But he's in no position to screw around because first I tracked down Ridout, gave him a call, told him that when we find Nathan there are a couple of ways we can handle it: quietly, no mention of MI6 in the indictment, and Nathan takes a plea – or Nathan and MI6 are all over the front pages. Then I told Ridout I needed a favour and two hours ago he signed an affidavit swearing that MI6 did not – repeat, not – provide Otto Schnell or anybody else with Mandrake's fingerprints. *Then* I called Otto and told him that the—'

Flint cannot believe what Cutter is saying and she cannot help herself. 'You've cut a deal with *Ridout*? He's as bad as Schnell. No he's not, he's worse—'

'Get real, Grace. This isn't a perfect world.'

'I don't believe this! You've promised Ridout—'

'I didn't promise him anything I wasn't going to do anyway. I want Nathan's ass in jail, you bet I do, but I'm not getting into a public pissing contest with the Brits.'

'You're going to cover it up?'

'Damn right I am. Now, stop shouting at me or I'm hanging up the phone. And you'll regret that, Grace.'

Flint is pacing the terrace as though she's in a cage. All that she sees is Ridout's smirking face and what she hears is his mocking taunt.

*My whore? Oh, very good. And what does that make you, my dear?*

'Ridout,' she says in not much more than a whisper, 'he's not off the hook, Mr Cutter.'

'No, he's not,' agrees Cutter. 'And he never will be, so long as you and I draw breath.'

He gives her a moment to absorb what he's said and then, 'You did well. You worked it out – about Mandrake, I mean.'

'A bit late in the day,' Flint says ruefully.

'Still counts because you got there first. Now all you gotta do is bring him in.'

'Oh, believe it, because . . .' she begins, an automatic response, and then something about Cutter's choice of words and their flat delivery grabs her attention. '*What did you say?*'

'I said, bring him in.'

Hardly daring to ask the question, Flint carefully says, 'You know where Mandrake is?'

'I know how you can find him.'

Flint is forgetting to breathe and she forces herself to swallow a gulp of air. 'How?'

'I told you, there's a lot more on Gröber's laptop than just his account details.'

'Mr Cutter, *for Christ's sake!*'

'I'll tell you, Grace – I'll give you the lead just as soon as you and I have a deal. I don't care how personal this is, you're a cop and you're gonna give me your word that you'll do this the proper way, the *only* way.'

'The only way?'

'That's the deal, Grace, the bottom line: you'll bring Mandrake back alive.'

Flint thinks but does not say, Gotta have a Plan B, Mr Cutter.
*I will find you, Ben.*

# La Rochelle

# sixty-five

It is after lunch and the traffic is snarled as the town returns to work, and Mandrake abruptly switches his direction, darting across the road, squeezing between the bumpers to reach the opposite pavement where he slips into a pharmacy. There is a line of customers, allowing him ample time to browse the racks of lotions by the window while he checks the street for any sign of Gröber's men. That they are out there hunting him he has no doubt, for in the last twenty-four hours they have come very close to killing him.

He knows it was his own stupid carelessness that almost cost him his life. Having read of Gröber's death in the newspapers, Mandrake had hoped that the danger was over, at least from that quarter. Even so, just to be sure, he had kept his head down in La Rochelle for three more weeks – using the time to work on the boat – and then, with scarcely a glance over his shoulder, he'd travelled to Bordeaux to empty his bank account. It was not until he was back in La Rochelle, and back on the boat, Gröber's money wrapped in plastic and safely stashed in the bilge, that he knew he had been followed. Some sixth sense had alerted him, and he'd put down the bottle of wine he was opening to celebrate and emerged cautiously on deck just in time to see three men approaching the slip; three swarthy hoods out of Central Casting who, in their unbuttoned shirts and loose-fitting jackets, had made no effort at all to look like pleasure sailors. But for the happenstance that the engine was running to charge the batteries, and that the *Lady Jane* was secured only by the aft mooring rope, he would never have got away – and even as he did, even as he slipped the mooring and rammed forward the throttle and dived for the deck, he had felt the rush of air as a fusillade of bullets narrowly missed him and peppered holes in the superstructure. It was their reckless indifference to who saw them firing their guns, attempting murder in a crowded harbour in broad daylight, that had convinced Mandrake that, whatever the papers said, Karl Gröber was not dead.

He had spent the night offshore, running without lights on a broad reach until he found shelter in the lee of the Ile d'Oléron. Riding at anchor, keeping a wary eye on the radar for the approach of any other boat, he had sat at the chart table and filled a dozen pages of notepaper, writing down everything he knew about Gröber – every last detail that might enable someone to track him down.

Someone who was obsessively determined; someone who would never rest if there was the slightest chance that Agent Ruth Apple's killer was still alive.

And then in the late morning, when the sea was full of boats among which he could hide, he had sailed the *Lady Jane* back to La Rochelle as part of a loose flotilla, and moored outside the harbour, and gone ashore in the dinghy and very carefully made his way to the main post office to mail the pages to New York – his parting gift to Grace.

Now Mandrake is ready to leave La Rochelle, to begin a voyage that has no itinerary and no settled destination. All he has to do to frustrate the hunters and stay alive is get back to the *Lady Jane*.

He buys a bottle of sunscreen and checks the street once more before leaving the pharmacy, falling into step with a group of English tourists heading in the direction of the harbour, pretending to be one of them.

Mandrake makes no assumption that the three men who tried to kill him are Gröber's only hunters, nor does he assume that only those who look like *mafiosi* pose a threat to him. Almost everyone he sees is suspect, almost every face is examined.

But reaching the harbour, breaking away from the tourists and hurrying towards the steps where the dinghy is tied up, Mandrake barely glances at the slight figure hunched in a wheelchair, a man wearing a beret and a threadbare black suit with a white shirt buttoned to the neck and a blanket on his knees; an old man, apparently, who is trying to get warm in the sun.

As Mandrake gratefully clambers into the dinghy and starts the outboard motor, Inspector Gilles Bourdonnec speaks softly into the microphone that is concealed within the sleeve of his jacket: 'On his way.'

*  *  *

In the Bay of Biscay, out of sight of land, Mandrake turns the bow into the wind and allows the boat to drift on the swell while he transforms the *Lady Jane*.

Climbing on to the transom, he removes the carved nameplate from the stern and tosses it into the sea. Now he installs a replacement plate that declares her to be the *Anna Magdalena* (the names of Bach's second wife) and registered in Panama – which indeed she is, the property of an anonymous shell corporation that has only nominee directors and no possible link to Mandrake.

Now, equipped with a template and two pots of paint, he boards the dinghy and works his way along the hull to erase her British registration number and stencil a new one on each side of the bow. And back on board the yacht, the dinghy stowed, he lowers the Union Jack and raises in its place the Panamanian flag – and to all intents and purposes the *Lady Jane* no longer exists. At his first port of call, wherever and whenever that might be, Mandrake will have the yacht hauled from the water and repainted, changing the colours of the hull and the superstructure and the deck. He will have the tiller replaced with a wheel and larger, electric winches installed and new life-lines and, perhaps, a new, taller mast – and there are a dozen other cosmetic changes he has thought of that will make the boat unrecognisable to those who may seek the *Lady Jane*.

Pleased with himself, Mandrake goes forward to raise the sails and then returns to the cockpit to set his course. The Bay of Biscay is notorious for sudden, violent storms and monstrous seas but for now there is a ridge of high pressure over this part of the Atlantic and the weather forecast is fair to good: only modest seas and light-to-moderate northeasterly winds. So, he has decided, he will take advantage of the conditions to sail due west until he is clear of the Continental Shelf and then, in much deeper water, where the seas are less confused, he will turn south to head towards the northern coast of Spain where there is any number of ports in which he can find shelter if needs be. Or, if the weather holds, he will turn west and continue to La Coruña and then turn south once more to pass along the coast of Portugal and into the warmer waters of the Mediterranean. It is a voyage of fifteen hundred miles, and perhaps twenty days at sea, but the yacht is fully provisioned and equipped with an autopilot and self-steering gear.

And a lot can happen in three weeks while Mandrake is at sea and beyond the reach of the hunters. With the ample leads he has given her, it is not too much to hope that Grace will find Karl Gröber.

He has set a large head sail and even in these light winds the *Anna Magdalena* is making seven knots and there is a black tern skimming just above the bow wave. Soon, he hopes he will see great shearwaters and storm petrels and perhaps secure an escort of leaping dolphins.

With all well and not another vessel in sight, he sets the autopilot and goes below to the main cabin to prepare himself a late lunch.

He's turned on his short-wave radio to double check the weather forecast while he chops tomatoes for a salad and he does not hear the door to the forward cabin open.

'Hello, Mandrake,' says Grace.

# sixty-six

It seems important to Flint that she can see his eyes clearly and since the light in the cabin is lacking she orders Mandrake up on deck, pointing the way with the gun that Gilles has given her.

He tries to stall but he gets no further than, 'Grace, I want you to know—'

'Shut up,' she says, though without raising her voice. 'And move.'

Now he sits alongside the tiller with his back towards the stern, and she sits at the other end of the cockpit, ten feet away, with her back against the bulkhead and the gun casually pointed at his chest. Still under the command of the autopilot, the *Anna Magdalena* continues on her westerly course.

For several minutes Flint keeps silent, staring at Mandrake with an expression that tells him nothing of what she's thinking, taking in his deep tan, the beard he's grown, the short-cropped hair that makes his face look gaunt. Then conversationally, as if she doesn't really care, she asks, 'So, what's your name – your real name?'

Mandrake smiles and answers, 'Does it matter? Won't Ben do?'

'Yes, it matters and, no, Ben won't do – and don't you ever use that name again. It doesn't belong to you.'

He nods his head as though he understands. 'My name is . . . let me see . . . Rayland Tully or Jeffrey Stamp or, before that, Christopher Morgan and, before that, Christian Myers, and then sometimes I'm called Mandrake – as you know, evidently. I've had many names, Grace. Take your pick.'

Now she nods, as though what he's said is perfectly reasonable, and then in a matter-of-fact voice, her tone flat, she says, 'Listen to me. You think you know me but you don't, not really, not any more. And so you have no idea what I'm capable of doing to you, what I will do if you make me. I'll ask you again and for the last time. What is your real name?'

'If I tell you, you won't believe me.'

'Try me.'

He hesitates and then, 'Errol Flynn,' and quickly, before she can react, he adds, 'I swear it, Grace, it's true. Blame my mother – she adored him.' Now he offers her a wry grin. 'You can see why I changed my name the first time.'

'Where were you born?'

'Melbourne, Australia.'

'When?'

'May of 1967. At least that bit was true.'

'Your father's name?'

'Joseph Flynn.'

'Mother?'

'Françoise, it really was – and, Grace, her folks really did come from France,' he adds, as though he's eager to emphasise that not every word he told her was a lie.

The wind has shifted by a couple of degrees and the mainsail is flapping and he leans towards the winch to tighten the line.

'Leave it,' says Flint.

'But look at the—'

'I said leave it. I'll tell you when I want you to move.'

He folds his arms in resignation and leans back against the transom and Flint says, 'So, Errol,' causing him to wince.

'Not that, please. Call me anything but that.'

'How about tart? Hooker?'

'What?'

'That's what you are, isn't it? Ridout's tart, Ridout's hooker? You fuck for money, don't you?'

He stares at her and from the look on his face she can't tell if his pride is hurt or he's puzzled or surprised, until he says, 'Oh, then you know about Ridout. I was hoping you did.'

'Really?'

'Yes, because then you must know why I did it, why I *had* to do it. Why I had no choice.'

*Here we go*, thinks Flint. *Here comes the only chance he's got.*

When she doesn't respond, when she merely shifts her position so that she can rest her gun hand on one knee, and while her face remains inscrutable, his voice takes on a pleading tone. 'You *do* know, don't you, Grace? You *do* know about the hold he has on me?'

Not a flicker of expression from Flint, not a word.

'Then I'll tell you anyway. Before you judge me you have to know.'

He seems undecided as to how to begin and the flapping of the sail is getting on his nerves. '*Please*,' he says, gesturing at the winch and this time she does not stop him from adjusting it. He tightens up the headsail too and runs his eye over the rig and fine-tunes a little more until he's satisfied. He checks the instruments and then he says, 'The wind's getting up. The forecast's pretty good but you never know in the Bay. If we're going back, it might be a good idea to come about pretty soon.'

'As things stand, you're not going back,' says Flint.

'Where do I start?' Mandrake asks rhetorically. 'Begin at the beginning, I suppose. That's probably best.'

He waits, watching her face, but there is no feedback from Flint and she hopes she's getting through to him that she's not going to help him, that he has to do this on his own. Eventually he begins.

'Okay, I left Oz when I was nineteen. Like most kids, I couldn't wait to get out because Australia seemed like it was at the end of the world. My folks weren't happy about it, not least because I hadn't even started college, but I told them I was going to the University of Life – ha, ha – and they finally gave me an airline ticket and a couple of thousand dollars to start me on my way. I bummed around Indonesia, Malaysia, Vietnam for a few weeks, and then I moved on to Thailand. I couldn't stand Bangkok so I went north to Chiang Mai and decided that was pretty cool, and that I'd stay there for a while. I was running out of money, so I had to get a job but I didn't have a work permit. Had to take whatever I could get.' Mandrake pauses and shifts in his seat. 'I ended up as a bouncer in a girlie bar . . . well, to be honest, more of a brothel than a bar. Most of the customers were tourists – Germans, Brits, a few Americans – and some of them would ask me where they could buy dope and . . . Well, not to beat about the bush, I started dealing on the side. Marijuana mainly, occasionally heroin. Small quantities, nothing big. Anyway . . .'

Flint is sure her expression hasn't changed but her contempt must be showing in her eyes for he heaves a giant sigh. 'I know, Grace, I know. You think that all drug dealers are scum, but I was still a kid, I had no idea what I was doing.'

*Worse than scum*, is what she's thinking.

'Anyway, after about four months I got busted. It must have been a set-up because the police came to the place where I was staying and went straight for my stash, knew exactly where it was hidden. And I wasn't even questioned in Chiang Mai. They threw me in the back of a van and took me straight down to Bangkok where I was put into a prison called Bang Kwang. God, was that a shithole! The police wanted to know who my supplier was and I told them I didn't know his real name. But of course I did and I also knew that he was the son of a very senior Thai official, and he'd warned me that if ever I got busted and implicated him he could reach me in any jail and he'd have me killed in about five minutes – and I believed him. The police beat the crap out of me, and when they got tired of that they said, "Fine, we'll just throw away the key and you can stay here for the next fifty years," and I still wouldn't talk because I was always more scared of Vicharn than I was of them. Vicharn,' Mandrake says again. 'That was my supplier's name.'

*This is what you married. This is what you thought you loved.*

'They left me to rot for ten months and then, one morning, out of the blue, I was pulled out of my cell, given my things and taken to the airport. They said I could have a ticket to anywhere I wanted to go so long as it was Amsterdam. I knew that Vicharn, or his father, must have fixed it and as I was being escorted to the plane one of the officers gave me an envelope. There was a note inside that said, "Silence brings its own reward" and a thousand dollars in cash. Wasn't much of a reward for ten months in stinking Bang Kwang, but I didn't think that at the time. Grace,' he says, breaking off from his story, 'I really need to take a piss,' and without waiting for her go-ahead he stands up and turns his back on her and now she can't see his hands, and she cocks the hammer of the gun. 'You know Gröber's still alive,' he says over his shoulder conversationally, apropos of nothing.

No response from Flint because she's been expecting him to pull some kind of stunt and she's not going to rise to his bait.

Still with his back to her he continues, 'I wrote to tell you that; that and everything I know about Gröber that might help you find him. I mailed it today to your office in New York.' He laughs. 'Of course, if I'd known I was going to see you . . .'

Now he acts as though he's zipping up his trousers, making a meal of it, and now he's turning and she's got pressure on the trigger, and if she sees a weapon in his hands she will shoot him, no question about it – and a large part of her really wants him to be holding a knife or a gun.

As if he's read her mind he holds up his hands to show her they're empty.

'Can I ask how you found me?' he asks and when she doesn't answer he adds, '*Please*, Grace, this is important.'

'I didn't find you. Gröber's hoods did. I just tagged along behind.'

'Right, that's what I thought. So you know they're out there?'

Not any more they're not, she thinks, but she doesn't tell Mandrake that; doesn't tell him about last night's gunfight with Gilles' men that left two of them dead and the third unconscious in the prison hospital and not expected to live.

'So?'

'So that means Gröber must be alive because he always pays by results, never up-front. If he was dead they wouldn't get paid, and – trust me, Grace – people like that don't work for free.'

'Trust you?' says Flint abstractedly as though the concept has no meaning for her.

'All right, okay, bad choice of words, but listen, I can help you, help you find Gröber. I'll do anything you want. And, don't forget, he was the one who killed Ruth. I had nothing to do with that and if I'd known what he was going to do I would have stopped him somehow.'

'Somehow?'

'I think I might have found the courage to tell you. Grace, you don't know how many times I wanted to tell you what was going on, what Ridout had forced me to do.' Mandrake rubs his face with both hands. 'I couldn't bring myself to do it because I couldn't bear the way I knew you'd look at me – the way you're looking at me now.'

Again he turns his back on her to stare at the *Anna Magdalena*'s creamy wake.

'What are you going to do?'

'Hear you out. Listen to what you have to say.'

'And then?'

Flint doesn't yet know the answer to his question but she keeps that thought to herself.

\* \* \*

'Amsterdam was where I first changed my name. I was never charged in Thailand but my cellmate in Bang Kwang told me the Thais always circulated the names of dealers – through Interpol, or however you do it – and I figured that every time I crossed an international border I'd get hassled. This guy, my cellmate, was from Quebec and he told me about a bar in Amsterdam where I could buy a Canadian passport in any name I wanted – and after sharing a cell with a Canadian for ten months I had the accent down pretty well.'

'A bar on a street called Herengracht?' Flint asks and catches the surprise in his eyes.

'Hey, that's impressive. How did you know?'

'What was the name of the man who sold you the passport?'

'Klaus. You know him?'

Klaus Fischer, to be precise and, yes, she knows him, for Flint has also had occasion to buy one of his well-forged Canadian passports. This is another thought she keeps to herself. She ignores Mandrake's question. 'Go on,' she says.

'Well, as it happened Klaus already had a passport made up in the name of Christian Myers that he was willing to let me have for three hundred dollars, so that's how I became a Canadian, and I've been one ever since. Of course, you never know how good fake ID is until you try it out and, just in case I got blown, I thought I'd do a trial run to somewhere reasonably civilised – somewhere they didn't have jails like Bang Kwang. Klaus said he could fix me up with a cheap ticket to London so that's where I went and, no problem, I sailed through Immigration. Then, as I was walking through the arrivals hall, who should I bump into but my old friend, Vicharn. "Fancy meeting you," he says. "Where are you staying? Why don't you come and stay with me?" Pretty amazing, yes?' Mandrake's voice is suddenly harsh. 'A pretty fucking amazing coincidence, don't you think, Grace?'

'No.'

'No?' – a bitter laugh. 'You're damn right it wasn't a coincidence.'

He lapses into silence until Flint says, 'You need to get on with your story. You don't have that much time.'

He swallows hard and it looks to her as though he's going to make a fuss but then he thinks better of it.

'Okay. Vicharn was sharing an apartment in Eaton Square with four other rich kids: a couple of Saudi princes, a banker's son from

Dubai and another Arab, an Egyptian, whose father owned the apartment. They were supposed to be in London to study but all they ever wanted to do was get high and get laid. Getting women was easy if you had drugs, and getting drugs was where I came in, because they didn't want to take the risk of being ripped off by some dealer or busted by the cops. They wanted a gofer they could trust and Vicharn knew he could trust me, so that's what I became – the absolute Candy Man who bought them their crack and their smack and anything else they wanted, and they could get their junkie girls and fuck themselves stupid. Are you getting the picture, Grace? Are you beginning to see why I didn't have the guts to tell you?'

Flint feels as though there is ice water running through her veins and she doesn't trust herself to answer.

'I was never a user, Grace. I tried crack just once and it made me puke. So whenever they had their *parties*' – Mandrake spits out the word – 'I'd make myself scarce until one or two in morning. And then one particular morning I came back early, not long after midnight, and they were still at it and I went to my room and there was a girl lying on my bed. She was stark naked and her skin was blue and she wasn't breathing. There was an empty syringe in her arm and I guessed that she'd overdosed on heroin or her heart had given out. Either way, she was definitely dead and she was nothing but trouble – boy, was she trouble.' He stares at the deck and shakes his head as he relives the memory. 'She wasn't just any junkie, you see. She was eighteen years old, still at college, and her father was a junior minister in the government. Well, Vicharn and the others, they freaked out when I told them. I practically had to tie them down to stop them running for the airport. I got all of the other women out of there and then I told Vicharn what we had to do – which was to get the dead girl back to her own place; her father had bought her an apartment in Chelsea. The problem was, we couldn't find her keys. Her purse was gone, stolen by one of the junkies, I suppose. They were like that,' he adds. 'They'd steal anything they could pick up, anything that wasn't nailed down.

'We had to put her somewhere, anywhere, and Vicharn was begging me to do something. Finally I dressed her, wrapped her in a blanket and took her down the service stairs and put her in the trunk of Vicharn's car and set off driving and I had no idea what I was going to do with her, and . . .'

That mask of hers must have cracked because he says, 'Please, Grace, don't look at me like that, as though I've crawled out from under a rock. Do you think this is easy for me?'

Flint coughs, trying to clear whatever it is that's caught in her throat.

'Do you want to hear the rest or not?'

'Uh-huh,' she manages to say.

'I drove to the river, near to where her apartment was, and tried to find someplace I could get her down on to the bank without being seen; someplace she'd be spotted before the tide came in. Well, I found a place but there was nowhere to park the car so I just left it with the lights flashing while I got her out of the trunk and over the wall, and I guess that's why a police patrol stopped – because of the car. I'd got her down by the water's edge when they found me. There was nothing I could do, nowhere to run. And my first thought was, "Can Vicharn have people killed inside a British jail?" because no matter what I said I knew they would trace the car back to him. Fucking Vicharn. Do you know what he did, he and his friends? They got hauled down to Chelsea police station, where I was in a cell, and they denied knowing anything about the girl or how she came to be dead. They said she was *my* girlfriend, and the last time they'd seen her she was going into *my* room with *me*, and that something must have happened after they'd gone to bed – oh, and that I'd stolen Vicharn's car. If I'd chosen to fight it, it would have been their word against mine, four against one.'

From her episodic memory Flint is calling up a front-page headline from the London *Evening Standard*: MINISTER'S DAUGHTER FOUND NAKED IN RIVER THAMES.

'The girl,' she asks, 'did she have a name?'

'A name? Sure. Kay or Kate – I think it was Kate.'

'You *think*?'

'Grace, I didn't know her! I'd seen her at the apartment maybe three times and she'd barely said a word to me.' He smiles with his eyes and adds deadpan, 'She didn't fancy me, I guess' – and Flint, who had fancied him, he means to remind her, feels a rush of shame, of something close to self-loathing.

'The police said they were going to charge me with failing to report a death and illegally disposing of a body – nothing too heavy, or so I thought. And then the next night – I was still being held at the police station – this guy I'd never seen before came to the interrogation room. He just let himself in and locked the door and the first thing he said was, "The heroin you gave the girl was contaminated with a lethal toxin, and that's what killed her and what you're looking at now is a charge of murder." And the second thing he said was, "The very best you can hope for is a reduced charge of manslaughter, and bearing in mind who she was – who her father is, the influence he has – that still means you're going down for fifteen years, minimum." When I got my breath back I started to say that I hadn't given the girl any heroin, and he opened this file of photographs he had with him and started showing them to me one by one; surveillance photographs of me meeting with my supplier, buying the smack. And the third thing he said was, "There is only one person on this earth who can help you, and that's me." And that's when I knew I'd been set up – and that I was totally, totally fucked. I thought he was a detective but he wasn't, of course.'

'Ridout?' Flint assumes.

'The very same,' says Mandrake.

'What did he want?'

'It was who more than what – Kamal Tohami, the Egyptian who owned the apartment. He was a big-shot industrialist but, according to Ridout, he was mixed up with a terrorist group in Lebanon and he was also selling arms to Iraq – this was just before the Gulf War – and he was using the apartment as a message drop and for occasional meetings. I was in an ideal position to monitor what was going on and that's what Ridout wanted. I was taught how to open Kamal's mail so that he'd never know and photograph the contents. I tapped the phone – with a hard wire, not a transmitter, so it was almost impossible to detect – and whenever Kamal came to town, and we had to clear out of the place until he was gone, I bugged every room in the apartment. Again, no transmitters to detect, just passive microphones hard-wired to voice-activated tape recorders hidden behind the skirting boards. It was the perfect set-up but it could only work with somebody on the inside. Me.'

'So, not in prison charged with murder, apparently,' says Flint.

'No. As soon as I agreed to do what he wanted, Ridout's photographs went back inside the folder and without them there was no evidence I'd supplied the heroin. I was charged with dumping the body but I got bail – Ridout saw to that. He also saw to it that I was welcomed back to Eaton Square with open arms, and not only because I'd kept my mouth shut about Vicharn and his friends. I was still the Candy Man, you see. Thanks to Ridout, I had a new supplier, one who didn't contaminate smack with toxins.'

For several moments Flint is very still while her mind furiously absorbs the implications of what he's just told her. Then cautiously she asks, 'Are you saying that Ridout – that MI6 – supplied you with heroin?'

'I'm saying that he supplied me with a name and a telephone number.'

'What name?'

'Orchid.'

'And you met this person, bought heroin from them?'

'I didn't buy, I was given it.'

'How many times?'

'Ten, maybe twelve.'

'Where? Where did you meet him?'

'In a pub, in a mews, just off Hyde Park Corner – and it was a her, not a him. I'm pretty sure she works for Ridout,' he adds carefully.

'Describe her.'

'White, early twenties, not English, I think – maybe Irish. Tall, red hair, very pale complexion. She didn't look anything like a dealer, which I suppose was the point. Ridout didn't want me getting busted, did he?'

'Could you identify her?'

'It was ten years ago – but, yes, I would think so. She had good bones and good skin, and she definitely wasn't a user so she won't have changed that much.' In fact Mandrake knows she has hardly changed at all, for he has seen her very recently, through the porthole of John Flint's barn – but Flint's father is not a subject he wants to go anywhere near. 'Yes,' he says, 'I'm pretty sure I could identify her.'

'Good answer,' says Flint, speaking mainly to herself.

'Why?'

Now entirely to herself she says, Because you might – just *might* – have found a reason why I shouldn't kill you.

It is not only the wind that is getting up. The Atlantic swells are becoming steeper and once in a while a crest breaks over *Anna Magdalena*'s bow causing the boat to shudder, and spume sprays the cockpit, drenching his shirt. Mandrake says the barometer is falling and that on the horizon that Flint won't turn around to see, because she won't take her eyes off him, the sky is turning an ominous shade of dirty grey.

'Then you better hurry,' says Flint.

'I spied on Kamal for four months, meeting Ridout every few days to give him the product.'

'Where?'

'Regent's Park, St James's Park, Victoria Station – always somewhere different. At the end of each meeting Ridout would set the time and place of the next rendezvous. If something urgent came up in the meantime – if, for example, Kamal turned up in London unexpectedly – I had a number to call and then we'd meet two hours later the colonnade outside the Ritz. Same thing if Ridout needed to see me urgently. I'd get a call at the apartment – "Your order's ready for collection," something like that – and two hours later I'd go to the Ritz. One day I turned up and Ridout said, "It's time for you to pay your dues." He meant go to jail. I had a few days to settle my affairs, and Vicharn threw a party for me, and then I went to court and pled guilty to the business of disposing of the girl – of Kate,' he quickly corrects himself – 'and I was given two years. Or, rather, Christian Myers was given two years. I never reached prison. That same afternoon, while Vicharn was being busted for possession of two kilos of uncut heroin that Ridout told me to plant in the apartment – Vicharn's doing eighteen years, by the way – I had a new name and a new Canadian passport, and I was on my way to Dublin to sell the IRA a consignment of rocket-propelled grenades. I didn't have any choice. Any time he wanted to, any time he wants to, Ridout can pull those pictures of me out of the file and I'm on a murder charge – if I get to live that long. Grace, listen to me: two days after I went to Dublin, Kamal and his son were killed in a car wreck on their way to Heathrow. Hit and run. I understand the driver of the other car was never found.'

Flint will not be diverted by the death of Kamal. 'You sold weapons to the IRA?'

'What? No, we ripped them off. The deal was they paid half up-front and half on delivery – and there never was a delivery, Ridout made sure of that. There are some things even he won't do.'

'Are you sure about that?' Flint asks, and Mandrake laughs, though her question wasn't meant to be humorous.

'Tell me about Gröber,' she says – and now that they've reached the critical moment his face takes on a solemn set. He looks almost stricken, as though he knows that every word he is about to say will cause her pain.

'I was in Moscow, getting close to one of the crooks in the Kremlin – this was in Yeltsin's day and there was no shortage of them in his entourage – and I kept hearing Gröber's name. It was clear that he was big, that he was moving money out of Russia for all and sundry, and Ridout got very excited about him. He wanted me to get inside Gröber's organisation but I had nothing to offer, and Gröber was very, very careful. I put out some feelers but nothing came back. And then Ridout yanked me out of Moscow, called me back to the UK, and told me that he'd found the key. You, Grace – you were the key. Ridout said that you were going to be investigating Gröber and that if I could get close to you then I would have something to offer him; something huge that would get me inside. I didn't think it would work. I didn't think I had a ghost of a chance of getting close to you, and not only because you were a cop. I'd seen pictures of you, of course. Ridout even had some movie footage. But until I followed you to that bar in Miami I had no idea how stunning—'

'Oh, stop it,' Flint says, derision in her voice.

'Why? You don't want the truth? You *were* stunning, and not only to look at. Afterwards, after you and I first met, I told Ridout that his plan was never going to work because so far as I could see you could have any man you wanted, and if you didn't have a boyfriend it was because you didn't *want* a boyfriend. If you want the whole truth, I wondered if you might be gay. If you hadn't called me—'

'You know, you really are a piece of work.'

'I can't change what happened, Grace. All I can do is try and make it come right.'

'Come right? What you did to me? No, never mind me – what you did to my father. How do you think you're going to make that *come right*?'

'Oh, Christ! You know it was me. I didn't dare to ask. I was afraid I might have . . .'

He turns his face away, unable to bear her relentless scrutiny.

'Might have what? Killed him? If you had, believe me, you'd be dead by now.'

'Then he's all right?'

'No, not all right. Because you put him in a dog cage and left him for dead, you bastard, and it was hours before they found him.'

'No! That's impossible.'

'Excuse me?'

'Ridout's people, they were there, and I left the barn door open to make sure that they found him and . . .' He dares to look at her again while he races to explain. 'Grace, listen. The woman I told you about, the one who gave me the heroin . . . I don't know her real name but her codename is Firefly, and she *definitely* works for Ridout. After I left the States, after Ruth was killed, Ridout ordered me to go to the UK and he put me in a safe house – except it wasn't safe, because I knew too much, and I knew that Ridout was going to get rid of me; a heroin overdose, a hit and run on the way to the airport; whatever pleased his sense of symmetry. So, I escaped and I went to your father's house, because I'd hidden some money and a passport in your bedroom, and your dad insisted that I stay, and the last thing on my mind was to hurt him. I just wanted to retrieve my stuff and slip away, and I came downstairs in the middle of the night and he was on the phone trying to call you and . . . I panicked, Grace. I swear I never meant to hit him that hard. I moved him down to the barn because I was going to stage a robbery and then trigger the burglar alarm as I left – and then they turned up, Firefly and a man called Fellowes, who'd been at the safe house.'

*'Andrake says you like to uck'* – Nick Fellowes, having trouble with his Ms as well as his Fs.

'While they were up in the house I got away, and I didn't dare trigger the alarm because of them, but I knew they were bound to find your dad, call an ambulance, do something, *help* him. This was five in the morning, Grace. It wasn't *hours*, for Christ's sake.'

Again he turns away to avoid her stare and he hears a moan that sounds as though it comes from the grave and he quickly turns back to see what he has achieved, and her expression hasn't changed. 'It was just the sound of the wind,' she says.

*I don't care how personal this is*, Cutter had said. *You'll do this the proper way, the only way. You'll bring Mandrake back alive.*

'This is the deal,' says Flint. 'The only one on offer.'

Mandrake watches her broodingly, like a man in the dock waiting to hear the sentence of the court.

'First, you will help me bring in Gröber, dead or alive, and if that means using you as live bait, if that means taking risks with your life, so be it. If we get him alive, and if you survive, you will testify against Gröber in court in any jurisdiction as often as necessary. You'll be a protected witness, which means you will never be alone, and you will do exactly as you're told at all times. You will sign a memorandum agreeing to all of these conditions and if you break that agreement – if you fuck up in any way – you will be prosecuted for the murder of Ruth Apple, which is a capital charge and, so help me, I will do everything I can, pull every string there is, to make sure you get the death penalty. Do you understand?'

'Yes.'

'Second, you will help me bring Ridout to account – whatever that takes. Again, I will use you as live bait if I have to but first you're going to swear an affidavit that sets down everything you know about him, everything you did for him, every conversation and dealing you had with him or any of his people. You will hand over to me any and all evidence you have to support what you say and you will submit to polygraph examinations and any other kind of examination that is required to test your veracity. You will testify in court, or before a judicial inquiry or a parliamentary committee – or, if none of these comes about, if there is an attempt to hush this up, you will talk to whichever journalists I choose. You will stand up, Mandrake, even if it means you are prosecuted for Kate's murder – and if you don't, I will make damn sure you *are* prosecuted. Is that clear?'

'Crystal clear, Grace.'

'Third, you will go to jail for what you did to my father, and you will not put him through the strain of a trial. You will make a full, written confession and you will plead guilty to whatever charges are brought. Is *that* clear?'

Mandrake nods.

'And, fourth, you will not even think of contesting our divorce, and if it's possible to get the marriage annulled on the grounds of your deception you will agree and, in any event, you will not claim any money or property from the marriage, you will make no claims whatsoever on me. And finally, when this is all over, when you've paid your dues, you will not attempt to contact me or my father in any way, shape or form, ever. Because if you do,' she adds after a pause, 'I will kill you.'

Mandrake shivers, perhaps because he's cold.

'That's the deal. Take it or leave it.'

'And if I don't?'

'Then I'll shoot you now,' says Flint, and if he knows her at all he knows that she means it.

*Gotta have a Plan B, Mr Cutter.*

'I agree.'

'Agree to what? Say it.'

'Everything you say, Grace, all of it. I will get Gröber for you, and Ridout, whatever it takes, and I will pay for what I did to your father. And when it's done I'll crawl away' – a sad smile – 'and never try to see you again.'

'Turn the boat around.'

And now the *Anna Magdalena* is on an easterly course running before the wind, Mandrake standing tall and silent at the tiller, Flint standing in the hatchway, her arms resting on the cabin top, flexing her knees to counter the motion as they ride the chasing swells. The sea is turning from green to black.

There is no warning – nothing she can do to stop him.

Almost lazily he leans against the tiller, and Flint has the briefest impression that the wind has shifted and then, out of the corner of her eye, she sees the boom of the mainsail swinging towards her head like a giant baseball bat and instinctively she ducks, but not fast enough, and she feels a savage blow to the top of her skull that sends her sprawling halfway into the cabin and she's trying to get her balance when the momentum of the boom causes the boat to veer on its side, losing way as though it has hit a wall. She is dangling inside the cabin, hanging on to a rail with one hand, trying to find the steps with her feet, stunned, half-blinded but vaguely aware that Mandrake is coming up the cockpit, coming for her, and she still has the gun in her free hand, and she fires wildly in his direction – and she fires again, and again, and again, and again, until there are no more deafening explosions, until all of the bullets are spent.

Now she lets go of the rail and drops into the cabin, falling on to her knees, scrabbling across the floor like a frightened spider towards the forward cabin where there is a knapsack Gilles has given her that contains a Very pistol and six star shells; signalling shells that, at close range, will burn a hole the size of a melon in Mandrake's chest. She fumbles to load the pistol, struggles to clear her head.

The movements of the boat are unpredictable and Flint is thrown this way and that, lurching through the main cabin, heading for the deck, prepared to fire on sight – but there is no sight of Mandrake and no place for him to hide. The cockpit is empty, no sign of blood, and he is not on the cabin top nor on the forward deck. He has abandoned ship – or fallen overboard.

She cannot think in all this din. The boat has turned into the wind and the sails are flapping furiously, and she knows that she must get them down. Her knowledge of yachts and rigging is not even rudimentary and, climbing on to the cabin top where the main mast is stepped, she has no idea which of the jumble of lines she should untie. Dumb luck is her only guide as she tugs at the first knot and the line is released, and the top of the sail sags.

It still seems to take forever to get the sail down and tied like an untidy bedsheet around the boom; to get the headsail furled; for her to figure out how to start the engine and how the throttle works. But at last the *Anna Magdalena* is more or less under Flint's control and she makes a slow, broad turn, searching the water for any sign of Mandrake.

And as the boat rides on the top of a swell she sees him. He is to her left at nine o'clock, maybe two hundred feet away, bobbing in a trough like a cork, one arm raised, waving to her. Then, as the boat drops, she loses sight of him until the next swell lifts her and now he is at eight o'clock, a little further away.

Flint increases the throttle and pushes on the tiller, turning the boat to port, guessing at a course that will bring the boat to him. It is not a good guess for the next time she sees him, as he is lifted by a swell, he is still to her left and no closer.

She makes a large course correction and this time she gets it right and the fourth time she sees him the *Anna Magdalena* is heading directly towards him and the gap is closing.

*You will stand up, Mandrake. You will make things come right.*

And then she feels herself engulfed by a gale of emotions as intense as – no, worse, far worse than any physical pain. She hears a screaming voice, a voice inside her head that is saying, *No! No!*

*No!* She is paralysed and the hand that moves to close the throttle is not under her control.

The boat drifts, rising and falling, as Mandrake rises and falls, his mouth frozen open in a rictus of fear and despair.

*Grace, you cannot do this. You cannot let him drown.*

*Why?*

*Because you're a copper. Because you took an oath. Because you promised* Cutter.

*Still the boat drifts.*

*Grace, you must—*

*He tried to kill* me, *for fuck's sake.*

*Because he's slime. Because he's a dirty lying coward. Because he doesn't have a conscience – doesn't even know what a conscience is.*

*Exactly right.*

*But you're not like that, Grace, you're not slime. You do have a conscience and how are you going to live with yourself if you let the—*

*SHUT UP!*

Suppressed deep inside her there is a kernel of knowledge that is growing like a tumour into visceral certainty – a certainty that is simply too awful to acknowledge.

Mandrake is lying on his back trying to stay afloat, trying to keep an arm raised though he clearly doesn't have the strength. His time is running out and the carping voice inside her head tries another, more subtle tack.

*Fine, let him drown – and let Ridout off the hook. Is that what you want, Grace? You want Ridout to walk away? Because without Mandrake you don't have a hope in hell of getting Ridout.*

*Not a hope in hell,* Grace agrees flatly.

*Well, then?*

*With or without Mandrake, nothing's going to happen to Ridout. Nothing ever happens to the Ridouts of this world.*

This is another bit of knowledge that has turned into certainty and there is nothing she can do to suppress it. Even if she wasn't paralysed she couldn't move because she feels so very, very tired.

*So, all this was for nothing. You just came here to kill him and now you're going to let him die?*

*Yes, no – I don't know.*

*Grace, don't do this, please. Don't make yourself as rotten as he is, as rotten as Ridout is. They left your father to die in a cage. Don't leave Mandrake to die.*

*You'll bring Mandrake back alive,* says Cutter.

Her limbs feel leaden and moving them – standing up, pushing the throttle forward, pulling on the tiller to bring the boat around – seems like a Herculean task. But now the *Anna Magdalena* is underway, closing the gap, and Flint is taking a life preserver from the locker, attaching it to a line.

Mandrake is fifty feet away, now forty, now thirty and Flint adjusts her course so that she doesn't run him down and tries to judge the moment to put the throttle into neutral, and she gets it wrong and the boat's momentum takes her careering past the spot where she meant to stop and when she throws the life preserver over the stern it lands far short of Mandrake's reach.

*Shit!*

She rams the throttle forward and hauls on the tiller and the bow pitches and catches the crest of a wave and she is temporarily blinded by the spray. When she can see again she's on a sweeping turn that should bring the boat to Mandrake and half of her wants to slow down and make a gradual approach and the other half of her is saying, *You better hurry, girl, because what's in the water there looks to me like a body.*

And then common sense takes hold – because bodies don't float, or not to begin with at least – and she puts the throttle into idle and as the boat slows she goes to the locker and pulls out all of the life preservers, holding them in her arms like a bunch of giant yellow chrysanthemums that she will scatter on the water when she reaches the spot.

Except there is no spot – no sign of Mandrake.

Flint clambers on to the cabin top and runs recklessly towards the bow, frantically searching the water.

Searching, searching, searching, until there is nowhere else to look.

# sixty-seven

A cross a leaden sky heavy with the threat of rain, one brilliant red light and then a second arc and fall like spent stars.

Flint's flares fired from the Very pistol, her come-and-get-me signal to Gilles, and signal evidence of her failure.

He waits aboard a Gendarmerie patrol boat that maintains radio silence somewhere over the easterly horizon towards which the *Anna Magdalena* now plods at half-speed, Flint at the tiller huddled inside an oilskin jacket that she's found hanging on a peg in the cabin. Mandrake's oilskin, she assumes. Her late husband's jacket.

Gilles will know that she has failed because he'd given her the Very pistol *just in case* things went very wrong; *just in case* Mandrake had refused to surrender and return to port; *just in case* he'd attacked her and she'd been obliged to shoot him with the gun Gilles had also reluctantly provided.

'But please, Grace, you will not shoot him unless it is absolutely necessary,' Gilles had said.

Well, at least she hadn't done that. No need to shoot a drowning man.

She can taste the sour flavour of her failure.

No live bait to lure Ridout and then Gröber into the open. No testimony in court, no evidence to lay before a judicial inquiry. She knows there is nothing she can do to Ridout because all she has against him is the unsupported, unrecorded word of a self-confessed pathological liar – a *dead* self-confessed pathological liar. And as for Gröber, even the knowledge gained from Mandrake that Karl did not die on Korcula, that he *must* be alive, is no more than a Pyrrhic-victory prize.

She would have found that out for herself sooner or later for even now, at her dogged insistence, forensic technicians in Washington are comparing the DNA of the victims of the Villa

Dora explosions to the genetic fingerprint of Karl's mother, provided by the few strands of hair that Flint had removed from the hairbrush in Ilse's shrine.

*So, no prizes for that, Grace.*

*Oh, stop it.*

*No bouquets, no balloons.*

*STOP IT!*

Flint stands up and struggles out of the oilskin, as though she is trying to physically escape from the torpor induced by her self-pity.

'I will find you, Karl,' she says.

*Sure.*

And now she finds within herself the strength to make a pledge – a pledge that she shouts into the wind – that, come what may, whatever it takes, she will find Karl Gröber and bring him to account within the next seven months.

And, by so doing, by giving her quest the edge of a race against time, Flint finally admits the truth; what her body has told her for weeks; what she has struggled to deny; what, nevertheless, has gnawed at her with mounting evidence every single day; what she would never, ever have admitted to Mandrake; what she would have obfuscated with wanton claims of office affairs and one-night stands.

That she is pregnant. That she carries Mandrake's child.

# Coda

In the sprawling megalopolis that is Greater São Paulo there reside more Italians than there are in Rome, twice as many Portuguese as live in Lisbon, more than a million Eastern Europeans. There are substantial clusters of Spaniards, French, Belgians, Germans, Dutch, Swiss, British – and though it is true there are also one million Arabs, and more Japanese than in any city outside Japan, and Chinese and Africans and immigrants of more than fifty nationalities, including Americans (and in the state of São Paulo there is even a town called Americana), Brazil's largest and most cosmopolitan city retains a distinctly European flavour that is much to Karl Gröber's liking.

Expensive cosmetic surgery has changed the shape of his nose and the set of his ears and the passport that he holds in the name of Peter Braun declares him to be a Swiss national from the city of Bern.

A wealthy Swiss, apparently, judging by the imposing house he has purchased in the exclusive district of Jardim Europa, his elegant soirées that are attended by many of São Paulo's leading personalities, the generous donations that he makes to many of the city's fine museums.

So, well-disguised and well-connected, just one soul among more than fifteen million, Gröber was not at all alarmed to learn from his source at the *Agência Brasileira de Inteligência* that the woman Flint had arrived in São Paulo bearing clues from a laptop computer that suggested the city could be his hiding place. Nor did he react when she returned a second time, and a third.

But then his source – his very well-paid source – reported that she had returned a fourth time; that with uncommon, almost unnatural obduracy she was *demanding* that the Brazilian police intensify their so-far lacklustre inquiry; that she had persuaded the

American Consul to lend his considerable influence to her campaign; that the word coming down from their political masters said that even the *Agência* might have to get involved.

Sitting with his source in a car parked high above the city, witnessing a sunset of spectacular beauty, Gröber had openly considered whether he should have Flint killed, a transaction that would surely not be difficult to arrange in São Paulo, he thought.

Best not, said the source. Best not kill a cop, a *foreign* cop, a *female* cop, and one who was so obviously pregnant – and he'd run his hands over his midriff in an exaggerated curve to describe the swelling of Flint's belly. Best, perhaps, if Gröber took a vacation, the source said; a trip to some other continent until nature took its course, to distract Flint from what was clearly an obsession.

And after a prolonged silence, as the dying light of the sun set the city on fire, Gröber had nodded his agreement.

'Where will you go?'

'Europe. Flint has reminded me that I have matters to attend to in Leipzig.'

'Business?'

'Family business. Long overdue.'

Tonight the house on Karl-Heine-Strasse seems to stand in total darkness. There are candles burning in Ilse's shrine but their dancing light does not penetrate the hardwood boards nailed tightly to the window frames. There are ghostly shadows on the wall, cast by gnomes that are positioned like mourners at the foot of the bed on which Ilse lies motionless, dressed in a white shroud, a single blood-red rose on her chest. The shroud is diaphanous, similar to the one worn by the woman in Fuseli's *The Nightmare*, but there is nothing remotely erotic about Ilse's appearance or her pose. In this light she looks almost child-like, like the adoring little sister Karl once had who would never have betrayed him to the police.

He sits beside her on the bed, monitoring the steady, lethal trickle of morphine into a vein in her arm. He does so tenderly for, despite her treachery, he has no wish to cause her pain. As he waits for her to die he strokes her thin hair and whispers a final, comforting word to remind her of what she always was to him and could – and should – have remained. His favourite.

*Liebling.*

# Acknowledgements

Jarrett Crawford of the Financial Strike Force bears only a passing resemblance to his namesake, who is a veteran homicide detective with the Miami Metro-Dade police department, but his character was informed by the real-life Jerry, my friend.

Thomas Tyler bears no resemblance at all to Thomas Urquhart, the former executive director of the Maine Audubon Society, but the authentic Thomas was unfailingly generous in sharing his wondrous naturalist's knowledge for Mandrake's benefit. I'm also grateful to Thomas and his wife, Amy MacDonald, for their friendship and hospitality in Maine.

The full title of the anthology from which Mandrake absorbed some of his faux passion for birds, including Alexander Wilson's description of an encounter with grackles, is *An Exhilaration of Wings: The Literature of Bird Watching*, edited by Jen Hill. To express his appreciation of Bach, Mandrake borrowed a passage by John Eliot Gardiner published in *Granta*.

Dennis Stock was my guide in Connecticut and his glorious home (which Grace did not burn down) was the inspiration for Miller's Reach.

Dallett Norris guided me to many locations in New York. The Marscheider building exists but has no connection with law enforcement.

In Leipzig, the staff at the *Runde Ecke* museum were extraordinarily helpful in answering questions about the activities of the Stasi. My interest in the Ministry for State Security goes back ten years when Wolfgang Veith introduced me to Normannenstrasse, the Stasi headquarters in Berlin, and shared with me his experiences of the regime, as did professors Thomas Meyer and Hinrich Meyer of the University of Greifswald. I also drew on long interviews with Joachim Gauck, head of the Special Commission set up after reunification to review the Stasi files, and Professor Heinz David, former Dean of the Medical Faculty at the Charité Hospital in East Berlin, who was forced by the Stasi to inform on his colleagues. When it emerged that he had been a collaborator his life was effectively ruined and it was in his garden – not Ilse's – that I saw a vast collection of gnomes which, in his despair, he had smashed to pieces.

Ed Victor and Andrew Nurnberg provided the kind of unfailing support you would expect from the very best of literary agents, and Andrew corrected the German that Ilse and Grace speak. Any errors that remain are mine, not his.

Neil Nyren (in New York), Rosie de Courcy (in London) and Bill Massey (in both) were my editors and collectively saved me from many narrative follies, particularly in the final stages. This was heroic of Bill for while the manuscript was going through a difficult labour his wife, Helen, was giving birth to their first child – and yet my anxious emails never went unanswered.

I doubt it, but if your father was at all distracted during your arrival, my apologies to Alfred Elwood Marriage Massey.